MW01531219

SHEM's QUEST

BILL ECKEL

SHEM's QUEST

TATE PUBLISHING
AND ENTERPRISES, LLC

Shem's Quest
Copyright © 2014 by Bill Eckel. All rights reserved.

No part of this publication may be reproduced, stored in a retrieval system or transmitted in any way by any means, electronic, mechanical, photocopy, recording or otherwise without the prior permission of the author except as provided by USA copyright law.

The opinions expressed by the author are not necessarily those of Tate Publishing, LLC.

Published by Tate Publishing & Enterprises, LLC
127 E. Trade Center Terrace | Mustang, Oklahoma 73064 USA
1.888.361.9473 | www.tatepublishing.com

Tate Publishing is committed to excellence in the publishing industry. The company reflects the philosophy established by the founders, based on Psalm 68:11,
"The Lord gave the word and great was the company of those who published it."

Book design copyright © 2014 by Tate Publishing, LLC. All rights reserved.
Cover design by Arjay Grecia
Interior design by Mary Jean Archival

Published in the United States of America

ISBN: 978-1-62994-075-5
1. Fiction / Action & Adventure
2. Fiction / Fantasy / General
13.11.25

DEDICATION

This book is for everyone who has a story in them, yearning to be told. I say godspeed and a successful journey. You know who you are. Get on with it.

There for the first word,
Still here for the last.
Thank you, my friend

THE MAKING OF A SUN FATHER

Un Tier clans kept their homes in the lair as did all Westerners. When they travelled for either raids or forays, they slept either in the open or under crude lean-to structures, but this particular gathering had a semi permanent look—and smell to it. Clan Leader U'bad and his mate, U'mee, had the largest lean-to. Paths leading away in several directions identified it as the center of activity. This turning a visitor had taken possession of the spot and commanded the attention of the U'bad clan.

"Under Priest Vlad, what is the reason of this visit?" asked U'bad coming out of his lean-to. Vlad had been the one to give the orders for the U'bad clan to raid the farmsteads of the soft skins. It had been the Under Priest's guidance that had kept the clan in the southern area so long. "New orders?"

"New enough, or soon-to-be, Clan Leader," began Vlad. "I bring news of coming change and to get a report of your success. First the news. Father Marteen has been called to Mieze."

The Un Tier looked about in confusion. None had heard the wail of passing that always preceded the moment of leaving, though none dared dispute the word of Under Priest Vlad. U'bad, when he could bring himself to think at all, a practice shunned by Un Tier, invariably ended up on the short end of the decision stick. He nodded to Vlad in acceptance of the statement.

"Who will be the new Sun Father?" asked U'bad.

A slow grin spread across the face of Vlad. The promise he had made to Mieze and the hints she had revealed of what lay ahead assured Vlad of that outcome. With his hands on the Auge Ose, his goddess, Mieze, had planted the slow eating cancer that was now consuming Sun Father Marteen.

The air stilled. A slowly building wail was crossing the threshold of audibility. It continued to rise in the minds of all Westerners. Higher it rose in pain wracked ecstasy before dying suddenly. A red tinged glow surrounded Vlad, growing bright. U'bad and his clan dropped to their knees. Under Priest no longer, Vlad was now Sun Father.

"Rise clan of U'bad! Serve Vlad, Sun Father, servant of Mieze!" The words of U'bad had not even faded before they were replaced with a thunderous cheer from the clan.

Vlad basked in the adulation. This was why he schemed, plotted and subverted. The glow strengthened as the power of the Sun Father filled Vlad. Completed, the aura winked out. He raised his hands. His mental voice replaced that of the wail and reached the minds of all in the West.

"I, Vlad, have been chosen by Mieze. I am now Sun Father."

Vlad lowered his hands. "Clan Leader, I will now hear of your progress."

At a motion from U'bad, a young Central Lander was drug out from under a lean-to. He was brought to stand before Vlad.

"The soft-skins along the forest edge fear the rising of Mieze!" boasted U'bad. "All except this young cub who has yet to believe in the might of U'bad's clan or that of the Sun Father."

Vlad closed his eyes, concentrating. When he reopened them, they once again held a wicked gleam, his face a menacing smile. "Do you know what a larvaling is, cub?"

The young Central Lander gave a quick, terse shake of his head. His ears filled with the mocking laughter of the Sun Father.

"You will, cub. And you won't like it. What is your name?" The willful silence of the Central Lander child amused Vlad. He turned his attention to U'bad.

"It is either Ham or Shem. The soft skin female called out both before I slew her."

At hearing of the demise of his mother and by whose hand, the child turned dark, smoldering, hate filled eyes upon the Un Tier clan leader.

Vlad chuckled, "You have made no friends this turning, Clan Leader." He placed his hand on the top of the lad's head and entered his mind. The boy's eyes grew big, innocence supplanting surprise, at the intrusion. He looked up into the depthless eyes of Vlad.

Vlad saw two boys fleeing in the night. One was struck a glancing blow from a bola and fell face first. The other crawled through the grass. Finding his brother bleeding on a rock, he picked it up as his brother opened his eyes and stared accusingly.

Into this memory Vlad projected the image of Shem. Slowly morphing the child's face. He showed the ears enlarging into the bat shaped ears of a Sol Dat. He showed the nose growing longer, the skin becoming pebbly. Vlad then changed the image into that of a fully grown Sol Dat still with recognizable features of Shem. He could taste the abject fear Shem projected. *This will be your fate, Shem. You are now one of mine. Shem o' the West. I will see you everywhere you go. Feel your every thought. You cannot hide, cannot escape.* Vlad released Shem.

Shem collapsed to the ground, the mocking laughter of Vlad ringing in his ears.

THE MAKING OF A LARVALING

S hem floated in and out of consciousness. *Where am I? What's happening? I was in the woods...the woods...the Western Forest! I've got to escape!* Shem sat up suddenly. Too suddenly, the forest swam before his eyes. He slumped back to the ground.

A pair of hands touched his face. Comforting, vaguely familiar, they gently but hurriedly probed his face and head, searching.

"Shem? Are you alright? Shem! We have to keep moving."

Shem winced as the fingers touched a knot on his head. Whose hands were they, and that voice? He had heard it before. *Rebecca.* It was Rebecca's voice! *Becky! Beautiful Becky.* Skin as soft as the finest cloth and warm to the touch. Luscious lips that begged to be kissed, but hid a sharp tongue that was just as quick to belittle as praise. Shem worked hard for the praise and usually got it. Liquid eyes that one could drown in, they held a merriment that twinkled and danced, but now was clouded with concern. Becky was everything that Shem had ever looked for in a woman. Since Shem had found her and been accepted by her, his life had been one blissful moment after the next. Well, nearly, anyway. At present his head hurt, his brain was foggy, and he and Becky were in the middle of a forest where they shouldn't have been, both armed to the teeth and, apparently, running for their lives. One thing he had to say about Becky, life was never boring around her.

"Becky, what happened?"

"You were hit by a glancing blow from a bola. You've got to get up, Shem. We've got to keep moving. They're right behind us."

Groggily, Shem rose to his feet. His sword was still at his side and his sling tucked into his belt. The bag of trinkets they had collected from the abandoned campsite they had discovered lay spilled on the ground before them. He bent to retrieve them.

"Leave them. We haven't the time," urged Becky.

"But..." Shem looked up, sniffing the air. The unmistakable smell of Sol Dat, Hunters as they were known in the Central Lands, filled his nostrils. He spied the distended snout and the bat-like ears of a Hunter topping the rise above them. He grabbed Becky's hand and they dashed off in what he hoped was an eastward direction. The pair raced on through the forest, keeping to an irregular pattern of flight in order to provide a less predictable target. Gone were all thoughts of treasure hunting, what now mattered was survival. He leapt over a fallen log, threw up his arm to protect his face from low branches. He veered to the right in order to keep close to Becky, who ran as if with winged feet. They burst into a small clearing and skidded to a halt, face to face with their pursuers. Shem's heart skipped a beat. *U'bad!*

Before them stood two huge Mashers. Broad of shoulder and heavily muscled, their outer skin more closely resembled some sort of bony plate than the regular epidermis that covered him and Becky. Only the joint areas gave any indication of flexibility or vulnerability. Atop their shoulders, their heads looked disproportionately small. A sloping brow, tiny ears set low, snout-like nose severely upturned at the end and a protruding jaw emphasized by a set of menacing tusks all made for an extremely ugly individual. They couldn't look any more different from the Hunters, three on each side that accompanied them.

"Good job, I'van," grunted the largest Masher. "You herd them right to me. Now U'bad will smash soft skins. Goddess Mieze, She will be pleased."

I'van and I'gor stepped out of the woods behind Becky and Shem and into the clearing. The Westerners spread out encircling the pair of Central Landers. "So, I'van and I'gor do the work, so

U'bad can steal the glory? Many times we could have claimed the kill!" stated I'van.

"Does puny Sol Dat want to challenge U'bad? As soon as I'm done with soft skins, I will take it!"

Shem leaned close to Becky. He whispered, "We can use this. Back me up."

"You're crazy," she replied.

"Do you have a better idea?"

"No. Oh, Shem?"

"Yeah."

"I love you."

His heart melted. *Becky! You don't know how long I have been wanting to hear those words,* he thought. Shem stole a glance at his love. "You picked a fine time to tell me. Try to watch my back, please."

"If you get yourself killed, I'll never talk to you again."

"I love you, too." Shem stepped forward. He drew his sword. As it rang out of the sheath, all attention focused on him. He drove it point first into the ground. "U'bad, you think all soft skins inferior. I challenge you. One on one. Personal combat."

"Why should I accept, cub? Yes, U'bad remembers soft skin cub who ran away from clan like frightened rabbit. We fight, challenge or no!" said U'bad. His beady little eyes flickered back and forth between Becky and Shem. Saliva drooled from his short tusks.

Shem put as much menace and bravado in his voice as he could muster, "Then let us finish this now. After I win, me and my mate go free."

"Mate? You wait until now to name me mate?" whispered Becky.

Shem whispered back, "You just now said that you loved me."

"Men!"

"Women!"

"I lose, go where you will. Dead not care," declared U'bad. His Masher partner retreated to the edge of the clearing. I'van and

I'gor each took one of Becky's arms and escorted her to the edge of the clearing, keeping her between them.

Shem withdrew his sword from the ground, and stepped back to further assess his opponent. Cycles of living in U'bad's clan had taught him that Mashers, or Un Tier as they called themselves, did not harbor much in the way of intelligence, instead brutish, single-mindedness. Shem feinted a straight ahead thrust, then skipped to the side, narrowly avoiding the huge mallet as it smashed into the ground where Shem had been standing a moment before. *Fiona! I had forgotten how fast he was!*

Shem continued, circling and probing, searching for a weakness. His childhood training with the Un Tier cublings had proven that a headlong rush was useless. There were few places of vulnerability. His jabs and thrusts met little resistance from U'bad. More than once his sword point had come into contact with bony plate with little result.

"Ha! Puny soft skin's sword has no might!" boasted U'bad. He stood still, spreading his arms, opening his defenses. "Strike! Hurt me if you can."

Shem launched an overhead stroke aimed at U'bad's head. U'bad shifted slightly, the sword cut missing his head and slamming into the bony plate covering his shoulders. The jolt of the impact caused a tingling in Shem's elbow and shoulder. He could barely hold his sword at the ready as he circled the Masher. He made a couple of quick feints, more to try shaking some feeling into his arm than any intent to do harm. U'bad merely flinched, then brought his mallet across his body in a sweeping maneuver, not intended for Shem, but Shem's sword. The jarring impact of mallet on steel sent a flash of pain burning up Shem's arm once again. His sword dropped from nerveless fingers. U'bad stepped forward. Shem, his right arm hanging useless, reached into his bag of stones with his left hand grabbing the first one his fingers came into contact with. He put the stone into the pouch of his sling. He watched, for the moment unable to move, as the mallet rose and came down in a powerful arc. *I'm sorry, Becky,* he thought. Instead of smashing Shem into the next existence, the mallet came down on his sword, shattering it, leaving only about two hands of jagged broken blade attached to the hilt.

"Ha! Soft skin's sword is puny as soft skin!" U'bad bellowed, raising his arms over his head in victory.

Shem stepped back. With what feeling he had in his right arm, he spun his sling. He hoped it would be enough. The sling made two arcs before it loosed, the stone hitting U'bad square in the sensitive area of his upturned snout. U'bad roared in pain, dropping his mallet and clutching his nose. Shem scooped up the remains of his sword and drove it deep into the unprotected armpit of U'bad before pulling it out in a slashing motion, cutting through muscle and tendon. U'bad's arm dropped uselessly to his side. Shem's return stroke opened a deep gash in U'bad's neck and throat. Shem danced backwards out of U'bad's reach to assess the damage.

Shem's own arm was recovering from its stinger. He would soon have full use. U'bad's arm was merely dangling, the gash in his throat was spurting a rich red blood, his life expectancy measured in moments. He tried to speak, hurl one more bombast, but could only manage a choking gurgle before falling back, dead.

Rebecca, who had been released when U'bad hit the ground, dashed to Shem's side. "Your arm?"

Shem put the arm in question around her shoulder. His reply was drowned out by the keening wail of the second Masher. I'van and I'gor approached Shem and Becky.

"Soft skin, it would be best if you left now," said I'van. "U'bad, the Un Tier you slew, was her mate. She will not honor the agreement."

"Westerners have no honor?" questioned Shem, though he was well familiar with the system of justice within the clans.

I'gor stiffened. "We have honor, but she will soon remember the mate-gild. She will claim your mate as her blood-price."

Shem cursed inwardly. *Why did I name Becky mate? How could I have forgotten?*

"It was a fair contest," protested Becky.

"Fair or no, U'bad was the clan leader. He had never lost. U'mee's loss of status will drive her to the mate-gild. One last thing. Your name, soft skin?" asked I'van. "For the death song."

"Shem."

"Leave now, Shem," said I'gor.

Nodding in agreement, Shem and Becky turned to leave. Shem turned back. He looked into the eyes of I'van and I'gor, then clasped their hands.

"Next time we meet, friend Shem, one of us will die," stated I'gor. "Until then, good hunting."

"Good hunting," repeated Shem. He and Becky left the clearing.

They travelled eastward to the best of their reckoning. The keening of the Masher mate had been left behind for the better part of a candlemark when Shem noticed the silence of the forest. There should have been some sound. He and Becky had been moving at a steady pace and the trees had begun to thin, but Shem felt that danger was near. Becky was still loping ahead of him when he slowed to look behind.

The Masher mate came crashing into view followed by four of the Hunters. She bellowed in rage as she spied the Central Landers, then sprinted forward with renewed speed.

"Run, Becky!" Shem urged as he turned to face the attackers. He drew Becky's sword, she had relinquished it after they had left the clearing, and faced the onrushing Masher. Something was different. The Masher was carrying a spear, a huge spear, instead of a mallet. In disbelief, he watched as the spear was given a mighty heave. It wasn't aimed at him. He turned his head to check on Becky. She was still running towards the wood's edge. He watched as the spear reached its apex. It was impossible. No one could throw a spear that far, no one human. The Masher wasn't human. She was Un Tier.

"Becky, turn left!" Shem screamed, but she was too far away to hear. Shem watched in slow motion as the spear arced down. *Maybe it'll miss. Maybe it'll hit a tree.* Neither happened. Gaining speed on its descent, the spear impaled itself between Becky's shoulder blades, pitching her face forward onto the forest floor. After momentum ceased, she moved no more.

Emotion drained from Shem leaving behind a void. A cold emptiness. Becky was gone. Gone. Their newly declared love was no more. Rushing in to fill the vacuum was the desire for revenge. The only thing that now mattered to Shem was the complete and utter destruction of those that had taken her from him. He was now an unfeeling, calculating, killing machine. He faced the oncoming Westerners. No longer a threat, he considered them animals, animals led to him for slaughter.

The Masher mate was in the center of the group flanked on each side by two Hunters. None of the Hunters appeared to be I'van or I'gor, not that that would have mattered to Shem. The Masher mate had stopped to watch the flight of the spear. Seeing it strike the target seemed to have sated her lust. The Hunters continued towards Shem, intent on completing the death sentence of the intruders.

He flowed towards the nearest pair, the ones on his right. With deadly precision, he attacked. Not even their enhanced reptilian skin, less thick and more flexible than the Mashers, provided any safety. The loss of his love lent strength to his blows. Two swift sword cuts left one Hunter without his head, the other lying face first on the ground, hamstrung. Shem stood over the wounded one. He raised his sword, point down, and drove it into the back of the Hunter. It had taken mere moments. The second pair approached more cautiously. One had reached for his bola, but Shem was quicker, the stone from his sling struck the Hunter in the throat, crushing its windpipe. The second looked to flee, but found his path blocked by the Masher's mate, who had drawn her sword and was advancing on Shem.

Shem tucked away his sling. In a blur of motion he drew a dagger and flicked it at the last surviving Hunter. It flew true and took the Hunter in the center of his back, burying to the hilt. The calmness left Shem as he turned his attention to the Masher. Here was the source of his pain. Here was the cause of his loss. Here was the one who had taken from him all that he had cherished. This one was going to pay. The calm killer was replaced with a raging berserker. He did not wait on the Masher. He charged, caring little if he lived or died, only dealing pain and suffering.

Such was the mindless rage of his onslaught that the Masher had little thought for offense. Shem was everywhere. His sword was slamming into her with such force that it rended the bony plates protecting her body. She fell back in confusion. Upon seeing the mate-gild paid, she had lost the edge that had driven her to this point.

Shem had no coherent thoughts at all, just an all consuming need to inflict hurt and pain. He continued to strike and weave, never standing still. He watched as one stroke cleaved through the chest plates drawing blood, another struck the Masher's shoulder penetrating half the width of the blade. It had taken a good tug to free the blade from that cut, but the Masher was already falling back, confusion replaced by a growing fear. Shem surveyed the damage. The Masher was bleeding from nearly half a dozen cuts and looked as if she wanted to flee, but she had not suffered enough in Shem's reckoning. He targeted the inside of the elbow joint and struck. The Masher's forearm was severed from its body. Before it had hit the ground, Shem had spun behind the Masher and struck behind the knee. U'bad's mate crumpled face first to the ground, whimpering.

The snapping of a twig behind Shem caused him to whirl, blade coming down in an overhead swing. I'van barely evaded death. His quickness saved his head, but the blade caught the tip of his bat like ears, notching the right one.

"Peace, friend Shem! It is over."

Shem's breathing slowly returned to normal, the berserker relinquishing it's control over him. He sheathed his sword.

"I'van," reminded I'van. Shem nodded. I'van continued, "T'gor and myself, we tried to persuade her to let you leave, but it was not to be. She wanted blood, little guessing that it would be hers. I am sorry for the life of your mate, but gild is gild."

At the mention of Becky, Shem was once again overcome with sorrow.

"But before you leave, there is one thing more," continued I'van.

The presence of Vlad, Sun Father of the West, High Priest of Mieze, flooded into Shem inhabiting the bond he had placed in Shem's mind soon after the Central Lander child had been brought captive into U'bad's clan.

He was paralyzed.

"Shem. You return to the clan that raised you?" The insidious voice permeated all of Shem's thoughts. He was helpless to resist. Vlad slowly extracted information, the scavenging, the challenge, Shem's pain and suffering. Satisfied that he had gleaned all that was important, the Sun Father released Shem's mind, leaving his ghostlike apparition standing in front of the Central Lander. "So, a deal was made, so be it. Go from my lands, larvaling. And know this," the image of Shem morphed into a Sol Dat burned its way into Shem's memory. "That is your fate. I can find you anytime I wish, wherever you may happen to be. You cannot hide."

The apparition vanished, leaving Shem once again in control of his body. He spied I'van kneeling before the slain Hunters cutting off the queues of hair growing from the tops of their heads. I'van handed Shem the shorn locks.

"These are their queues. In breaking the agreement made between you and U'bad, these Sol Dat sacrificed their honor, thus their queues. Go now, Shem, and remember the words of I'gor, for I, too, am now bound by them."

Shem accepted the fallen Hunters hair and tucked them into his belt. There being nothing left to say, Shem left I'van and made his way towards Becky. He knelt to pick her up.

"She stays."

Shem remained kneeling beside Becky. The coppery scent of spilled blood was just beginning to rise from the ground making it past the sniffles that promised tears to come. "Why?"

"Her blood has mingled with the land, friend Shem. Were you to take her, her spirit would find no rest. She is now part of the land. Would you have her become a ghost?"

Tears trickled slowly down the cheeks of Shem's bent face. *Now she is truly lost to me. I cannot even take her back. I'm sorry, Becky. Sorry I failed you. My love. My mate. But there is one thing I can do. I can guarantee that I'll be back.* Shem drew his dagger and extended his arm. He pulled the blade across the inside of his forearm. He watched as the blood welled from the cut and dripped to the ground.

The moment Shem's blood hit the ground his bond awoke. In ominous tones Vlad spoke, "The fate of Shem, once of the Central Lands, by his own hand, has been sealed."

1

FIONA AND MIEZE

In the nothingness and everythingness of the void and the unending emptiness of time, the abode of gods and of goddesses, Mieze waited. Goddess of the Western Lands, maker and shaper of her people, she had been summoned. *Summoned!* How dare she! *Who did Fiona think she was?* Assuredly, it had been phrased as a request, but Mieze was one who could discern a slight, no matter how subtle.

Idly, Mieze created a small planet. She listened as the innocent life forms called out to their maker. "Mieze, Mieze, Mieze!" She gloried in the adoration. "Tierra!" *What was that?* Among the teeming throng of her creations, a lone voice cried the name of her sister. *This is MY creation! How can this be?* Focusing her will upon the new planet, she watched as it exploded, atomizing completely; leaving no trace it—or its inhabitants—had ever existed. She considered justice done. Mieze smiled. The smile evaporated as she became aware that she was not alone.

"Mieze, our sister awakens. Soon she will take her place as the head of this council."

Sarcasm dripped from Mieze's thoughts. "I can't begin to tell you how thrilled I'm not."

"Mieze! How can you be displeased?"

"Isn't it enough that I have to share with you, Fiona? Now I must give way to our sister, Tierra? Not as equal but beneath?"

"Mieze! How can you think such thoughts?"

Not wanting to contemplate the event, let alone discuss it with Fiona, Mieze left the void, reaching out to Vlad, the Sun Father of the Western Lands. "Tierra cannot fully awaken without the Hjerte. My Ascendency approaches. The Hjerte will be mine!"

"Mieze? Mieze! She is gone. I fear for our sister. Mieze bears her ill will. I must be vigilant." Fiona reached out for her High Priestess, El-lina, consort of the El, leader of the Eastern Lands.

2

SUN FATHER

"The Land is alive!"

Long narrow shafts cut in precise astrological positions provided light for the chamber deep in the heart of the mountain. The dim light illuminated Vlad, leader of the Western Lands, High Priest of Mieze, worshipped by the people of that land as Sun Father.

"The Land is alive!"

The eerie words echoed throughout the central chambers. Vlad stood atop the speaking rock, a tall flat topped stalagmite in the midst of an enormous cavern in the center of the Lair. Below him the chamber was crowded to capacity.

The Un Tier, brutish monsters, stood in clan ranks to one side. Sol Dat, smaller than the Un Tier and insanely jealous, stood to the other separated by gatherers, Stein Bauen and the Priest. All gazed up with rapt attention.

"The Land is alive!" thundered Vlad for the third time, arms raised and outstretched, "And it must bow to Mieze! Mieze approaches. Soon the Ascendency will be upon us and Mieze will take what is rightfully hers!"

Vlad lowered his arms, basking in the hissing roar of praise and approval rising from the throats of his people. *Yes, cheer me, fools. When the time comes, you will serve me well.* He could feel his power growing with every turning. Every night Mieze grew larger, her scarlet tinged surface slowly deepening to a rich ruby red, the color of blood. And it was blood that she demanded.

"We will cleanse the Land of the taint of the Central Landers! Those Fiona- worshipping infidels who blight the sight of Mieze. They will bow the knee and turn their hearts or they—will—die! So says Mieze. So say I, Vlad, the Sun Father!" The adulation of his people had seemed loud before. It now rose to thunderous proportions with a chant of "Mieze, Mieze, Mieze, Vlad, Vlad, Vlad," echoing and reverberating off the walls of the cavern. Vlad turned and descended from the speaking stone, his people continuing their chanting. They would keep it up for a candlemark or more. Vlad signaled Erik, his second, to accompany him. Together they strode from the cavern to the cadence of the chant.

Unlike the people he ruled, Vlad, and also Erik, retained human appearance. What was in his heart was another matter. Hatred. Deep, abiding, everlasting hatred. This was the strength of his link with Mieze, the source of his power.

"Do you feel the effects, Erik?"

Erik hesitated. Words came slowly to is lips, "The effects of what, Sun Father?"

Vlad smiled inwardly. *Do you fear me, Erik? You would do well to do so. I took no little pleasure in disposing of your father. I tolerated no challenge then and I won't now.* "The approach of Mieze. Does she not quicken your pulse, energize your very core?"

"I attribute that to your presence, Sun Father," said Erik choosing his words carefully.

Vlad glanced casually in Erik's direction. His second had his head bowed in submission, but his hands were clasped behind his back indicating little need for protection. *A self assured suck-up, then? Some is good, too much breeds ambition, Cub.* Vlad could have entered the mind of Erik with little difficulty and found out exactly what his second was thinking but saw no need to do so. Instead he turned his thoughts to the approaching times. "What do you know of the Ascendency, Erik?"

"It has been the life spans of ten Sun Fathers since the last Ascendency. Mieze lowers herself to get a better view of her subjects, to bless them all the more," responded Erik by rote. He had been well versed in the cycles of power during his priesthood training. "During the Ascendency, all will be more than they were, most especially the priest class."

"Yes, and the period of the Ascendency?"

"The Ascendency lasts for one moon."

"That is the length of time we have, Erik, to accomplish our mission." *Though this time, Cub, Mieze does not intend for the Ascendency to end.*

"Our mission?"

"To prevent the rise of the usurper Tierra. To convert all to Mieze—or kill them."

Vlad led a silent Erik through a high ceilinged cavern of natural origin with only the flooring being smoothed to the point of being nearly polished. That flooring ended at the edge of a chasm. Carved out of the stone walls of the chasm was a stairway leading down to the bottom of the pit. At the bottom rested the Auge Ose, the eye of Mieze.

All in the priest class knew of the Auge Ose. They were brought down during their initiation to touch the ruby red jewel and feel the power of Mieze, which in turn allowed Mieze to search their hearts. It was not unknown for an initiate to fail. In that occurrence, the body simply ignited and burned to ashes in a flash. None came lightly to the Auge Ose.

"What we are about to do is similar to a renewing," explained Vlad. "Only this time Mieze will release the Auge Ose to my will."

Vlad heard the sudden catch in Erik's breathing. He smiled. "Such a thing is possible to the Sun Father. *And any other of sufficient strength, but there is no need for you to know that.* Place your hands on the Auge Ose."

Vlad stood, his hands on the stone, facing Erik. Erik placed his hands on the Auge Ose. The presence of Mieze filled both immediately. Vlad's every synapse tingled with intense delight as she searched his every thought, every wish. No secrets could be held back. Her words resonated within him as in Erik.

"You've come to fulfill my desire."

"Yes, my lady," answered Vlad.

"Very well. It is yours."

The presence of the goddess faded away replaced by a vision of the Western Lands. Vlad directed the Auge Ose towards the border between the Western and Central Lands. The mountainous jungle landscape transformed almost immediately to the nearly flat, heavily wooded deciduous trees marking the border. He chose the third stone fortification and zoomed in closer. "That will be the first target."

Erik studied the layout. "Over topping the walls will be a problem," he said.

Vlad waved away the comment, "One for you to solve."

3

HAM AND SHEM

"The Land is alive!"

The words of Priest Duran, head of Fiona's Temple in Yakstown, rang out over the congregation, hurting Shem's ears as they pounded against his skull. The hairy coating inside his mouth distracted him, and he couldn't remember how or why he came to be sitting in the temple listening to the priest, at least to those words that penetrated the fog, which passed for coherent thought in his mind. *Why am I here? I've got patrol today. What's this moron blathering on about?*

"The Land is alive and she needs a hero. The awakening of Tierra, goddess of all the lands, approaches and a leader must stand. Stand against the Goddess Mieze of the West who will try to oppose her. This has been made known to us by our own blessed Fiona who looks forward with much joy to the awakening of her sister. Last night, bravely, with much meekness and humility— well bravely anyway, a hero volunteered. Brother Shem, rise. Give us a few words."

Shem gradually felt the expectant, eager eyes turned in his direction. He desperately sought an avenue of escape. He stood slowly with only a slight wobble.

"I did what?"

Ham was the serious one. Like all members of Baron Yakov's guardsmen, he was clean shaven and physically fit. He was also a Guardsman of the First File, a title bestowed upon the members of the first graduating class of Baron Yakov's arms school and one that he was very proud of. For the first two cycles, he had served without distinction patrolling Peddler's Way on the western border. Then his brother, Shem, arrived. Not that Shem himself was necessarily trouble, but Shem and trouble were never very far apart. If it wasn't for Shem's uncanny knowledge of the West, he would have been drubbed out of the guardsmen fairly quickly. Instead, Ham recognized that knowledge for what it was. Far superior to anyone else's that Ham had ever met. The fact that Shem shared this knowledge only with him, allowing him to take credit for it, had convinced Ham it was worth the price to take Shem under his wing. That price usually entailed inns and surprisingly small amounts of ale that caused big problems. Ham didn't believe Shem's military career was going to be either long or illustrious.

His brother was, however, well practiced in the use of knife, sword, and bow, but his specialty was with the sling he kept wrapped around his forehead. With that he was deadly. *Yes, Shem you are a skilled soldier. At least when on duty, but your fondness for ale will be your downfall. Either that or one of those crazy oaths you are forever swearing. Brother, your only redeeming social value is… Who am I kidding? Brother, you are a burden.*

Ham rode through the streets of Yakstown, his horse's hooves clopping leisurely on the cobblestones. He led another mount behind him. Shem's horse. Making his way through the throng of the market place, he marveled as he always did, at the clash of scents and aromas that assailed his nostrils, scents that invigorated him somehow. He often thought of becoming a merchant after his time in Baron Yakov's army had been served. Leaving the market square, he headed towards the Temple of Fiona.

"That should be where Shem is," he said aloud. "Or anywhere else trouble can be found."

—◦◦◦—

Shem stood in the middle of a boisterous crowd, topping it by at least a head. They had followed him out of the temple begging and pleading for him to stay and champion them, lead the awakening of Tierra. His frustration bordered on irritation as he tried to extract himself from the congregation, "I can't stay; I'm in the Baron's army."

"You swore an oath!" wheedled the priest.

Shem ignored him as he looked about for any excuse. He spied Ham riding out of the market square leading a spare mount. He breathed, "Thank Fiona."

"You can't thank Fiona anymore, Brother Shem. You swore an oath to Tierra!" admonished the priest, reluctant to let Shem go.

Shem wheeled on him. "Was I drunk when I swore that oath?"

"Well, yes, but…" Words of a convincing argument escaped the priest.

Ham reined in at the edge of the crowd. Shem took the proffered reins and swung up onto his mount. He leaned over to the priest, "Then, the next time I get drunk, I'll come back and fulfill it!"

The pair cantered back towards the marketplace. Shem exhaled, "You're a sight for sore eyes."

"They wouldn't be sore if you didn't drink so much ale and run off with the first acolyte that came around proselytizing," retorted Ham.

Shem winced at the words. "You don't underst—"began Shem.

Ham cut him off, "No, I don't. Nor do I care. We're patrolling south towards Third Stone."

Shem smiled. *Yes you do, Brother. I know you love me.* He waited. He had always been able to outwait his brother.

It took less than a quarter candlemark for Ham's broad, straight back to sag slightly. "What oath this time?" he asked.

"I'm the hero of Tierra."

The light of day slowly gave way to night's enveloping darkness as the two brothers rode down the road at a leisurely pace. On the east side of the road were cultivated fields for melons, greens, and grains. Small half sunken huts, the kind used to house tools or other farm implements, separated some of the fields indicating an orderly society of homesteaders. About an arrow shot off to the west was the beginnings of the Western Forest, the border between the Western and the Central Land. Eerie enough during the daylight hours, darkness brought a sensation of menace, of evil, emanating from the forest, especially of late.

The brothers were nearing Third Stone hamlet, three turnings easy travel south of Yakstown. Shem licked at his lips. He gave way to an exaggerated bounce in his saddle, the thought of washing the road dust out of his throat with a mug or two of ale enticing. He saw that even Ham was leaning forward in his saddle in order to get there the quicker. For at the Wayfarer, Third Stone's inn, worked Sheila, a dark haired, doe-eyed server whose personality and person were well rounded. She also had a fondness for Ham. Ham picked up the pace. A rumble from his stomach revealed his thoughts. "Midweek turnings, Sheila's made lamb chops. No one makes lamb chops like Sheila," remarked Ham.

Shem laughed. "And no one makes Sheila like Ham."

They reined in in front of the inn. They were met by the stable boy. The two soldiers handed over their reins.

"Care for them well, boy. I'll be checking later. Oats in the bag now," warned Ham. Shem winked and flipped the boy a half coin. "And you," Ham rounded on Shem, "keep your wits. I expect an uninterrupted night. I mean it!"

Innocent eyed, Shem touched his fingertips to the center of his chest a questioning look on his angelic face.

Third Stone's inn was open and airy for the most part. Though a two-story building, the upstairs rooms only lined the back of the inn and down the left side with a landing for access, leaving the common room with a very high ceiling held up by four huge tree trunks growing up through the floor. Lanterns hanging on four sides of the trunks and a large fireplace halfway down the right side kept the inn well lit except for "the shadow" the back left corner, which was shadowed by the wall of the kitchen. It was reserved for those patrons who wished a little privacy. Two long tables ran parallel down the center of the common room with tables scattered throughout the remainder. About half of the tables were occupied. Conspicously absent were any soldiers from the fort south of the hamlet.

Sheila pushed through the gate in the middle of the bar, a tray of full ale mugs in one hand, two more mugs in her other hand. "Ham!" she squealed. She shooed a farm hand away from the table near the bar. "You, move over there. You're sitting at my Ham's table." She moved off towards a table of thirsty farmers. "I'll be right back."

Sheila's father, Detrik, stood behind the bar. He nodded at Ham, a slight frown tugging down the corners of his mouth. Sheila returned and wiped off their table. The brothers sat down. Sheila sat in Ham's lap and gave him a big kiss.

"Lamb chops tonight. I saved you the biggest ones," she cooed.

"I wouldn't have missed them for the world," replied Ham. "No ale for him until after dinner."

Shem couldn't believe Ham would treat him that way. He squawked, "What?"

"I want to be able to enjoy my supper."

Shem mocked the superiority in his brother's tone, "I want to enjoy my supper."

Sheila returned with two heaping plates. She set them on the table. "Eat up, love. You'll need your strength…for dessert."

Ham grinned wolfishly and dug in.

"Sheila!" Detrik called out.

Sheila turned towards her father who nodded towards "the shadow". She shivered.

"What is it?" asked Ham, now alerted and peering into the darkened corner. Shem looked as well. All he could make out was a cloaked figure sitting at one of the tables.

"A stranger. He arrived right after nightfall and went immediately to 'the shadow'," answered Sheila.

"Any visitors?" asked Ham.

"None. He had two plates of lamb chops and wanted another, but dad refused. Then he started on ale. This will be his third."

Shem's ears perked up at the mention of ale. Sheila left to deliver the order. The two soldiers fell to their meal in shifts, one watching while the other ate, keeping their eyes on Sheila and the stranger in the shadow. Sheila returned.

"Could you make anything out?" asked Ham finishing up his plate.

"Nothing," said Sheila, "He keeps his hood up and his sleeves cover his hands. He whispers when he speaks and uses simple words. He makes me feel...it's like..." Sheila faltered, at a loss to explain, "I just don't want to be around him."

Sheila's stumbling explanation was interrupted by the arrival of another serving girl. Similar in appearance to Sheila, but a few cycles older, her arrival was met by the enthusiastic cheering of the inn's customers. Now they would have someone to laugh and toy with, without fear of angering the soldiers.

"Good, Janet's here," exclaimed Sheila. "I'll go wash the pots. Then we can go." The two girls met at the gate in the bar. Sheila leaned in and whispered into Janet's ear. Janet cut her eyes towards the shadow. She listened a little more and started laughing. Sheila disappeared into the kitchen. Janet filled two mugs of ale and brought them to the soldiers.

"Evening, boys. Enjoying yourselves?" asked Janet.

"I'm about to," declared Shem.

Two candlemarks and several ales later, Shem felt no pain. Sheila and Ham had disappeared over a candlemark ago, leaving Shem to regale the crowd with stories of his exploits. Each tale had gotten larger and more unbelievable. Shem launched into an account of how he and Ham had single-handedly saved a farmhouse from a raid of western creatures when the stranger emerged from the shadow.

"You lie," he hissed.

All eyes turned to the stranger. He had taken a step out of the shadow and was now visible for all to see. Shem saw that the stranger was neither short nor tall, and from the way his cloak hung about him, he was probably thin and wiry. He was also upset. From the way his eyes blazed noticeable inside his hood, he was more than upset. Positively livid.

The spark of a vague memory penetrated his wooziness. He tried to wrap his mind around it. Shem finally noticed the quiet of the crowd. Then it came to him, *I've heard that voice before,* but he couldn't quite place it. "Well, maybe there was only a Hand instead of two Fists, but twenty makes a better story," explained Shem staggering sideways.

At the same time the stranger's arm blurred forward, Shem stumbled onto a table and chair. The thunk of a knife embedding itself in the tree trunk behind him cut through his ale-induced fog. Shem stalled looking around for his sword. *Where did I leave it?* "C'mon, my story wasn't that bad!" Nothing else at hand, Shem flung the chair he was holding on to in the direction of the stranger. The stranger easily leapt up over the chair.

The *toon* of a compound bow was quickly followed by the thud of a bolt impacting flesh. The stranger spun around, the bolt meant for his neck sticking out of his shoulder. Landing nimbly on his feet, he made for the door and escape. The stranger sped past Shem who lurched sideways, reaching out to grab him.

"Gotcha!" Shem cried triumphantly. Without breaking stride, the stranger shed the cloak and continued towards the door. Shem, cloak in hand, stared, rooted to the spot, as patrons moving to block the door froze, stopped in their tracks by the sight of large bat-like ears and an extended snout. "A Hunter, a Sol Dat," exclaimed Shem stating the obvious. The Hunter burst through the door and escaped into the darkness.

"Is this what you call an uninterrupted night?" asked Ham dryly. Ham stood at the head of the stairs, blanket wrapped around him, his bow resting on his shoulder.

Shem spluttered in amazement, "What did I do?"

"Keep that cloak. The baron will want to see it." Ham returned to his room and closed the door.

Shem walked slowly through the crowd as they reseated themselves. His confused mind began sorting out the events.

He could hear the whispered comments,

"A Hunter!"

"In our inn!"

"Where's the baron's troops?" Shem muttered, "Sol Dat daring the Central lands. This can't be good." He stepped outside onto the porch, away from the accusatory eyes of the patrons that had followed his every step.

His eyes went to the ground. He could dimly see the tracks of the Hunter leading to the north, away from the fort on the south side of the village. *Ham is upset. It's all my fault. But I didn't invite the Sol Dat to the inn!* The tracks of the Hunter burned themselves into Shem's brain. Without a word he returned to the inn and retrieved his sword. He would redeem himself.

The tracks had continued northwards for about a league before heading west into the forest. The crisp cool air invigorated Shem, suppressing the effects of the ale. It reminded him of the carefree cycles honing his woodsman skills and wits against the Un Tier and, even more challenging, Sol Dat clans. Before he had found and then lost Becky. It was the losing that hurt. Losing always hurt. U'bad would mercilessly cuff him about the head when he lost bouts against the other Un Tier cubs. The pain had been motivation enough that he seldom lost, though by that time he had achieved his growth, possessing muscles hard and knotted. Strong as the Land! That is what he had become and happy enough in his innocence. Then he spied Becky exploring the woods.

His whole world changed. It wasn't that just the fact that she was a soft-skin like himself, she was female. Urges and desires he had never known overwhelmed him. He became clumsy and forgetful. More than once Shem had been caught in the woods trailing Becky when he should have been tending to other chores. U'bad had recognized the danger. Shem's initiation into adulthood had been near. To prove himself to the clan he had been ordered to kill the soft-skin interloper. Instead he had run off with her. Those had been the happiest cycles. His fall from those dizzying heights had been swift. He had discovered ale and its euphoria, its forgetfulness, and finally the deepening depths of its false promises. Now here he was.

Shem crouched at the point of entry. Since leaving the West cycles ago, he had never reentered unless it had been daylight and even then, he did not penetrate far. He knew better than to make the attempt at night. He sniffed the air as he thought. He caught a lingering odor. *Sol Dat alright. How did I miss it at the inn?* Because you were drunk, that's why! *That's not fair.* What's fair? *It helps me forget!* Shem shook the conversation from his mind. Despite the fact that he had found a cachet of herbs sewn into the cloak that absorbed the scent secreted by the Sol Dat, he knew that he should have known better. Besides, he couldn't afford to get distracted, *especially since I always lose this argument.*

The barely perceptible crack of a twig jerked Shem to full awareness. "I can't just sit here," he murmured. He retreated to Peddler's Way and headed north at a trot. Shem could barely hear the sounds of pursuit from the forest, but he knew it would be there. *The Sol Dat never disappoint and they always come in two's.*

He chose a clump of trees just off the road on the east side and headed for it. Entering, he looked around. *Yes, this will do.* He set a trip wire along the tree line, extending it a little way out towards the road. He was glad it was still another moon before the season turned completely and the real cold set in, considering he would be camping this night without a fire. *They will rest up, wait for Mieze to rise.* Shem settled in to wait.

The first red-tinged rays of Mieze brought a slight stench which stung his nostrils. He gripped his sword, with both hands. To his left, Shem heard the thud of a body hitting the ground, a hissing moan escaping the Hunter as it tripped over the wire. *That means,* Shem swung his sword to the right about chest high. It caught the Hunter right above its shoulders and cleaved through the neck. The Hunter's torso continued a few steps before falling over, the head landed at Shem's feet. Shem spun back to his left intent on the second Hunter. The Hunter was struggling to rise, clearly injured in the left shoulder. Shem was on him in an instant, sword to his throat.

The Hunter hissed softly, doom in his eyes, "Friend Shem, don't you recognize me?"

It can't be! Shem's right hand shot out exploding on the elongated snout of the Hunter. The unconsciousWesterner crumpled to the ground in a heap. Shem's gaze moved from the inert form to the bodiless head and back. Unable to shake the foreboding creeping over him, Shem sighed and trussed up his prisoner.

4

EL-LINA

Far above the city of Celeste, capital city of the Eastern Lands, in a tall, thin, needle-like tower known as the Aeryie sat Timothy El. The El. Who, along with his wife and Consort, El-lina, High Priestess of Fiona, ruled over his people with the blessings of their goddess. At present, the El didn't feel like it was much of a blessing.

The roof over his head provided shade from the midturning sun while the open sides gave a panoramic view in all directions. The El sat at the table drumming his fingers and staring at the spire. Surrounded by fingerlike towers with onion-topped domes, the spire soared even higher than the Aeryie, which was proper for the Temple of Fiona that it anchored.

El-lina had been summoned by the goddess and was holed up in the temple where she had remained sequestered for the last three turnings. That is what had the El contemplative. Never had their goddess required the attention of her high priestess for that extended a period. Something big was on the horizon, and something big usually meant something bad.

The El ignored the well-set table before him. Scattered among the books and scrolls he had been searching through were fruit juices, light wines and water, sliced meats and fresh tubers, and fruits and nuts. All untouched.

"It's all because of the deepening red of Mieze," he declared to the open sky. "An ill omen." He rose and paced, keeping his eyes at all times on the temple spire.

"More ill than you would believe, my love."

The El had missed the arrival of the lift with its occupant, but he recognized the voice. He turned slowly and beheld her. A vision of loveliness. Golden wind swept hair encompassed an oval face giving the appearance of a halo. Eyes, slightly atilt, shone with a bright blue radiance. Around her neck nestling into the cleavage of her bosom was the Azure, a setting of three diamonds catching and reflecting the sunlight like a cluster of stars, the connection between the goddess, Fiona, and her high priestess. Slender, but not overly tall, she was clad in tight fitting black gown and had her arms outstretched, palms up, betokening welcome.

He raised his arms from the elbow, palms up and bowed slightly. "High Priestess."

The pair sat at the table, El-lina helping herself to the tubers, fruit and nuts. The El's discerning eyes could see the concern visible not far beneath the El-lina's stoic features as he waited the pleasure of his wife. Sated, at least for now, El-lina pushed away her plate and filled a goblet of light wine. He could tell she did not look forward to this conversation.

The three turnings she had spent in the presence of her goddess had filled her with firm determination. He was not going to like her decision

"Mieze is in Ascendency. Her power grows as does her malice. Worse yet, Tierra has chosen this time for her Awakening. Fiona fears that Mieze will try to prevent it. It has been given to me to stop her," informed El-lina.

The El busied his hands touching and arranging the plates in front of him. He feared the answer to his next question. Steeling himself he lifted his eyes to look at El-lina. "You will be going up against the Sun Father?"

"Not head on, but yes, and his power is growing. I must see that the Central Landers reach the Hjerte first. The successful awakening of Tierra depends on it," she replied.

Though spoken with a trace of sympathy, there was no denying the determination that lay beneath the words. In the past he had always admired that trait in El-lina. Not now. "Do you know the location of this Hjerte?"

"By that you are asking how long I will be gone. I wished I knew, love. Yes, I know where it is, but not how to get it. Only Tierra herself knows. She will let it be known when she is ready. After she chooses her hero. I must by then be there to help," said El-lina.

The El felt the emotions play across his face finally settling on acceptance. He had never really had any other choice. While the El was considered the leader of the Eastern Lands by its people, the true leader was El-lina. The dictates of the goddesses demanded that only the true leaders of the lands could be high priest or priestess. In the Central Lands, that meant Chet Sinclair. *That will be a problem.*

5

CHET SINCLAIR

Chet Sinclair sat in the command chair. His once powerful frame had long since began to sag. He leaned back, resting his close-cropped grey-haired head on the high chair. His tired eyes are beginning to glaze over; he only half listened as Hotig, priest of the Shrine of Fiona at High City, addressed the Council of Barons.

"The Land is alive, Cap Tan. As you know that is our basic tenet. It has long been taught that 'the Awakening' would come. That time will soon be upon us." Barons Camdene O'Kelly and Enri Filip sat up in anticipation.

"Are you going to wait for that, too?" interrupted Baron Uri Yakov. "Cap Tan, all we have done is wait! Wait, wait and then wait some more!"

Chet ignored the outburst. "Yes, thank you, Hotig. I shall visit the shrine on the Turning of Rest. You can instruct me then."

Baron Uri Yakov rose from his seat, not waiting for the priest to retire. "What are we waiting for? A full scale raid? The Westerners to start killing people en masse? The time for waiting is over! I say we act!" Baron Yakov pounded his fist on the table to punctuate his words.

Chet Sinclair, the Cap Tan, wilted before the barrage. His arms limp on the side rests, trying to disappear into the command chair. *Uri, why do you press? Why so eager to plunge us into war with the West? At least you are not converted to Mieze.* He shook off his lethargy. "Please be seated, Baron Yakov. We are all well aware of your feelings on this matter."

Chet gazed across the table, gauging the reactions of the other nine Barons in attendance. He looked first to his two younger cousins and his nephew. Hap Simon, eldest of the three, only a couple of cycles younger than Chet himself, was solidly in his corner. John Marcus, a big, heavily muscled, middle aged man who had a tendency to speak first and think afterward, smoldered, barely containing his anger and contempt of Yakov. *Peace, Cousin.* Wilbert Lucas, son of his wife Minerva's sister and only a hand of cycles older than Chet's son, Malcolm, sat calmly, his eyes reflective, taking in and cataloguing the attitudes of the other barons. Chet knew they were his.

Next in line were the representatives from the Grimval Valley. Barons Ichabod Sulieman and Camdene O'Kelly, both clannish, rarely gave much concern or thought to happenings north of the mighty fortress, which guarded their valley. They attended the council meetings purely for the trade aspects, and usually voted with the majority or abstained. Chet judged they would again. Barons Arn Reis, Enri Filip and Juan Iago, all sharing the Western border or having close familial ties, would side with Yakov on this issue. That left only Baron Derrick Delbert.

Derrick Delbert was just approaching his middle age. His estate lie between High City and Baron Uri Yakov's manor along the Peddler's Way, the major thoroughfare in the north before turning to parallel the Western border, and the junction to Baron Filip's estates. Chet knew he tried to avoid conflicts, numerous as they were and becoming more so, between Chet Sinclair and Uri Yakov. Many times he had acted as the intermediate between the two, preferring compromise to conflict, but it was becoming increasingly more difficult as Baron Yakov asserted himself more and more. Chet felt sympathy for Derrick, especially now that the situation in the Central Lands was deteriorating.

"Cap Tan," began Derrick as Yakov reseated himself, "perhaps it is time to increase the patrols along Peddler's Way. Just to be safe. I believe it would reassure the people."

Chet sighed. He knew this was just the opening of the next round, the compromise. "You would have me raise another army?"

"Yes!" postulated Baron Uri Yakov forcefully.

"You would love that, wouldn't you Uri?" growled Baron Marcus. "I suppose you would insist on commanding it as well."

"Of course," answered Yakov.

"And what would you have next? Or are you finally regretting turning down being Ex Cek?" threw back John Marcus.

"What are you implying, John Marcus?" sneered Uri Yakov, eyes ablaze.

"Gentlemen, a little decorum?" interjected Hap Simon. "Cap Tan, can you do nothing?"

Looking as if nothing was exactly what Chet wished to do, he implored, "Peace, Baron Marcus. Baron Yakov, I'm sure there was no implication."

The council settled into an uneasy truce. Baron Arn Reis cleared his throat. Chet groaned inwardly. He knew Arn to be a skilled diplomat.

"Surely, Cap Tan, you would agree that we have the right to defend ourselves? Some would say, a goddess-given right."

Arn's oily words, smoothly delivered, were rewarded with nods of assent around the table, especially from Barons Camdene O'Kelly and Enri Filip.

Thank you, Arn. As is your wont, you have taken a simple question and littered it with thorns. Chet began carefully, "I have stated on many occasions that all have the right to defense, goddess-given or otherwise," he added with a nod to Baron Camdene O'Kelly before continuing, "Did I not endorse Baron Yakov's arms school?"

"Reluctantly," interrupted Uri Yakov.

Chet gave him a tired look, then continued. "Reluctantly, yes, because I was loathe to open Conundrum's container. How many is enough? How many is too much? I will not have the Central Lands filled with soldiers. While we may be sensible, will our children's children's children be as well? We have open cities. Will we enclose them for our own protection? Will we contest with one another on the field of battle? I would not have it so."

Baron Yakov gave a start at the mention of enclosing the cities. Regaining his momentary lapse of control, he replied. "I would hope that we teach our children well. I know that I have done so, but who can control the future? Our concerns are for the present and at present we have a threat."

A flicker of motion up in the rafters caught Chet Sinclair's attention. A bird had flown through one of the high narrow slits used for lighting. It spiraled downward finally landing on a sconce attached to one of the many the stone pillars that held up the high ceiling of the Great Hall. He could see that there was no message attached to the leg of the bird. *A summons then. Not the most convenient of times.* The bird made eye contact with Chet then flew away.

"Cap Tan?" asked Baron Hap Simon, gently, noticing that his cousin's attention had wandered.

Feeling overburdened, but glad for the excuse to get away from the council, Chet rose from his chair. "I will not raise another army. At least not at this time. Now if you will excuse me, gentlemen, I have other business to attend to. This meeting is adjourned." Chet left the room followed by Lieutenant Gilroy, leader of the Cap Tan's Hand, his personal guard.

—⟊⟊⟊—

Uri Yakov did not bother hiding his contempt. He groused, "Can he not even pay attention? A decision has to be made. We will not just sit idly by" he gestured inclusively towards Barons Reis and Iago, "while the Westerners raid our lands."

"The Cap Tan will make the right decision in his own time," offered Baron Lucas.

"He had better, or I will," muttered Baron Uri Yakov to himself.

———✦✦✦———

Chet was disappointed with himself. He knew he should be more forceful with Uri Yakov. The problem was that Chet doubted himself. He doubted as to whether or not he still had a firm grip on the needs of the people, their desires, and to be perfectly honest, his barons. "Perhaps Minnie is right. Maybe it's time to step down and let Malcolm take over."

"I believe you still have some good cycles left in you, sir," replied Lieutenant Gilroy.

Chet chuckled, "Even when I speak aloud unknowing?"

Chet made his way up the stairway to the second floor of High City Manor. Hotig would be waiting for him there. He felt the weight of the coming meeting, especially on the heels of the council meeting. The situation in the Central Land was changing too rapidly for Chet. He longed for the easier days of his youth. Chet stopped at the door to the library. He turned to Lieutenant Gilroy, "Gil, wait out here. See to it I'm not disturbed."

"Aye, Cap Tan," replied Gilroy, taking up station at the door.

Chet entered the library and took a seat behind his desk. He heard a panel on the outside wall open and close quietly. *I'm going to have to tell Malcolm about those passageways.* He heard the rustle of the priest's silken robes and smelled the lingering scent of incense that always accompanied him. Chet leaned back in his chair and exhaled tiredly. Without looking around he offered, "Priest Hotig, please be seated."

"Cap Tan," began Hotig without further preamble, "I apologize, but what I have to say cannot wait until the Turning of Rest."

"That's the problem, priest. Nothing can wait. It all has to be handled now. Uri's not going to be held in check much longer. He wants action now against the increasing pressure from the west.

The people of the Central Lands are turning to Mieze against Fiona, and now you want to tell me that the Mother Earth is awakening. Why now, priest?"

"I wouldn't presume to be in the counsel of the goddesses, Cap Tan," said Hotig in soothing tones.

Chet was in no mood for the roundabout ways the priest usually spoke in. He snapped, "Isn't that your job?"

"That is to say, the goddesses tell me what is happening, Cap Tan, not why," answered Hotig unaffected by Chet's outburst. He waited.

Chet resigned himself to the fact that the priest would do things his way. "What have they told you?"

"Not me, Cap Tan. As you know, I am Fiona's priest. She has directed me to assist only."

Chet waited for the priest to continue, but the man sat in silence. "When is this assistance supposed to begin?"

"Yes, my pardon, Cap Tan."

Chet then heard the hidden panel open again. *Maybe he is going to put me out of my misery,* thought Chet hopefully. A young boy of about eight or nine cycles walked around Chet's desk and stood before him. He bowed and then fell to his knees, eyes lowered.

"Cap Tan, this is Wybee, an oblate. I was training him to join Fiona's priests, but it turns out he belongs to another. Speak, young Wybee," ordered Hotig.

Wybee, kept his eyes lowered. When he spoke, it was in a soft low voice. "She stirs. Tierra's time is coming. She stirs. She warns of the menace of Mieze. The Ascendency must not come to fruition. The Hjerte must be found. Tierra wishes to awaken. Her high priest must be named."

Wybee's last words caught Chet's attention. The high priests or priestesses of the gods were also the ruling lords of their lands. He felt a sinking feeling. Against hope he asked letting the question linger, "And this high priest?"

"Will be the Cap Tan of the Central Lands," finished Hotig. Chet sagged back into his chair and closed his eyes. "I'm sorry, Cap Tan. It's the will of the goddesses. I shall leave young Wybee with you in case Tierra has more to say. We'll speak of this again."

Chet heard the hidden panel close. He opened his eyes and leaned forward. The priest had been true to his word. Young Wybee still knelt before his desk. He had hoped the child would be gone, too, that he had imagined the whole encounter. *I suppose things could have ended up worse, but I don't know how.*

"Tierra says not to worry. She won't give you more than you can bear."

Chet started at the words. Was his every thought now being read by Tierra? Was this what it meant to be high priest? He wanted to feel hopeful, but couldn't stop the helplessness that threatened to overwhelm him. *Why me?* "Get up, child. Come with me."

Lieutenant Gilroy raised his eyebrow at the sight of Wybee, but remained silent as he followed Chet upstairs to the third floor. The Sinclairs had gathered in the solar, the large high ceiling central room of the Sinclair personal quarters which took up the entirety of the third floor of High City Manor. Chet saw that Minerva had taken the center seat and was flanked by Malcolm and Angeline, daughter of Baron Hap Simon. Jonathon, Chet's grandson, played on the floor, setting up his tin soldiers for a frontal assault on a wooden keep. The entry of Chet and Wybee stopped conversation. Jonathon looked up and beamed at the sight of Wybee.

"Angeline, your father sends his greetings and asks after Jonathon," No one responded to the greeting. All attention was on Wybee. Chet continued, "Everyone, this is Wybee. He will be staying with us for awhile."

"Hello, Wybee. Welcome. Who are your parents?" asked Minerva bekoning Wybee forward.

Wybee shuffled forward, head down, though he did sneak looks at Jonathon and the toy soldiers. "I have no parents, milady. I was left on the steps of the shrine. Priest Hotig took me in."

"Well, you will stay here then and be welcome. I'm sure Jonathon wouldn't mind the company," stated Minerva. She glanced around at the group waiting for someone to oppose her will. No challenges forthcoming, she looked back at Wybee. He lifted his head and met Minerva's eyes, smiling sheepishly before cutting his eyes back to the toys and Jonathon. "Go ahead. It's okay," she encouraged. He wasted no time in joining Jonathon.

Chet sat opposite Minerva. He could tell by the calculating look in her eyes that he had been the subject of the conversation which his arrival had interrupted. Also, that an explanation for Wybee was still required.

"Why?" she asked.

Chet considered an attempt to buy some time. It had seemed inevitable at the time of hearing it, *You are going to be the high priest for a new goddess,* but now faced with the task of explaining it to one's wife, the plausibility kept slipping through his fingers. Chet was pretty sure he didn't want to be a high priest, especially not the high priest of a new goddess who was going to cause further upheaval in an already unstable populace. But apparently his approval wasn't necessary. "It would seem that Baron Yakov is but one of our problems, and maybe not the biggest."

"Go on," prompted Minerva.

Chet looked around. Malcolm and Angeline leaned in to hear better. "Tierra awakens..."

"Come on, Father! Don't tell me that you have been taken in by that noise. We have always served Fiona," expostulated Malcolm.

"Chet, dear, I don't think it would be wise to declare for this new goddess. There's enough confusion and unrest among the people now," added Minerva.

"We'll need a united people to face down Yakov, Papa Chet," said Angeline.

Chet smiled in her direction. Angeline had always been a source of comfort. Her informality kept him rooted in himself, providing him with a small measure of relief from the pressures of being Cap Tan. "Or at least loyal ones," said Chet. "Tell me, would the people be more loyal to their Cap Tan or to the new high priest?" He looked around the group, studying their faces as they worked out the question posed. He added, "What if they were one and the same?"

"What are you saying, Father? Are you the high priest of this new cult?" asked Malcolm, alarmed.

"Tierra is not a cult. She is destined to head the Council of Goddesses. Above both Fiona and Mieze," informed Wybee. None had noticed his rising, but the otherworldly quality of his voice had captured their attention and held them enthralled.

Chet explained. "He is a conduit. Tierra speaks through him, at least for now. Any more than that I don't know."

Wybee sat back down next to Jonathon and watched him move soldiers around.

"Does Tierra really talk to you?" asked Jonathon, whispering excitedly.

"Yes. She has told me a secret about you, too."

"What? What did she say?" asked Jonathon barely able to contain himself.

"I can't say. It's a secret,"

"I don't like you," Jonathon pouted, turning his back on Wybee.

"Putting that aside for the moment," Malcolm began, trying to ignore the exchange between the boys, "We are either going to have to appease Yakov or oppose him. He is building his forces along the border. Despite the fact that the converts of Mieze are clamoring for the Sinclairs to step down, I believe he means to attack the West."

"That would drag us all into war," said Chet. "What does he want?"

"Everything," said Minerva matter-of-factly, "Instigators are never satisfied with appeasement until they have it all."

Chet started to argue. He wanted to, desperately, but this was family. With them there was no denying the truth, "True. Mobilize the army, Malcolm. We will at least be ready to move. One way or the other."

"Papa Chet, I can understand opposition to Fiona, but why do those converted to Mieze hate the Sinclairs?" asked Angeline.

Chet sighed, "I wish I knew, Angel,"

———

The door of Heaven's Gate, the passageway used by acolytes to enter and exit the secret tunnel system running underneath High City, opened. A hooded figure, head bowed in supplication, stepped out then carefully closed the door behind it. Hotig grinned beneath the hood remembering the first time he had passed the lintel. He had been surprised that the stairs lead downward since Heaven was the other way, at least to the mind of a child just entering the priesthood. He could have used the Priest's door in the Sanctuary, but he wanted a little more time to think, and the quiet halls of the temple were the place to do it.

The Cap Tan had not taken to the idea of being high priest. Not that that had been a surprise to Hotig. It wasn't Chet Sinclair's devotion that was in question, rather his ability to handle the increased workload; especially now. It also disturbed Hotig that he had no answer to the Cap Tan's question, "Why now, priest?" In fact, he wondered why himself. Why now? Why did the young conduit insist on being taken to the Sinclairs and what of Priest Duran's claim. On the surface it seemed a little hard to believe. There were too many questions and not enough answers.

His contemplations nowhere near complete, Hotig entered his spartan office in the Shrine of Fiona. He was startled to find High Priestess El-lina sitting in the chair before his desk. He bowed low to his high priestess.

"High priestess, what a pleasure," greeted Hotig.

"I'll take your confession later, Hotig. I assume you have felt the coming Awakening?"

Hotig smiled. "Indeed, High Priestess. In fact there was a conduit within the Shrine. I was just now returning from delivering him to the Cap Tan." Hotig noted El-lina's disappointing slump, slight as it was, as he made his way around his desk. He remain standing awaiting permission to sit.

"Pity. I would have liked to have spoken with Tierra. No matter. How did the Cap Tan react?" The high priestess motioned for Hotig to have a seat.

"As he usually does, put upon."

"Will he fulfill the dictates," she wondered aloud, frowning.

"Willingly? Probably not. I did not get the impression that he had any desire to become high priest. But in the end, I think he will be compelled to." El-lina sat silently, waiting for Hotig to elucidate.

"Conversions to Mieze have increased sharply, especially along the western border. Baron Yakov has been trying to contain it, so he claims, but he is hell bent on attacking the West. A preemptive strike to use his own words. But it may be that the followers of Mieze will subvert those plans and turn him against the Cap Tan. Fiona's shrine in Yakstown is nearly under siege."

"The Ascendency of Mieze emboldens them," stated El-lina. "I must go to Yakstown and do what I can."

"Which reminds me, High Priestess. The young priest in Yakstown, Duran, if you'll recall, informs me that Tierra has chosen her hero."

"Indeed?" El-lina sat up straighter, interest clearly piqued.

Hotig studied El-lina. He saw the rapid decision making and determination take root. *She has always been decisive.* "Yes. A drunken soldier in Baron Yakov's army. Someone named Shem. Personally, I'm doubtful, but the priest is fervent and assures me that this Shem is the one. Priest Duran claims that this soldier has been touched."

"Send a message to Priest Duran. Tell him I'll be there tonight. Now if you will excuse me, I'll be in the chapel." El-lina rose to leave.

Hotig rose and bowed from the waist. "At once, High Priestess. It shall be as you say. Praise Fiona."

After El-lina left his office, Hotig turned and opened a cabinet door behind him. Inside the sheen of a spider's web lit the interior with a silvery glow. Hotig concentrated on Priest Duran. The shimmering web began to vibrate. He was rewarded by the priest's voice emanating from the silken strands.

"Priest Hotig, praise Fiona, what can I do for you?"

"It's what I've just done for you. Tonight, you'll have the pleasure of entertaining High Priestess El-lina…"

6

HAM AND SHEM

"Why am I still alive?" hissed the creature.

The Hunter sat leaning against the trunk of the tree with his arms bound behind him. His hood was pulled back revealing the notch cut out of his right ear, his gag pulled down past his chin. He nodded towards the headless body of his once living companion lying on the ground a few feet away.

"With I'gor you honor the edict. With me, you choose shame. Your manners have lessened somewhat, friend Shem. That must be the result of you living among your own kind."

Shem sat in front of a small fire stirring a pot of stew, his mid-turning meal. He had gotten over the initial shock of discovery. I'van. The last Sol Dat he had ever expected to meet this side of the Western Forest. The only Sol Dat that had ever treated him with respect. The only one still living he amended with a glance at the deceased I'gor. *What should I do?* By custom and in adherence to Western mores he should kill I'van. They were under edict, but Shem needed more information. The nicker of an approaching horse pulled Shem's attention southward. He saw Ham riding down Peddler's Way leading Shem's horse. Even from a distance, Shem could see the smoldering anger in Ham's eyes. He got up and walked over to I'van. He replaced the gag pulled the hood over his head.

"Not a sound from you or you'll be old and wrinkled before I honor the edict."

Shem waved towards his stewpot when Ham reined in before him. "Hungry?"

"We haven't got time. Mount up," ordered Ham.

Shem went to the saddle bags on his horse for a bowl. "Whatever it is can wait a few minutes while we eat."

Ham dismounted and walked over the simmering stew. He kicked it over with his foot. "Now, mount up. We have to get to Yakstown as soon as possible," he ordered, his voice tight.

Shem's own anger ratcheted up watching his meal spill over the ground. "What did you do that for? It took me nearly a candlemark to find those coneys!"

Ham rounded on him. "And while you were out here gallivanting about all night, the Westerners attacked and burned to the ground two farms south of Third Stone. The defenders at the fort rode out and finally drove them back, but suffered heavy losses. We have been assigned to report back to Baron Yakov."

At times Shem found Ham a little irritating. This was one of those times. He knew Ham burned for glory. He also knew that Ham blamed him for being assigned to train his little brother as a scout runner instead of leading a Hand at one of the forts. *He missed a battle, so that's what eating him. If you had ever faced an Un Tier on the field of battle, you wouldn't be so eager to do so again, brother.* Shem had taught Ham everything he knew about the Westerners, everything except the stark fear one felt going up against an Un Tier or Masher, one on one. One couldn't be taught that. It was something that had to be survived.

"What about our prisoner?" Shem asked.

"What about *your* prisoner?"

"How am I going to get him to Yakstown?"

"You can drag him behind your horse for all I care. Just don't slow me down!" Ham mounted up and set out north towards Yakstown.

Shem grabbed the I'van and slung him across the withers of his horse. He had considered untying his feet and making him walk behind on a tether, but knew that Ham had not been kidding about keeping up. He swung into the saddle and urged his horse forward riding hard to catch up. He looked down at his prisoner, "This might be a bad idea."

⚜

The morning had dawned fair and crisp with just enough chill in the air to make it invigorating. Baron Uri Yakov had nearly completed his morning ride around the growing walls of his manor. The inspection would conclude at the arms school where a new class was being sworn in. His attention was only partially focused on the walls, the rest was turning over the events of the previous day.

The Council of Barons had broken up after the departure of Chet Sinclair. Uri had had enough. Gathering his support, they had ridden in haste back to Yakstown. He didn't have the time or patience to waste in High City. As far as he was concerned the council had already accomplished everything it was going to, nothing. At least here in Yakstown he could do as he pleased, and only have to answer for it if the Cap Tan found out. If then.

No other estate or city, not even High City, the seat of governance and home of the Cap Tan, had an enclosing wall. None of the previous Cap Tans, all Sinclairs, had approved of enclosing the manors. They had believed in an open society with all citizens having free access to all other cities, manors and hamlets. *But the Sinclair's don't live close to the Western Border nor are they subject to the ever-increasing raids from the West. No, the Sinclairs did not approve of my walls*, thought Uri. *So what.*

Uri didn't approve of the Sinclair's handling of affairs. The Cap Tan was weak. He either couldn't or wouldn't make important decisions about what to do in the West! *If I had my way*, thought the baron, *I'd increase the fortifications along the border and use them for staging grounds to invade the West! None of this open borders, love*

54

thy neighbor, feel good fluff! A man has to recognize his enemies and deal with them!

He turned north after passing through the gate, the din of construction competing with the clacking of wooden practice swords brought on a satisfying smile. He rode past the orchard and into the western edge of the archery range. He paused a moment watching recruits practicing with the newly developed compound bows. These new bows, a product of Grimval, were a marvel. The increased range and penetrating power were sure to prove a nasty surprise to whomever they faced. The only problem was that there weren't enough of them. He continued on, ultimately arriving at the arms school's classroom area.

This was where the newly arrived students were admitted, and they were coming in droves, young and old alike. Fears of the West had farmers sending their sons to learn defense, field hands looking for a better way of life and lately, many of the other barons sending their sons for instruction. This was what he had been waiting for. Baron Yakov had heard that Chet Sinclair had actually been roused out of his usual lethargic state when he had learned of it. Sinclair had been positively angry. Uri was ecstatic. The baron dismounted, handing the reins to the waiting stable hand.

"A full house, lord, again," informed the stable hand.

"Some big specimens?"

"A few," answered the stable hand.

Uri chuckled wickedly. Being smaller than most of his people, though compactly built, he was highly sensitive about his size and took immense pleasure in proving his combat skills, with or without weapons. Especially against larger opponents. "Good."

He walked into the room. It was fairly large, longer than it was wide. Seating was provided along the side wall for any parents, especially the visiting barons, who wished to view the proceedings. The classroom was used for graduations as well as initiations. The tables and chairs had been stacked at the back wall, making a large open hall. The new recruits were standing in their assigned groups. Barons Arn Reis, Enri Filip and Juan Iago were seated on the side.

As Uri strolled across the room he could hear a few mutters, "Doesn't cut much of a figure," "Maybe it was a mistake coming here," and "Where's the rest of him?" Nearing Cadman Gallagher, the arms master, Uri spun, throwing a dagger and burying it, business end first, in the chest of a straw man set next to the door. The thunk of the knife silenced all mutters.

He cleared his throat. "Some of you may question my ability to teach you. Who wants to try me?"

The students shuffled their feet, looking around, up, or down, anywhere but at the baron. A large lad, a couple of rows back, dressed in worn homespun, one of the earlier mutterers, started forward.

Uri grinned.

"Your pardon, milord."

All eyes turned to the doorway. A young boy rushed over to the baron, handing him a note. Perturbed, Uri quickly scanned it.

He demanded, "Where are they?"

"In... in the stables, milord," the boy replied, scared by Uri's tone.

He turned to the visiting barons and all, but ordered in his brusque manner. "Milords, come with me," The currently visiting barons showed no offense. Having known and in many cases grown up with Uri Yakov, they knew him well, they rose, joined him, and left the building.

———⋘⋙———

The trip to Yakstown had been chilly. Ham still hadn't forgiven Shem for what he believed to be an opportunity lost, but he had at least softened at the prospect of presenting the baron with a gift he had never received, a Western prisoner. Shem was at least happy for that.

They had settled in at the back stall of the stables, as far from the horses as they could get, the smell of the Hunter causing the animals to be skittish, rolling their eyes in fear. The Hunter, still cloaked and tied hand to foot, lay on the floor in the corner of the stall.

"I'll wait up front for the baron," said Ham, his voice muffled by the rag he held over his nose, though it did little to stop the odor of the Hunter. "You guard the prisoner."

Shem walked over to the huddled figure. He kicked him, none too gently, in the wounded shoulder. The creature hissed. Shem squatted down. "I should have left you with your friend. And in the same condition, too," said Shem. "So don't get any ideas and don't try any of your Hunter tricks. I'll be watching."

"And do what? Dishonor me further?" hissed the creature softly, rolling into a sitting position.

Shem jerked the hood off the head of the Hunter. The tip of the right, oversized, bat-like ear was missing. He reached out a hand to touch the notch. It had been a parting gift from Shem commemorating the last time he and I'van had conducted business. *That venture didn't end well*, recalled Shem. *Becky!* Shem fought back against the tears. Only the fact that Vlad had instructed I'van and I'gor to let him leave the West had saved Shem. *They knew who I was. They had no right to be offended.*

The Hunters who had ambushed Shem during his last gathering expedition into the West had displayed body parts, fingers or ears, of soft skins as trophies. Shem knew the original intent of the Masher who had challenged him to combat was to claim Shem's, ears! But they reneged on their promise to free him if he won. Shem had nicked I'van's ear as he was making his escape.

"It's not too late to choose the Righteous Path," said I'van.

Shem dropped his hand back by his side. He responded accusingly, "Still lecturing me on honor, are you? Your kind just murdered all the inhabitants of two of our farms. Lots of honor there."

"That was-s war," hissed I'van matter of factly.

"I've heard of no war being declared," said Shem.

"It only takes one side to declare war," said I'van. "But between us…there is still the edict. One of us must die."

Shem heard the voices of Ham and the approaching barons. He didn't want I'van running his mouth and making Shem's situation even worse. He warned, "I'm counting on it being you. Speak a word of this and I'll do more than strip you of your honor, *friend*," He grabbed the hood and yanked it back over I'van's worthless head.

"That is what Lieutenant Benjamin Arn would have me say. For the second part of my report, there it is," said Ham leading the barons into the stall and gesturing toward I'van.

Barely able to contain himself, Uri Yakov studied the creature huddled in the corner. He addressed his fellow barons.

"Well, gentlemen, shall we feast our eyes on our enemy? See what it is that is causing our strife?" The other barons nodded, each eager to size up the foe. "Pull back the hood," ordered baron Yakov.

Shem reached out grasping the back of I'van's hood. He jerked it back. Baron Yakov stood riveted. The other three barons gasped.

I'van's head was basically humanoid in shape. Eyes, ears, nose, and mouth were in the correct positions on the face, but that's where the similarity ended. The Hunter's nose was slightly elongated with the end of it looking more like that of a dog's than a man's. His ears were much larger and extending out, the left one was missing a chunk at the top. His dark colored hair was cut short all around except at the crown where it grew long and hung down his back. This tail was gathered together at the top of the head with a piece of leather and tied close to the end. What was truly amazing was his skin. While similar in texture to those of the Central Landers', his seemed more reptilian. When Shem had originally pulled back the hood I'van's skin had been dark, now it was gradually lightening, blending in with his surroundings.

"By the goddess!" murmured Baron Enri Filip.

"Are they all like that?" asked Baron Arn Reis.

Baron Juan Iago stood still, mute, a look of shock on his face.

"Would a bath help?" asked Yakov.

Shem shook his head negatively.

"I thought they were larger," intoned Baron Reis clinically.

"This one is called a Hunter, Milord," explained Ham. "It's not their normal fighter. Those would be Mashers. They are bigger, stronger, and uglier. This kind is used mainly for scouting. They also serve as archers. We first saw him at the inn at Third Stone the night the raid was occurring. I shot him in the shoulder, but he managed to escape. We tracked him and his companion and then captured this one when they tried to ambush us on our way back to report."

"The other one is dead?" inquired Baron Yakov.

"Yes, milord. This one would be as well, but we thought it best to bring him to you," answered Ham.

"You did well, soldier. Your names?"

"Ham, Milord. This is Shem," he said indicating Shem with a nod of his head.

"We need more like…What's it doing?" Yakov was staring at I'van who had gone rigid, head slightly upturned, eyes rolling into the back of his head.

Shem glanced at I'van then hung his head down. "I was afraid of that," he said to himself.

—◦❀◦—

The Sun Father was pleased at the success of his plan. He had detected Shem travelling along the border and dispatched I'gor and I'van to guard the inn. There had been an anxious moment when he thought Shem would kill both Sol Dat, but just a light touch of the bond had been all that was required. Shem had not even been aware.

The physical body of Vlad stood grasping the Auge Ose. His astral body was standing behind the barons looking at I'van.

None in the room could see or hear him, save I'van or Shem. At present he was shielding himself from the big Central Lander.

"And that is what you will do," he instructed. Vlad then walked around in front of Baron Yakov. He committed him to memory then withdrew.

Vlad watched as I'van was led out of the stable. So far the one called Shem had been the only Central Lander to touch the Hunter. But that would change. I'van had his orders. He would touch the one called Yakov, no others, then Vlad would have access to the puppet he needed.

———⟨✦⟩———

Yakov's Great Hall was filled nearly to capacity. At the head table, situated at the front of the hall on a raised platform, sat Baron Uri Yakov, Barons Enri Filip, Juan Iago, Arn Reis and their wives. Also joining them was Yakov's eldest son; Will, Ham, Shem, and Cadman Gallagher the arms master. Three large tables ran nearly the length of the hall. At the benches sat those soldiers who were off duty, the lesser parents of students, and the manor's craftsmen. At the far back of the hall was a table set up for the students themselves. The night's meal was in honor of the newly arrived students who were about to embark upon their training. After this night their meals would be taken at their barracks or mess halls.

The aroma of roast boar and fowl mingled with the sweat of all the bodies packed into the room, but no one seemed to mind. Ale flowed freely at the three large tables encouraging a festive atmosphere. Shouts and jests hurled from table to table as comrades often will. News of the latest raid had not yet become common knowledge.

At the head table Baron Uri Yakov held court. "Baron Filip, as you can see, we are going to be needing more mounts. How are you progressing with the herd?"

"It's been a good cycle. By spring I should be able to deliver a hundred more."

"That's not going to be nearly enough for all to ride," interjected Gallagher. "My lord, I believe we are going to have to go forward with infantry. I know you wanted fast mobile units, but the force is growing too quickly."

"Infantry means army. That will be harder to disguise," said Baron Reis.

Uri scoffed in contempt, "Then why bother? Sinclair isn't going to do anything about it. That would require him making a decision."

"I wouldn't sell Sinclair too short," moderated Baron Iago. "Even a whipped cur will turn and fight if you prod it too hard."

With a dismissive gesture Uri waved off the comment and sneered, "Speaking of the Cap Tan, I say we act first and ask permission later. We haven't got the time to wait around for Chet Sinclair to do nothing. We can always apologize later if need be." The other three barons nodded their agreement.

Baron Arn Reis's wife, Cynthia, touched her husband's arm. "If you please, My lord, perhaps it is time to excuse the ladies. All this militaristic talk is bad for the digestion. I'm sure we could find a place to speak of more familial matters." Baron Reis looked to Uri.

"Yes, of course," granted Baron Yakov. "My apologies. Being a widower, I have no one to steer me towards more refined conversation."

"You are forgiven, My lord," said Cynthia standing. The other wives stood as well. "I pray that someday you may find someone to fill that void." The men stood as the ladies departed.

Happy to be rid of the women, Baron Yakov bid the men reseat themselves. He shouted out, "More wine!" Then cast an inquiring look at Baron Reis.

"She suffers hearing ill directed at the Sinclair's. She's Minerva's third cousin I believe. But don't worry. I screen all of her correspondence. Besides she has grown accustomed to the luxuries provided by all the foodstuff you buy from our barony," offered a smiling Baron Reis as a house attendant refilled the goblets of the men at the head table. After the attendant departed Baron Reis continued, "Now that the by way between the Napir and the August rivers is complete you will be seeing even more shipments by barge."

Satisfied with Baron Reis's explanation and eager to move on to subjects more his liking, Uri pressed on, "Excellent, Arn, but getting back to business, most of you have seen the prisoner. We will now hear the details of the capture." He motioned to the two soldiers seated at the edge of the table. "Gentlemen, meet Ham and Shem. They are the ones who brought the prize."

"A live one?" interjected Will eagerly. His father continually found excuses to keep him away from the border patrols.

"Yes, alive," said Ham. "Two of the creatures, this particular breed are known as Hunters..."

"Breed? You mean there are different kinds?" asked Will.

"Yes," answered Ham. "I've seen two breeds, Hunters and Mashers. Mashers are the heavy infantry..."

"And the Hunters are more like scouts?" interrupted Will.

"Yes, and archers," answered Ham.

Uri's impatience got the better of him. He wanted to hear the story straight through. "Enough! There will be time for questions after. Soldier, report."

"We saw the prisoner for the first time at Third Stone Inn," began Ham. Shem sat at the end of the table, his face in his cup. Ham looked at him, giving him a worried frown. "He escaped after being wounded. He was then joined by another and trailed us until we camped for the night. They came for us after Mieze rose. Shem killed one. I captured this one and we brought him here."

"So, why did the creatures enter into our lands?" asked Baron Arn Reis whose face showed alarm that the creature, especially with its outward appearance, could sit unchallenged in an inn. Of the three visiting barons, his estates were the closest to the Western border.

Ham looked to Baron Yakov. As of yet, no mention was made of the two farms or the attack of the fort. Ham had been instructed to relate only the capture of the prisoner.

This was the opening Uri had been waiting for, the reason for bringing Ham and Shem to the front table. He planned to attack and needed to know how many of the Barons would declare their liege. "It seems that the West has made its largest foray to date a few turnings ago. Two farms were raided and burnt to the ground. Lieutenant Reis then led a sortie out and drove the Westerners back into the forest." He paused to let the news sink in and to give a nod of appreciation to Baron Reis. "It's past time for debate. This calls for action. The question is, what action do we take?"

The gathering was shocked. Will's face began turning red in anger.

"We strike back!" demanded Will, pounding his fist on the table for emphasis.

Thank you, tiger. Uri knew that part of his son's anger was directed at the fact that he had missed the fighting. *Now let's push them over the edge.*

"I don't know," said Baron Reis. "Popular support may be difficult to rally. Every turning the crowds favoring Mieze get larger. I doubt they would condone an invasion of the West."

"Then all the more reason to attack now!" declared Will, still hot.

"While the rest of us still have the favor of Fiona," added Baron Iago.

"What about Tierra?" inquired Enri Filip.

Uri noted the fervor of Enri. *I need to keep an eye on this one. I can't afford to be divided by someone chasing the latest religious fad.* He gambled that none of the others felt the same way. He didn't want to lose Enri's horses, but better that than lose this opportunity. Even so, he tried to keep derision out of his voice. "What about her? This a war council, not a religious retreat." He turned to the others. Barons Reis and to a lesser extent Iago held forts along the border. He directed his comments to them. "Have your troops been infected by this new goddess?"

"No, nor by any great fervor for Mieze or Tierra as far as I can tell. At least not as yet, Uri," said Arn, "but I can't say the same for the homesteaders. I just don't know." Iago nodded his agreement.

Uri chose to take that as an approval of his plan. "Then all the more reason to strike quickly," He turned to his arms master, "Cad, prepare to reinforce the border. Have them ready in two turnings."

"Aye, Milord," answered Cadman Gallagher.

Shem sat bleary eyed at the end of the table. He hadn't been following much of the conversation. He waved for a refill. Ham glared at him.

"I'm more interested in hearing about this prisoner." The change of subject drew the eyes of all the barons. Will looked eager, "I'm the only one that hasn't seen it."

At the mention of the prisoner, Shem lifted his head. He staggered slowly to his feet.

"Don't touch him!" shouted Shem. The next sound heard was that of Shem's large body hitting the floor.

Uri snarled, "Get that drunk out of here."

———✦✦✦———

It was surprising really. Shem had expected Ham to be furious with him, but when Shem had finally woken to Ham's shaking instead of being dismissed he found himself guarding the door of I'van's cell. Shem felt certain that his good fortune rested partially on the fact that the baron did not want the Western prisoner becoming common knowledge. At least not until he had a chance to learn everything he could about them.

Not many Central Landers, outside of soldiers at the border fortifications, had ever seen anyone from the West. Their raids, until lately, had been in isolated, sparsely populated areas along the border. Few people, in fact, had ever seen a Westerner and lived to tell. Shem's case had been an exception, an experiment that, to his knowledge, had not been repeated, but while few saw them, all knew of the results of a Western visitation.

The sounds of the cellar door opening and footsteps on the stairs alerted Shem to someone making their way down to the newly excavated cellar. Out of the corner of his eye, he saw the baron's son, Will. His gait, posture, and the look in his eye all indicated that he was most eager to see the creature. Shem had been expecting him. Opening the door, Shem pleaded, *I hope he doesn't mention anything about last night.* Will walked through without a glance. Shem slid in behind him and closed the door.

Torches burned brightly in wall sconces, illuminating the Hunter from the West who was manacled to the far wall. Four chains, attached to an iron ring embedded in the stone above the head of the prisoner, ran to each of his ankles and wrists, enabling minimum movement in a limited space. At present he was huddled on the floor directly underneath the ring, wearing nothing but a loincloth.

Uri Yakov sat on a stool off to the side, peering intently at the prisoner. Another stool sat next to the baron. Uri turned upon hearing Will enter. Will had frozen, practically in mid step. Uri motioned towards the stool.

"It's a good thing you didn't clap eyes on them for the first time on the field of battle," laughed the baron. "You would have been run through a dozen times."

"That is an ugly creature!" exclaimed Will regaining his wits. "Can't you do something about the smell?"

"I've soaked him down, myself, three times. I suggest you commit that smell to memory. You'll be the one leading the attack."

"Thank you, Father. Has it said anything?"

"Nothing of import. Surprisingly, it seems to speak our tongue or a version of it. It's hard to tell with all the hissing," informed Uri.

"Yes-s, I s-sspeak. What makes-s it your tongue? Perhaps-s you s-speak ours-s," said I'van.

Will stopped before the stool. In a blink he had a dagger in his hand. He lunged towards the Hunter. Faster even than Will, I'van caught the thrust between his manacled wrists, deflecting it up and above him. Will pulled back beyond the chains.

"It's fast," he remarked.

You don't know the half of it, thought Shem watching from the rear of the group, nerve synapses ready to explode into action.

Baron Yakov said nothing. He stared at the Hunter as if mesmerized.

———❦❦❦———

Vlad looked at the baron through I'van's eyes. He enticed the baron to move closer. Uri moved his stool closer. *Closer,* willed the Evil One, *Move within my grasp.* Uri continued staring at the Hunter.

Baron Yakov reached in.

———❦❦❦———

Shem watched, a sense of impending doom overwhelming him, as Baron Yakov reached towards I'van. He couldn't take it anymore. *I know you're here, you bastard. You can't block me out completely.* He knew what was about to happen. He had to stop it. He lunged forward, thrusting with his sword.

"No! He's here!" Shem shouted. His sword took I'van in the chest.

The baron stared at the results of Shem's interference. I'van's hand shot forward to the very extent allowed by the chains. He grabbed the baron by the wrist.

Shem groaned inwardly. He knew what had just happened. He had been too slow. Vlad, the Sun Father, had transferred his presence from I'van to Uri Yakov. I'van slumped over, dead.

Will recovered and spun on Shem, drawing his sword.

"Peace!" demanded Baron Yakov.

"But, father..." began Will.

"Leave be, son. It's alright," soothed Uri Yakov. "Shem. Leave us. In the morning be gone," ordered Baron Yakov.

Shem looked the baron in the eye. He saw the presence of the Sun Father glittering back and forth behind the orb. *I've failed*, he thought. "Aye, sir," Shem sheathed his sword and left.

———

Vlad came out of his trance. *Now I have a weapon. Now I can stop the Awakening.* He smiled and raised his hands off the Auge Ose.

7

EL-LINA

The darkened skies were briefly illuminated by a flash of lightning from the building Harvest Storm. Shadowed by that illumination was the silvery flash of an object dropping down to the surface coming to land behind Yakstown's Shrine of Fiona. El-lina dismounted from her winged steed. There to meet her was Priest Duran who threw a blanket over the horse to shield it from prying eyes. The winged steeds, considered mythical by Central Landers, existed only in the Eastern Lands. They willingly served the high priestess or others on her request, but their presence was a beacon announcing Fiona's high priestess. Neither El-lina nor Duran wanted to gin up any more hostility from the supporters of Mieze than already existed, hostility that both knew would be heightened by the known presence of the high priestess of Fiona.

Duran raised his arms from the elbow, palms up and bowed from the waist, "High Priestess, well met."

El-lina merely nodded, her glance scanning their surroundings, She studied Yakstown's spiritual leader. *Young for a priest. Bright eyes. Let's hope their fervor is for devotion and not the mindless passion that passes for reverence these turnings.* "Well met, Priest Duran. Let us hurry inside. This storm is moving in fast."

As they passed through the chapel, El-lina was surprised at the number of people in attendance. She whispered to Duran, "Are there always this many?"

"Not in the past, high priestess, but now they are afraid. Afraid of the rapid growth of Mieze among them," he replied. "Also they are confused about Tierra. They don't know who they should call upon."

"I see," said El-lina. She reached up to touch her Azure. Instantly she knew what she had to do. "Give me a moment, Priest Duran. May I use your pulpit?"

"Of course, high priestess."

El-lina made her way to the dais. Once behind the pulpit she spread her arms wide, palms upward, "Children," she proclaimed to the assembly.

Though spoken in a normal voice, her words were amplified in the hearts of those before her. They raised heads to stare at the pulpit. As one they raised their arms palm upward, "High Priestess!" they chorused.

"Trouble not your hearts in these times. The awakening is upon us! And it will be glorious! Our beloved Fiona bids us welcome the arrival of her sister, Tierra. Though the travail may be bitter, what birth isn't, better, more peaceful times await! Therefore be glad, my children. Our beloved Fiona wishes it so!"

El-lina lowered her arms. Already she could feel an easing of the people's hearts. *These will spread the word. Hopefully it will be enough.* El-lina left the dais and followed Duran into his office. She sat.

"Thank you, High Priestess. I have said much the same, but coming from you it sounded so achievable."

"Praise Fiona."

"Praise Fiona, High Priestess, but now if I may ask about the reason for your visit," asked Duran.

"You may ask, but what I really want is a report on this *hero* you've named, Brother Duran." Duran visibly relaxed at her use of the Informal Acceptance in calling him Brother. "Is it true?"

"Oh, yes, Sister. I was there when she touched him. He staggered to his feet and drew his sword. He looked majestic," Duran added in an aside, "Then bellowed, 'None will prevent the Awakening as long as I draw breath!' A spot of green appeared above the hero. It grew to the size of a marble. The purest, most vibrant green I've ever seen. Then it plunged itself into his chest!"

She had been sensing the priest, since he began his story. She discovered that he absolutely believed that what he had just recounted was true. *I have to find this hero.* "Quite dramatic. Who is he and where would I find him now?"

Duran shrugged. "His name is Shem, but I don't know where he might be at present. He left the next morning not remembering a thing. Said he was part of Baron Yakov's army and he had patrol. Another came with a horse and they rode off. That is the last I saw him."

El-lina reached up and touched her Azure. *In Yakov's army. Yes, that should work.* She dropped her hand. To the booming accompaniment of the unleashed Harvest Storm raging outside she made a request of Duran. "I'll need a peddler's wagon and a few other things..."

———⟨⟩———

Shem had known this day would come. He had known it since the day he first arrived and Ham had only reluctantly agreed to help him, but knowing did not fill the emptiness. He had proven his brother right, again. Even worse, he had failed. Failed to prevent Vlad from bonding Baron Yakov. As a result the largest army in the Central Lands was now indirectly controlled by the Sun Father of the West. Shem would have left even if he had not been dismissed. He would not, could not serve the Sun Father. He only wished he could find some way of making Ham believe him, but he couldn't do that without telling Ham that he himself had been bonded. And that was something that he never told anyone.

So Shem stood before his bunk, his meager possessions rolled up in his blanket. He wrapped his sling around his forehead and settled his blanket roll across his back. Looking around one last time, he sighed and left the barrack. The first person he met stepping out of the door was Ham. *Oh, great!* "Don't start. I don't want to hear it," said Shem.

"You never do, Brother, but I just wanted you to know, I didn't even try to save you this time!"

Shem hung his head. He didn't want Ham to see the relief that was building up within him at the thought of leaving. *Good, I didn't want you to save me.* "I'm sorry, Brother. I didn't mean to bring any shame on you," he mumbled.

"You never mean to, then you do. Well I've had it. I've looked after you longer than I care to remember. The time has come to look after me! As of last night you are on your own. Here," Ham handed over a small leather purse. "The bursar said that this is all your wages up to yesterday."

Shem hefted the purse. It felt light to him. "They must have taken out for breakage." He tied it to the inside of his belt.

"That and a little extra for your trouble. Where now?" asked Ham.

"I thought I'd go south. I've seen some land on our patrols. I thought I might try my hand at farming," answered Shem.

"Then we'll probably pass you on the road," said Ham, "The baron's reinforcing outposts down Peddler's Way. We leave in the morning. Don't bother saluting when you see me."

Shem looked at his brother's tunic sleeve. *How could I have missed the Leader patch?* "Civilians don't salute."

The morning sun shone brightly, bringing a bead of sweat to Shem's forehead as he walked leisurely down Peddler's Way feeling freer than he had in cycles. Up ahead something shimmered in the distance. *I'm going to have to make me a hat,* thought Shem bringing his hand up to shield his eyes. *That looks like a wagon up ahead. It must have broken something to be stopped in the middle of the road. Maybe I can help him out.* Shem adjusted his blanket roll, which contained his sword, and continued on.

By the time Shem reached the wagon, he had determined that it was a peddler's wagon. Longer than most and enclosed, it had four wheels, a folding down sidewall that doubled for a table to display wares, and a door in the back with three steps leading down. It was painted bright red. One of the wheels, the left rear, had fallen off.

The peddler sat on a camp stool on the shaded side of the wagon. He had a long thick staff lying on the ground next to a log that when set on end would come up to the wagon floor. The log was rounded and grooved on one end. The wagon wheel was leaning up on the side of the wagon. The peddler, himself, was on the down side of his prime, flecks of gray beginning to be noticeable in his hair, his eyes were a brilliant blue.

Shem greeted the wagon, "Good morning, traveler,"

"Good morning and well met," returned the peddler.

"Might I be of help?" asked Shem.

"You might," answered the peddler. "I can lift the wagon up, but I can't put the wheel on. I could put the wheel on, if I could lift the wagon up. You see my problem."

Shem tried not to chuckle aloud at the manner of the peddler's speech, but there was no way to keep the amusement out of his eyes. "Indeed." He moved to the left corner and tested the weight of the wagon. It was heavy.

"You will need a healer if you try it that way," stated the peddler. He set the log on end behind the left corner of the wagon. He took the staff and placed it in the grooved end with about a third of it under the wagon. He grasped the long end out as high as he could. Shem, who was taller, grasped the staff further out.

"Pull it down," ordered the peddler. Both men pulled and the wagon rose. "Hold it there," said the peddler. Shem held the staff down. It was surprisingly easy. The peddler took the wagon wheel and slid it onto the greased axle. He took a nail and put it through a hole in the axle, then bent the end over with a hammer. "Let it down easy."

Shem eased off the staff. The wagon settled down on all four wheels. The sound of approaching horses caught his attention. From down the road, off towards the west, came the rhythmic clopping of horses coming at a trot. He suggested to the peddler, "I'd get the wagon off the road."

"They can go around," replied the peddler.

"I doubt they'll want to," said Shem. "That's probably Baron Yakov with the reinforcements for the border forts."

"Do tell. Nothing for it then," The peddler stowed the log and staff then led the pair of horses hitched to the wagon off the road leaving it clear.

Shem had no desire to see either the baron or his brother. He felt the eyes of the peddler on him as he ducked behind the wagon. From his hiding spot he heard the peddler call out.

"A good morning, Milord. Could I interest you in anything?"

Despite his feelings to the contrary, Shem was unable to resist. He peeked around the corner and observed Baron Uri Yakov ignoring the peddler. The column moved on.

"Where might you be about?" asked the peddler after Shem had reemerged.

"Nowhere in particular."

"Imagine that. I've been there myself, you know. And...I'm on my way back. Join me?"

Shem considered the offer. He searched his feelings and found no animosity towards the peddler. *If I join him I can at least ride,* thought Shem as he peered down Peddler's Way watching the last of Yakov's guardsmen as they disappeared southward. He shrugged and stuck out his hand. "Why not. I'm Shem."

The peddler smiled. "I'm called the Peddler."

⧫

El-lina was pleased that her gambit had worked. She would have liked to reveal herself, but it was too early; however, now that Shem was travelling with her, she could probe him at her leisure, undetected. She whistled a lilting tune.

The wagon rolled out of Third Stone heading south. Shem sat next to the Peddler leaning back and resting against the wagon front his newly acquired hat pulled low over his eyes.

The Peddler held the reins of his team loosely and from time to time cut his glance in Shem's direction studying the former soldier. He raised his hand to his throat as if fingering an object that hung there. The sensing complete, El-lina smiled. *He does indeed carry the touching, but has no idea what to do with it.*

Passing the fort just south of Third Stone, Shem roused and looked around. The men from the fort had broken into groups and were practicing archery, some rode with lances circling a quintain, other practiced with swords. Shem spotted Ham leading a Hand around the quintain.

The Peddler noted his interest. He asked, "Friend of yours?"

"Once," replied Shem, "At least as much as a brother could be."

"What happened?"

"I guess he got tired of babysitting me," replied Shem with just a trace of regret.

"Care to talk about it?" asked the Peddler.

"No."

What a troubled choice, Fiona. Will he accept guidance? El-lina had complete faith in Tierra's decision. She wished she had the same for the decisions of Shem.

The sickly scent of rotting flesh too long unburied announced the farm before the Peddler saw it. Shem was still huddled under his hat as the wagon rounded the slight turn in the road.

The Peddler observed, "Not a pleasant sight...or smell."

"War never is," Shem responded.

"War? I've heard of no war."

"You will. Baron Yakov will not let this go unavenged."

The Peddler jumped on the opportunity to discover the extent of Shem's political acumen. "But what of the Cap Tan? I've heard he is opposed to war with the West."

"What of him? Is he here?" Shem looked around. "I don't see him."

Provincial and pragmatic, she assessed.

When the farm came into sight, she saw a handful of people were busy burying the remains of those killed in the raid. Graves already dug and filled with the last remains of the former inhabitants were surrounded by people with bowed heads. An acolyte was giving a benediction for the deceased.

"Blessed Fiona take these into your bosom to rest the rest of the faithful," intoned the acolyte.

The Peddler whispered under his breath, "Amen."

"This wouldn't have happened, if they had accepted Mieze!" shouted a man at the back of the crowd.

"Blasphemy!" said another.

"Look around you. Is this salvation? Or the just reward of the unfaithful? The next farm down was spared. Spared because they converted," asserted the first man.

"Lies! They will be damned for their heresy!" the second man responded.

The people around the grave sites separated into two loose groups. The acolyte tried to diffuse the growing argument. "Peace, my good people. There is room for all, and all will be healed with awakening of Tierra."

"Tierra," responded the first man derisively, "I see no Tierra. If Tierra was here then why does Mieze grow larger with each turning? Why is she becoming blood red? To cleanse the land of the unfaithful! That's why!"

"Stop the wagon," said Shem as he reached for his sword belt.

Surprised, the Peddler asked, "What are you going to do?"

"I don't know," Shem replied. He hopped off the wagon and walked up to the gathering of people. He singled out the man supporting Mieze. "Who would deny Tierra?"

The people surrounding the accuser pulled away leaving him standing alone before Shem who was a head taller and forty pounds heavier.

"Who are you, some kind of hero?" He sneered.

Shem flinched as if struck. His sword flashed out of its scabbard in a direct arc towards the man's neck. It stopped inches away from impact. The muscles in Shem's neck and arms corded with sustained effort. Sweat trickled down the sides of Shem's brow, but he could move the sword no farther.

The man laughed. He turned and walked away. Nodding his head in Shem's direction he said to his followers, "Hero."

Mocking laughter followed Shem back to the wagon. His face burning in embarrassment, he climbed back aboard.

The Peddler said nothing. El-lina had felt the will of Tierra as it stopped the blade. The time for the letting of blood in her name had not yet come. *Hopefully, it won't.* El-lina could sense the confusion raging within Shem. His embarrassment and anger at his inability practically emanated from him in waves.

She felt sorry for Tierra's hero. El-lina snapped the reins to urge the team forward. "Did she say anything to you?"

"Are you going to mock me, too?" asked Shem bitterly.

—◦◊◦—

Shem sulked. None of his decisions had turned out well this turning. *Why wasn't I able to complete my stroke? If I hadn't killed I'van I would have been at the fort at Third Stone. If I hadn't agreed to travel with this peddler then he wouldn't be mocking me now. How did he know that I heard something? Or did I?* It had actually been more of a feeling, a sense of wrongness that had swiftly built the moment his sword cleared his scabbard and solidified just before his stroke landed. He hadn't actually heard anything. He had also felt the color blue then green. *How do you feel a color?* Shem didn't know, but it was the last thing that caused him to scratch his head the most. A thought had been implanted in his mind. A seed that had easily taken root. *The Hjerte. I have no idea what or where it is, but I've got to find it.* He understood none of it. He looked at the Peddler closely. His eyes were a brilliant blue.

—◦◦◦—

The Peddler broke the silence that had settled over them since the burial. "It's a couple of candlemarks before dark, do you know what is ahead?"

"Fourth Stone. There is only a couple of steadings, almost a hamlet, unless the people fled after the raids."

The Peddler looked about. To the east, all he saw was fallow fields with no sign of agricultural activity, to the west the ever present forest. He pulled the wagon off the road on the east side. "This looks like as good a place as any to stop," he declared, setting the brake and climbing down off of the front bench. He looked at Shem, who had long since shed the peaked hat, and pointed to the sling Shem wore wrapped around his forehead.

"Are you any good with that?"

"Fair," said Shem.

"Why don't you see if you get us a couple of coneys? I'm thinking a little rabbit stew would go down well."

Shem reached under the bench to retrieve his bundle. He pulled out a pouch of stones and attached them to his belt. He gave a look towards the forest then headed into the fallow fields unwinding the sling from around his forehead.

The Peddler busied himself making a fire, getting out a stew pot and selecting some vegetables from his provisions. The vegetables were still fresh having been traded for at Third Stone and were soon simmering. The same could be said for the thoughts of the Peddler as he entered the wagon. *How to teach him without revealing myself. That's the problem.* He opened a cupboard door. In the corner of the otherwise empty cupboard was a silvered spider's web. The lilting voice of El-lina caressed the web. "El, Love."

"Yes, dearest," he immediately responded.

"I have found him. The hero of Tierra."

"Are you sure?" He asked.

"Aye, Love. I've sensed the touching. I feel the draw. It is strong."

"Does he know?"

"He's struggling," she answered.

"Isn't it always so? I have sent Il-ar to gather the riders. They should be ready by the cold solstice."

"I have one more test, but I am positive of the results. Then I'll nudge this hero in the direction of the Sinclairs and see what happens."

"Be careful," said the El, signing off.

"Aye, Love," El-lina closed the cupboard door and returned to tend the fire and stewpot. She settled in to wait for Shem.

—✥—

The sun was nearing the horizon when Shem ambled in out of the fields, idly swinging his sling in a slow arc, two coneys in the other hand. *Movement!* Suddenly a covey of plump field fowl burst from a tuft of grass, taking wing. Faster than eyes could follow and describe, Shem spun and loosed. Two of the fowl fell to the ground. Shem smiled. *U'bad would be proud. Shem's step faltered. U'bad? Why not my father? Why do I need to make someone proud of me anyway?* Shem's pleasure at his achievement dimmed somewhat. He collected the birds and walked to the fire, dumping the birds and the coneys at the Peddler's feet.

"I killed them. You clean them. I prefer the birds."

"Fair enough," said the Peddler reaching for the coneys first. "Wine in that jug if you want some," he added.

No, Shem said to himself, *Say no, say no, say no!* Shem froze. He was midway between the fire and the wagon with his back to the Peddler. "Thanks, friend, but if I had one cup I'd drink it all."

"Then drink it all," the Peddler replied.

Shem sat before the fire, face flushed with the effects of the wine. His inhibitions had left him long ago and he had just finished regaling the Peddler with one of the many stories of his youth that he had so far recounted. One that had involved Ham as well, back before the estrangement.

"You and your brother seemed to be pretty close," remarked the Peddler.

Remorse flooded Shem taking up what little space the wine had left. He couldn't keep it out of his voice or thoughts. *But that was then. Before I became a burden to him.* He remarked, "Yes, once upon a time."

The Peddler poured the last of the wine into Shem's cup and changed the subject abruptly. "Drink up! Tell me about Tierra."

Shem tossed the wine down his throat with one gulp. His face lit up with excitement. "I'm her hero."

"You don't say," replied the Peddler, "what does that entail?"

Shem shook his head as if trying to clear it. *The Hjerte.* He struggled to fit a complete sentence together. "I…uh…haven't got a clue. Something…about a stone…no, a heart? Not real sure. 'N don't wanna to get tangled up with bunch of priests to find out!"

"And yet, you became this *hero* while visiting a shrine," prodded El-lina.

"Well, was drunk. Don't 'member lot 'bout it."

"Like right now?"

Shem beamed with pride, "Tes! I mean, yes! Like now."

"What if I could find you someone to help you understand?" asked El-lina.

Shem sat weaving back and forth, a stupid drunken grin on his face. The air around the Peddler shimmered. When it cleared El-lina sat before Shem. Shem's eyes grew big and he leaned forward slowly. *So beautiful.* Just before he toppled into the fire El-lina reached out and touched him, gently pushing him back into a sitting position.

Shem felt the warmth from El-lina's fingertips spread through him, centering on his chest where he felt something else, similar and sympathetic to the touch of El-lina. He didn't know what it was, but it was proud of him. He grinned a sloppy grin as he slowly toppled over backwards, unconscious.

———◦◦◦———

It had been the deepest and most complete sensing El-lina had ever given anyone. It almost assuaged the guilt she felt for abusing Shem's weakness for alcohol, but her need had been great. At least that is what she told herself. She sat back and sighed. She had felt the still growing kernel of touching and had sent what comfort she could through it. What had disturbed her, though, was another link she had sensed. A very old one, little used. One between Shem and Vlad the Sun Father. This could prove to be troublesome. She had no way of knowing how strong it was, but she did know this, Shem must be kept out of the West at all costs. Ironically, they were now and had been travelling for the last two turnings within a sling's throw of that very place. At least El-lina now knew what must be done. "Tierra seeks the Hjerte, the heart stone, the link between her and her high priest. I wish now that Hotig had not been so hasty with the conduit, but that is where we go next."

———◦◦◦———

Shem woke with his head pounding like a kettle drum. The sun was already halfway up in the sky. He rolled over to get up and discovered the only thing pounding worse than his head was his bladder. He stumbled over to the nearest tree. He was still there when the Peddler walked by with their freshly filled water skins.

"Shem! Good morning, Brother."

Shem groaned. Whatever fuzzy thing it was that had taken up residence in his mouth and throat had yet to move on allowing him the ability to make coherent sounds.

"Feeling that good, huh? I have to say this about you, you sure are entertaining!"

Shem groaned again and leaned his head against the tree.

"When you are done there, I've brewed some tea that will fix you right up," the Peddler offered as he walked to the wagon. He gave a last parting shot, "Oh, Tierra is pleased to have you as her hero."

The almost hamlet of Fourth Stone consisted of four cottages built close together, two on each side of the road. The inhabitants shared an animal pen between the houses and farmed the field on the away side. It was a typical steading designed for expansion that was favored by the farming communities. As more home owners moved onto the land they purchased the steading grew, but the commerce center remained near the original holdings.

Fourth Stone was still intact. The Peddler waved at the people working the fields as he rode by, but none indicated that they wanted him to stop. Shem, sitting on the bench beside him, was beginning to feel human. He stirred. *What happened last night?* Some vague memory of a woman flitted through his fragmented thoughts, here then gone. *No more! I'll not touch drink again.* "Where are we going?"

"High City," answered the Peddler.

Shem grunted and settled back into the wagon bench and fell back asleep.

Ba-boo-oom! The concussive blast from the thunder clap jolted Shem out of a deep sleep. Lightning crashed, followed immediately by the exploding sap of the struck tree which came crashing down next to the road. Instantly alert, he looked around. It was impossible to determine the time of day as clouds covered the sky as far as the eye could see and it was unnaturally dark underneath. "What time is it?"

"A couple of candlemarks past midturning," replied the Peddler, voice tight with suppressed fear.

Shem looked around uncertain. Something didn't fit. He chuckled. "We are still short of Fifth Stone, I see."

"I'm glad at least one of us finds our present predicament amusing. I for one have no desire to be caught in a Harvest Storm," said the grim-faced Peddler.

Harvest storms were no laughing matter. They were dangerous, killing storms occurring about a moon and a half before harvest time and lasting for half a moon. One was said to have nearly burnt High City to the ground about a hundred cycles back. Fire from the lightning strikes was the biggest threat, but the torrential rains didn't help much either. How the fires kept burning in them was a mystery to all. However, what survived the storms gave overabounding crop yields. People usually took to their homes and rode them out, praying lightning didn't strike.

"Nor I," acknowledged Shem. "I was just looking around for a very large, very old tree. I just now realized that it was lying on the ground." Another bolt of lightning smashed into the ground ahead of them on the west side of the road punctuating Shem's revelation and showering them with clods of dirt.

"And the import of this landmark?" asked the Peddler hopefully.

"Shelter. Right past that blasted tree you'll find a trail going into a copse of trees. Take it."

Suddenly the sky opened up and the rain poured down. The two travelers were instantly drenched. Forward visibility was reduced to near zero. A third bolt struck the ground. Shem wasn't exactly sure where but it was so close he could feel the shock wave and taste the gritty ozone of the spent lightning. The horses' eyes rolled up in their heads and they bolted. Despite the best efforts of the Peddler with the reins, all they could do was to hold on as the horses raced into the darkness through the pouring rain, bouncing the pair around on the wagon bench. Shem looked around. The lightning moved on. The rain lessened. They were now surrounded by trees and were no longer on the road. "I hope these trees are from the thicket."

The Peddler frantically tried to get the horses to turn around, but they refused to reenter the lightning-filled skies beyond the woods. An arrow thunked into the wagon between the heads of Shem and the Peddler. Shem's hopes sank. They were in the West.

—⟨◊◊◊⟩—

The meeting wasn't very productive. They seldom were when Vlad opened them up to his Clan Leaders. The inevitable bickering and squabbling, like two dogs fighting for the same bone, didn't take long to break out and would continue until Vlad raised his hand in commanding silence. Even though Vlad was in attendance, the meeting was being run by Erik and it was obvious that Erik needed the practice in dealing with high level conflict resolution. It would still take him awhile to realize that in the West conflict was best dealt with with the point of a sword or the convincing power of Mieze.

"The Un Tier, they wish to drive straight through the soft skins puny little forts. The soft skins, they are too few and too weak. I say smash them head on! Forget bridge!" roared the Un Tier Clan Leader, thumping his massively muscled chest.

The Sol Dat Clan Leader, not having nearly the Un Tier's muscle mass or the protection of their bony exoskeleton, generally put some thought into his decision making. Not much, but some. His bat-like ears twitched, "The soft skins will ride their horse soldiers out the back gate. Then we would have to fight and chase them all the way to bridge and some will escape," argued the Sol Dat Clan Leader. "Better to go around out of sight, burn bridge and everything else on way back. The soft skins will be confused seeing fight come from behind."

"No! Attack from front!" bellowed the Un Tier Clan Leader.

Vlad caught Erik's eye and gave him a piercing look. *End it, cub.* The Sun Father had reached the limit of his patience. Erik gave the slightest of cringes.

"Gentlemen, thank you for your input. You both have strong points. We will use the pincer movement, burn the bridge, and everything else on the way back," stated Erik.

The Un Tier Clan Leader began a protest. Erik's voice became soft and menacing, "You wish to question me?" The Clan Leader of the Un Tier hesitated, sucking in his cheeks and pulling on his smallish ear set low on his jaw. Erik continued, "I thought not. If the Sol Dat plan fails, you can use them for sword thrust practice. Mieze would be pleased. One more thing. You will use the new rock throwers. I want you to knock the walls down."

The Sol Dat Clan Leader's smug expression evaporated as the Un Tier Clan Leader nodded his agreement, saliva drooling down in ropy strands from his tusks.

"*Noooo!*" Vlad's piercing, infuriated shout rang out, audible in the minds of all in the Western Lands. All covered their ears, wincing in pain. The shout died away. Vlad's astral body raced to the area where El-lina had entered the Western Lands. He saw her. She and another, one from the Central Lands. His anger nearly caused Vlad to miss the deeply buried bond in the soft skin. *Yes, it was the one called Shem.*

El-lina was fighting the fear of the horses, her glamour unable to disguise her from Vlad's eyes or senses while in his lands. Vlad's rage increased. "Get her!" His sending reached all Westerners in the border forest and included her position. A pair of Sol Dat near the intrusion point picked themselves up off the ground and raced towards the site.

Vlad slumped back into his chair, emotionally drained. *How dare she enter his lands!* However, he now had proof of what he had long suspected. The Easterners were in league with the Central Lands. He needed to know how deep their councils ran, how much the Central Landers knew. He sent another sending, "Capture the woman or kill her, but bring me the other one. I would like to...talk...to him."

Vlad turned to Erik before dismissing his commanders, "Launch the attack"

—◦◦◦—

El-lina tried to get the horses under control, but not even the sending of soothing thoughts to them could override their terror. She could sense the helplessness of her Eastern mount while in the traces of the wagon's harness. Even he fought her control. She also kept an eye on Shem marveling in the calmness he displayed. It was as if he were an entirely different person.

Shem reached under the bench pulling out his bundle and strapping on his sword. He unslung his sling and tucked the loose ends in his belt, affixing the pouch of stones next to it. He looked around wistfully.

"A bow would be nice," he muttered softly.

The Peddler opened the front sliding window and reached into the wagon. He pulled out one of compound bows used by Baron Yakov's forces and a quiver of arrows. He passed them to Shem.

"Where?—" began Shem.

The Peddler returned his attention to the horses, "No time, but I am a trader."

Shem studied the angle of the arrow stuck in the wagon, then looked back into the woods, nocked and fired. No more arrows came from that direction.

"You can give up on those horses," said Shem putting a hand on the reins and looking the Peddler in the eye. "Unless you can convince them that the sun is shining, they are not going to move. You know where we are."

"Yes, and I've got to leave as soon as possible!"

"We are about a furlong, furlong and a half in. I'd say we probably have a candlemark..." Shem was interrupted as another arrow thunked into the wagon, just missing his head. "or less before we are overrun." He slid from the bench and crouched near the front wheel, looking westward. El-lina bailed on the other side, keeping Shem in sight while she made her way forward, releasing her eastern mount from the traces. Free of confinement the horse calmed down. Shem scanned the woods towards the back of the wagon. He raised to a kneel and loosed.

Anxious, El-lina asked, "Did you get him?"

"Yes, why do you ask?" inquired Shem.

El-lina placed her hand on the top of Shem's head. "Because I have to go. Now. I'm truly sorry, Brother Shem. You will remember none of this."

Shem's eyes widened then he slumped, unconscious, to the ground. The air around the Peddler and the unhitched horse shimmered. An arrow narrowly missed the shimmering air and imbedded itself into the wagon's bench. The air returned to normal revealing El-lina sitting on the back of a black, winged steed.

She commanded, "Now, horse. Fly!"

The horse leapt into the air, its powerful wings driving El-lina swiftly upward towards safety. She looked down at the rapidly shrinking figure of Shem. Abandoning him tugged at her conscious. She knew that she would have to spend many candlemarks atoning for the wrongness of her actions, but she had been forbidden direct conflict and above all else she could not be captured by the Westerners. There was nothing else she could have done.

8

BARON YAKOV

The lightning flashed, piercing the predark gloom above the Sixth Stone fort briefly illuminating Baron Uri Yakov and his son Will as they stood looking over the crenellations. At the edge of the dusky darkness Uri could make out fleeting glimpses of forms crossing into the Central Lands from the Western forest. The skies opened up instantly drenching the two men and masking any further observations. They strolled towards shelter. Uri, unperturbed by the pouring rain, asked his son, "What do you make of it?"

"Hard to say in the dark, impossible in the rain. It could be a raiding party or worse," replied Will.

Uri nodded his agreement. "Inform Leader Bickford. Double the watch and put everyone on alert. Quietly."

"That's not going to make anyone happy," assuaged Will.

As they entered the dry protection of the watch tower Uri said, "No one's here on vacation. I'll be in the keep."

He studied the faces of the huddled men who had ducked into cover as the rain began. It was easy to distinguish the reassigned veterans of Third Stone from the new replacements. There was a hardness to them and a healthy amount of respect for the foe. The others displayed either anxiousness or fear. Stories had been told of the clash at Third Stone. Stories of arrows bouncing off the bony skin of the Mashers. Stories of soldiers getting pulped by a single blow of the Masher mattocks. Lastly, stories of the cavalry's charge and eventual victory. Uri suffered from no illusions. *If this is an attack, I cannot afford to be trapped here.*

A candlemark later Will entered the main hall of the keep, dressed for battle. Uri and Bickford stood at the head table, maps laid out before them. Both men turned to watch as Will made his way to the table.

"The lightning has moved off towards the north and the rain is easing," Will reported. "There's a faint glow of fire off to the east."

Uri asked, "Lightning strike?"

"Could be," answered Will.

"Attack! Attack! To arms! Mashers to the east!" The alarm shattered the calm. The three men raced outside heading for the nearest watch tower. From the northeastern tower Baron Yakov watched the approaching horde. In the near darkness it was impossible to count accurately but judging from the torches scattered throughout the Western army, Uri determined that they were outnumbered. Men continued to scramble into position on the east side of the fort.

"Attack! Attack! Mashers to the west!" came the alarm. It was accentuated by a crushing whump of a stone hitting the walls of the fort. "They're throwing huge stones against the fort!" came the call.

"What?" muttered Uri. "What devilry is this?" He felt a slight shudder run through walls as another huge stone struck the west wall. Cracks were beginning to appear in the masonry. He did not believe the fort would hold out against a bombardment. "Bickford, have the cavalry mount up. We're going to have to punch through and make our way north. We'll open a hole in their lines for the infantry. Hurry!"

Bickford hurried off, shouting orders. Uri and Will descended the stairs of the watch tower, joined by increasing numbers of soldiers streaming down towards the bailey. Only those with compound bows remained on the walls.

They mounted just before the east facing gate. Cavalrymen with lances couched waited for the gate to open. Every third man also carried a compound bow, a grim face, and quiet desperation. Uri leaned over and whispered to his son, "Stay by me, Will. If we have to make a break for it, I want you close."

"Bickford, give us two volleys from the walls and then get down here as quick as you can and follow us. We head north." Uri waited as Bickford left to carry out his orders.

"Father, do you think the Cap Tan will approve?" asked Will.

Uri snapped, "We don't need permission to defend ourselves!"

"No, Father. I meant approve of the West attacking. I'm sure they didn't ask his leave," laughed Will as the command to fire was given to the archers above.

The gate opened and the mounted men swept out. The Mashers had dropped the torches they had been carrying, many being dropped by dead fingers. The column of cavalry clattered across the drawbridge and turned north. They slammed into the Masher position, lances lowered and powered through the Westerners lines. Wheeling, the column returned to widen the gap. The baron's infantrymen were beginning to fight their way through the gap. Mashers gave way to the lancers allowing Hunters to slip through with their bolas to bring down the horses when they could be found in the night.

⟡

Vlad stood behind the Auge Ose with his hands upon the stone. He could sense the presence of Uri Yakov among the defenders. He didn't like it, not one bit. He was going to have to change his plans. *It won't do to have my puppet killed.* He sought U'cha, leader of the Un Tier. *Let the soft skins escape. Chase them northward.* He monitored the fleeing Central Landers. When they neared the next fort, he would unleash the next wave of his attack. He would drive them all the way to his puppet's city, Yakstown. Vlad smiled.

———〰〰〰———

Will materialized out of the misty darkness, his last lance shattered a third of the way down. Weariness accompanied him as he rode up to report to his father. They were joined a moment later by Bickford.

"The Mashers show themselves just enough to draw our attention then give way in the darkness only to rematerialize a different spot down the line," said Will. Bickford nodded his agreement of the assessment.

"They are also squeezing us eastward away from the road and the fort at Fifth Stone," added Bickford.

Uri pondered, "So, we're being driven, but where?"

"Either the river—" began Bickford.

"Or back to Yakstown," finished Will.

Uri looked up, judging the night sky. The Harvest storm had gradually eased while it moved north. The cloud cover had yet to break completely, but where it had the increasingly red glow of Mieze burst through lending strength to the arms of his enemies. At present the cloud breaks showed a lightening sky. Uri said, "I judge a candlemark or less until dawn. We should be at Fifth Stone by then."

"But what will we find?" mused Will.

Uri replied, "We'll find out how widespread the attack is. Pull the forces back."

Like his son, he wondered what the dawn would bring. *The stone throwers had been a new development. Did the West have any more surprises? The fort could have been held if not for those.* Though truthfully their chances of withstanding a siege had been considerably less than Uri wanted to admit. That more than anything else necessitated Uri's current plan of action. Still the why of it all bothered him.

The rising of the sun found Uri's forces a furlong to the east of Fifth Stone fort. Through the lifting mist he saw that the fort was surrounded. The Mashers and Hunters that had been pressing him all night had amassed themselves between the fort and his men. Uri watched as a single Masher and Hunter approached the fort under a flag of truce, escorting a dark robed figure. Some unknown force lent strength to the speaker's voice. All could hear.

"Soft Skins, do not die in vain! Accept Mieze and live. All others will perish. Decide!"

Will cantered up to his father's side. "A religious war, then," he said.

Not well pleased, Uri answered, "The worst kind. It will divide our forces. Your thoughts?"

"One goddess is as good or bad as another, I guess. I fight for the Yakov cause!" declared Will, the last fervently.

Gesturing in the direction of the men, Uri asked, "As do I, but will they?"

Father and son watched as the envoy returned from the fort. Instead of stopping within the ranks of the Westerners, they continued towards Uri. The baron said, "It looks like it's our turn."

Bickford appeared at the side of the Yakov's. Together the three rode out to meet the envoy who had stopped midway between the forces. The features of the priest were hidden in the depths of his hood. His cloak was emblazoned with a red moonrise on his breast. His voice when he spoke had a slight hiss that was missing in his proclamation to the occupants of the fort.

"Baron Uri Yakov, like your men behind me, you have a choice. The Sun Father knows of your desires. He too would see you sit the Command Chair in the Central Lands. All you need do is to accept him as your liege-equal." Unlike his address to the fort, this time the priest's voice was only for the ears of the parley.

Uri felt a growing pressure in the back of his head, one he hadn't felt since the turning he had been touched by the Hunter. It irritated him, *I don't have time for a headache!* Before he could respond, the priest continued.

"Your time of choice is not yet upon you. Watch, and learn."

The gates of the fort opened, and three Fists of soldiers, about a third of the contingent departed. None with weapons drawn.

They milled around before the line of Mashers and Hunters, unsure of what to do. The big voice of the priest was heard once again.

"Kneel! Accept Mieze."

The group fell to their knees as one. Uri could not hear their voices at this distance, but apparently the priest could.

"Rise! Take your weapons and go your way. Return at my calling."

Uri and the rest of his soldiers watched in amazement as the converted soldiers walked through the lines of the Westerners unopposed. Uri couldn't hear it, but he knew that there was muttering within his own battle weary troops as they watched those converted be allowed safety.

Uri asked, "What of the rest of those men?"

"They made their choice. They will die."

Uri sat uneasy in his saddle, the pressure in the back of head increasing. *I can buy time with the lives of those men. Is it worth it? What does this priest mean, 'liege-equal'? What about the forts at Fourth Stone? or Third Stone?*

"As we speak, the armies of the Sun Father offer those forts the same choice as these men here. Retire to your stone city and those that do not convert will be sent to you. Or attack and take your chances."

The ultimatum stung Uri almost as much as the realization that this priest knew his thoughts. He had to get away. Maybe distance would hinder that particular advantage. For now he had to keep his thoughts unvoiced even to himself. He made another attempt to save his men, "Very well, I will return to Yakstown. I would have the men of this fort as well."

"You may have the men of the others. These will die...as a reminder of the importance of your choice."

Uri slumped in his saddle, defeated. Without further words, he turned his horse and made his way back to his lines.

The angry shouts of the growing crowd outside Uri's manor walls could be heard in the Great Hall. Uri sat with Will, Cadman

Gallagher, his arms master, and Lance Takoda, his bailiff. Uri didn't need to hear the shouts to know that unrest was on the rise. It had intensified with the arrival of the surviving troops from Fourth and Third Stone forts. The tales of the huge army had sent fear pulsing through the populace as much as the reports of the converted being allowed freedom. Neither of these events sat well with Uri. Neither fit his plan. Uri needed to beat back the West and use the victory to wrest leadership of the Central Lands from Sinclair. He had to win. The problem was the followers of Fiona who up until Uri's return had seemed to regain the upper hand were now in a definite minority. The only good thing was that the pressure in Uri's head was gone.

"Scouts say that the Westerners have made no attempt to cross the August River. It seems the attack was confined from Middle Road northward," reported Will.

"The outriders say the Masher army is moving towards us from First Stone village and their numbers are growing. With the city walls only half completed, there is little hope we can hold them off when they arrive," said Cadman adding to the dark news.

Uri asked the group, "What do you suppose is his definition of *liege-equal?*"

"I can only surmise that if you convert to Mieze then you would be subservient to their high priest or Sun Father of the West. At least in religious matters," said Will with a shrug.

Uri expostulated, "Which is what? A marionette with half the strings?"

"How many do you have now?" asked Cadman.

Uri chafed. He had not appreciated being under the heel of Chet Sinclair. He doubted he would like being under the heel of the Sun Father, either. *There is only one heel that can do the grinding and I don't intend to be under it!* The sounds of the angry crowd punctuated his thoughts.

———⌘———

High Priestess El-lina had been very specific. Once her requests had been fulfilled she had told Duran to save as many as the faithful as was possible and Priest Duran considered himself nothing if not dutiful to his goddess and her high priestess. The situation had actually improved for a while after she had delivered her sermon, but it had been short lived. The fall of the border forts had brought the Western priests. At first covertly but now they were operating in the open instigating the converts, whipping them up to a frenzy.

"The evacuation of Fiona's supporters from Yakstown needs to begin," suggested Priest Duran speaking into a box, which contained his spider's web. The strands vibrated as he continued, "Already, we are openly attacked in the streets as we make our way to the shrine. Last night at the rising of Mieze a deluded rabble tried to burn us out. Only a fast rising Harvest Storm prevented it. It will only get worse."

The voice of Priest Hotig at High City answered from the web, "Whatever you think best, Brother. We will miss the daily updates. Where do you intend to go?"

"I will send some up the river to Bridgetown, others east along Peddler's Way, eventually to find their way to High City. Has there been any word from the high priestess?"

"None. The last I heard was three turnings ago. The night of the attacks," came the reply of Hotig.

A knock on the door halted further conversation. Duran put the lid on his box and put it back on the library shelf behind his desk. "Enter."

A minor acolyte entered, his head bowed and his hands clasp before him. He stopped just inside the door. "Priest Duran, I'm sorry to intrude, but there is a crowd gathering outside the walls of Baron Yakov's manor. They are all shouting for Mieze and threatening to burn the homes of the faithful. It's also said that the Western forces are approaching."

Duran hesitated only a moment. He had known that it would only be a matter of time. If the Westerners took Yakstown, they would slay the followers of Fiona. It was not a matter of if, but when. "Ring the bells, Brother. Open the tunnels. It's time to leave."

The acolyte bowed out of Priest Duran's office. The priest looked longingly at his box with the spider. He fervently wanted to talk to the high priestess. The ringing of the bells brought him out of this reverie. He had to prepare for the tunnels.

<hr />

The outrider hurried through the crowded throng growing in front of Yakov's manor. The shouting people grudgingly giving way to the horse and rider. Voices kept calling out to him, "Are you with Mieze?" Ignoring the queries, he forced his way through the crowd, a crowd being made larger by the steady stream of people flowing along the backside answering the bells of the Temple of Fiona. He was stopped by the guardsmen holding the gate through the wall surrounding the manor.

"Are the Mashers coming?"

The messenger nodded in the affirmative as the guardsman let him through. Word passed quickly among the soldiers behind the manor walls as the messenger made his way to the manor house. Unease grew.

"Milord, an outrider," announced Lance Takoda, Baron Yakov's bailiff, as he showed the rider into the baron's presence. Conversation halted as the rider made his way to the big table. The outrider watched the demeanor of the baron as he crossed the room. *He knows it's bad news.* The outrider dropped to his knee in front of Uri. "Milord, I bring ill news."

"Of course you do, man. Otherwise the news would be being shouted out on the walls. There would be cheers instead of this infernal chanting for Mieze!" declared Uri. "Come, come. Give the news."

"Their army approaches, Milord. At a crawl. The people of the countryside flock to them. They bend the knee, accept Mieze, and the security promised by the Sun Father. The people march before the Western army as shields."

"None stay true to Fiona? The West turns my own people against me. This must be dealt with now, before we lose all." Uri turned to Cadman, "Reinforce the city walls. We'll stand there first. Ready the cavalry. We'll try to turn the flanks. If we can't protect Yakstown, we can't protect the Central Lands."

"As you will, Milord," said Cadman, the ghost of a smile playing across his lips.

"You find the situation amusing, arms master?" asked Uri.

"Not so much amusing, Milord, as apropos," replied Cadman. Uri's raised eyebrows suggested he continue. "It's been heard on some lips that Baron Uri Yakov resents authority. Yet here, you are given a choice of masters to serve and you take the middle fork."

"Resent authority? Me? I believe authority is a needful thing. As long as I hold it."

"As you will, Milord," said the arms master, bowing his way out of Uri's presence. He was followed by the outrider.

—◦◦◦—

Uri had been considering the words of the Western priest. *The Sun Father also desires I sit the Command Chair. His support could be more valuable than any in the Central Lands, but at what cost?* Uri could only go down one path. If he started down that one, there could be no returning.

Will watched the struggles play out across his father's face. "Father, forgive me, but we both know that we cannot hold the outer walls," began Will.

Uri was not willing to take that step just yet. He acknowledged, "True. With the people demonstrating for Mieze both before us and within the walls, we cannot hold. Therefore, we shall call upon Fiona. This is, after all, her fight. Get me the priest."

As the door of the hall closed behind Will, Lance brought Uri a cup of 'Feine, steam still rising from the liquid. He set it on the table. "Milord, what will you do if Fiona doesn't prevail?"

Uri ignored the still steaming cup of 'Feine. "What I must, Lance. What I must. But not before. For now we fight." He strode purposely out of the Great Hall.

Atop the walls enclosing the Yakov Manor, Uri looked out over the gathered crowd. It had quit growing, but it's sheer size gave Uri pause. *Fiona's priest had better have something to offer.* The crowd had not yet discovered Uri looking down on them. Their chants were still unfocused. Uri knew that would change as soon as they saw him. A small knot of people pressed their way through the crowd. Uri saw that it was Will and his guards. *Where's the priest?*

⟞⟝⟞⟝⟞

Ham had been promoted to Leader for the capture of the Hunter. His heroics at Third Stone had been rewarded by selection into the elite First Guard and now personal guard of Will Yakov. His rise had been swift since he had shed himself of his brother. He was now point man, leading the group as they forced their way through the crowded street. The anger and the tension of the crowd enveloped him as the group made their way towards the gate in the manor wall. The nearer they got to the gate, the more insistent the wild eyed agitators in the crowd pressed in on them. Hands attempted to reach in and grasp the baron's son.

"Save us!"

"Accept Mieze for our sakes!"

Ham knew what the crowd wanted. Safety. He had fought valiantly at Third Stone, but had been shocked at the ease in which the West had overrun them. And now Yakstown was threatened. Ham intended to deny the West this victory. He knew that there would be no reprieve this time. But first he had to get Will through the crowd. He and the rest of the guards drew their swords. The rasping sound caused the crowd to move away, but only slightly. A cloud of acrid smoke from one of the many burning homes drifted across the crowd tearing his eyes and leaving an ashy taste in his mouth.

Ham muttered, irritated. "Where's your Tierra now, Brother?"

"Look around you. This rabble is removing all traces of her and those who supported her!" said Will between clenched teeth.

Ham started at Will's response. He hadn't realized that he had been speaking aloud. He wasn't sure if Will was upset about the disappearance of the supporters of the newly proclaimed revered goddess or that the unrest caused by an unruly mob threatened his position as the baron's son. He did know that any hope of invading the West was shattered. They were now in a fight for survival and the enemy had the high ground. *I wonder if you got caught up in this, Shem? On the other hand, I'm better off without you.*

The progress of the group was halted by the sudden appearance of a large man in a dark homespun robe a depiction of Mieze on his breast. His eyes danced with feverish intensity. His voice when he spoke seemed distant, far away, and not his own.

"Your time grows short soft skin. Your decision is..." The man's words gurgled to a stop as Ham withdrew his sword from the chest of the now dead priest.

"That may have been hasty, Leader Ham," said Will. The crowd parted before the group as the dead priest fell to the ground.

Ham answered, sheathing his sword, "I hope not, Milord, but at least the way is clear now."

"The temple was empty, Father. All were gone with no trace," reported Will.

Uri and Will stood atop the manor wall looking over the city flanked by Ham and the rest of the guard. Ham had never seen anything like it. Not even during the worse Harvest Storm. The city was dotted with seemingly random fires in every quarter. The smoke hung like a cloud over the city, increasing with each new fire that revealed itself as tongues of flame biting through the murky pall.

"Did they burn their own houses before they left?" asked Uri.

"Near as we can make out the burning homes are of those that professed for that new goddess, Tierra," said Will, "but they did not start the fires. The western priests did."

Ham shivered at the sight. It brought to mind the fire and brimstone promised those who were found lacking of proper faith. He wondered if this was the beginning or the end of his afterlife. "Judgment Day."

"What's that?" asked Uri.

Ham had not realized he had once again spoken aloud. Out of the corner of his eye, he noted a fiery speck high in the sky, growing larger with each beat of his heart. It was headed right for him. He apologized, "I'm sorry, baron, but that priest I slew in the crowd. I think he was about to tell me that today is Judgment Day."

The crowd quieted with the words of Baron Yakov from atop the wall. As his words faltered to a halt, all eyes turned to the sky to see what their baron was staring at. A rapidly growing red speck became a fiery red projectile trailing flames and smoke behind it. It was headed right for them. When it appeared that they could nearly reach out and touch it, it exploded.

Above their heads hanging in the mid turning sky was the red moon depiction worn by all the priests of Mieze. It settled slowly as the out-flung rays of the moon turn to ash and drifted downward. A voice boomed out from the sky. The voice of Vlad.

"Central Landers! This will be your only opportunity. Kneel now and accept Mieze or accept your fate!"

A guardsman shouted from the outer city walls. "They are here! Mashers and Hunters outside the walls!"

The crowd before Uri's manor dropped to their knees. It spread outward like ripples on a pond. They raised their voices in supplication. They called out not to Baron Yakov or Fiona. Neither to Tierra. In increasing strength they raised the name of Mieze.

The voice of Vlad boomed within the mind of Uri. No growing pressure, no gradual overriding of his own thoughts, but powerful and insistent. "Choose now, baron." Without thought or hesitation Uri dropped to his knees and called upon Mieze.

———

In the pit of the Auge Ose, Vlad smiled. It was an evil thing to see as his skin grew taut over his skeletal features. The almost constant use of the Auge Ose had taken a toll on Vlad. But he didn't care. The reward for preventing the rise of Tierra would be well worth the loss of a pretty face, not that he had had one to begin with. It would be nice to be a demigod.

"You have done well, priest," rang Mieze's words in the mind of the Sun Father. "Now this is how you will proceed."

Vlad finally withdrew his hands from the Auge Ose. Power surged through his body, a gift from his goddess. "Erik, attend me," he sent. It was time to plan the demise of the Sinclair clan.

9

SHEM

Shem woke to the none-too-gentle prodding originating from the foot of a Sol Dat. Shem rolled over to protect his already sore ribs and opened his eyes.

"Get up, soft skin. *He* wants you."

Shem didn't have to ask who *He* was. Memories of the voice in his head made that quite clear. What wasn't clear was what had happened. The last he remembered before slipping into darkness was fighting to protect himself and the Peddler... The Peddler! Shem struggled to his feet, grasping the traces of the horse's harness to help him up. Why was he so weak, and why did his head hurt? As he rose above the horse's haunch, he saw that the second horse was gone. At least the Peddler had been able to make a break for it. Shem hoped that he had made it.

The Sol Dat had retreated away from the horse and wagon, in fact he seemed extremely reluctant to approach the horse, and had nocked his bow. "Get that wagon out of here. It doesn't belong."

"I'll have to move to the other side of the horse to fix the harness," Shem informed the Sol Dat. *Maybe he'll stay on this side and I'll be able to slip out a knife or load my sling*, hoped Shem, but the Hunter followed him around, giving the horse a wide berth. As Shem was adjusting the straps and gathering up the traces left by the missing horse, he noted additional Sol Dat arriving. His chance was gone. He threw the empty traces up on the wagon bench. Perhaps the new owner would be able to use them.

"Your sword, too," ordered the Sol Dat.

Shem complied, dropping his scabbarded sword to the ground next to his bow, adding to it his knife and quiver. He then tied the reins loosely to the side ring and smacked the horse in the rear. It took a few tentative steps, adjusting to pulling the wagon by itself then took off at a steady pace towards the east.

Watching the wagon retreat, Shem reseated his belt, tucking the pouch of stones up under it. *If I'm lucky no one will recognize my sling for what it is. After this turning I'm due some luck.* He turned to face his captors.

"Bind him," the leader ordered.

The party consisted of four Sol Dat, led by I'mam, and Shem. Shem's hands were bound leaving only enough rope between them to allow him to grasp something for support, which I'mam assured him was going to be necessary before the trip was through. Shem had also been searched. His wide leather belt had been taken from him, revealing his pouch of stones and the hidden queues that had ignited the wrath of the Sol Dat and had earned him a few well placed kicks from his captors. All except the young one, Row. None, however, had discovered that the leather wrapped around his forehead was actually his sling. They moved out, Shem in front.

Shem felt I'mam's eyes boring into his back. He thought of I'van. He had once named Shem friend. *Perhaps I'mam could be reached, but how to approach him?* He said, "Friend..."

"You presume much, soft skin, to name me friend. Did you also name those Sol Dat whose queues you took *friend?*" asked I'mam.

"My name is Shem. No, I did not name them friend. Nor did I take them. They were given to me by I'van, whom I did name *friend* and he me."

"Shem? I've heard of that name. Yes, and I'van as well. It was he who sung the death song of U'bad and his mate, slain by the Central Lander named...Shem. The song had also included four Sol Dat who had broken pledge."

Shem could hear the awe creeping into I'mam's voice. *If I can't win friendship perhaps a little fearful respect might make one of them slip up.* He raised his voice enough that all might hear. "That's right. I am that Shem. I was raised in U'bad's village as little more than a slave. I slew U'bad and his mate to win my freedom. Those queues belonged to the four Sol Dat who tried to renege. You've heard the song."

"So you say," said I'mam eventually. "And where is I'van now? Was his queue among those we took from you?"

Shem sighed. This was not the way he had hoped the conversation would go. "No, I had, however, been placed under edict. Were we to meet again, one of us would die. We met again."

"Yet you still live," said I'mam. "Do not speak again, *friend.*"

The ground continued to slope upward, the trees growing more numerous, changing from ordinary deciduous to a larger more exotic jungle-like canopy. The topography changed as well. The gentle upward sloping land became more rugged. Chasms suddenly revealed, plunging downward hundreds of feet to river bottoms where turbulent currents roared and crashed, further sculpting the landscape below before disappearing into subterranean caverns. It was if the land was molded, mirroring a dark chaotic mind, or the mind of a goddess. It was before one of those chasms that they now stood as the last rays of the setting sun disappeared over the tree tops. Wider than any that they had previously encountered, this one could not be jumped or poled over.

"We will rest here," announced I'mam. "Tie the soft skin to that tree."

Row jumped to do I'mam's bidding. Shem was sat at the base of a large tree overlooking the chasm and his arms tied around the bole. Row had done his job well. Shem's arms were tightly stretched behind him.

"Sleep well, soft skin," mocked Row.

"I'll take the watch," said I'mam, "Be ready to move with the rising of Mieze."

The three Sol Dat settled in to sleep. I'mam took up a position near Shem who tried to sleep but found that his arms were too tightly stretched for him to find any comfort. His mind blazed with thoughts of escape. *Great! On my way to see Vlad. Only this time he is the Sun Father. There has got to be a way out.*

—⟨∿∿⟩—

Shem's eyes swam into focus. He found himself staring at a pair of well defined quads, strong and toned, bathed in a silvery light. He had no idea how long he had been studying them. Gradually he realized that they were his. He raised his head as he became aware of another presence. Comforting. Motherly. Immersed in the silvery light outlined by a hint of green luminesence was a face. Shem wished he could see it clearly. He knew it would be beautiful, more beautiful then any he had ever seen.

"You've grown, Shem. How strong and brave you are."

Shem reached out to touch the silvery green figure and discovered that he couldn't move his arm.

"Fear not, my hero. Help is coming."

Shem struggled, but could not move. The figure retreated, devolving back into the silvery light. Before the face vanished recognition came. His sudden cry violated the quiet of the night, "Tierra! Come back!"

The crack of I'mam's fist back handing across Shem's jaw jerked him fully into wakefulness. Looking around Shem realized his surroundings and that he had been dreaming. The dream, no, actually more of a vision, had been so vivid and real. Tierra was proud of him. He would get out of this current situation and go find her. This he swore to himself.

"Do not ever utter those words here again!" hissed a Sol Dat before him, eyes blazing, his knife, which more closely resembled a short sword, gripped tightly in his other hand. It was I'mam. He continued angrily. "We serve Mieze and her Sun Father. So will you or you will die." Shaking with pent-up rage, he stalked off.

Shem wished he could rub the ache out of his jaw, but his hands were still bound behind the tree. A small voice sounded in his ear.

"Chill, Hero. We'll spring you."

Hero? "Who," began Shem in a whisper. His words were cut off by a sharp pain in the lobe of his ear.

"Quiet! You asked for help, we're here."

Shem could feel two stones placed in his hands behind the tree. He rolled them around in his fingers. *They will fit my sling nicely.* The sling tied around his forehead began to loosen. *Tierra has sent aid!*

The strains of a melancholy melody drifting through the night air reminded Shem of his reality. The little voice by his ear disappeared.

> Mieze, second in the night, unwanted and unloved
> Watch over our travels this night.
> Though shunned be you by others
> Who care not for your offerings
> We, the mighty Sol Dat, bask in your light.
>
> Mieze, oh wise one, though you rise not first
> You chase the cruel one from the sky.
> We ask this strength from you
> We, too, are unloved and unwanted.
> We, too, outlast our enemies underneath your light.

In the waning light of Fiona, he saw a group of Sol Dat and Un Tier materialize on the far side of the chasm. Bolas were thrown by the Sol Dat. They consisted of three equally sized rocks with holes bored through them. Knotted ropes of equal length secured the rocks at one end and attached to a center ring at the other. A coil of rope trailed behind them as they raced across the chasm to wrap around the branch of an overhanging tree, securing the contraptions tightly to the branch. I'mam called out, motioning towards the tree branch.

"Remember that, soft skin, should you try to run. The bola, it will wrap itself around your legs and if you are lucky, the stones, they will not break your bones."

Shem flinched inwardly at the use of the term 'soft skin'. He had failed to make any inroads with I'mam.

I'mam's warning was followed by a pair of Sol Dat who swung across the chasm. They secured anchor pegs and swiftly erected a rope bridge. As the two groups of Westerners prepared to cross the dim silvery light of Fiona gave way to an increasingly reddish tinge. Mieze was rising. The Un Tier crossed first. Their leader paused briefly before I'mam, flicking a glance towards Shem before moving on. The Sol Dat leader stayed longer. He stared openly at Shem.

"He claims his name is Shem. The Shem," offered I'mam.

The Sol Dat leader shifted his gaze and looked longingly at the chasm.

"Tempting, isn't it? But the Sun Father wants him," said I'mam.

"Too bad," responded the Sol Dat leader. The last of his men had dismantled the bridge on the far side and swung across the chasm. "I would have left it for you, but we'll have need of it again. We go to clean out the soft skin's walled city. Good hunting!" The Sol Dat leader touched his hand to his forehead and extended it towards I'mam.

"Good hunting!" said I'mam repeating the gesture.

"Yakstown! They are attacking Yakstown! At least Ham is at Third Stone. He watched through the red tinged night as I'mam went to rouse his companions who had in the manner of soldiers at rest slept through the passing of the Western troops. The ropes binding Shem's wrists fell away. He was free.

"Now, Hero. Get 'em!" came the cry at his ear.

Shem's sling fell down off his forehead. He caught it as he rose. Despite the protest of his aching muscles, now fueled by adrenaline, he slung the two stones he had. *I'm going to pay for this later,* he thought as he watched the stones strike their targets.

I'mam had turned slightly at the sound. The stone hit him in the temple between the eye and the ear with such force that he immediately dropped to the ground. The second struck one of the Sol Dat guards in the center of his forehead just as he opened his eyes. They glazed over as he slumped to the side. That left one soldier and Row.

Row had frozen, terror stricken by the attack of the fabled soft skin warrior. The remaining soldier was swatting at something or many somethings buzzing around its head. Shem moved forward quickly, scooping up I'mam's knife as he charged past. The Sol Dat's hands were still swatting the air when the knife plunged into his abdomen. Shem ripped it upward before withdrawing it and turning on Row.

Row fell to his knees pleading. "Spare me! Please!" He made a pitiful sight in the red tinged darkness rocking back and forth touching his head to the ground in supplication. His loose hair falling over his face. The scent of fear strong in the night air.

Shem felt a pang of pity. Row had not yet gone through the Fa Sung, the ritual binding of his top knot. He was not yet a warrior. *If he has any sense, he will choose something else after tonight.* Shem didn't hold out much hope for him. While more sensible than Un Tier, Sol Dat were just as stubborn.

Shem commanded, "Rise, boy." Row got slowly to his feet. "Drop your weapons." Row complied. Shem picked up a bola and connected a rope to the center ring. He swung it over his head and launched it towards an overhanging branch on the far side of the chasm. The bola flew true anchoring itself on the branch. Shem handed the rope to Row. "Over you go. When you get to the other side drop the rope."

"But I'll be stuck there," whined Row.

"Not my problem, boy," said Shem. "Now move!" As Row swung over the chasm Shem retrieved the two stones he had slung earlier. On the other side Row clung to the rope. Shem loaded his sling and slung it. The stone whistled past Row's head causing him to flinch.

Shem shouted across the chasm as he reloaded his sling, "That was a warning, boy!"

Row dropped the rope. It hung from the branch over the chasm out of Row's reach. Shem nodded and turned retracing the steps he had taken earlier. He had not gone far into the forest when he heard the tiny voice at his ear.

"I don't know about that, Hero. I think you should have whacked him and been done with it."

Shem spun around. He could see nothing. The protest of his muscles finally overcame the adrenaline rush that had propelled them during the attack. His knees buckled and Shem dropped to the ground. Rolling into a sitting position he began messaging his legs. There was little he could do about the ache in his shoulders for now.

Shem said wearily, "Show yourself."

"Hold out your hand," came the small voice.

Shem extended his hand palm up. He watched in amazement as a tiny man-like figure easily descended from his shoulder to stand in the center of his palm. Shem brought his hand closer to his face to see better. He couldn't believe his eyes. Standing before him was a man no taller than his pinky finger. "Who or what are you?"

The tiny man straightened to the extent of his height. In the gloom Shem could faintly detect a gossamer sheen of insect-like wings folded up on his back.

"We are the Nem Elt-til. The first creations of Tierra," he declared proudly.

"We?"

The twitter of little amused voices surrounded Shem. The little figure smiled.

"We."

"Do the Nem Elt-til have names?"

The little man looked confused. He gazed around. "Hmmm, well...uh. Not as yet, but we will. We are newly created. You cried out to Tierra. She sent us. And a message. Other than that...well, these things take time!" he ended a little indignant.

A glimmer of a smile threatened Shem's lips, "I see." He waited a moment. "And that message might be?"

"Look, Hero. You may be huge, but you needed us! A little appreciation might be in order."

Shem bowed his head to the little man, as much to hide the laughter that threatened to burst from of his lips as it was a show of respect. "The bravery of the mighty Nem Elt-til is beyond dispute. My deepest thanks."

"That's better! Tierra said to tell her hero to seek Wybee."

Shem knew of no one named Wybee or any thing or place for that matter. "Who or what is Wybee and where might this... Wybee be found?"

The tiny man sat down on Shem's palm, hand to chin, obviously deep in thought. He sat that way for some time, not moving. Finally he rose to his feet.

"I can't say." He bowed from the waist, "But I do know it's time for us to go. Later, Hero." The little man turned to leave. He turned back for a parting shot, "Oh, Tierra depends on you. And time grows short. This moon may be the last for free peoples. Don't blow it." The little man spread his wings and launched himself into the night followed by his people.

The buzzing of their wings faded into the night. Shem continued to massage his legs and to what extent he could his shoulders. He put the strange speech of the Nem Elt-til behind him, but not the warning. Finally his muscles felt some semblance of normalcy. He rose. "I'll go back to the wagon. Maybe I can find the Peddler. At least I can get my weapons back."

What funny little people, Shem thought. With that he disappeared into the forest retracing the route that brought him to the Nem Elt-til.

Shem arrived at the clearing where the wagon had been and he had been captured. His bow and sword still lay where he had dropped them as did his pouch of stones. Reclaiming his weapons, he said, "Thank Tierra for small favors."

He felt a warm sensation within him. Since his encounter with the Nem Elt-til he had taken to acknowledging her presence in the small things. Apparently it pleased her. He scanned the ground. The tracks of the wagon were still clearly visible. He headed out of the forest.

—✦—

Further to the north, between Fifth and Fourth Stone, in a shallow cave beneath a copse of trees, nestled a peddler's wagon, safe and dry. Wisps of smoke from lightning struck trees still hung in the air while the remaining runoff from the Harvest storm trickled past seeking lower ground.

Inside, the mellifluous voice of El-lina vibrated the silken strands of her spider's web. "At least no one found the wagon."

"Yes, my love, fortunate indeed. I shudder to think of you unprotected among the elements. It would displease me if anything were to harm that beautiful head of yours." The voice of the El emanated from the web.

"It was a narrow escape. I was driven into HIS realm. I lost the hero."

"There was no masking from HIM?" asked The El.

"None, Love. Within moments HE knew and was not well pleased. I could not reveal myself to the hero at that time. I had to stun him, then leave him behind. Fiona made it clear that I was not to directly encounter the high priest of Mieze."

"If it could not be helped, it could not be helped. This is merely a setback. I suppose it means you will have to stay longer. Do nothing to bring attention to yourself."

"Aye, Love. Perhaps it would be a good time for Il-Ar. I would hate to waste the wagon. An extra set of eyes would be a big help."

"We'll see. He has yet to return from his last errand."

"The Avians are resisting?"

"You know they do not like to leave the East."

El-lina sat back, biting her lower lip. When she spoke again, it was if still deep in thought. "This may be a problem. I caught a glimpse of his mind when he saw me. They are marshalling their forces. I may have to return."

A soft knock at the wagon door ended the conversation. El-lina said, "We'll speak later." She closed the cupboard. The air shimmered around her. When it cleared the Peddler once again stood in the middle of the wagon. She opened the door.

"Thank Tierra, you still live."

The Peddler gasped, "Shem!"

"Are you going to ask me in? I'm kinda hungry," informed Shem.

The Peddler recovered from his surprise. He stepped back to allow Shem entry. He asked, "Of course! Come in. How did you escape?"

The wagon creaked under Shem's weight as he mounted the steps and stepped inside. "I'm Tierra's hero," he said nonchalantly. *Something has happened. Tierra rolls easily from his lips and with conviction.* He encouraged Shem to keep talking, "Which tells me a lot and nothing. Give."

Shem ignored the request. "You travel a lot. Have you ever heard of a place or thing called Wybee?" He turned to look at the Peddler.

El-lina startled, nearly losing control of her masking. She asked another question, stalling for time, "Why do you ask?" Shem remained silent while she halved a loaf of bread and scooped out the middle making two trenchers.

"I hear a lot of questions being asked, none answered," stated Shem matter of factly.

El-lina offered, "I have a pot of stew on the fire behind the wagon. Let's eat. Then talk,"

"Good enough. Lead the way."

El-lina studied Shem as the two ate in silence. Shem had indeed been hungry. He was just finishing his third trencher. *He seems a lot more comfortable or perhaps accepting.* El-lina had been harboring reservations from their previous journey. Then Shem had been unsure and at times insincere with his role at least on the surface. Whatever had happened in the Western woods had changed him. He stuffed the last of the trencher into his mouth and chewed.

El-lina commented, "Apparently, they didn't feed you very well in the forest."

Shem wiped his mouth with his sleeve. "I wouldn't recommend their hospitality to the faint of heart," Shem responded a slow grin spreading across his face. "This stew, however, is top notch. Now, about Wybee."

"Why do you want to know?" El-lina hadn't meant to question Shem, but it was hard to break the habits of tens of cycles of being high priestess. The smile evaporated from Shem's lips.

"If you continue to answer my questions with questions this may take a while. Time that I may or may not have." Shem eyed the Peddler who was of similar size to himself. "We could have a contest of arms or wrestle here in the dirt, but someone has to start answering questions."

El-lina laughed, "I'm sorry, Shem. Ask your questions. I will answer."

"Who are you?"

She had been stunned by the directness of the question. *He cuts to the heart of the matter. Much has indeed changed within him.* She opened her mouth to speak, about to launch into her prepared spiel of a wandering Peddler. Instead the voice of Fiona spoke through her.

"Go outside! Look to the north."

El-lina and Shem rose as one and headed out of the shallow cave. Standing in the middle of Peddler's Way they turned northward. A fiery streak was descending out of the sky. Suddenly it exploded. Both El-lina and Shem recognized the symbol of Mieze as it burst over the northern sky.

"Blessed Fiona, save us."

"Tierra, protect us."

The air shimmered around the Peddler. When it settled El-lina stood before Shem. "I am El-lina, High Priestess of Fiona. We have much to discuss."

10

CHET SINCLAIR

The Cap Tan looked down from the window of his office on the third floor of the Jeffson Administration building as the influx of evacuees from Yakstown swelled the populace of High City nearly beyond its capacity to house them. With more arriving every turning, Chet Sinclair's anxieties were running high. To make matters worse, the tales of atrocities and violence directed towards the followers of Fiona by converted Central Landers had the citizenry of High City looking askance at each other. He turned away from the window and redirected his attention to the Priests Hotig and Duran who were attending himself, his son Malcolm, and Lieutenant Gilroy leader of the Cap Tan's Hand.

"Then it exploded filling the sky with a depiction of the moon burst of Mieze. I'm told that Baron Yakov fell to his knees and converted on the spot," concluded Duran.

Hotig joined in. "Already there are those in High City openly talking about converting. Saying that serving Mieze is better than dying. There has been no violence as yet, but..." he let the implied threat hang.

He took in the travel stained appearance of Yakstown's priest. The dusty robes and footwear along with his bedraggled hair told Chet much. *He didn't even stop to freshen up. He fears for High City.* Chet leaned back in his chair and sighed.

"I always knew that Yakov was craven!" said Malcolm hotly.

"No, son. Uri is many things, mostly troublesome, but he is not a coward. What of the City Guard?" asked Chet.

"Loyal so far," reported Lieutenant Gilroy. "Though I have taken the precaution of adding a member of the Hand to each patrol to ensure it remains that way."

"Good." Chet turned back to the priests. "What can we expect in the form of aid from the high priestess?"

"I don't know, Cap Tan. We haven't heard from her since Brother Duran provisioned her per her request," replied Hotig. "What of young Wybee? Has he offered anything?"

"So my father is now to take counsel from a child?" chided Malcolm still stinging from his father's mild rebuke.

Chet stepped in, "Gentlemen, I would not start High City's civil war here in my office. Malcolm send out scouts towards Yakstown. I want to know what's happening, especially with Baron Delbert. Inform him of all that is going on if he doesn't already know. I want those reports immediately, and put the Hand on alert."

The door had barely shut behind Malcolm when it opened again admitting Baron Wilbert Lucas and Ma Ne, the latter bearing a platter of refreshments for the Cap Tan and his guests.

Ma Ne was a free goatherder. The free goatherders lived in the high mountains at the northern base of Mount Fiona. While acknowledging the existence of the Office of the Cap Tan and the Council of Barons, they gave allegiance to neither. Their autonomy had been accepted by the first Cap Tan, Jonathon Sinclair, and in recognition of this the free goatherders provided the Office of the Cap Tan a personal protector. This protector's job was to ensure the free goatherder's autonomy remained. Were a Cap Tan to revoke their self rule, that Cap Tan's life was forfeit. Such was the original agreement and it had never been compromised. He set the tray on a side table and began pouring mugs of 'Feine for the Cap Tan's guests.

"Wilbert, I'm glad you are here. I assume Ma Ne has filled you in?" asked Chet. In the twenty cycles that Ma Ne had served as Chet's protector and valet Chet had yet to discover exactly how it was that Ma Ne knew everything that was going on around the Cap Tan. He had long since quit being amazed and now depended on it.

"Yes, Uncle."

"Good. I want you to send word to Hap and John Marcus. Also call a council meeting. I need to know where the rest of the barons stand and how they are faring," said Chet.

"They are already on their way, Uncle."

Chet nodded in acknowledgement. Wilbert was very efficient. When he stepped down, he intended to make his nephew Ex Cek to Malcolm. But for now, a way had to be found to preserve something of the Central Lands to leave. "Ma Ne, what is the position of the free goatherders?"

"Cap Tan, it is widely believed that the ambitions of Yakov," he spat after saying the name, a seldom seem display of emotion, "do not coincide with the desires of the free goatherders. The Life Giver must rise!"

Hotig and Duran sat back pleased with the pronouncement. Wilbert turned to Ma Ne in surprise.

"You believe in Tierra?" he asked.

"As should you, Baron Lucas," Ma Ne replied nonplussed.

"The Hero comes."

Everyone turned to the sound of the voice. Wybee stood in the center of the office. None had noted his arrival. Ma Ne was the most surprised of all. Usually nothing happened that he was not aware of first. He studied the young boy then dropped to one knee and bowed his head in reverence. Chet barely heard Ma Ne's first remark.

"He seeks the Hjerte," he said under his breath. Rising, he said louder, "Cap Tan, High City must be held. For as long as possible. We must buy time."

The scouts ordered out by Chet had returned the previous turning. Their reports had been less than favorable. Hap and Marcus had arrived at the same time and had joined Wilbert, Malcolm, Lieutenant Gilroy, and Chet in the third floor office. Maps were strewn across the desk and table with markers indicating the approaching forces of Yakov and the West. They appeared to have made camp about three candlemarks west of High City and were waiting. What they were waiting for was unknown. An argument about how to deal with the threat, which had begun the previous night was still in full swing. Chet slumped back into his chair. He was wearied by the long dispute. He knew that Malcolm sided with John Marcus and Wilbert with Hap. The decision would ultimately fall to him and he desperately wished that he could see a way out. The thought of giving up part of the city was distasteful, but the the reports of the Western might left him fearful.

"Look, John Marcus, if we try to set our defenses on the west side of the Majestic River to protect High City we'll be fighting in open ground. I don't care how good a defensive perimeter you set, it won't be as good a river! You've heard the stories. Those Mashers are big and hard to kill. And that was before Yakov joined forces with them," argued Hap taking up what seemed to him the only sensible solution.

"So you surrender a third of High City? Not even fight for it?" retorted Marcus.

"Yes!"

John Marcus spared a glance for Ma Ne then turned to Chet for support. "I thought we were suppose to hold High City for as long as we could. Cap Tan, are you willing to give up the western part of the city?"

Chet tried one last gambit. "Ma Ne, your thoughts?"

"I would say that you had the clarity of twenty cycles ago. The Central Lands are your affairs, not mine."

Chet muttered under his breath. "Thanks for nothing,"

"Just last turning you said we needed to hold High City for as long as possible!" said Malcolm accusingly.

Ma Ne bowed his head, humbled. "My apologies, Ex Cek. I overstepped."

"Father, if you want me to decide just say so," offered Malcolm.

"Yes, I want that!" said Chet hotly, ashamed by the realization that he was not cutting such a fine figure. "But Ma Ne is right. This is my affair. The only way to hold High City is to give up part of it." He stiffened his spine and sat up. Grabbing a pen and paper, he scribbled a note and sealed it.

"I'll offer the people a choice. Those who want to convert can stay on the west side. Those with us will remain in the eastern part. After we are sorted out, burn all the bridges. Everyone has until tomorrow to be where they're going to be. Post the notices."

"How do we know that we won't be infiltrated?" asked John Marcus.

"We don't," answered Chet, "But even if we are, it won't be with as many as it would have been had we allowed all to pass over." He handed the note to Wilbert. "See that this gets to Priest Hotig immediately. Now leave me."

"But, Father," began Malcolm.

Chet said with finality. "You wanted a decision, Malcolm. I gave you one. Carry it out."

As his war council left the office Chet sought out Ma Ne. His usual expressionless eyes held a glint of approval, his lips the ghost of a smile. He slumped back into his chair. *After this is over I'm handing the reins to Malcolm*, decided Chet.

When Chet arrived at the solar in the Cap Tan's quarters, he found the family already gathered. He stationed the two members of the Hand, his personal guard, outside the entry and closed the doors. His family's looks told him that Malcolm had informed them of the meeting, at least his version of it. He took his seat. Minerva was first.

"Chet, is it true? You're abandoning the western part of the city?"

"Yes, Minnie. It's true."

"Is that wise?"

Chet replied wearily. "What is wisdom, but doing that which necessity dictates. It is our best hope."

"Father, I still believe that we can hold the entire city," said Malcolm respectfully.

Chet countered, "But I don't, son. Yakov, who crouched behind walls, walls that I forbade being built, could not stand. What makes you think we can prevail without them?"

"Because High City has braver men! Loyal to Fiona. Loyal to their Cap Tan!" asserted Malcolm.

"This is not a contest of men, Malcolm. Goddesses are involved."

"We have one, too! Fiona will aid us."

Chet could discern the fervent belief of his son's words. "It is good that you believe, my son. I am not so sure. What is happening now is beyond our ken."

"Fiona will aid us," asserted Malcolm stubbornly.

But it would seem that Fiona has given us over to Tierra, thought Chet. "Speaking of which, where is Fiona's high priestess?" The question met stony silence. None could say because none knew. "Until such a time as guidance is forthcoming, we must use our own. Having said as much, Minnie, I want you to take Jonathon, Wybee, and Angeline to John Marcus' estate. Be ready to leave with the rising of the sun. You will have an escort. We'll join you after this is through. Oh, don't hold dinner for us."

"Yes, dear," Minnie replied.

Malcolm started to object. Chet cut him off with a gesture. "Malcolm, please join me in the library. If the rest of you will excuse us?"

The stroll down to the library on the second floor was made in silence. Outside the door Chet bid the members of his Hand to remain. The leader of the two man unit took a quick peek inside to assure himself that there was no danger to the Cap Tan. Inside the library as Chet already knew were Barons Simon, Marcus, and Lucas. Lieutenant Gilroy stood looking out the window.

"Cousins, nephew," Chet greeted his kin receiving curt nods in response, "What you see and hear in this room, stays in this room. No exceptions. Malcolm, be seated." Chet looked around the room. When all were seated, Chet began.

"First, no interruptions. Some of you believe that I am surrendering too much of High City without a fight." Chet raised his hand to forestall John Marcus and Malcolm. "No interruptions. I have listened and thought much during our discussions. We will pull back east of the Majestic, but we will not totally abandon the western side." The kin exchanged confused glances. Chet called out to the seemingly empty air, "Priest Hotig, enter."

The gathering turned towards the doors of the library.

"Cap Tan," said Hotig.

The heads of the kin whipsawed back. Standing next to the outside wall, head bowed to Chet, was Priest Hotig.

"How?"

"Where?"

"What kind of magic is this?" Startled voices asked.

Only Wilbert was silent, studying the bookshelves in the vicinity of the priest. Chet was pleased. Lieutenant Gilroy was not.

"This is how I believe we can do the most damage to Uri and the West," said Chet. Further explanations were delayed by a knock on the door. The door opened and the leader of Chet's guard stepped through.

"Cap Tan, a messenger from Baron Yakov."

"Where is he?" asked Chet.

"He waits in the Great Hall."

"Gil, will you see to it. Feed him and apologize for the delay. I'll see him when I can," ordered Chet. Lieutenant Gilroy hesitated. Chet asked, "Was there something else?"

"Begging your pardon, Cap Tan, but I'd rather not—apologize, Milord," he said.

"I see. Then don't." Chet waved him out of the room. After the door closed, John Marcus spoke.

"Cousin, you're too easy on your people."

Chet replied, "I believe that Gil originally hailed form Yakstown."

"So?" said John Marcus in a questioning tone.

"So, unlike you, Cousin, he is ashamed," explained Hap. John grunted.

Chet let the grumbling settle back into silence. The eyes of family went back and forth between himself and Hotig. Satisfied that he now had their complete attention, he spoke. "Priest Hotig, can you tell us what you have learned about the happenings in Yakstown before the conversion." *Make it good, Priest.*

Hotig began without preamble. "Most of you know that the people of the countryside, those who didn't convert on the spot were driven by the Western Army slowly to Yakstown. The influx of the survivors caused unrest in the city. So called Miezian priests showed up and fanned those flames and an ultimatum was delivered." So far the tale wasn't new. In fact the same tale, with the exception of the Miezian priests, could be told about the happenings in High City.

"The houses of the holy, those who preached of Fiona and the coming of Tierra, were set to the torch as an example. It was most effective. The faithful were ordered to flee, to escape the city. Afterward even the Temple of Fiona was razed to the ground, leaving not a stone on top of another." This last was spoken sorrowfully. His own Temple of Fiona was on the western side of High City.

Malcolm had shown little regard, looking up and rolling his eyes, at the mention of Tierra. However, hearing about the razing of Fiona's temple, his ire returned.

"Priest, why does Fiona or the high priestess allow this to occur?"

"That is a question many have asked, my son. I have no answer," said Hotig.

Malcolm was not mollified. John Marcus joined in.

"Cap Tan, you spoke of damaging the traitor Uri. What did you mean?"

Chet looked to Hotig deflecting the question to him. Hotig clapped his hands. The corner bookcase silently swung outward revealing a passageway behind it. Two acolytes stepped out. The bookcase returned to its original position. The silent surprise was broken by Wilbert's chuckle.

"I take it these passageways are widespread?" he asked.

"Indeed, young baron. You are most perceptive," said Hotig.

"That is how the faithful escaped Yakstown?" asked Hap.

"Yes, Baron Simon. They disappeared beneath the very noses of Baron Yakov. Unfortunately the entrances, most of them anyway, had to be destroyed afterward to prevent discovery."

The advantages of the new discovery were a little slower coming to John Marcus and Malcolm, but when they did both became excited. "How widespread?" asked John Marcus.

"Extensive, Baron Marcus. Every major building older than a hundred cycles. A few of the newer ones as well. As long as they were built on the same foundations." High City was very old. Most of the major buildings fit into this category.

"Horses?" asked Malcolm.

"Unfortunately, no, Ex Cek. The tunnels were originally used to protect the citizens from the danger of the Harvest Storms. The main arteries are wide enough to travel four abreast and have many storage rooms, but the ceilings are not high enough for horses."

Malcolm and John Marcus got up and walked to the far side of the library, heads huddled together talking excitedly on how to use the new information. Wilbert and Hap remained with Chet and the priest. Chet's eyes had followed his son and cousin as they moved off to cook up their latest brainstorm. He knew it would happen, in fact he had expected it. Still, he looked uncomfortable. Whatever was planned would reveal the tunnels he had hoped and still hoped to keep secret, but there was no other way. *A weapon unused is no weapon at all.*

"Hotig, you understand why I have to do this," said Chet.

"Yes, Cap Tan. I expected as much," Hotig answered. "It's not easy being responsible for the masses."

Chet breathed, "Amen."

"Besides a new temple would have had to have been built anyway. You don't expect Tierra to want a used one, do you?" offered Hotig, smiling, though it was bittersweet.

Chet squirmed in discomfort. The ease in which Priest Hotig deferred to Tierra unnerved him. Chet had no desire to become a high priest while Hotig seemed to relish the idea.

"The question that comes to my mind," said Wilbert, "is whether or not Yakov will use one of the buildings for a command center. I doubt very seriously that the Western commander will."

"Why not?" asked Hap.

"It's my understanding that the people of the west shun above ground structures" said Wilbert.

"You continue to impress, Baron Lucas. If you had spent more time in Fiona's temple perhaps I would have recognized your talent the sooner," said Hotig. Wilbert's embarrassment deepened with the exploding laugh of Chet.

"Well said, Hotig! Well said." He continued to chuckle. "Truth is, Wilbert has his own shrine. He doesn't like to display his devotion on his sleeve."

"So I have heard," replied Hotig, "but the young priests who attend him have not reported his studious nature. I shall have to have a talk with them."

"Getting back to the point," said Hap speaking to Wilbert, "You don't think we will be able to listen in to any strategy meetings."

"Precisely," said Wilbert. "But that's not to say that we still couldn't hear something useful If Yakov quarters in High City."

"I shall assign someone to watch. Ah, our fiery combatants return," said Hotig.

Malcolm approached his father while John Marcus took his seat. "Father, I withdraw my objections to your plan. I ask only that I be allowed free use of the tunnels."

Chet studied his son. He could see the recklessness in his eyes. He also knew that he would not be able to control it. "So be it, Malcolm, just don't do anything rash." Chet knew his hope was false.

Malcolm turned to Hotig. "Priest, I would like a look at these tunnels."

At a gesture from Hotig the two acolytes stepped into the passageway, Malcolm and John Marcus on their heels.

The door of the library opened to admit Ma Ne bearing Chet's dinner. Chet turned to Hotig to ask him to join him. The priest's eyes were gazing off at nothing, his lips moving silently as if speaking to someone the rest couldn't hear. *Why does my heart tell me it's not good news?*

————

Priest Fitzpatrick closed the lid to the box containing his spider and it's web. He had to inform Baron O'Kelly immediately. He knew that the baron was not going to be pleased. The Council summons had arrived that very day and he was preparing for departure. Now he was going to have to choose between the orders of the Cap Tan and the request of the high priestess. Somehow or another Fitzpatrick was going to have to convince the baron to seal the Grimval Valley.

11

WYBEE

The toy soldiers were scattered about the wooden keep in disarray. Jonathon was patiently trying to explain military tactics to Wybee. "You have to keep your soldiers together in formation. That is their greatest strength."

Defiant, Wybee challenged, "Says who?"

In the manner of young boys, it hadn't taken long for Wybee to feel comfortable in his new situation. Even Jonathon had forgotten his earlier declaration of dislike for Wybee and the two now played and squabbled like long time siblings.

"My Father! That's who!"

"Well, maybe..." Wybee's voice immediately cut off. He sat staring at nothing for several moments.

"What is it?" Jonathon pouted. "Is Tierra talking to you? I wish Tierra would talk to me." Feeling left out, Jonathon's fascination with the talent of his playmate had turned to envy.

Wybee returned to himself. "The hero is coming. We have to be ready."

"We? Me, too?" asked Jonathon, breathlessly.

Their conversation was interrupted by Angeline who swept by with an armload of clothing. "Jonathon! You can't play with your soldiers there. Stay out of the way!" admonished a frustrated

Angeline. Though the morning was half spent, the manor servants still hadn't completed packing the belongings of the Sinclairs.

"C'mon, Wybee. Let's find somewhere else to play," said Jonathon scooping up his soldiers. Wybee grabbed the wooden keep and followed Jonathon to an unoccupied corner.

They settled into a space that was clear of traffic for the moment. Wybee squatted where he could keep Angeline in his sight. "Why is your mother so cross?"

"They don't think I know, but I heard them talking last night. Baron Yakov is camped outside of town with an army of Western monsters. They think he will burn High City to the ground. Momma is afraid," said Jonathon. He dropped his soldiers and drew the slender rapier-like sword he wore at his side. "But I'd protect her!" He declared bravely.

Wybee looked admiringly at Jonathon. He was beginning to like the young Sinclair. "You will be a mighty Cap Tan and high priest," he said. "Just like your great great great...I don't know how many greats but like the first Cap Tan. His name was Jonathon, too."

"How do you know?" asked Jonathon.

"I dunno," said Wybee, "but Tierra says so."

"Huh," replied Jonathon with a hint of jealousy. Minerva strolled into their rooms carrying a tray of 'Feine and surveyed the progress. She set the tray on a small table and called Angeline to join her.

"Dear, I think we are going to have to leave some of this," she said to Angeline. "The wagon is almost full and we are running out of time."

"I know Aunt Minnie," said Angeline falling into her lifelong method of addressing her mother-in-law. She accepted the proffered mug and sat down. "I'm just worried that Malcolm will do something foolish, like getting himself killed!"

"Yes. I know what you mean. The heat of the Sinclair blood. Chet had better remember his age. If he confronts Uri thinking he's a hero and survives, I just might kill him myself. Just for putting me through the worry. Men!"

Angeline broke into a nervous giggling fit, nearly choking on her 'Feine. When she subsided enough to speak coherently, she asked, "Aunt Minnie, how did this happen? I mean, I know that the Yakov's or at least Uri Yakov resents us. I know that he is ambitious, but his ire had almost always been towards the Westerners. Why does he want us dead now?"

"Yes, why? I hate saying it, dear, but I think it's because of this Tierra nonsense. I didn't want to believe it. We have always been faithful to Fiona, but I'm beginning to believe this Tierra is real. The Westerners believe she is and they desperately want to prevent her arrival. What distresses me the most is that we are caught up in it. Why the Sinclairs? But bemoaning fate has never been productive. We are Sinclairs and we must deal with it." Minnie patted Angeline on the hand soothingly.

"I don't want to deal with it. If this upheaval is her fault then I don't want her to rise either!" said Angeline bitterly.

Wybee, absorbed in the women's conversation, neglected his turn to move his soldiers. He stared at Angeline. His eyes took on a faraway look. Jonathon pounced on the hesitation, capturing the Leader of Wybee's forces.

"Aha! You should never hesitate in battle. My father says so. Hesitate and you lose!"

Wybee turned back to the game. He was crestfallen at the capture of his leader and by what Tierra had told him. "Your mother has displeased her."

Jonathon ignored Wybee's words. He was busy setting up his forces again.

"There's nothing we can do about it, Angeline. We can only take care of what we can take care of," said Minerva still trying to placate her daughter in law. She clapped her hands to get the attention of the servants. "That's enough. Load what you have. We must leave. Boys gather your toys, we have to go. Now."

Jonathon put his wooden keep and soldiers into a cloth bag and tied it. He and Wybee picked up their small bag of provisions and made for the door. Minerva and Angeline retrieved their cloaks and followed the servants towards the stairway. As they passed the door to Minerva's quarters, the elder Sinclair stopped.

"I have to get my barter bag. I never go on the road without some trade items. You boys go on ahead and get on the wagon. I'll just be a moment, Angeline."

Jonathon rushed ahead. "I'm getting the best seat!" He called over his shoulder to Wybee.

Wybee hurried to catch up. As they approached the second floor landing, he called to Jonathon. "Wait! Stop a moment."

Jonathon waited at the second floor landing. "Alright, but I still get the best seat."

Wybee pushed past him and left the stairway entering the dining room on the second floor. He began searching the outer wall. "We can't get on the wagon. Follow me."

"What do mean?" asked Jonathon. "If we don't get on the wagon we'll be in big trouble."

Wybee ignored Jonathon's protest and continued his search of the wall offering no explanation. He looked back at Jonathon urging him to follow with a wave of the hand. "We'll be in bigger trouble if we do! Follow me."

Looking confused, Jonathon followed. A few steps away from the entrance to the stairway Wybee stopped. He looked up at a statuette of Fiona displayed in a little niche just out of his reach. He looked around to make sure no one was in sight. "Help me. Lift me up."

"Why?"

"I need to move that statue."

"Why?"

Wybee commanded. "Just do it! Hurry!"

Jonathon, who was a little taller than Wybee, reached up. His fingers barely reached the statuette. He grasped the base and pulled it towards him. A click sounded from the wall paneling and a hidden door swung open slightly. Wybee opened it further revealing a passageway. Jonathon's eyes registered surprise. All protests about the wagon evaporated.

Wybee entered the passageway. "Come on. Pull that lever and follow me. Make no noise."

Jonathon, right on Wybee's heels, complied and the door closed behind them leaving the two boys in the darkened passageway. Mostly by feel, Wybee led Jonathon unerringly to a flight of stairs and down to the first floor. A pool of light beckoned ahead and reaching it they found themselves back behind the fireplace in the Great Hall.

"I think we should get back to the wagon," said Jonathon, hesitating.

"We can't."

"Why not?" asked Jonathon.

Wybee looked around. He found the iron ring to the trap door and pulled it up. He grunted, "Tierra said to use the tunnels." The trap door came up a few inches then fell back down. Wybee looked to Jonathon imploringly. "Help me. It's too heavy."

"Not until you tell me why," said Jonathon crossing his arms and refusing to budge.

During the short time that he had been with Jonathon, Wybee had discerned Jonathon's envy whenever talking to Tierra was mentioned. Wybee looked at Jonathon, a sly glint in his eye. "Once we get in the tunnel, She'll tell you why."

"Tierra?" asked Jonathon excitedly. Wybee nodded. Jonathon reached for the iron ring. Together both of them pull it up and climbed down into the tunnel. Once they were down below the surface totally encompassed within the bowels of the ground a dim green glow surrounded Jonathon. A look of delight spread across his face. A moment later the look evaporated. Jonathon's features deteriorated into grief. The glow winked out.

It didn't take Tierra to tell Wybee that something horribly bad had happened to his companion. All he, Wybee, had been told was to not get on the wagon and to use the tunnels. He hadn't been told why. "What's wrong?"

Jonathon collapsed into a sitting pile on the floor of the tunnel. His tears flowed freely.

———⟨φ/φ/φ⟩———

Deep in the pit of Auge Ose in the heart of the Lair, Vlad grasped the stone and watched as Minerva's wagon, parked just beyond the manor's back door, was being loaded under the watchful eye of five members of the Cap Tan's Hand. He sent his mental commands. Three men stepped out of the steady stream of refugees fleeing the west side of High City. They motioned to others in the crowd who slipped out of the stream to join them. The three groups then made their way towards High City manor. In all, they numbered twenty. *I gave you an opportunity, Sinclair. Now experience the price of defying me.* The three groups came together just out of sight of the rear of the manor. As Minerva and Angeline stepped through the back door, Vlad gave the command. Bows hidden beneath cloaks appeared and fired a volley.

12

SHEM

Like peeling layers from an onion, the revelations had been nearly non-stop. First had been when the hulky Peddler had turned into an exotically beautiful woman right before his eyes. Only to find out that she was the High Priestess El-lina. He had been aided by little men with wings that could fly and the high priestess's horse also had wings and could fly. There was fighting in the heavens between goddesses that now encompassed all the lands and worst of all Un Tier and Sol Dat camped just outside High City were being led by of all people, Baron Uri Yakov.

The last was what irritated Shem the most, made the deepest cut. Baron Yakov had the largest contingent of forces of all the barons and, as far as Shem knew, the best trained. Now they were arrayed against the Central Land.

"Thank you, Tierra," he breathed.

He had just escaped being a part of that army. In fact, thinking back, he had a lot of close calls and near misses every since that night in Yakstown when he pledged as Tierra's hero. It was as if he'd managed to stay one step ahead of catastrophe. He hoped that trend continued.

Shem found the acceptance of the Westerners by the populace intolerable, and it must have shown on his face because all gave him a wide berth. None had challenged him or prevented him from going where he wanted to go and right now he wanted to go to High City Manor to pick up Wybee.

The streets were clogged with citizens loyal to Fiona, or so they claimed, escaping from the Westerners. Most headed east or south. Shem left Peddler's Way and guided the wagon onto the wide boulevard which lead to the manor. He planned to go to the back and enter the servant's door. They would know if a young lad fitting Wybee's description was staying at the manor. It was Shem's intent to get in and out as quickly and quietly as possible.

Shem heard the commotion before he saw it. Still, it took a moment to process the scene unfolding before his eyes as he rounded the corner leading to the back of High City Manor. An armed rabble had engaged the guards of a heavily laden wagon. Horrified, Shem witnessed the slaughter of two women cut down from behind as they fled. He noted guardsmen, weapons still sheathed, whose arrow perforated bodies lay about the wagon a testament to the surprise nature of the attack.

He dropped the horse's reins and leapted from the wagon as the last two guardsmen went back-to-back. They were immediately set upon by the attackers. Shem sensed the influence of the Sun Father in three of the attackers. He had his sling off his forehead, loaded, and whirling above his head by the time he rounded the horse giving him a clear field of fire.

"That one, then that one over there."

Shem looked around to identify the voice causing his stone to sail over the head of everyone.

"What kind of hero are you? Can't you aim any better than that?" groused the tiny voice. Shem finally located the source. It was the leader of the Nem Elt-til. He had a hold of a lock of Shem's hair and was hanging on for dear life.

"I could if you'd shut up!" Shem quickly slung two stones taking out two of Vlad's pawns.

"Whack attack! Whack attack!" The little man screamed excitedly, jumping up and down on Shem's shoulder.

Frustrated by the distraction, Shem growled, "If you don't be quiet I'm going to load you in my sling!"

"Oh yeah! A big brave man! My hero," sassed the little man.

The ambush had proved costly. Before Shem could fling his last shot, he saw the two guardsmen fall. Fueled by anger, Shem's last stone completely embedded itself in the forehead of the Sun Father's last minion. Deprived of their leaders the rest of the mob fled back towards the stream of refugees. Shem let them go. He had killed those that had been touched by Vlad and finding the rest in that stream of humanity would be impossible. Instead Shem wrapped his sling around his forehead and knelt at the side of one of the fallen guardsmen. Though fatally wounded he hadn't yet breathed his last.

Shem tried to comfort the man. "Friend, can I get you anything?"

"More time," gasped the man.

Shem sympathized. "I would if I could."

He probed the man's chest trying to ascertain the extent of his injuries. His fingertips tingled. A pale, nearly invisible green glow emanated from them before settling into the stricken warrior. The man's breathing came a little easier. Surprised, Shem jerked his hand away. "What just happened? What did I do?"

"She did it, Hero. Hurry, he hasn't much time," said the tiny voice perched on his shoulder.

"Friend, Milady, did she escape?" The soldier's voice was weak and breathy.

Shem glanced over at the fallen bodies of the two females then back at the soldier. He didn't lie. Not exactly. "You did your job, friend. You did it well." The soldier relaxed, closed his eyes and breathed his last. "Wait! I need to find the Cap Tan." The ringing sound of a sword leaving it's scabbard answered Shem's question.

"I can accommodate you, stranger. Rise slowly and keep your hands where I can see them."

Shem looked up. A towering form bearing the insignia of the Cap Tan's Hand stood over him his sword pointed menacingly at Shem's neck.

"See ya!" came the voice of the Nem Elt-til into Shem's ear. Shem said bitingly, "Thanks a lot,"

"You may not want to thank me before this is over, stranger," replied the soldier. "Now get up."

—⟨⟨/⟨/⟨⟩⟩⟩—

"Life giver, life taker, protector of all. We beseech you this turning. Give strength to our arm, so that we may preserve the office of the Cap Tan." Ma Ne's mid-morning ritual atop the Jeffson Building was interrupted by the metallic sounds of swords clashing. He rose from his cross-legged sitting position and went to the edge of the roof. He watched as High City manor came under attack.

"It has begun."

Abandoning the rest of the ritual, Ma Ne left the roof to prepare himself for his duty. He felt saddened. The attack had come early. Sinclair's forces had been caught unawares. Ma Ne gave little chance for the Cap Tan's survival and if his fears were true it would be time for Ma Ne to return to the Council of the Free Goatherders and report this change of status.

—⟨⟨/⟨/⟨⟩⟩⟩—

Its a sad tragedy, thought Hotig as he watched the scene unfold. *And my part perhaps the saddest.* High Priestess El-lina's orders had been specific. Delay. Cost Baron Yakov as much time as possible even if it meant sacrificing High City, its temple, or even himself. Offer him a plum he cannot resist plucking. The hero was on his way to get Wybee and he had to have time to get away free. That was why he had not protested the treatment of Yakov's messenger. He hoped it would enrage the baron enough that he would spend time sacking the city. Time the baron didn't really have.

The crowded office of Chet Sinclair seethed with barely restrained tension. A full squad of the Cap Tan's Hand surrounded the beaten and bloodied form of Yakov's messenger who lay in crumpled heap before Chet's desk. John Marcus, Wilbert, and

Hap were grouped off to one side trying to calm the furious Malcolm who had just finished beating the messenger senseless.

"Father, you know it's an ultimatum! It's the death sentence of the Sinclair family!"

Lieutenant Gilroy stood next to Chet who sat behind his desk holding the crumpled parchment in nerveless fingers. "The Ex Cek is right, Cap Tan. You cannot possibly consider handing yourself and your family over to him," said the Lieutenant.

"No, of course not," said Chet wearily, "but we could have sent this messenger back with a counter proposal. Tried to enter into negotiations and buy some time for Minnie and the kids to get away." He looked at the messenger and shook his head. He turned and glared at Malcolm. "Not now. Not in his present condition. It would provoke an immediate retaliation."

"I'm not sorry. He's a traitor! A convert! He deserved that and more!" said Malcolm.

"Yes, but we are not in a position to pass judgment. We must see to survival first," Chet reasoned.

The office door opened. Hotig felt a stirring of wrongness as he watched a large man, hands bound behind his back, being escorted in by two members of the city guard. They marched him up to Chet's desk. One continued around to bend over and whisper in Chet's ear. The big man looked at the pain wracked figure on the floor. He cocked his head to peer closer as if he recognized the beaten messenger.

"Ham?" he said. Ham rolled over and peered up at Shem through blackening swelling eyes. He groaned.

Lieutenant Gilroy came around the desk to stand before Shem. "Do you know this man?"

"He's my broth... oof!" Shem's breath exploded out him driven by the force of Lieutenant Gilroy's fist buried in his midsection. "No! *Noooo!*"

Hotig watched as Chet launched himself out of his chair. He stared at the gasping figure of Shem who had fallen to his knees trying to catch his breath. Stared as if trying to impale him, flay him, and eviscerate him through sheer will. Ma Ne burst through the door, sword drawn and held horizontally over his head, looking for a place to put it. Chet sank wearily back into his chair and buried his head in his hands. "No," he mewled weakly.

"Father! What is it? What's wrong?"

"They're dead. They're both dead. If I had just read this last night." He tossed the crumpled ultimatum away as if it were burning his fingers.

"Who's dead? Father, who is dead?"

"Minnie. Angeline." Chet would say no more. He could say no more. The sobs and tears pouring down his cheeks prevented even thought. Chet Sinclair, the Cap Tan, was broken.

The blood rose from the neck of the already infuriated Malcolm Sinclair, climbing slowly from neck to lower jaw. Hotig could see that the young man was about to explode, unleashing a mighty fury of anguish and despair. His uncles moved in to restrain him. Lieutenant Gilroy took charge.

"Get these two—-men," he spat derisively, "out of here. Now! Put them in chains. I'll see them later." Two of the Cap Tan's Hand grabbed Ham. The city guardsmen took Shem. Both were dragged out of the office, neither able to make the trip under their own power. As Shem was dragged past Ma Ne, he looked up. Hotig was the only one who witnessed the recognition in the eyes of Ma Ne as he gave the prisoner the slightest of nods, barely perceptible. *It cannot be. Have we just put the Hero in chains?*

After the door closed on the prisoners, Malcolm's uncles released him. He rushed immediately to his father's side. "We'll get through this, Father. I swear! We will have vengeance for this. Starting with that messenger!"

Lieutenant Gilroy helped Chet out of his chair. The Cap Tan rose slowly, shakily as if in great pain. He placed his hand on his son's shoulder, his other arm hung limp by his side. "Nothing will bring them back, Malcolm. The deed is done. Lead the Central

Lands well." He turned to leave. His knees buckled and he fell into the arms of his son.

Malcolm gently lowered his father to the floor. He placed his hands on his father's chest. He bowed his head tears falling freely. Priest Hotig knelt beside Chet's lifeless body. He checked for signs of life. Finding none, he made the sign of Fiona over the body.

"The Cap Tan is dead." He rose and addressed the room. "Malcolm Sinclair is now Cap Tan of the Central Lands," he intoned solemnly.

Ma Ne slipped silently out of the office.

—⟨⟨⟨⟨⟩⟩⟩⟩—

The prison was no more than an empty store room, one floor below the manor. It provided no air circulation and no light. It had apparently been used by the kitchen staff to hold vegetables. The rank smell of rotted greens and tubers still permeated the air. *The place could use a good cleaning, but then prisons are dark, stinky and unpleasant. Aren't they?* Shem should know. Ham had gotten him out of more than one dark hole during his short army career. He looked around. He could barely discern his brother's huddled form about two or three arm lengths away curled up in a fetal position.

Somehow Ham had survived the invasion of the Westerners. This pleased Shem though he didn't know why. Ham had abandoned him, cast him out to fend for himself. Still Ham was the only family Shem had and that meant something. Didn't it? Shem stretched his arms and legs to test the extent of his movement. "Not much," he said aloud. His wrists had about a shoulders width, his legs less. Worst of all, his arms and legs seemed to be connected by a chain short enough to disallow standing erect. The manacles chafed where they rubbed against the skin of his wrists and ankles. They also made a goddess awful clanking noise. The noise awakened Ham who had been in a semi- conscious state since his arrival.

"Why are you always waking me up?" groused Ham, the effort splitting his lips open again.

"Uh, because you sleep too shallow?" asked Shem. His only response was the clinking of chains as Ham tried to shift positions, quickly followed by a moan of pain. "Why were you beaten?" he asked his brother.

Ham's answer was slow in coming. When it did, derision cut through his pain. "Because the Sinclairs have no honor."

Shem was not sure what his brother meant. Though, to be honest, he couldn't really argue the point. Shem had come to aid of their guardsmen. It wasn't his fault he had been too late. His reward had been to be bound and brought before the Cap Tan as a prisoner, given no chance to speak, beaten, and then thrown into this dark room in chains. He had gathered from the Cap Tan's actions and words that the two women had been part of the Sinclair family. Decisions made in time of grief could be irrational as he well knew. *At least Wybee wasn't attacked.*

He tried another tack with his brother. "The last I saw you, you had been promoted and were serving at Third Stone. I'm glad to see that you survived the Western attack and were able to escape to High City."

Shem and the High Priestess El-lina had had to back track to Middle Road to get around the invading forces, neither being willing to risk discovery. They had been able to gather a lot of rumor, but little real information from the people in the countryside. Not even El-lina's spiders had been much help. Some unexplained interference kept contact with her fellow priests to a minimum. She had tried to explain, but the doings and machinations of goddesses were beyond Shem's area of expertise. "Just give me a weapon and point me in the right direction!" had been Shem's usual response. Ham's painful laughter surprised Shem.

"Escape? Brother, I didn't escape. I was sent by Baron Yakov to deliver his ultimatum to the Sinclairs."

The pieces came together for Shem. "You converted."

"Yes. I like being on the winning side."

Shem spoke without thinking, "It's doing you a lot good right now."

"I may be uncomfortable at the moment, but in two turnings I'll be sitting at the left side of Will Yakov, Governor of High City. While you will still be rotting here and what's left of the Sinclairs, if any, will be running for their lives. However short that may happen to be."

"Perhaps," said Shem, "Perhaps not."

"Don't think I'll save you. I told you the last time we parted that I was through saving your carcass. I'll leave you here just like you left me lying in the field that night!"

"That's unfair Brother. I was being dragged away practically by the hair in the clutches of the Un Tier!"

"So you say," Ham sneered.

—◁◦◦▷—

The flames grew higher illuminating the darkness, revealing flickering scenes of horror that flashed before the eyes of Shem as he and his brother Ham, hand in hand, ran for their lives. The last words of their mother still rang in Shem's ears. "Run! Escape in the darkness. I'll find you. Ham! Take care of your brother!"

Their mother never found them. What did find them was even worse than the bedtime bogey man stories their parents had told them to keep them from exploring the Western woods. Tales of giants made of stone and bat men who appeared and disappeared in the darkness like shadows, taking what they wanted and killing everything else. One such stone giant appeared before the boys. Ham cut left, Shem to the right, pulling their hands apart as they attempted to run around the huge monster. Somehow the stone giant, or Masher as the Central Landers living near the border referred to them, didn't see them or perhaps was more intent on the burning farm house to pay any attention to two puny soft skin cubs. Shem didn't know nor at the moment did he care. He heard the whuff of Ham's exhaled breath and a low moan of pain.

He scrambled desperately on all fours towards the sound finally locating his brother in the tall grass. Rolling him over Shem discovered that Ham had hit his head on a rock and was bleeding profusely from a cut on his scalp just above the hairline. Shem picked up the offending blood smeared rock just as Ham's eyes flicked open. His brother opened his mouth to say something, but the only sound he could manage was another moan of pain, this one louder than before.

Shem was near panic. The crackling of flames as his family's farm burned, the guttural shouts of the Mashers, and now his brother's moans, which could lead to their discovery had Shem almost completely unnerved. Fear flowed through his veins, nearly as much as adrenaline. "Hush, Ham!" he mewled. "You'll bring the Mashers."

Shem looked around for something to wipe off the blood streaming down Ham's face and spied a darker shadow in the night moving towards them. Terror gripped him. Ham's eyes opened wider. Shem could see the shock and disbelief in them as his brother threw up his hands as if warding off a blow. It took Shem a moment to realize that Ham saw him sitting atop his chest bloodied rock in hand. "It wasn't me, Ham. You fell."

Ham's eyes rolled back into his head and he slumped unconscious just as a huge hand grabbed Shem by the hair lifting him off his brother. "It wasn't me, Ham!" wailed Shem as the Masher dragged him off into the night.

—◦/◦/◦—

Shem shook away the painful memory. He had tried to make amends. He gave Ham all the credit for his knowledge of the West, but despite all his hopes of reconciliation, that had apparently not been enough. But that was then, right now Shem suffered from the disbelief that Ham had converted to Mieze. It made him feel as if everything he had done for his brother had been for nothing. Yes, Ham had looked out for him, keeping him out of most trouble. "It hasn't been the one way street you've rubbed my nose in, Ham. You've benefitted from me. Besides, I've survived worse. I will survive this, too," said Shem though it sounded lame even to his ears.

"Don't tell me that you still think you're some kind of hero," said Ham.

His mocking laughter burned Shem's ears. It hurt. "Believe what you will, Brother."

Ham settled in to as comfortable a position as he could manage and lapsed into silence, leaving Shem with his thoughts. Shem knew that his being taken prisoner was merely a mistake by the Sinclairs. It would be remedied as soon as rational thought ruled once again. *But how much time would it cost?*

That gloomy question and Ham's soft snoring kept Shem company until the door to the store room opened slowly. *It's the free goatherder,* thought Shem recognizing him from the Cap Tan's office. Lightly, Ma Ne touched Shem on the chest.

"It is true. The Life Giver is in you. You must be him." He drew his sword. It was single edged and had a round cross guard that protected a two handed hilt which was ornately wrapped in leather. "Hold your hands out as far and as wide as you can, and your feet," he ordered Shem.

At first Shem had thought that the free goatherder had come as executioner. He now realized that he had come to free him. "This isn't necessary. The Cap Tan will come to his senses."

"The Cap Tan is dead. His heart burst with grief. There are no cool heads, only hot blood. Now hurry."

Shem complied. Ma Ne's sword flashed. The silver blur went across and down severing the chains as a scythe through ripe wheat. With the clatter of the chains Ham opened his eyes. He had awakened at the opening of the door but had remained silent, listening.

Shem was free, though sections of chain were still attached to the manacles on his wrists and ankles. He motioned towards his brother. To the accompaniment of clattering chains Shem said, "Him, too."

"No. That one stays," said Ma Ne.

"He is held unjustly. Sinclairs do not punish messengers," said Shem. He did not know whether or not that was actually true, but if it wasn't it should be.

"Save your breath. You're talking to a goatherder," said Ham, derisively.

"Your friend lacks manners," said Ma Ne, making no effort to release Ham.

"He is not my friend. He is my brother."

"My sympathies, Protector." Ma Ne studied Ham in the dim light. "Mieze is in him. He is filled with hate. Leave him." Shem refused to budge. Ma Ne gave in. "Very well. Hold out your arms and legs."

Ham complied and Ma Ne's sword flashed again. This time the down stroke flayed the tip of Ham's nose. He eyed Ma Ne with murderous intent, but when he spoke it was to Shem.

"We will meet again, Brother. When we do, one of us will die."

Shem stiffened, thinking of I'van. "I've heard those words before, Ham. I still live."

"For now," Ham's hate filled laughter followed them out of the door.

They stepped gingerly over the unconscious body of the city guardsmen who had been on duty when Ma Ne arrived and walked over to a bundle sitting at the base of the stairs leading out of the cellar. The rattling of Shem's chains echoed despite efforts to muffle them. Ma Ne reached into the bundle and pulled out a hooded cloak. It was an acolyte's robe.

"Put this on. It won't do anything to silence the chains, but it will hide them until I can strike them loose," ordered Ma Ne.

"What about weapons?"

"We'll just have to get you some on the road," said Ma Ne.

"Where are we going?"

"South for now, out of immediate danger. Then we will decide."

It was the *we* part that disturbed Shem. He was grateful that the Free Goatherder had freed him, though he still didn't think that it had been absolutely necessary, but Shem did not recall asking for a travelling companion. He was supposed to be finding Wybee. Fleeing south wasn't going to bring him any closer to Tierra's conduit, and he most especially did not like being without weapons.

"Perhaps I can be of assistance," came a muffled voice out of the shadows behind the stairs.

The sword of Ma Ne seemingly appeared in his hands, so swift was the draw. "Step out of the shadows," ordered Ma Ne.

"Priest Hotig extends his sympathies, Ma Ne. He says you have been a faithful protector for many cycles, but one cannot protect against grief," said the voice out of the shadows. Ma Ne relaxed and lowered his sword. A young acolyte stepped out of the shadows. Though it couldn't be seen from the depths of its hood, the voice of the acolyte revealed a smile at seeing Shem garbed in the religious robe.

"Blessed Fiona would be proud to shelter her sister's hero beneath her wings, but perhaps these would serve you better." A bundle dropped at their feet.

Shem dug in. He found his sword, his compound bow, and best of all his sling and stone pouch. Smiling hugely, he removed the robe and donned his weaponry. "My thanks, friend, and to Priest Hotig."

"Further, Priest Hotig would have you know that which you seek has taken to the tunnels." Shem looked at Ma Ne. He saw no recognition of the acolyte's words. What worried him most, though, was the thought of Wybee travelling alone. If something were to happen to the conduit he would have no clear way of knowing what Tierra wanted him to do. Wybee must be found.

"There is more," continued the acolyte, "the heir travels with him."

"Life Giver, protect him," breathed Ma Ne.

"Yes, though Priest Hotig would ask that you do so now that you are presently unemployed."

"For the time being," said Ma Ne. "I will do this."

Now that Shem had his weapons, he wished that the chains and manacles could be stricken from him. He asked, "How about these?"

The acolyte held out its palm. Upon it lay a key. Shem snatched it up with a huge smile on his face.

As he relieved himself of the burden of confinement he said, "You're a good man. For a religious sort."

"Actually," said the acolyte throwing back the hood of her robe, "I'm not a man." Her voice, now free from the confines of her hood, had a pleasant melodic sound to it. Her laughter was filled with gaiety as she took in Shem's shocked expression. "If you will follow me."

As she turned to go, Shem wondered how he could have mistaken her voice for that of a man. He started to follow then stopped, feeling an unease. He looked back towards the door of the storeroom that had been his cell. Ham had opened the door and was watching. *Leave him*, his mind screamed! *Like all the times he left me?*, his heart replied. *That was before he converted.* Shem hesitated. He knew he should just walk away, that freeing Ham would only cause future trouble. *But he is my brother.* Shem held the key to the manacles between his thumb and forefinger. He dropped it at the foot of the stairs. Ham withdrew back into the room and closed the door. "Okay. Now let's go."

The acolyte beckoned them behind the stairs. In the shadow was an open trap door. She disappeared into it followed by Shem, then Ma Ne who closed it behind them.

—◊◊◊—

Ham spied on his brother through the cracked-open door, burning with impatience. He wanted to leave as soon as possible to get back to Baron Yakov with the news of Sinclair's death. He knew the manacles would be a problem, especially if he ran into any of the barons, but he thought that he could bluff his way through any guardsmen. He strained to hear what his brother and that waste-of-good-food goatherder were saying, but they were too far away to be clearly heard. Then there were three. He heard the clatter of chains.

He opened the door a little wider. Shem turned and looked him straight in the eye. He held a key out so that he could see it, then dropped it on the floor. Ham shut the door. *Damn you, Shem! I'll not be beholden to you. I'll take the key, but it changes nothing.* When he opened the door once again, they were gone. Where they went didn't matter to him, only getting the key.

He moved as swiftly as his sore body would allow. At the bottom of the stairs he found the key. He wasted no time freeing himself and kicking the manacles out of sight behind the stairs. Straightening his clothes as best he could, he left the cellar and walked purposefully across the first floor to the main entrance. He saw only a few manor servants who paid him scant attention. At the door he summoned all his bruised dignity before stepping out. His parley banner leaned against the wall just past the guard who had turned to see who had stopped in the doorway.

Ham held out his hand without looking at either guard and demanded, "My banner." A moment passed in silence as the guard sized him up.

"It looks like negotiating is a tough job nowadays," said the guard with the banner. The other laughed under his breath. Ham remained silent, not moving, his outstretched hand unwavering. The guard gave the banner into Ham's hand.

"Come back anytime, convert," sneered the other guard. Ham took the banner and solemnly stepped away, his departure followed by mocking laughter. *I'll be back. We'll see which end you laugh out of then.*

13

MALCOLM

Tension was palpable in the office of the Cap Tan with grief simmering just below the surface. While Malcolm held court with his uncles and cousin, Priest Hotig's thoughts dwelt on Shem and the plan he had let loose. Acolyte First Selene was one of the brightest and most resourceful of his priestly candidates. *She must not fail,* he thought. *High Priestess El-lina said Wybee was in the tunnels. If anyone can find him it would be Acolyte First Selene.* Lieutenant Gilroy's stern, disapproving countenance brought Hotig's attention back to the conversation around him. Hap was arguing.

"Malcolm, your plan is insanity!"

"Cap Tan."

Hap bowed his head in submission. "Cap Tan, your plan is insanity. Especially the part where you lead it!"

"I will not submit to Uri Yakov! I will not lead from behind nor ask my men to take any risk I am unwilling to," he averred.

"That is a noble sentiment, cous—-Cap Tan," began Wilbert, placating. He had just returned from overseeing the burning of the south bridge. The smell of smoke and soot still clung to him. "but we have already lost your father. To lose you so soon after might be unrecoverable."

"And it delays the destruction of the north bridge," added Hap with a little more heat.

Priest Hotig had brought word that Baron Uri Yakov had taken residence in the custom house, the largest building on the west side. It also overlooked the north bridge and gave an observation point to invade the eastern side of the High City. Uri's son, Will, was also in residence there. Access could be gained by two tunnel entrances.

"It's perfect! It's what we've been waiting for," said Malcolm with conviction. "A perfect opportunity for a hit and run strike. We'll be there and gone before they realize anything's even happened."

"I agree with the Cap Tan," said John Marcus. "We cannot pass on the opportunity to take out both Uri and his son. We could end this thing in one stroke. If it's just a matter of leadership I'll lead it."

Priest Hotig stepped in. He was, of course, in favor of the raid. The loss of Baron Yakov would set back the plans of the Sun Father, which is what Hotig and High Priestess El-lina wanted, but it would not end the battle. He had to make that clear to those assembled. "The Sun Father of the West would only replace Baron Yakov with one of his Mashers or Hunters. Whether that would be preferable, I don't know. However, the war would go on. It's Tierra they are after. Not the Sinclairs. You are just the bait for Yakov."

"Then let's dangle in front of him," said Malcolm.

"Let someone else lead, Mal—-Cap Tan," said Hap hoping against hope.

"My mind is made up," he declared.

Baron Enri Filip's advance riders had ridden in with the rising sun reporting that the baron would arrive on the next dawning. Hotig knew that Malcolm wanted to greet him with a victory, no matter how small, and was unwilling to give up his part in it.

"The men would be heartened by their Cap Tan's direct involvement. It would stiffen their spines!" growled John Marcus eager for the fight.

"This is getting us nowhere," said Hap, exasperated. "Instead of arguing we should be fortifying the east side of the river. Not to mention looking for Jonathon." Malcolm went still as death. Resentment at the reminder his son was missing plainly visible. Hap noted his error. He bowed his head.

"I'm sorry, Cap Tan."

"I'm going," said Malcolm.

Lieutenant Gilroy stepped forward. "Cap Tan, as leader of your Hand I shall accompany you. I'll put together an elite guard."

"No, Lieutenant. As I have been so bluntly reminded, someone has to find Jonathon. That is your task. Do not fail." With that Malcolm got up and left the room, leaving it in silence, Lieutenant Gilroy right behind.

"Good job, cousin," said John Marcus.

Priest Hotig rose. "Before you all fall back into bickering I will depart as well. My place is with my remaining flock at the Temple. I shall sent Priest Duran to you."

Wilbert knelt before the priest. "You will be missed."

Priest Hotig knew Wilbert was really saying goodbye. "It is the goddess's will, my son. Worry not. I have spoken with High Priestess El-lina. She has returned to the East." The pronouncement brought looks of despair upon the company. "She goes to amass the might of the East. She will return with much needed aid." The collectively held breathes exhaled in renewed hope. Hotig made the sign Fiona over all and walked to the door.

"He goes to his death," said Wilbert, softly.

"Don't we all?" added Hap.

"Not if Tierra rises," said Hotig under his breath as he closed the door.

14

IN THE TUNNELS

Wybee felt at a loss. He desperately needed some advice. Taking care of a grieving child was beyond his area of knowledge, especially with him being no more than a child himself. The soothing steady voice of Tierra now felt far away and very weak. It had happened right after she had talked to Jonathon. Wybee didn't know why, only that she wouldn't or couldn't answer and that he and Jonathon had to find some place to hide. He said sympathetically, "I'm sorry, Jonathon, about your mother and grandmother. I don't remember mine, but I'm sure it must hurt an awful lot."

Jonathon nodded slowly, the tears still dripping from his nose and chin. Wybee let him sit there as long as he could. So far, no one had travelled this particular tunnel, but the steady footfalls of people moving along the main arteries echoed continually. They couldn't risk being discovered.

"Jonathon, we need to move. Can you get up?"

Jonathon looked up at Wybee with reddened tear-filled eyes. He nodded still unable to find words. He struggled to his feet with a little help from Wybee.

"Let's go down this way. Maybe we can find some place to rest until you feel better. If someone should come along, do not tell them who you are, okay?"

"Okay," choked out Jonathon between sobs.

Wybee was worried, but he couldn't let Jonathon see it. The two made their way down the tunnel towards the main artery. Wybee started several times in false alarm as he thought he heard someone coming down their tunnel. He trailed his fingers along the wall, trying to sense what was behind the doors they passed. He had led Jonathon down into the tunnels confidently enough. It wasn't that he had grown up in the tunnels or had memorized their layout, Tierra had guided him. Now, it was as if she slumbered.

A growing glow cut through the dim darkness. As the two boys turned a slight bend, the main passageway came into view. It had been well lit. Torches placed in sconces tended by temple members directed the believers to safety. Wybee put out his hand to halt Jonathon. It came to rest on a wooden door. He pushed and the door swung inward. "Jonathon, in here quickly."

The darkness in the room was daunting. Wybee left the door open a crack to give them some courage, but it wasn't enough light to explore their refuge. He asked Jonathon, "Can you start a fire?"

"Sure," Jonathon replied. He dug around in his bag of provision and pulled out a flint and a striker. "I'm going to need something to burn."

Wybee scrambled around in the darkness. His hand came across a bundle. *Torches! Thank you Tierra!* He pulled one out and brought it to Jonathon. After a few tries a spark from the flint landed on the head of the torch. Jonathon blew gently on it. The glow brightened and reluctantly caught. The light from the torch revealed that they were in a small storeroom. Bundles of torches lined one wall, kegs of something along another.

Safe for the moment, but we risk discovery when it comes time to refresh the torches in the tunnel. Wybee closed the door to the storeroom. He took the torch and climbed up on one of the kegs to reach a wall sconce. He put the torch in it and climbed back down to sit next to Jonathon. "At least we won't have to worry about light," he said cheerfully then added, "We can stay here for a little while, then we have to move on."

The pounding sound of many feet on the march penetrated the door of their refuge. Wybee opened the door just enough to look out. Troops were in the main passage hurrying northward going against the flow of the refugees who were flattening against the wall giving way to the troops. Wybee caught a glimpse of the troop leader. *Jonathon's father. He's going to battle.* A quick peek at the glum and dejected Jonathon decided him to remain quiet. He closed the door and returned to Jonathon's side.

The troops passed quickly. With the echoing sound of their footfalls receding Wybee spoke. "Are you okay?"

Jonathon had stopped sobbing and only occasionally had a catch in his breathing. Wybee was felt relieved. A sobbing child would cause too many questions to be asked. Questions Wybee didn't want to have to answer. He was counting on being able to disappear into the flow of fleeing people without much notice.

"I don't have time to go to your council. I have to find Wybee. And soon!"

The two boys looked at each other, fear in their eyes. Both raised their fingers to their lips for quiet. Wybee hadn't detected any menace in the voice, but he was afraid to open the door and find out. Other voices responded to the man looking for Wybee, but they were spoken softly and their muffled words did not penetrate the door. The voices moved on.

"Jonathon, we are going to have to leave here soon. When we do, we cannot tell anyone our names. Do you understand? Let's pretend we are spies!"

"Okay,"

—⊷⟋⟍⊷—

Pre-battle excitement filled Malcolm as he waited on the first floor of the Jeffson building with his uncle, John Marcus and the twenty men he had provided. They had joined the two detachments of the Cap Tan's Hand sent by Lieutenant Gilroy and were awaiting the arrival of Priest Duran who would lead them through the tunnels. Malcolm used the time to go over the plan one last time with his uncle, mostly for the benefit of his attack force.

"After we secure the building, we'll set fire to the upper floor. When you see the smoke send the lancers across the bridge. They must make it past the customs building. We'll cross behind their charge during the confusion. Have people ready to burn the bridge when the lancers return."

"Aye, Cap Tan," said John Marcus. He clasped Malcolm's forearm and leaned in close. "Good luck, Malcolm. Be careful."

"I will, Uncle."

The door of a small side office opened. Priest Duran stood in the doorway. "Cap Tan, if you are ready."

Malcolm turned to his men. "We travel fast once we get in the tunnels. Keep your eyes ahead and stay alert. When we get under the custom building remain silent. There are two entrances. Move fast and kill everyone. Alright, let's go."

Priest Duran led them into a closet, a grimly determined Malcolm followed. Once inside he found the back section of the closet removed revealing a stairway down. Malcolm waited below the Jeffson Building as, one by one, the detachment exited the stairway and reformed in a column of twos, the torchlight reflecting off expressions of amazement at the discovery of a whole other world existing beneath the streets they used to patrol. He took his place at the head of the column, Priest Duran next to him to lead the way.

"At the double march, go."

The march took less than a candlemark. Once the troops had gotten into the main passageway, the orderly flight of citizens, despair and impending doom writ across their faces, readily gave way to the armed men. Malcolm's uplifted eyebrow inquired of the priest.

"They are Fiona's faithful. Most came from Yakstown. This is not the first time they have had to escape through tunnels."

Beneath the custom building the troop halted and split into two groups. They were met by two acolytes. Malcolm and the Hand leaders huddled with Priest Duran and his watchers.

"At the top of this ladder, the passageways run along the outer edge of the building. There are peepholes. Stairs at the far end go to the second floor. There are levers at the doors, which are disguised as sections of the wall. They open outward. The Yakov's quarter on the second floor," one of the acolytes reported.

Malcolm asked, "How many men?"

"It's hard to say, sir. Maybe twenty on each floor. About half soldiers."

Malcolm pressed, "Any Westerners?"

"I don't believe so, sir, but I cannot be sure."

Malcolm looked to his Hand leaders who nodded their understanding. Malcolm ordered. "Toleck, you take the first floor. Jacabo and I will take the second. We'll leave first. Wait until we are all up the ladder, Toleck. Then move out."

"May the goddess be with you Cap Tan," said Priest Duran making the sign of Fiona over the troops before departing with the two acolytes.

Malcolm stood before the secret entrance on the second floor, his troops squeezed into the passage behind him. His look through the peephole had revealed little. Muffled shouts and sounds of battle from below came to him. He pulled the lever. The door swung outward, and he charged into the room, drawing his sword.

He spied Will Yakov in the center of nine of his leaders, huddled over a table in the corner. The table was littered with maps and the remains of a half eaten breakfast. Will looked up as Malcolm charged towards him.

"What the...Malcolm?"

Malcolm shouted as his men fell on the unprepared group, "Will Yakov is mine!"

"You're a bigger fool than I thought, Malcolm," said Will drawing his sword. "You were never able to beat me."

Most of Will's leaders were cut down before their swords cleared their scabbards. Those who had managed to were quickly overwhelmed. Only Will remained. He was allowed to walk to the center of the room where Malcolm waited. He cut his eyes towards the still open door.

"I don't know how you managed that, but it won't help you now," said Will lunging into his attack. His overhead stroke was met with a ringing clang as Malcolm blocked and sidestepped, his counterstroke swinging neck high. Will stepped back as Malcolm's sword whistled past missing by inches.

"I see you've kept your lessons up," taunted Will.

"You killed my mother! And Angeline!" Malcolm punctuated his words with hammering blows.

Will gave way to the onslaught, circling around Malcolm, a look of confusion on his face. "I don't know what you're talking about." He started a feinting thrust at Malcolm's chest.

Malcolm gave no thought to defense. He stepped in, taking a shallow cut in his shoulder. His fist shot out connecting with Will's jaw. Will, taken by surprise, was knocked back a few steps. Before he could recover Malcolm's sword slid into his chest below the solar plexus.

"I'm talking about the assassins you sent to kill the Sinclair family while under parley." He gave his sword a vicious twist.

"It wasn't me," Will gasped weakly sinking to a knee. He was unable to remain upright and slumped back sliding off Malcolm's sword.

"You still paid. As will your father. Where is he?" Blood welled up and out of Will's mouth drowning any response he was going to make. "Jacabo, take five men. Go upstairs and set the fires. The rest of you with me."

Still filled with blood lust, Malcolm and the rest of his men rushed down the stairs. On the first floor the melee was coming to a close. The large room was littered with fallen bodies. Malcolm spied two Hunters among the fallen. There were also three of his own men. Toleck withdrew his sword from the chest of one of Yakstown's soldiers. He came over to join Malcolm.

"We surprised them at first, then a group of five Hunters came through the front door. They fought like devils. Two of them escaped. We can expect company soon," he reported.

Malcolm reassured his leader, "The fires are lit. We can get out and get back before their friends arrive."

⸻ ◈ ⸻

The wait had done little to improve John Marcus' nerves. Not known for his patience to begin with, anxiety for his nephew's safety put him in an ill mood. The hazy smoke from smoldering homes on the east of the river drifted across Peddler's Way partially obscuring John Marcus's view of the custom building. He groused, "Why can't we have a Harvest Storm when we need one."

He looked over at his lieutenant, Nils P'edar, whose attention was focused on the west side of the river.

"What's that, baron?" asked Nils, pointing in the direction of the Customs building.

"What?"

The smoke cleared momentarily revealing a group of Hunters entering the building.

"Should we attack?" asked Nils.

John Marcus considered. His inner voice screamed at him to attack, instead, though his voice lacked conviction, he said, "We don't know that Malcolm's in yet. We wait for the signal." In truth, John Marcus was having trouble restraining himself. His immediate urge was to charge head long into a conflict and sort it out later, but this time was different. If he attacked too soon it could ruin the raid or trap them all on the west side of the river. *Patience is a virtue,* he thought. Problem was, John Marcus was not very virtuous.

Two figures ran out of the customs building and fled westward towards the Masher encampment. John Marcus swore, "Damn! Give me the signal. Give me the signal."

His horse sensed his impatience and began prancing about eager to charge. John fought the reins as he struggled to stay mounted and at the same time keep a hold of his lance.

"Baron, they're coming," informed Nils pointing past the customs building.

Twenty or more Mashers were rapidly making their way towards Malcolm and his men. This was not the way the plan was suppose to work. *Thank Fiona I sent Tanya to the Free Goatherders.* John Marcus looked up at the third floor of the customs building. *Was that smoke?* A thin tendril was spilling out of a window. It rapidly increased to a brownish black roil as the fire gained strength. The baron put his spurs to the flank of his horse. He screamed, "Now! Charge!"

⚜

The guard watching at the front door of the customs building called out. "Cap Tan, Mashers coming. They're coming fast."

Malcolm ran to the door, cursing. He saw the Mashers and the unraveling of his plans. He looked back towards the bridge. John Marcus's mounted men had begun their charge. It was going to be close. He had considered escaping back through the tunnels, but he had already ordered the signal fire lit and had no way of informing John Marcus of the change in plans. He didn't want to needlessly throw away his uncle's life. The die had been cast. "Everyone get ready. We're going to have to fight our way out."

It looked like the two forces would meet right at the front door. He and his men should still be able to slip out in the confusion of battle without anyone realizing that they had come from inside the building. As his uncle's force cleared the bridge, Malcolm watched in disbelief as Hunters streamed out of the warehouse across the street from him swinging their bolas. The weapons were thrown low and tangled the feet of the leading horses bringing down half the force and throwing their riders. Most rose immediately but without their lances they would be no match for the Mashers. Malcolm wished they had brought compound bows. He made his decision. Charging out the of door, he ordered, "Cross the street. Get the Hunters,"

They passed between the remaining lancers and the approaching Mashers falling on the Hunters with ferocity. Their unexpected appearance took the Hunters by surprise, but more kept pouring out of the warehouse. Malcolm surveyed the battle. His uncle had not risen after being thrown. The lancers crashed into the Mashers taking out many, but not enough. The riders were being pulled from their horses and hacked to pieces. The Hunters had pulled away from Malcolm's initial charge and strung their bows. Malcolm knew he would lose.

"Hold!"

Icy fingers of fear clawed their way down Malcolm's spine. The bitter taste of the inevitable filled his mouth. He knew that booming voice. *Uri Yakov.* The Westerners pulled back further, surrounding Malcolm's few remaining forces, none of them lancers. Uri rode up to Malcolm.

"Tell your men to drop their weapons or I'll kill them where they stand."

Malcolm couldn't find his voice. He let his sword drop from his fingers. His men followed suit. A whooshing sounded from the bridge. Thick black smoke permeated with bright orange yellow flames rose from the center of the span.

"It looks like you are stuck here," Uri told Malcolm. He turned to the leader of the Mashers, "Seize this one. Kill the rest." He dismounted and walked towards the customs building.

—⦿⦿⦿—

Shem was simply amazed. The acolyte laughed. *She does that a lot, but it's not unpleasant.* He asked again, "These tunnels have been here for how long?"

"As I have said, Hero. What is your name? Anyway, they have been here a long time. Since the beginning or nearly so."

She also talks a lot. Shem smiled. He liked the sing song way the acolyte talked, running her thoughts together, and the fact that she talked to him. "My name is Shem, and yours, priestess?"

"I'm not a priestess, at least not yet, Shem," she said demurely, trying Shem's name on for size. "I am Selene, first level acolyte. Our Free Goatherder companion is called Ma Ne."

"You are the one. Chosen of the Life Giver. You must come with me. The Council will want to speak with you." The group turned at a slight bend in the tunnel. They could see the main passage up ahead.

The Free Goatherder was beginning to frustrate Shem with his insistence on going to this Council. When he spoke, his voice was a little louder than he had intended. "I don't have time to go to your council. I must find Wybee. And soon!"

"Yes, and the heir. We'll find them and take them to the Council. There is much they can tell you. The land of the Free Goatherders would also be the safest place for the heir."

Shem looked around for another alternative. He eyed the acolyte. "What about you, Selene? Where do you go?"

"Priest Hotig has instructed me not to return to the Temple of Fiona. The Westerners were attacking it as I left. We have no way of defending it. I fear it has been taken. In short, I have nowhere to go."

Shem smiled sheepishly, "To quote a peddler friend of mine, 'I've been there myself, you know, and I'm on my way back. Join me?'"

With a nod Selene accepted.

Entering the well-lit passageway, Shem looked around. He knew that Wybee and the heir had a head start. Going north against the flow felt useless to him. It would have attracted too much attention. If he were running he would have wanted to blend in. That meant south, surely. He tried to settle into a state of calm like the high priestess had told him during their time together. Tried to feel the presence of Tierra, but something was wrong. *I must not be doing it right.* His gaze passed over then lingered on Selene. *Or maybe I'm just distracted.* Selene and even Ma Ne seemed to be waiting on his decision.

Shem singled out the Free Goatherder. "Ma Ne, you are the only one of us who has seen them. If you would, describe the boys."

"Waist high, the heir a little taller with dark hair. Wybee has hair the color of straw, maybe a little lighter, slight of build."

It was the acolyte's turn. Shem asked, "Selene, where do these tunnels end?"

"On the south edge of town. They come up at a small sanctuary. People will only be able to leave one at a time," she replied.

Shem made his decision, "South then. Keep your eyes peeled."

He took off moving down the center of the tunnel, walking slightly faster than the stream of people. Selene took the left, Ma Ne the right, eyes swiveling through the refugees looking for the boys.

Two candlemarks later found them empty handed close to the end of the tunnel. People sat on the floor in an orderly manner, awaiting their turn up the ladder and out through the sanctuary. He had seen many children the size and coloring of Wybee and Jonathon, but each time he pointed one out to Ma Ne, the Goatherder shook his head negatively.

Shem scrubbed his hands through his hair. He was beginning to think that maybe the boys did go north. As the group stood in a loose huddle near the end of the line of refugees, Shem said, "I say we question everyone here. Someone must have seen them."

"Then you alert everyone to the fact we are looking. We don't want to bring attention to them. Or ourselves for that matter," said Ma Ne.

"I have a better way," said Selene. "Follow me." She pulled her hood over her head and crossed her arms, putting her hands in her sleeves. She headed through the crowd murmuring, "Excuse me, child. Fiona's blessing upon you." Word quickly spread and a pathway opened up before her. Shem and Ma Ne followed in her footsteps. They reached the ladder where two acolytes were instructing the refugees on what to do. The acolytes stepped aside at a word from Selene and Shem led the trio up.

At the top Shem was met by an elderly priest standing behind his dais. His short cropped grey hair and beard framed kindly eyes, tiredness evident in them as well as devotion and determination. He felt good about the old man as he watched him help Selene from the ladder.

"Sister. Are you well?" He took in the size and girth of Shem then Ma Ne as he climbed up through the entrance.

"I am well, Father, but I fear for Priest Hotig."

"Fear not, Sister. It will be as Fiona wills," he said. "How may I help you?"

Shem listened to the pleasantries. It was obvious that Selene had everything under control. Ma Ne stood silently to the side.

"Father, we seek two children. Boys. One fair haired the other dark, about this high," she held out her hand a little above her waist.

"I have seen many children pass by, Sister. Too many. Most as you have described them."

"The fair haired one is... special. It is discernible," she said.

The priest turned to Shem. A smile peeked around the corners of his mouth. "Special," he mused, "Like this tall warrior here?" Shem no longer felt surprised. In fact he had come to expect those sensitive enough to recognize him.

"Yes, Father. The other is," she leaned in close and whispered, "the heir."

All amusement left the priest. He nodded understandingly. "I have seen no one like that, Sister," he said.

"Thank you, Father. If you should, could you...contact me?"

"I will, Sister. Now if you excuse me, there are many below who would like out."

"Of course, Father" Selene bowed her head in deference. The three walked around the dais and made their way out of the sanctuary. Shem looked back. The priest was bending over helping raise a child out of the outstretched arms of its mother. He then assisted the women off the ladder offering Fiona's benediction.

"No one will get out of the tunnel without the father seeing them," said Selene.

The trio left the sanctuary. Shem raised his arms to shadow his eyes from the bright midturning sky. Being in the tunnels for as long as they had been with nothing but torch light to see by had left their pupils dilated. He quickly scanned for any signs of a Harvest Storm. What few clouds there were were high and wispy. There would be no storm this turning.

"I believe the storms are over. Harvest should begin soon. It's a good time for traveling," said Ma Ne.

Shem asked, though, coming from Ma Ne, he already knew the answer. "Going where?"

"To my land. To see the Council."

Shem wished he had the spider High Priestess El-lina had given him. Especially now. Their failure to find Wybee and the weakening of Tierra's presence left him with a sense of urgency. But the spider was in the peddler's wagon along with most of his foodstuffs. If he left right away he could be back before nightfall. Selene and Ma Ne could stay here in case the priest located the boys. He didn't want to concede too much ground to Ma Ne, but he wanted his wagon. "If we are going somewhere I'll need my wagon. It's back at the manor."

"If it's still there," said Ma Ne.

"If it is then Wybee and the heir wouldn't have to walk to wherever it is we're going," argued Shem. "And we would have supplies."

"If it's not, then you will have wasted half a turning," countered Ma Ne.

Selene had been staying out of the discussion merely listening to both men, weighing their words, reading their body language. "Is our need for haste that great, Ma Ne? Shem, what's really in that wagon that you need or want?"

Shem studied blades of grass and leaves on the trees, ignoring Selene's question. Ma Ne answered first. "The Life Giver has long been known by the Free Goatherders. Even though we revere the blessed Fiona, we have been awaiting the arrival of the Life Giver. The Council has...some knowledge. They have been awaiting the time and the sign."

Ma Ne's words brought Shem's attention into focus. *What knowledge? How much do they know?* "What sign?"

"You."

Frustration crashed down on Shem's shoulders. He rubbed the back of his neck thinking. He already knew he was the hero. What he didn't know is what he was supposed to do. All anyone would ever allude to was hints, hopes, and good wishes. What he needed was direction! He asked, "And the significance of this sign is?"

"The beginning. There are tasks that—no. I can say no more here. It is for the Council."

Shem hadn't realized that he had been holding his breath. With Ma Ne's refusal to say more, it burst out of him. Selene asked gently.

"The wagon, Shem. What is in the wagon?"

"The spider that the high priestess gave me."

"A mighty gift, Shem. Why was it left behind?" she asked.

Shem could see that Selene immediately regretted the last question. He tempered his own flare of anger. "I had expected a somewhat different welcome in High City. But what's done is done. Now I wish I had it." He also hoped that whatever had been interfering with it could not reach this far into the Central Lands.

"I believe something can be done about that. Let's go back and talk to the priest."

Shem brightened immediately. *Why hadn't I thought about that?* His smile was reflected by Selene. Even Ma Ne seemed pleased now that talk of going back was averted. In the sanctuary the priest was helping a young mother off the ladder. He stepped back from the opening to talk to Selene.

"Father, we have need of speaking with the high priestess."

"Of course, Sister, but she has been uncommunicative of late." He glanced at the ladder. A grown man was just climbing up through the opening. He led the way to his office, a small cubby just off the dais, closing the door behind him once they were in. Four people made for cramped conditions. He squeezed his way to a shelf and secured a wooden box that was tucked between two old tomes. He placed it on his desk and took off the lid.

Shem took the wooden box in his hand. He could see the sheen of the web. His hopes grew. The high priestess could give him direction. He thought hard trying to remember what El-lina had told him about using the web. *Just concentrate on me. Clear your mind of all other thoughts and think of me. Speak and I will answer.'* He set aside all the worries and doubts that were swirling around in his head. He thought of nothing else but El-lina. He spoke. "High Priestess. This is Shem." Nothing happened. He tried again. The shimmering strands of the web faded slightly then they all heard.

"Shem! Where are you?" It was El-lina.

———⟡———

They called her Na Na. It seemed to please her. She was older than Angeline by about ten cycles but still had a pleasant face and disposition. When she wasn't talking about the converts, that is. This is what had drawn the boys to her. They had rejected many while traveling through the tunnels. Some because of the fear and despair they displayed, mannerisms indicating they no longer trusted anyone, or just the emptiness in their eyes. Na

Na was different. She was none of those things. She had also protected them from the scrutiny they had been beginning to receive traveling alone.

"They are with me!" she declared to the overly aggressive man who had attempted to take charge at one point, wrapping her arms around them and hustling them away. "They are beasts!" she confided to them. "They tore my own boys out my very arms in Yakstown. Took them for Mieze! You two stay away from him. He has the look. Na Na will take care of you, poor dears."

Wybee had accepted her right away. He asked innocently, "Where are we going, Na Na?"

"Home," she said. "Back to the valley. We should never have left it in the first place, but Na Na had been swept away by the pretty face. He was a good man, my husband. Until they came. Then he feared and converted. He gave our boys over to them. But not you, Na Na will protect you."

The valley turned out to be Grimval Valley. Na Na had been a member of Camdene O'Kelly's clan and it was to her clan that they were returning. "It's far away from all this trouble," she assured them and that was good enough for the boys. At least for now.

Finally, it was their turn at the ladder. The acolyte instructed them to climb up and go out the door. There would be someone at the top if they needed help. He blessed them and sent them on their way. Wybee first, then Jonathon and Na Na. They followed a grown man up the ladder careful to stay far enough away from him that he would be unable to grab one of the boys and run. When Wybee emerged from the trapdoor behind the dais there was no one at the top. He heard the closing of a door off to his right. With no other help available, the two boys assisted Na Na off the ladder and they walked out the door into the sunshine.

"Head for the river, boys, we'll try to find a barge. Na Na's legs won't carry her all the way to the valley," she instructed Wybee and Jonathon.

They followed the road southwest keeping the river in sight. It was near dusk when they came upon a group of soldiers disembarking from several barges. Na Na went up to a barge carrying an O'Kelly pendant. She hailed the captain.

"Na Na MacDuff of the O'Kelly clan. Are you heading home?"

The captain came to the rail, "Aye, as fast as I can unload," he yelled back.

"Passage for three? I can cook, two for the holystones."

"It'll be three if ye displease me!" he yelled back.

"Done! Up the gangplank, boys. Mind you steer clear of the soldiers."

15

HIGH CITY

The Westerners had taken easily to tents, being similar enough to the lean-tos they preferred in their own country, and the Fair Green was now littered with them. Uri sat in the tent of U'cha, the Masher Clan Leader assigned to him for the conquest of High City. Uri had wanted to hold the meeting in the customs building, but had been unable to convince the Mashers or Un Tier as they called themselves, to enter it. The meeting would begin as soon as he finished receiving the orders from Vlad whose astral projection stood before him bearing a stern countenance. His orders sounded firmly in Uri's mind.

"You have taken the Temple. Send the Un Tier. Raze it to the ground. Leave no stone upon another. It will be as if it had never existed. Your men and the Sol Dat will cross the river today and beat back the forces of the enemy. This will be done."

The last words were implanted with a little more force, making Uri wince, but he had learned to close off a small kernel of his own mind whenever Vlad "visited" him. Wayward thoughts were to be guarded against at all times. Failure to do so resulted in agonizing mental pain. "Yes, Sun Father."

The pressure inside his head eased somewhat. "I have good news for you. Sinclair's women are dead." Uri could feel his facial muscles tightening into a smile.

"Thank you, Sun Father."

The image of Vlad faded. His presence left Uri. Free now to think his own thoughts, Uri contemplated all that the Sun Father had told him. Baron Filip had chosen Chet Sinclair and was even now mustering his forces south of High City. This did not really surprise him. Enri was devoutly religious and that overrode his fealty to the Yakov's. Baron Reis was moving against the lands of the Free Goatherders, *Damn them! They will pay for their devotion to Fiona. They all will,* and Iago was moving against the Grimval Valley. He didn't like that his forces were split, but augmented by the armies of the West he still had the largest force. All in all that left him in a very favorable position.

He knew that no one on the Sinclair side had as complete an overall picture as he. Uri rose and brushed aside the curtain giving him privacy. He looked around the tent. U'cha and U'tam of the Un Tier, I'ron of the Sol Dat, and Lieutenants Cutler and Keith of his own forces stood around the table in the center of the tent awaiting their daily orders. There was another man, by himself, trying to look both important and invisible at the same time. *The envoy. What was his name? Yes, Ham, that was it. Will's new favorite.* Uri asked, "Where is Will?"

Lieutenant Cutler answered. "Still at the customs building last I heard, Baron. The envoy we sent to parley yester's turning has returned. He has news."

"Bring him forward."

Ham walked as proudly as he could, though it was still obvious that his hurts pained him. His face was bruised, his eyes swollen but open, and the tip of his nose bore a cut. Uri smiled. He had intentionally worded the ultimatum harshly to goad the Sinclairs. It had apparently worked. That Ham had survived was a testament to his skills.

"Report."

"Milord, the Sinclairs reject your proposal, utterly. However, I have news that their Cap Tan, Chet Sinclair, is dead as is his wife and the wife of the new Cap Tan, Malcolm Sinclair."

"You have seen this with your own eyes?" asked Uri.

"No, Milord, but I was present when Chet Sinclair received the news. He was rendered incapable of command. Later while imprisoned, I heard of his death. They said it was from grief." Ham lifted his fingers to his nose then inspected them. "I have reason to believe the reports are true."

"Grief, you say," Uri smiled again, "and how did you manage to escape?"

Ham paused. He continued hesitantly, "With the aid of my brother."

"Your brother." Uri thought furiously. "You are the one who brought the prisoner. The big man, the drunk, that was your brother." It was more of a statement than a question.

Ham bowed his head to Uri then looked him in the eye, "Aye, Milord. I would like to add that when crossing the bridge to return, I noticed a detachment of lancers. I believe they are going to attack."

Uri recognized Ham's attempt to redirect the conversation. He was about to probe further when two Sol Dat dashed into the tent unannounced. The first one blurted out.

"Clan Leader I'ron! The soft Skins attack the customs building. They came out of the walls. We were caught by surprise!"

Uri reacted swiftly. Will was in that building. "U'cha, send some men, Now!" A runner was dispatched. He was about to commit a second force under his command when he remembered the Sun Father's orders. "U'tam, go to the Temple. Destroy it utterly. Bring me the priest. Alive." On his way out of the tent he said, "Well done, Lieutenant Ham. See to your wounds. We'll talk later."

"Aye, Milord," said Ham.

The battle was nearly over by the time Uri, now mounted, rode up behind the Un Tier. He could see that the Sol Dat had Malcolm and about six or seven others surrounded in the street. The Un Tier had already dispatched the lancers. *Posting the Sol*

Dat in that warehouse had been a good idea. He rode up to edge of his troops. "Hold!"

Malcolm looked at him knowingly. The Sol Dat pulled back further keeping Malcolm's few remaining forces surrounded. Uri rode up to Malcolm. "Tell your men to drop their weapons, or I'll kill them where they stand."

Malcolm let his sword drop from his fingers. His men followed suit. A whooshing sounded from the bridge. Thick black smoke permeated with bright orange yellow flames rose from the center of the span.

"It looks like you are stuck here," Uri told Malcolm. He turned to the leader of the Sol Dat, "Seize this one. Kill the rest."

He dismounted and walked towards the customs building. The street was littered with bodies, both Central Landers and Westerners. Inside the customs building, it was worse. Most of the dead were his men. *What was that Sol Dat had said? 'They came out of the walls.'* Uri found that hard to believe, but Malcolm's men had gotten there, they had definitely achieved surprise.

He searched among dead. Not finding Will, he went up to the second floor, which was beginning to fill up with smoke. It was much the same. Very few of the dead were Malcolm's. Uri stopped in his tracks. That which he had begun to fear became true before his eyes. Will was slain. He turned on his heel and left.

U'cha was the first person he saw. "Burn the building and everyone in it." The customs building would be Will's pyre. His joy at learning of Chet's death diminished, but he still had Malcolm, now Cap Tan of the Central Lands. *For the time being.* He looked over at where Malcolm's men had been captured. They lie dead in the street with their throats slit. Only Malcolm remained, standing straight and defiant. He walked over.

"I killed him!" Malcolm spat. "Vengeance for my father. My mother. And for my wife!"

Uri backhanded him savagely. "Shut up, boy. Gag him and bring him with me."

—◦/◦/◦—

U'cha grudgingly gave his tent over to Uri. Malcolm sat tied and gagged in the chamber Uri had used earlier to receive his orders from Vlad. The count from the battle stood at seventy four Central Lander dead to ninety seven of his own. The losses were sustainable. Uri knew that the Sun Father didn't care how many he lost and was more than willing to use his troops as fodder as long as they won victories and today had definitely been a victory. The Sinclair family had been reduced to a single child. A child of nine cycles. Not exactly leadership material.

Still, Uri did not like losing so many men. Especially not in the manner in which he lost them. He had been lucky. If they had not learned of Malcolm's attack, the results would have been very different. Malcolm had been bold. Uri had to find out how it had happened. The runner had said the attackers had "come out of the walls".

"I should not have burned the customs house," he mused aloud. But he had been angry at the death of his son.

"Sir?" asked Lieutenant Keith who was acting as his adjutant in Will's absence.

Uri didn't realize that he had spoken aloud. "I said, I should not have burned the customs building, but no matter. There are still a lot of buildings on this side of the river. Pick one. Tear out walls from the inside. See if you can find anything."

"Aye, Milord," said the Lieutenant. As Keith was leaving, Lieutenant Cutler entered.

"Milord, the Temple is destroyed. Even now the, uh, Un Tier…" he stumbled over the term, "are completing the leveling. Nothing will remain. Here is the priest as ordered."

The tent flap was pushed aside and Priest Hotig, hands tied behind his back, was forcefully shoved inside. He nearly stumbled and barely managed to keep his balance. Straightening, he stood proudly defiant.

"Baron Yakov, what a pleasure it is to see you," he said amiably.

Uri was in no mood to banter words with the priest. "That remains to be seen. You will be required to recant your devotion to Fiona and accept either Mieze or the consequences."

"I will accept neither. Nor will I recant. I may not be able to prevent your actions, but they will occur without any willingness on my part or the part of my goddess, Fiona."

Uri smiled. He had never liked the priest anyway. "So be it, priest. You've sealed your fate."

"My fate has long been sealed, Baron. Since first I bent the knee to the blessed Fiona. Yours, forgivingly, still hangs in the balance. It is not too late."

Uri walked around Hotig. He took a rag out of his tunic pocket and wrapped it around Hotig's mouth, tying it tight. He leaned in and whispered, "You talk too much and say too little." He led Hotig to the curtained area where Malcolm sat seething. He sat the priest in a chair and secured him. Before pulling the curtain to, he informed his guests, "Your new accommodations will be ready soon. Until then, enjoy each other's company."

Uri was in a good mood. The scaffold was nearly complete. He had had it built near the site of the customs building ruins and made it tall enough to be clearly seen from the east side of the river. He had also brought up his rock throwers, displaying them prominently. They were to be used to drive home his point of futility to those still opposing him by returning the fallen High City soldiers.

He had spent the remainder of the turning planning the assault across the river. It had taken three buildings to find the hidden tunnels, but he now had access across the river. Tomorrow as the people of High City watched their Cap Tan swinging from the gibbet his troops would be pouring out of buildings and into their streets. The Sun Father had ordered him to cross this turning, but there were no bridges left standing. Uri had at least found a way that was quicker than building bridges. He hoped it would be enough to satisfy Vlad.

Hap now looked back upon Chet in a different light. There had been times when he couldn't understand the decisions or lack thereof made by his cousin. Times when he had wanted to shake him and scream, "Do something, even if it's wrong!" Now the decisions were his to make. Faced with no good decisions, no possible good outcomes, how did one decide which catastrophe to embrace? Should he abandon High City? Should he make his stand in its streets?

The lines of Hap's face had deepened overnight. He had hardly slept. At first it had been thought that the construction across the river was to span the bridge for the pending attack. The arrival of the huge arms that threw rocks had reinforced that thinking, but it was now evident that Uri was building a gallows. The proclamation naming Hap Simon acting Regent followed swiftly on the heels of that recognition.

"I hear that there are two ropes," said Wilbert.

"The other would be for Priest Hotig," said Priest Duran.

Hotig, High City's leading priest and trusted advisor. Hap added him to the list of a baron and soon to be two Cap Tans and their wives. *This war is rapidly becoming too expensive to fight,* thought Hap. "So now the question is how soon after Uri's gruesome display will he attack and where will it come from?"

"If he's found the tunnels the attack could be from anywhere. I think it's time to pull back," advised Wilbert.

Hap agreed. But Ma Ne's last cryptic warning had been to hold High City as long as possible. But how? His contemplation was diverted by Priest Duran whose attention had appeared to be wandering, but was now sharply in focus.

"Regent? The high priestess has just informed me that we should evacuate the city."

"What?"

"Evacuate High City, quickly."

"Why? Where?" Hap knew the first question was foolish, but he had been surprised by the sudden communication. He knew little of priestdom mysticisms, but he had heard nothing.

Priest Duran ignored the first question. "She did not say where, only that it is time to go. She talked with me as long as she could, but something seems to be interfering with her ability to do so. She apologizes. She believes the Ascendency is increasing the Sun Father's power."

Hap understood little of what the priest had just said, but he did recognize the urgency in his voice. "Is there more?"

"She has mobilized the East and soon expects to be able to send aid. In the meantime her flying scouts have been scouring the Central Lands. Baron Reis will soon bring the battle to the Free Goatherders. Baron Iago attacks the Grimval Valley from the west. She will try to talk again, but she doesn't know when. Lastly, she says Tierra weakens. She doesn't know why, but is very concerned."

Priest Duran looked as if there were more, but Hap didn't press. Barons Reis and Iago's defections had been expected, but not the speed in which they had coordinated their attacks. He now had limited choices, the Free Goatherders who may or may not allow them into their strongholds or the Grimval Valley, both of which were currently or soon to be under attack. Neither choice was good. On the other hand neither land had ever been successfully invaded. *Winged scouts? Is there a winged army?*

"Uncle?" said Wilbert gently.

Hap roused himself. "Yes, yes. Where would we go? The roads south are clogged. Baron Filip says he cannot advance for all the people fleeing south."

"Then have him hold as a rear guard. Cover the evacuation while gradually moving back towards your estate. We'll take our men and head southeast towards John Marcus's estate loop around and meet up. It's a longer way but we should be able to move faster," offered Wilbert.

Hap concurred, "Very well. Ask Nils P'edar and Sloan Quinn to come in."

"Yes, Uncle," said Wilbert.

Hap turned to Priest Duran, looking for support, encouragement, or perhaps validation. The priest was lost in a faraway stare. Nils and Sloan entered and stood before Hap's desk.

"Regent."

"Sloan, we're pulling back. Take your men south. Join Baron Filip. You will be the rear guard. Protect the road for as long as you can, then pull back to the estate. I'll join you there. Send a runner to the baron."

"Aye Milord." Sloan saluted, fist to chest, then departed.

Hap waited until Sloan had left the office before addressing Nils. Nils had been with John Marcus for some ten cycles and had vehemently argued for another rescue attempt. His face still betrayed the bitterness of losing the argument.

"Nils, John is dead. There is nothing we can do for Malcolm. We have to live to fight another day." Hap's words made no dent other than the bitterness morphing into a stony silence. "Wilbert and I will be with you. We will head southeast passing close enough to John's estates to ensure that Tanya and the kids have fled. Then turn towards my estates."

The mention of John's wife Tanya had brought only the merest of flickers in Nils eyes and a slight relaxation of his posture. Hap wished it were more, but that was all he could offer. "Send a scout ahead to try and locate them. We leave at once."

"Aye, Regent." Nils saluted and left.

Hap Simon, Nils P'edar, and Priest Duran stood on the east side of the Majestic river overlooking the gallows. From their vantage behind the shield wall held by the remnants of the Cap Tan's Hand, they came to pay their last respects to Malcolm, John Marcus and Priest Hotig. The two nooses were plainly visible, swinging in the slight breeze which brought the sickeningly sweet stench of the decaying bodies stacked beside the rock throwers.

As Priest Duran gave the sign of Fiona the order to fire came from the west side. The arms of the rock throwers swung upward hurling their loads. Cheers and jeers rose from the west side. Amidst the rain of dead Central Land soldiers, the party turned and left the city. None were left to witness Baron Uri Yakov's display. None would see their Cap Tan hang.

⚓

Vlad was displeased with his puppet. Uri had woken in a jubilant mood. Vlad quickly changed that. The blinding flashes he caused behind the eyes of Uri had reduced him to helplessness, little more than a writhing worm skittering across a hot paving stone, but it was short lived. Just a reminder of the importance of following orders. No, he had not been pleased at the delay in crossing the river, and so withheld the fact that the Central Landers would not be around to witness Uri's celebration.

"Let him savor his empty gloating," mused Vlad aloud. "Let him have his empty ritual."

He would deal with that later when it would be more appreciated. Punishment for failure would be sweeter when prolonged.

Hands on the Auge Ose he watched as Malcolm and Priest Hotig were brought to the gallows.

⚓

Uri stood atop the gibbet in full view. He had hoped to see Malcolm's people lining the street to witness the spectacle. *The Harvest Storm (or rain of bodies from the rock throwers) have them cringing out of sight, but not out of view*, he told himself, pleased with his metaphor. He raised his hands.

"People of High City…You know who I am, Baron Uri Yakov! You are about to be given a choice." He spoke the words in measured tones, measured phrases. He didn't want any to misunderstand. "The same choice which is about to be given your Cap Tan!" he continued.

He motioned to Lieutenant Ham. Uri had given Ham the honor of escorting Malcolm as repayment for the harsh treatment he had received at the hands of the Sinclairs. Ham led the hooded Malcolm, hands tied behind his back, up the stairs and positioned him next to Uri. Uri untied the hood and pulled it off Malcolm's head. Malcolm stared back defiantly, muffled sounds coming from the gag still inserted into his mouth.

"Your time as Cap Tan has come to an end, Malcolm Sinclair," stated Uri loudly enough for all to hear, "however, you still have a chance to save your life. Kneel and accept Mieze and your life will be spared." He removed the gag from Malcolm.

"I'll see you burn in the afterlife first!" Malcolm shouted hotly.

"Perhaps, but not first," Uri said softly, tightening the noose around Malcolm's neck. He motioned to Ham.

Ham pulled on the rope, raising Malcolm off the ground. He took his time, protracting the agony of the man who had beaten him. Uri smiled. Ham would fit in well. They both watched as Malcolm's face turned red and his feet began dancing the gibbet. Uri signaled for Priest Hotig to be brought up.

Uri stood beside the priest untying the hood. He pulled it off and removed the gag. "Hotig. It's been a while. I don't believe I received your last invitation to festival. I trust you will be as entertaining as the soon to be late Cap Tan."

Hotig stood composed and serene as Uri settled the noose around his neck and tightened it. The baron gloated, "I would say how much this pains me, Priest, but then I'd have to repent." Uri turned to address the crowd. "Citizens of High City, behold your priest…who has labored these many cycles…teaching you falsehoods! But…who now has the opportunity to come to the light…as you all have. What say you, Priest?"

"Goddess, forgive them for they have sinned…" Hotig spoke in a normal voice. His words, enhanced by Fiona, boomed over the entire square penetrating to the soul.

The Goddess's Prayer ended abruptly, choked off as the noose tightened. Hotig was suddenly jerked off his feet and left dangling in the air, turning in the slight breeze.

"I believe that was a no," said Uri to Hotig. "Secure the ropes." Uri walked off the gallows as the ropes were tied off. The bodies would remain until sunrise.

Across the river Sol Dat burst through secret doorways, wall panels, and closets into High City Manor, the Jeffson building, the Bursary, and other empty buildings. They were followed by Un Tier where the doorways were large enough. They looked around frantically for an enemy to engage. The city was deserted.

16

SHEM

"**I**'m in a shrine, south of High City at the end of the tunnels. Where is Wybee? Where are you?" asked Shem unable to keep the excited relief from his voice. Selene and Ma Ne crowded in closer.

"You must find Wybee as quickly as possible. Tierra weakens," said El-lina. She sounded calm, but disappointment tinged her words.

Shem spoke without thinking. "Easy to say. It's total chaos down here."

Selene gasped, her face a portrait of shocked disbelief that anyone would address the high priestess in such a flippant manner.

"I'm sorry, Shem, but you must do what you can. Who is with you?"

"Selene, High Priestess, Acolyte First from High City and Ma Ne, Free Goatherder."

First Selene, then Ma Ne took their turn at the web asking and answering questions, speaking hurriedly. Shem listened to the give and take without interruption. It wouldn't do to waste the strength of the spider with argument; besides, direction was what he was seeking and his companions were covering those bases. By the time Ma Ne had outlined his plan the web was beginning to fade and El-lina's voice weakened.

"Very well. Shem, would that I had some wisdom to share. I agree with Ma Ne. Selene, stay with them. I will send aid to quicken your journey." The last words were barely audible as the sheen of the web faded away.

"I've never been to the home of the Free Goatherders. Is it pretty? Are there lots of flowers?" she said gaily in an obvious attempt to lighten the mood. She took the box from Shem's hands and tucked it into the sleeve of her robe.

"Not many have," said Ma Ne. "I fear that it will be but another of the many changes that have been thrust upon us."

Shem could not resist needling the unflappable Free Goatherder, "Sorry now, Ma Ne?"

"One should not pray for rain then curse the flood, it makes the goddess angry," he replied.

"That would be a wise man," said Selene as they left the priest's office. "We could use more of those. These ambitious ones are killing us."

The fatherly priest was helping the last of the refugees out of the tunnel. He blessed the old couple and sent them on their way. He closed the trap door and moved the dais back on top it. "They were the last. I am sorry," said the priest. Neither Wybee nor the heir had been among those the priest had assisted. Going to a statuette of Fiona on the back wall, he pulled it forward. They could hear a rumble from underneath their feet.

"The entryway has been sealed," the priest explained. "Will you be leaving now, Sister?"

"Yes, Father," Selene replied. She removed her hand from her sleeve revealing the spider's box.

"Keep it with Fiona's blessing. Your need will be greater than mine."

"Thank you, Father."

Outside the sun was shining in direct contrast to Shem's darkening spirit. Their feet may have followed the path towards River Road, the main throughway south out of High City, but Shem's mind retraced everything that had happened since entering High City. Passing unit after unit of first Un Tier then Sol Dat, witnessing their pleasure as they randomly burnt out homes of Fiona's faithful, his reception by the Sinclairs, and not finding Wybee. None of it was encouraging.

The faces of the fleeing denizens of High City depicted a simular spirit. Some dogged determination, but mostly disbelief and despair, which did not change once they crossed the river bridges. He had not been surprised, rather it had settled heavily on him that he could do nothing to stop it.

That was the beginning, Shem thought. *That was when the seed took root.* It had gotten worse after his arrest and imprisonment, and even more so in the tunnels. No Wybee. No heir. Shem couldn't say exactly what or when, but something bad or unexpected had happened. Even the high priestess had felt it.

He truthfully admitted to himself that he hadn't known what he was doing when he first offered himself up to be Tierra's hero, and he didn't know much more now. He knew the players, but not their parts; he knew he had a path, but not the direction to take nor the destination to reach; he knew he had enemies and they seemed to be always ahead. His frustration was growing. Every step of the journey seemed to take him further away from his goal. The shining of the sun didn't illuminate his way, only his mounting failures. He had asked Ma Ne if he was sorry. What Shem hadn't added at least aloud, was that he was beginning to be.

Shem had nothing to show for his efforts and a new task to fail at. He knew he had to shake off the impending feeling of doom, not allow whatever it was to sink it's claws deeper into him, but he couldn't help it.

"Why so glum, Shem?" asked Selene as they joined the tail end of the flood of refugees.

"I would just like something to go right for a change," he said. After a moment he added, "Have you ever failed, Selene?"

"No, Shem, I haven't. Nor will we now," she said after a moment.

Shem refused to be buoyed by her confidence. "I have. It feels a lot like this."

"Accepting defeat is the path of losers," said Ma Ne. There was no trace of either recrimination or condemnation in his voice.

Shem looked sharply at Ma Ne, remembering the countless times Ham had accused him of being just that. "You're not helping," he said.

"That was not my intent," Ma Ne replied.

Just before nightfall, they approached an army camp. Shem perked up at the sight.

"Who do suppose it is?" he asked Ma Ne.

"Part of Baron Simon's forces perhaps. Maybe Baron Filip's," Ma Ne said.

"I'll go find out," Shem offered.

"I think it would be more beneficial if I went," said Selene. "I'm sure that whoever it is, will have a priest or at least an acolyte with them."

"I agree. Shem and I will find a place to make camp."

Shem's disappointment was clearly evident. He mechanically went through the motions of preparing for their evening. After their bedrolls were set out, he informed Ma Ne, "I'll see if I can find some firewood. If this army has left any about, that is."

—◦⁄◦⁄◦—

Selene had discovered that they were in the camp of Baron Filip who was charged with holding the south road. While the baron had been busy with meetings, Selene had been able to have a short, but unfruitful conversation with Priest Conyn. Other than the promise of supplies, there had been little gain from the visit. It was just as well as Selene's thoughts kept drifting back to Shem. She was worried about his state of mind. Dwelling on failure usually produced it, like a self-fulfilling prophecy. So she had hurried back to their campsite as quick as she could.

Shem wasn't there. Ma Ne had scrounged some wood and had a small fire going. The pleasing aroma of a simmering camp stew blended in with the wood smoke to remind Selene of how hungry she was. She looked around. "Where is Shem?"

"He went out to gather some wood, but it was trouble he was searching for," Ma Ne answered.

Selene found herself annoyed, "Why didn't you stop him?"

"He is a man and the protector. Who am I to interfere with the goddess?" said Ma Ne matter of factly. Selene was about to protest when the sounds of a commotion reached them. "Whatever he was looking for, I think he found it," said Ma Ne.

They followed the sounds into the army camp. As they got closer they could distinguish laughter and catcalls amidst the bellowing of Shem. They approached the edge of a circle of soldiers.

"Over here, hero!"

"No, over here!"

"Stand still and fight!" came the slurred words of a very drunk Shem.

Ma Ne pressed through the circle making a way for Selene behind him. The elbowed soldiers started to protest until they saw it was a Free Goatherder and priestess that had joined them. They gave way. In the center of the ring stumbled Shem, turning this way and that, balled fists ready to pummel someone, anyone.

Dispirited and disappointed, mostly with herself for not having been there to prevent it, Selene asked the crowd, "How could you let him drink so much?"

"Forgive us, priestess, but he only had two ales. Then started telling this wild tale about being a hero," answered a soldier. He shrugged his shoulders in confusion. "We thought it was a joke. He didn't appreciate our laughter." The soldier walked away as the crowd broke up leaving Shem standing alone in what was once a circle.

Shem squinted at Selene. Recognition dawned, piercing his fogged brain. He dropped his fists. "They laughed. They laughed at me. I've failed again," he said morosely.

"It's alright, Shem. No one's failed. Not yet," soothed Selene. "Forget about them. Come back to camp. Everything is alright."

The look Ma Ne directed at Shem gave the indication that he thought differently, but he remained silent and led the way back to camp. They were met there by a stranger. Selene gasped, in his hands was Selene's box containing their spider. Ma Ne's sword flashed out in an instant, leveled at the stranger.

"Explain yourself, Easterner," Ma Ne demanded.

The Easterner was similar in appearance to Ma Ne, long dark hair and a slight up tilting at the corner of the eyes. Placing the box reverently on the ground he stepped away and bowed slightly. "The Free Goatherder. You are very perceptive," he turned and bowed to Selene. "The acolyte, first level and," he did not bother bowing to Shem, "The Hero. Though I must say he is somewhat less than expected."

Shem did not even register the insult. It was all he could do to stay upright, leaning against Selene. The Easterner continued.

"I was sent here by my mother, El-lina, Consort to the East and High Priestess of Fiona. I am Il'ar, at your service."

Ma Ne sheathed his sword.

Selene said hopefully, "You've come to journey with us."

"I've come to aid you on your journey," corrected Il'ar. "May I be seated? That camp stew smells most inviting and I doubt that our hero will be partaking. In fact, judging from his present condition, it would be best if he did not."

"How did you find our camp?" asked Ma Ne.

Il'ar glanced at the spider's box. "I know my mother's tools. I sensed it. It led me here."

With a satisfied look, Ma Ne started filling three bowls of stew. He handed one to Il'ar. Selene slipped out of Shem's grip. He found the ground with a thud and a moan. Rolling over into a sitting position, he paid the arrival of Il'ar little attention. Selene joined the other two men by the fire, accepting her portion of the stew. She blessed their meal and they began eating. Once everyone was finished Selene took the bowls and scoured them with sand.

"You were talking about aid," she said when she returned.

"Yes. I know where you are bound. My mother says speed is of the essence. I will have you there before Fiona's setting," he cut his eyes to Shem and frowned. "We must be there before Mieze rises."

"This night?" asked Ma Ne as if he didn't believe that Il'ar understood distances. Il'ar nodded in the affirmative.

"That's quite a mount, Il'ar," said Ma Ne. "It's three turnings from here by the fastest mount."

"Not for mine," said Il'ar cryptically.

They half carried, half drug Shem through the large encampment. In a copse not far from the river and out of sight of the army elements they met up with another Easterner guarding five mounts. Not much larger than the horses of the Central Lands, these were definitely more muscled, especially around the front shoulders, and they were black as the night sky.

"Ip'star, to me," said Il'ar. "Help me with this one. He'll have to be tied in."

Ip'star led the mounts clear of the trees and went to assist Il'ar. "Which, Il'ar?"

"Cyst."

Together they heaved Shem up onto Cyst's withers and secured him tightly. Il'ar stood by Cyst's head and stroked his neck. "Do not let him fall, my friend. There will be an extra cane for you this evening."

Cyst threw back his head and huffed, clearly understanding the words. Selene and Ma Ne were soon mounted. Both noted the strangeness of the saddles, especially the stirrups which were half the normal length and very uncomfortable, buckles tied to the horn and two extra leather straps attached to the saddles rear. Il'ar spoke to each animal in turn.

"Fugol, you carry a very special passenger," he said to Selene's mount. "Rodor, you carry a noble warrior. Don't bite!" Il'ar bowed to the mounts. "Worthy Avians, our thanks for this night."

He then stepped back. The air around the three riders shimmered. When all was normal, Selene gasped. The reason for the muscled shoulders of the horses was clear. They had wings.

"These beasts will not let you fall, but if it would ease your mind you can secure the belts to the horn," informed Il'ar. Both did. Il'ar mounted his own horse, but did not reveal its wings.

"Ip'star, fly with the wind. Be there before Mieze rises." Ip'star bobbed his head in acknowledgement.

Selene asked again, hoping the high priestess's son had changed his mind, "You're not going?"

"No, Acolyte. My business is with Baron Filip," he said and cantered off.

"Where to, Free Goatherder?" asked Ip'star politely.

"Sho ku," said Ma Ne.

"Fly, Jo, fly!" commanded Ip'star and his horse leapt into night sky followed closely by Cyst, Fugol and Rodor.

Once airborne, Selene looked back at Shem. She could see that the beauty and exhilaration of flight was lost on him. He had his eyes closed tight and clung desperately to his saddle horn. Even though securely strapped to his mount, Shem's weight swayed and shifted in the saddle, causing much consternation in Cyst, who let his displeasure be known.

Wanting to feel the wind in her face, Selene shifted her attention to the scene unfolding below. The encampment fires twinkling in the dark like a starlit sky as they faded into the distance behind them, the rising of Fiona bathing the landscape in her glorious silvered light, the ribbon-like appearance of the Majestic river giving way to the expanse of grasslands belonging to the Baron Enri Filip.

Selene's face shone with rhapsodic delight. The whinnying of Cyst brought her back to the here and now. Checking on Shem, she saw that despite the precautions of Il'ar in denying Shem food before the flight, his stomach had heaved.

Ip'star brought Jo in close to Fugol and Selene. "The hero has made no friend this night!" he yelled in a laughing tone. "He shall have to bathe Cyst when we land."

Selene could barely hear the Easterner above the sound of the wind, but she could hear the relish he had for flying in his voice. Looking at Shem, she saw complete and utter misery. Ip'star shrugged his shoulders as if to say 'Oh well' then pulled away and took point once again. Selene watched as the land below began slowly rising, morphing from plains to rolling hills. Up ahead the hills grew larger and larger.

The night wore on. Ip'star scanned the horizon. Fiona was already before them having passed her zenith. Mieze would be peeking her head over the edge of the world at any time. They must find Sho ku soon. Very soon.

The rolling hills had become the foothills and valleys of the Mount Fiona region. The land claimed by the Free Goatherders. Nestled in one of those valleys lay the hidden Sho ku, city of the Council. Ip'star appealed to Ma Ne in a gesture. Ma Ne pointed to a valley opening up to the northwest of them. It was little more than a darker shadow in the night, but Ip'star guided Jo unerringly towards it and began descending. They entered just as the first rays of Mieze made their way over the foothills behind them.

The night sky in the valley was darker than at any part of the flight, but the darkness did not hinder Ma Ne. He urged Rodor to fly up beside Ip'star. He motioned downward. They landed beside a stream. Ma Ne untied himself and dismounted. Ip'star and Selene followed suit.

Selene looked around at the empty valley. "This cannot be Sho ku." She sensed motion. Materializing out the darkness, five Free Goatherders surrounded them. They wore black, tight-fitting clothes with black cloths tied over their heads and faces with only a narrow slit revealing their eyes. All had drawn swords at the ready.

"Make yourselves known," ordered the leader. The order had been given without emotion, but the night air dripped with menace.

Ma Ne dropped to one knee, his still scabbarded sword held out horizontally before him. He bowed his head. "Ma Ne, Protectorate of the Cap Tan, returns...with friends," he said.

"Ill news in ill times, Ma Ne, Protectorate of the Cap Tan. Rise."

Ma Ne rose and returned his sword to the sash at his waist. "I would have a bucket."

The leader of the Free Goatherders flicked his eyes. One of men went to the river and returned with a full bucket. Ma Ne took the water and went over to Shem. He threw the water over the hero and his mount cleansing them of Shem's previous gift. The icy cold water revived Shem somewhat. Selene and Ip'star untied him and helped him dismount.

"Ya Ma, I must speak with the Council," said Ma Ne.

"Of course." He turned and headed up the valley following the stream. The other four remained on guard, disappearing into the night. Ma Ne and the rest followed after Ya Ma leading their mounts.

Selene made her way up beside Ma Ne. "That man frightens me."

"He should," said Ma Ne. "His name means *God of Death*. He is my son."

Selene was incredulous, "You named your son *God of Death*?"

"It is his title. Bestowed only upon the best."

The valley curved off towards the east. Around the bend rose an imposing wall of stone. A narrow switchback trail snaked up its face. In the darkness it was impossible to see how far up it went. Ya Ma had already mounted the stairway and was making his way slowly up. Ma Ne halted the group.

"The stairway is very dangerous. Pay close attention and step only on the stairs that I step on," he instructed.

"What of the mounts?" asked Ip'star.

"They remain here. None will harm them," said Ma Ne. Ip'star stood as if rooted to the spot arms folded across his chest. Ma Ne continued, "You have fulfilled your duty. You have shortened the journey. Do not presume more."

"What's to prevent me from just flying over the mountain?" he asked stubbornly.

"The Ya Ma," said Ma Ne.

Selene watched in silence as Ip'star considered. Already the Ya Ma had disappeared in the darkness of the stairway, and who knew where the other four were at this moment.

"Very well, perhaps there is more aid I can render to the Council," said Ip'star relenting, but his body language said that leaving Jo unattended in the valley did not sit well with him. He turned to Jo and stroked his forehead. He murmured softly in his ear. Jo huffed in reply. "Let's go. Just drop the reins," he instructed Selene and Shem.

Even with Selene hovering over Shem ensuring that he stepped only where he was supposed to, it took better than a candlemark to navigate the way safely up the winding stairs. Mieze was directly overhead by the time they made it. At the top was a cave-like entry hidden by an overhang. It protected the entry from the prying eyes of Mieze. If any had been watching it would have seemed like the travelers had simply disappeared.

Inside the way was lit by some luminescent moss growing on the walls. The end of the short tunnel split in opposite directions and headed downward. Ma Ne chose the right-hand path and led them down.

The downward descent ended suddenly on a rising. A nearly one hundred eighty degree turn, a quick left and they exited the cave-like tunnel. There wasn't much to be seen. Mieze had passed over the mountain ridge while the group had been in the tunnel and it was still at least two candlemarks before sunrise. *Not that sunrise would shine directly on this valley until mid turning*, thought Selene. *But the sky would at least lighten enough to see something other than shadows.*

Ma Ne led them down another stairway carved from the mountainside. At the bottom he led them into a one room stone structure. It wasn't a barrack exactly, but it did offer a line of cots along one wall that looked inviting. They hadn't slept all night and Selene, for one, was tired.

"Rest here," said Ma Ne. "In the morning someone will be sent to guide you. Do not try to leave the building." Having given them that final piece of advice, though it sounded an awful lot like a warning to Selene, Ma Ne left.

Ip'star took in the bareness of the windowless room. "I would say this establishment just oozes hospitality," he said.

"People, too," added Shem.

Selene reminded, "You two just remember that we are guests."

"What did I do?" asked Shem.

—◦◦◦—

Shem's eyes opened. Instantly alert, he looked around the barracks-like room. Something was pulling at him, urging him to rise. He didn't know what it was, but it desired to be discovered. That much he knew for certain. *Have I found Tierra?* He wondered. Soon a young lad arrived. Waking the others, he directed them to the building where they could clean up and prepare for the day. Shem ducked out of the doorway with an eagerness in his step. The sun had broken the top of the valley and had just begun to chase away the shadows. Evenly spaced stone houses speckled the mountainside in what seemed at first glance a randomness, but closer inspection revealed that each house could give covering fire for the ones below, in front, or to either side. Not only were the homes evenly spaced, but they were also the same size. At regular intervals were larger structures, dining halls, like the one not far from where he now stood, and others that Shem had yet to determine their uses. All in all a very ordered society, at least on the outside. What struck Shem as odd was that there were no discernible buildings for government, or inns, or shops readily apparent. Didn't they practice commerce?

Very few people were about and those that were around were down on the valley floor, which was fenced on both sides, running the length of the valley as far as Shem could see. They tended the goats which dotted the valley like splattered paint. A stream ran through the center of the valley crossed by numerous bridges. The stream originated from a large pond not far below Shem's feet. Ip'star joined him as did Selene and the young lad who had awakened them.

"Zing, here, says that after our meal we will be taken to the elders for "disposition" as he terms it," said Selene.

Shem asked, "Where's Ma Ne?"

"The Protectorate is with the elders now," said Zing.

"I don't like the word, 'disposition'," said Ip'star. "I thought we were allies. The high priestess might look upon these Free Goatherders in a different light if she knew."

"Lead the way, Zing," said Shem ignoring the complaint at least for now. Besides, his treatment at High City had been worse. "I'm starving."

Inside the dining hall it was light and airy. A handful of tables with bench seating filled most of the interior. The place was empty with the exception of a single unarmed Free Goatherder who sat at the far end of the room drinking tea.

Selene, Shem, and Ip'star took a seat at the first table. Immediately a server came out of the kitchen area bearing a large platter. He set the dishes down in front of the visitors. Eggs and some sort of hash filled most of the plate with a side of sautéed mushrooms and a thick slab of goats cheese. A mug of steaming tea rounded out the repast. The aroma made Shem's mouth water. He dug in before Selene had finished the blessing. Shem was pushing away his second plate and reaching for the tea when the Free Goatherder approached.

Shem watched him as he neared the table. He was dressed in a simple robe woven from the silky strands of a long haired goat, a sash at his waist holding it closed. Dark haired, not overly tall, he was lean and hard-muscled and moved with the assured grace of the extremely confident. Looking into his eyes Shem could see traces of Ma Ne. The man stopped before Ip'star.

"Your mounts are well. They are being provided for," he informed.

"I wouldn't get too near them," said Ip'star.

"That has been learned," said the man without going into any detail of the lessons. A ghost of a smile haunted Ip'star's face.

"You are Ya Ma," said Selene.

"I am," he said.

The three rose from the table wiping their mouths.

"Then it must be time for our 'disposition'," said Ip'star stressing the word.

"It is our way," said Ya Ma. "Follow me."

Stepping outside Shem looked up. He stopped in his tracks, immoveable. Above him perched on a ledge overlooking the large pond and the valley beyond was a large building. It looked like several houses stacked one atop the other for five stories, each house slightly smaller than the one it sat upon. Their identical overhanging roofs rose in perfect symmetry. One level from the top, a flying bridge connected the structure to the mountain face. From the top house, a spire with a silvered depiction of Fiona reflecting the light of the sun completed the magnificence. It took his breath away.

"It is Fiona's Temple and the protectorate of the Life Giver," stated Ya Ma.

Shem's eyes cut towards Ya Ma at the mention of the Life Giver. Was this what he felt pulling at him?

"This way," said Ya Ma.

The three tore their eyes away from the temple and followed Ya Ma to a set of stairs carved into the cliff. Unlike the one leading to the valley entrance, this one was wider and rose straight to the ledge.

"It is called the 'hundred steps'. On Holy Days pilgrims climb the steps pausing at each one to reflect on their lives and service to Fiona and requesting the hurried arrival of the Life Giver. You are not pilgrims. We must make haste."

They were met at the top of the stairs by a young boy who could have been Zing's twin. He pressed his palms together and bowed before Ya Ma. Turning on his heel he then led them into the temple. There an older initiate of indeterminate age replaced the young boy. Shem was struck by the strong smell of some sort of incense. It seemed to promote a sense of calm within his mind. He looked around and saw that even the tense lines of Ip'star's jaw had appeared to relax a little.

The initiate stopped before a wooden door which had some sort of thin papyrus material for its panels. He went to his knees and bowed, then knocked lightly. "Enter," came a command from within. The man slid the door to the side and bowed once again. Rising, he led the group into the room.

Inside they were met by a wizened man in a robe closely resembling Ya Ma's only more ornate. He had a thin, wispy, grey beard growing from the end of his chin to mid chest. He sat cross-legged on a cushion, his hands tucked into his sleeves. Beside him sat another similarly attired old man that Shem could only conclude to be a priest of some sort. On his other hand sat Ma Ne. The bearded one gave a respectful nod to Selene and a cursory glance at Ip'star before settling his gaze upon Shem. He closed his eyes. When he opened them again he said to Ip'star.

"Please accept our apologies for the hospitality you have endured. Those of the east have long enjoyed our mutual respect. These are, however, trying times. One must be sure. You may call your mounts into the valley if you so desire. They are indeed glorious animals."

Ip'star bowed his head to the old man. "Thank you, your Holiness, and please accept my own apology for my short-sightedness." The old man gave a slight bob of his head in acknowledgment.

"First Selene, welcome to Sho ku. We would be most pleased to have you stay with us here in the temple."

"Thank you your Holiness, but I would prefer to stay with my friends," she replied.

"As you will. Perhaps another time." He finally returned his attention to Shem. "So you are the one."

Shem felt a compulsion within him to speak openly and to speak the truth, but it was warring with another feeling. A feeling from deep within and long ago in his past. He knew it wasn't Tierra. That sense was still lying nearly dormant with only a faint glimmer of hope emanating from it. Suddenly he groaned and collapsed to his knees. He knelt there for a moment then slumped over unconscious.

———⟨⟨⟨⟩⟩⟩———

"Sun Father!" The sharp command tore Vlad away from the battle he had been directing on the southern side of High City.

Only one power could wrench the Auge Ose away from his will. He answered, "Yes, goddess."

The image of the stone shifted to reveal a large man inside a temple somewhere in the middle of the Central Lands. The man seemed vaguely familiar. Vlad sensed a bond within him. He concentrated on the bond and an image of a young boy came to mind. It was rapidly replaced with a grown man trapped in his woods, fighting beside the high priestess of Fiona.

"Shem. Shem 'o the West I had named him."

"Kill him," ordered Mieze.

Vlad concentrated with all of his will, but he was meeting resistance. Something or someone else had also put a bond on Shem and it was stronger than his. He felt the power within him grow as Mieze joined the struggle trying to overcome the resistance; a red glow encompassed his hands, which were firmly grasping the stone. Sweat beaded from his forehead as he concentrated. "Die, Shem! Die!" he willed with all the enhanced power that Mieze was directing through him. A sudden green flash arose from the Auge Ose breaking contact between his hands and the stone. Vlad collapsed to the ground beside the pedestal. His last coherent thought before unconsciousness was that of Mieze in his mind.

"Interesting. She can still refuse me. No matter, the bond has been strengthened. My power grows with every turning. While hers weakens. Soon the threat will be ended."

Shem woke up lying in a bed. *It must be a bed*, he thought. *It's too soft to be stone or ground.* He felt linen sheets, a coarse blanket, and a comfortable pillow whose case was soaked through with some kind of moisture. He opened his eyes and moved his head to look around. He wished he hadn't. His groan woke the small boy who had been sitting near the door, dozing while he supposedly kept watch on his guest. The boy slid open the door and dashed off.

Selene was the first to enter. Following on her heels was a temple initiate, a pouch of herbs at her side. Selene stopped at the foot of the bed. She looked at the wan and pasty face of Shem, dry streaked with the sweat that had poured out of him. The healer moved past her and gently extracted the pillow from under Shem's head. She tossed it to the boy who now stood once again by the door.

"Bring another. And more water, hurry!" she ordered.

She took a cloth from the bedside stand and dipped it in a basin of cool herb infused water. She bathed his face, cleaning the sweat streaks and brushed his hair from his eyes. After rinsing the cloth, she folded it and placed it across his forehead. Shem stirred, but did not try to rise. The initiate peered deep into his eyes.

"The fever has broken. There is still something haunting him from behind his eyes, but I believe the danger has passed." The boy returned with a clean pillow and some water. The healer took the water brought by the boy and searched through her pouch. Finding the packet of powder she wanted, she stirred some into the water and lifted Shem's head to drink.

After Shem had taken enough to satisfy her, she turned to leave. Selene came up beside Shem and took his hand in hers. Shem's eyes tried hard to focus. They flitted back and forth as if seeking out an enemy.

"Shem, it's Selene. What happened? You look terrible. You're safe now."

"He needs to rest. He is too weak to talk now," said the healer.

Shem relaxed at the sound of Selene's voice. She took the clean pillow and put it under his head.

"We'll let the draught work and come back later. He should be able to speak then." She turned to the boy, "If he tries to get up, you come get me, quick." With that she left. Selene gently placed Shem's hand by his side and followed.

Shem let his head sink into the comfort of the pillow thinking of Selene's words. *Safe. If you only knew.* The healer had been right. Dancing behind Shem's eyes was a vision of Shem with bat-like ears, a snout, and pebbly skin. Shem dozed off to the taunting laughter of his demon.

—⟨⟨∅⟩⟩—

His Holiness, Priest of Fiona, Protectorate of the Life Giver, sat on a cushion in the center of Fiona's Temple surrounded by Ma Ne, Ya Ma, the initiate healer, and Selene. He was troubled. The rest of the Council would soon arrive. They were anxious to hear word of the Protector and what had caused his recent illness. Tensions were running high. It had also been reported that a small group of refugees had been sighted travelling towards Sho ku. It was said the party was being lead by Hen Was. If it were true then the party could only be Tanya and her family. Hen Was would lead no others to the Free Goatherder city. He would deal with that, but right now he had other pressing matters. Namely, the healer. He addressed her, "So you believe that the Protector had been bonded at an early age by this Vlad who is now Sun Father, High Priest of the West?"

"Yes, Holiness. There can be no other explanation. I can sense the touching of the Life Giver, fresh and pure, as is the Protector's response. I can feel a——-a pull as well. A beckoning of some sort," she said the last guardedly, "and underneath it all, festering, is something that I have never felt, but can only be the bond of the one called Vlad. In his fevered ramblings, the Protector spoke of him. Fear and dread was in his voice at the remembrance."

Quiescent, His Holiness asked, "When will he be strong enough for the Council?"

"Physically?" asked the healer. The high priest nodded. "Soon, but if he's bonded to Mieze's high priest, should it be done at all? We could be revealed," answered the healer.

17

HIGH CITY

Hollowness. That's what Uri Yakov felt. His elaborate display on the gallows had been for naught. Runners had returned saying that High City was empty. There had been none to witness. *I have been cheated of my triumph!* Uri felt a familiar tingle in his mind. He cleared it of all thoughts. The presence of Vlad took its time before speaking.

"So you've crossed the river with no significant loss of life. Impressive, but know this. Time is more important than life. Move south swiftly. Crush all before you. Do not waste time with tactics. Don't concern yourself with triumphs. Mieze will own the ultimate triumph."

"Yes, Sun Father."

"Keep the rest of the Un Tier on the west side of river. Move south, bringing the catapults. There is a bridge. Take it."

"Yes, Sun Father."

Uri felt the departure of Vlad. He waited a moment just to be sure before retreating to the one place in his mind he felt secure. He had no desire to repeat the punishment he had suffered the previous morning. *I did not bend the knee to Mieze to become the slave of the Sun Father!* he fumed. *One day,* he promised himself and Vlad, *One day you'll pay.* Uri left his thoughts of vengeance in that private spot. "Life doesn't matter, huh. Very well, I'll lead with the Westerners," mused Uri aloud. He smiled. "Guard!"

The guard stepped inside of Uri's tent and saluted. "Bring me Lieutenant Ham and a Sol Dat runner. One who knows those tunnels," ordered Uri. He knew the bridge that the Sun Father was talking about. It was the Middle Road crossing. It led to Hap Simon's manor. "This could work out nicely."

Lieutenant Ham was quick to arrive. He stepped through the tent flap unannounced, "Milord, you wished to see me."

"Yes, Lieutenant. I want you to organize the Un Tier on this side of the river. Move them as quickly as you can to the bridge at Middle Road. Take it and allow none to cross." Uri handed him a written set of orders. "These will instruct U'cha to follow your orders. Leave at once."

""Aye, Milord." Ham saluted and left.

Next the guard brought in a Sol Dat. He looked young to Uri. His top knot was new as if recently promoted. *Put them in their place early,* Uri demanded more harshly than was needed, "Your name?"

"I'row, milord," he said.

"I'row, take me through the tunnels." I'row bowed from the waist and turned to leave. On the way out Uri ordered the guard, "Have this tent struck and moved over to the east side of the river."

The trip through the tunnels was uneventful, though Uri did look around in amazement. This must have been the way the followers of Fiona and the new goddess escaped Yakstown. He made a note to tell arms master Gallagher to find them and map them out. He watched as masses of Sol Dat passed them on their way through the tunnels to assemble on the east side of the river. They would be used to press the attack southward. Uri was pleased with the numbers. I'row led him to High City manor where Lieutenant Cutler and I'sim shared command. Uri found them in the Great Hall poring over maps.

Uri took command at once. "Lieutenant Cutler, who holds the road south?"

Cutler straightened to attention. "Baron Filip, milord. I'sim and I were putting finishing touches on a flanking maneuver—-"

Uri interrupted, "How many Un Tier on this side?"

"Twenty, milord," said I'sim.

"They will be the point of the spear," said Uri. "Send them straight down the road followed by the Sol Dat forces. Yours will bring up the rear. Hit them hard and keep hitting them until they collapse."

"But, milord—-," began Lieutenant Cutler.

Uri's steely eyed gaze bore into Cutler. "But what, Lieutenant?"

"As you will, Baron," said Lieutenant Cutler, swallowing his complaints. "When?"

"At once." Uri could see that his lieutenant did not like the orders. Too bad. Uri didn't necessarily like them either, but obedience was required. "Are you still here?"

"No, sir!" said Lieutenant Cutler. He left without saluting, I'mam on his heels.

Uri looked around at the Great Hall. He would have liked a little time to go through High City Manor properly. To see if there had been any more secrets left behind by Chet Sinclair, but he had a war to execute.

―――◆◆◆―――

The guard at the tent was disinclined to disturb Baron Filip at this late hour, least of all for a foreign looking envoy who professed to be from the East. Il'ar knew that other than the high priestess of Fiona who hailed from Celeste, capitol city of the Eastern Lands, none or at least very few Central Landers had any dealings with the East. Most believed that Easterners were a secretive lot who kept to themselves. Some even said Easterners were arrogant and thought themselves above those in the Central Lands, or so Il'ar had been told. He waited patiently.

"I'm sorry, Ser. The baron left orders not to be disturbed. You will have to wait."

"Then I will wait," said Il'ar, giving all indications that he would indeed wait. Wait until Fiona returned to bestow the reward of the faithful, eternity with her on her moon paradise.

"You can wait over there by your mount," said the guard.

"I will wait right here."

"You cannot wait right here," said the guard. The tautness of his body giving away his irritation and belief in what was said about Eastern arrogance.

Further discussion was halted by the jerking open of the tent flap. Sloan Quinn poked his head out. "Is there a problem?"

"No problem, Sir," answered the guard smugly.

Sloan cocked his head and peered closer at Il'ar noting the knee length tunic split up the front, tight trousers, no sash, and most importantly no single edged sword. "Sir, you are obviously not a Free Goatherder. Where are you from and what unit are you with?"

Il'ar gave the slightest of bows from the waist. "I am Il'ar, from the city of Celeste in the East, son of High Priestess El-lina."

The guard wilted with the pronouncement. Sloan stepped out of the tent and straightened, buying some time to absorb and judge Il'ar's words. "I see. I am Sloan Quinn. Commander of Baron Simon's forces. Why do you stand outside this tent?"

A smile flickered across Il'ar's lips. "Your faithful and ever-diligent guard has instructed me to wait. We were merely discussing where this wait would occur."

"Might I suggest that you wait inside the tent. Baron Filip would be most grateful to hear your words," offered Sloan. With a nod to the guard Il'ar entered the tent.

All eyes were on Sloan as he reentered the tent. Baron Enri Filip, his son Beltran, and Priest Conyn all waited for the introduction of Il'ar with anticipation. They had all overheard the conversation at the tent flap. An air of expectancy and hope hung thick choking the breath of the occupants.

"My lord, gentlemen, may I present Il'ar of Celeste in the East, son of High Priestess El-lina," said Sloan.

"Praise Fiona, help's come," said Priest Conyn.

"Do you really have flying mounts?" asked Beltran, excitement and disbelief competing for the tone of his voice.

"Is the high priestess well? Will she be joining us?" asked Priest Conyn.

"Flying mounts? Really?" pressed Beltran disbelievingly.

With fervent devotion blazing from his eyes Baron Filip raised his hands to forestall any further questions. "Gentlemen, peace." He turned to his son, "Beltran, do you doubt the wonder and grace of Fiona? If the high priestess says she has flying mounts, then her mounts fly! Fiona has provided." He turned his attention to Il'ar, "Il'ar, welcome. Have you eaten? Would you like wine? If you have any needs, you have but to ask. Everyone please be seated. Let us hear what the high priestess' son has to say," said Filip.

Il'ar could see why Baron Filip had broken with Uri Yakov. This man would never convert. He knew he would be able to work well with him. He looked about the tent, assessing the rest. Priest Conyn looked kindly with his long grey hair and close cropped beard. *Why are all the priests so old?* Il'ar knew that was unfair, not all were old, but it seemed so. Beltran was just approaching his prime. Old enough to have some experience, but still young enough to express wonder. He was well muscled and graceful as well. Sloan was an old war horse, solid and reliable. Il'ar wondered how many of them would survive the war.

"First, let me say, yes, Beltran, the Avians fly," he paused while the chuckles died down. "I'll be receiving their reports starting on the morrow. I also wish to extend condolences from all of us in the East for the loss of the Sinclairs. Now if there are any specific questions I'd be happy to answer as I can."

All deferred to Baron Filip. "How many have you brought, and how can they best be used?"

"I have brought three flights, about thirty. More will arrive later. Scouting will be their most useful asset, but we can mount an aerial assault, which would be more effective than any on the ground."

"What of weaknesses?" asked Sloan.

Il'ar could see that it had cost the old warrior much to ask the question. One did not immediately ask how you could be beaten, but tactically it had to be known.

"We bleed, Sloan Quinn. Our mounts also. In addition flying takes a lot out of the horses, two turnings recovery time usually. Three flights allow daily patrols. That limits the number we can put in the air, except at great need." All nodded their understanding.

"Why so few? Are there more?" asked Beltran.

Il'ar knew that no offense had been intended in the question. He smiled. "You would know all our secrets in one sitting? Truthfully, we are a far-flung people. It takes a while to muster. Flying horses do not grow on trees." Beltran had the good grace to blush. "Now I would like to know of your preparations," finished Il'ar.

The men gathered around the map spread out on Baron Filip's camp table. They spent the next two candlemarks going over what to expect from the enemy and how to best counter it. The red tint of Mieze was beginning to make its appearance on the northern horizon when the meeting broke up.

Il'ar threw back the tent flap. He noticed the guard had changed. Over towards his Avian, standing before a newly erected tent was the last guard. He beckoned Il'ar over.

"Begging your pardon, Milord Il'ar, I didn't know if you had been quartered, so I set up this tent for you."

Il'ar saw that the guard's hand had been bandaged. He looked inquiringly into the guard's eyes.

"Your horse refused to be picketed," he said.

"That's just like Anwar. Stubborn as an Easterner, he is," Il'ar said. The guard flinched. "What is your name, sir?" asked Il'ar.

"Rafal, if it please milord. I—-I'd like to apologize for earlier."

Il'ar smiled and clapped Rafal on the back. "No need to apologize for doing your job, Rafal. Oh, there's no need to call me, milord. That's what the 'Il' stands for. Loosely, it means 'oldest son'"

"As you will, mil—-Il'ar. You have guests inside," said Rafal.

Il'ar looked to the tent. As if summoned, two Easterners stepped out. "Shura, Ahern."

"Il'ar," they both said.

"Report."

Ahern glanced at Rafal then began, "Camp has been made to the south. Ulf commands. We await the rosters."

"The last of the scouts have returned. They report a mustering of Un Tier not far north from here. Sol Dat behind them, then men," said Shura with an eye to Rafal.

"Are they ready to attack?" asked Il'ar.

"Unknown, Il'ar. It was too dark to tell. They were seen just as the scouts were returning," said Shura.

"Who's the most rested?" asked Il'ar.

"Second, then Third," replied Ahern.

"Have Second up before dawn, in full battle gear. Third on standby. I'll be there shortly. Anwar, to me!" said Il'ar. The two men left. Il'ar turned to Rafal, "Rafal, if you would act as my runner. Inform Baron Filip of all you heard here. Then you might want to strike that tent, just in case we need to move in a hurry." Anwar trotted up to Il'ar. The Eastern Lord leapt into the saddle.

Rafal stood staring at Anwar's wings, unable to move.

"Impressive isn't he? Stand back."

Rafal stumbled back a few steps.

Il'ar commanded, "Fly, Anwar!"

Anwar gave a mighty leap, beating his wings strongly. They rose quickly into the air. Rafal turned and ran towards Baron Filip's tent.

The predawn darkness revealed little to Il'ar as he glided over the road in front of Baron Filip's front lines. No revealing fires had been lit by the Central Landers. None wanted to be a beacon to guide the attacking forces to them. *The baron paid heed to Rafal's warning. Hopefully a sleepless night will be the only price paid,* thought Il'ar. Further north, Ulf and the second wing continued an elliptical patrol searching for any signs of movement from the enemy camp. Il'ar glanced towards the northern horizon. The first hints of a rosy glow were beginning to lighten the skyline. Soon the darkness would fade enough to see clearly.

The attack started suddenly. It was as if the entire enemy camp began moving at once. A vast shadow roiling silently towards Baron Filip's troops, spreading out rapidly for a furlong. Il'ar brought his horn to his lips. It was an aggravating sound meant to gain immediate attention, to encourage all who heard it to do whatever was necessary to make it stop. It was effective. Before the last strains, faded movement could be detected amongst the baron's position.

Il'ar lowered the horn and patted Anwar's neck. "Bring the Third wing, my friend," he said. Anwar relayed the message mentally. At Il'ar's encampment ten more riders lifted into the sky heading towards the battle. Ahern joined with Il'ar.

"Another few moments will bring enough light to aim, Il'ar," he said as they hovered over the soon to be battlefield.

"Another few moments and the battle will be started," said Il'ar.

In the growing daylight the two men saw the main body slow their approach. A group of twenty detached itself and headed straight down the road towards the center of Baron Filip's line.

"Un Tier!" called out Il'ar.

The wing brought out bows and fired down on the advancing Un Tier. Il'ar watched in disappointment as most of the arrows, not only from the wing but those fired by Filip's troops, bounced off the Huge warriors. "Lancets," he said tight lipped. The throwing spear had a head about half an arm's length, double edged, and razor sharp. It was the only weapon the wing had that could penetrate the tough skin of the Un Tier. The problem was the riders would have to get close in.

Ahern led the flight down. They would get just one pass before the Un Tier made it to Filip's men. Il'ar hoped that Filip's men remembered whose side the Easterners were on. The Sol Dat behind the Un Tier scattered at the sight ten winged horses swooping down from above them. They had never seen such a sight. Ahern and his flight threw their lancets just as the Un Tier crashed into the baron's line. Eight struck true. The rest would have to be dealt with by the baron. Il'ar watched as Ahern's flight continued straight, overflying the Central Landers before pulling up. They had been lucky. The Sol Dat would not panic again.

The remaining dozen Un Tier tore through the Central Landers creating a sizeable gap in the line. Men fell back before them until archers with compound bows arrived to slow them down and finally cavalrymen with lances to finish them off. Sol Dat poured into the very nearly severed line. It held, but barely.

Il'ar watched from above, directing first Ahern's flight then Ulf's into the areas where the fighting was fiercest. The flights would swoop low and fast over the enemy raining down arrows, leaving a swath of death in their wake, only to see more of the enemy take their place. First it was Sol Dat, then men, but always more. Inch by inch, foot by foot the forces of Baron Uri Yakov pushed back Enri Filip.

The battle stopped late afternoon. Yakov's forces had simply stopped attacking. Il'ar watched from above as the enemy started making camp just out of bowshot. He sent his flights back to their camps. It had been a brutal day. Six men and horses lost. Over a quarter of his force. He couldn't afford many more battles like this one. He was about to return when he spied a cloud of dust from across the river. He urged Anwar higher to get a better view.

Landing at the rear of Baron Filip's men, he made his way to the command tent. Beltran was there as was Sloan, both had minor wounds. They were going over the day's losses with Baron Filip.

"So that makes at least a third?" asked Enri.

"Yes, Father. It would have been worse if they had more Mashers or if we didn't have the Easterners," said Beltran with a nod to Il'ar.

"Your warning was timely, Il'ar. You have our thanks," said Enri.

"As long as we have some daylight left we should erect some barricades for when they renew the attack tomorrow," suggested Sloan.

"Will your forces be available?" asked Enri.

"Not for flying. I'll barely be able to put two scouts in the air. One on each side of the river, but we're capable on the ground as well; however, I wouldn't spend too much time building barricades," said Il'ar. "At least not here. Are there any fords across the river? Where's the nearest bridge?"

Sloan shook his head in the negative. "No fords. The nearest bridge is at Hap Simon's estate. It's about a two turnings ride south. Why do you ask?"

"We're being flanked. A large force is on the west side moving south," said Il'ar. "We need to pull back to the bridge."

Sloan looked to Enri, his eyes full of concern. Enri dithered. Beltran rescued his father.

"Il'ar there are two problems with pulling back," he said.

Il'ar waited for someone to pick up the conversation. "And those are?" he prompted when no one did.

"We've been tasked with two missions," said Sloan. "Rendezvous with the Regent and buy time for Tierra's hero. Regent Simon evacuated High City towards the southeast. We were hoping to split Baron Yakov's forces and Regent Simon wanted to ensure his cousin's family was protected."

"I've met your hero," said Il'ar contemptuously. "The only thing he is using this time for is to sober up or find more ale." The Central Landers were shocked. Il'ar continued, "Yes, I know my mother vouches for him."

"Where was he?" asked Enri.

"When?" asked Sloan.

"Right here in this camp. I flew him and his friends out last night. We had to tie him to a horse that was more noble than him."

"We? How many were with him?" asked Enri eagerly.

"He had two companions. A first level acolyte named Selene and a Free Goatherder named Ma Ne. All three left last night per my mother's orders."

Enri relaxed at the mention of the acolyte and Ma Ne. "Well at least they are on their way. Ma Ne is a good man and the hero has spiritual guidance. That just leaves the Regent."

"And the heir," added Beltran.

"Nothing we can do about the heir. We don't even know if he made it out of High City," said Sloan. "Besides we are in a bit of a bind ourselves," he added.

"One thing we do know is that Uri doesn't have him. If he did he would be crowing about it," said Enri with certainty.

"Which gets us no further in deciding what to do now," said Il'ar. "But if the Regent went southeast there's a chance he is behind or at least on Baron Yakov's flank. If we pull back to that bridge on a quick march Yakov may rush forward and the Regent could hit him from behind. If he doesn't dog our heels we'll have a turning to prepare for the forces on the other side of the river or burn the bridge."

"We can't burn it. It's made of stone. But it will take the Westerners longer than two turnings to get there. They have a marsh that they are going to have to go around," informed Enri.

"Then let us act. Let's make for the bridge," urged Il'ar. "Unless you want to attack. We can coordinate with the Regent and hit him from two sides. Whichever we choose, let us do so. Sitting here is courting disaster."

"So would be attacking," said Beltran. "We haven't enough men. How would we coordinate with the Regent? Il'ar, you said you will only be able to send up two scouts. How will we tell the Regent, whatever we decide?"

"Does the Regent have a priest with him?" asked Il'ar.

"Yes. Priest Duran. He took over for Priest Hotig before—-before we left," said Sloan.

Il'ar looked knowingly at Baron Enri Filip.

"Priest Duran, you say? I'll inform the Regent," agreed Enri. "We pull back to the bridge and may Fiona bless us all."

⌘

It had been clear that U'cha hadn't liked the orders he had been given, placing him under the soft skin commander, Ham. He also resented missing the fighting on the east side of the river. So did his clan. Anticipating trouble and remembering Shem's tale about challenging a clan leader, Ham issued one of his own. At first he thought U'cha was going to accept, but he had backed down in the end. Ham now thought less of his brother's tale. *It was the ale talking, wasn't it, Shem. You never fought, let alone defeated a Masher.*

Getting out of the city had been easy enough, but soon the road degraded into a large path. The rock throwers became harder to haul. They began losing too much time. By the end of that turning they had only reached the swamp. Ham called a halt and summoned U'cha. "The good news first, Clan Leader U'cha. We're ditching the rock throwers."

"The Sun Father won't like that, Soft Skin," he hissed.

Ham pressed, "How large is this swamp? And how long would it take to drag those things through this muck or around it?" He already had a good idea. "Too long if we're to reach the bridge first. Which do you believe the Sun Father would like least?" Ham knew very little of their Sun Father, but he didn't know of any commander who liked failure. "If we need them at the bridge, we'll build new ones. Rest now. We cut through the swamp at first light," ordered Ham.

"There will be enough light at Mieze-rising. Leave then," said U'cha.

Ham considered. If the Mashers only wanted a few candlemarks rest that was okay with him. U'cha spoke again.

"The Sun Father says that we are being watched," he pointed to a speck in the sky.

Ham looked in the direction the Masher was pointing. He could barely make out something. It was moving westward. Then it changed its direction and moved eastward. Ham wasn't sure what troubled him the most, aerial scouts or the fact that the Masher could somehow talk to the Sun Father and he couldn't. Either way he was going to have to adapt. He ordered, "Wake me when it's time to leave, no fires."

Ham woke with the first red tinged light of Mieze. He found the Westerners ready to move out. While he had slept they had disassembled the rock throwers dragging the huge timbers into the forest to confuse the watchers of the Central Lander forces. He was impressed with their efficiency. Now it was time to move out. "Stay close to the river just inside the trees. That will be the quickest way through. Be as quiet as you can. Move out."

U'cha led the way with Ham following a few ranks back. The huge Masher clan leader traveled quickly, keeping an exact distance between his route and the river regardless of the terrain. At times they sank into the muck up to the knees of the great creatures. Other times they waded through brackish water up to their chests. During those passages, Ham had to ride on the shoulders of the Westerners, but none complained aloud.

Keeping quiet seemed to be a matter of relativity, especially in the waterways. It wasn't so much splashing sounds as it was the battles with the nocturnal swamp creatures. The snakes were just batted away without concern, their fangs unable to penetrate the tough skin of the Mashers. The large reptilian beasts were another matter. Some were as long as the Mashers were tall and they would try to drag them under the water. The Mashers would plunge their arms down regardless of the noise, grab the reptiles by the neck and choke the life out of them before tossing the lifeless creatures back where their companions found an easier meal.

U'cha came back to Ham. "Un Tier do not like soft skin's water. It tastes bad, smells worse. We do not like soft skin's creatures, but they like us even less!" He bragged. "We will soon be through." He waded back up to point and continued.

U'cha's words proved true. In just a short time the waterways became the sucking muck once again and then firmer land. The trees thinned as they neared the edge of the swamp. Ham looked up at Mieze to judge the time passed. Two things struck him as odd. The red tinge was growing deeper and while he was seldom if ever up at this time, Mieze seemed to loom larger in the sky. Both were troubling. Near as Ham could reckon it had only taken three candlemarks to get through the swamp. He had not realized that the Mashers had been making that good of speed. He called a brief halt and sought out U'cha. "We made amazing time through the swamp."

"Mieze makes us strong," said U'cha.

"Does that have anything to do with the red light?"

"Mieze is always red," said U'cha.

"Not this red and she doesn't usually loom as large in the sky as she does now. She appears to be growing larger."

U'cha made no response. Ham was beginning to think that the clan leader had not understood him. He was rephrasing the question in his mind when U'cha suddenly spoke.

"The Sun Father wishes to speak to you. Take my hand." U'cha put his huge meaty paw out for Ham to grasp.

Ham hesitated. He looked at the extended hand that would dwarf his. What did U'cha mean? How was the Sun Father going to speak to him? U'cha just sat there with hand out. Slowly Ham reached out his hand and placed it in the Clan Leader's. He felt a gradual tingling in the back of his mind. More a warm sensation spreading slowly through his head as if searching. It felt like it was everywhere, just looking. With painstaking slowness it seemed to grow larger, pushing his thoughts and awareness to the side and finding a place to call its own.

"So, Shem is your brother," said a voice inside his head.

Ham recoiled in shock, jolted as if in pain though he felt no physical blows. *How does he know that! And why is that important? Why not say hello to me!*

"Easy, easy. Do not fight me. Hello, Ham. I *am* pleased to see you. Let there be no doubt. I can see all of you."

Ham saw himself lying in the grass, blood streaming into his eyes from the cut on his head. The image of a young Shem looming over him with a bloodied rock in his raised hand. Ham feebly trying to block the next blow before he passed out. He felt again the sheer terror he had felt that night. The betrayal of his brother.

The image shifted. He found himself in a brightly lit cave facing Shem. He had a sword in his hand. This time it was he looming over his brother who was sprawled out on the floor of the cave, helpless before him.

"I know your thoughts, your feelings, and your desires. Trust me. They will be fulfilled with my help. You will triumph over Shem."

The voice was reassuring, soothing. Ham began to relax. Whatever or whomever was in his head was on his side. He could feel it.

"Leaving the catapults was a good decision. You were right. It would have displeased me more to be late to the bridge. I can use resourceful men like you. As long as you are right."

The last had a tinge of warning to it. Just a slight feel as if telling him that pain could be delivered as easily as pleasure.

"You are wise, Ham. And intelligent. Yes, Mieze grows larger. She grows stronger as well. The deepening red is an indication of her growing strength. Serve me well and she will reward you. We shall speak again."

The voice was gone along with the presence. One moment it was there and the next gone. Ham continued standing with his hand in the hand of the Clan Leader.

"Unless you wish to challenge my mate, I suggest you let me go," said U'cha in a hissing laugh.

Ham snatched his hand away from the Clan Leader. "No thanks. We have two more candlemarks. Let's get moving."

The Mashers kept a good pace for the remainder of the night, most humming a barely audible marching song. Having been carried through most of the swamp, Ham was able to keep up, but only just. Mieze was sliding past the horizon when he called a halt. They had just enough time to erect some concealing shelters for the day.

Ham went down to the river to wash away as much of the decaying stench of the swamp as he could. He squatted down in some reeds as he washed. He listened to the night air. The light breeze sent an occasional clomp of a horses hoof or jingle of harness from the other side. They had caught up with the High City defenders. He smiled knowing he would beat them to the bridge.

The sudden clash of arms brought him upright. He listened. *Only a skirmish,* he decided. Baron Yakov had caught up to the retreating army and was harassing them. He returned to his own camp with the news and an admonition for silence.

Priest Duran left Hap's tent. He had delivered the morning's messages. Sure they had been peppered with all the "by your leave's" and "if it pleases you," but it was obvious that at the moment Filip was running the defense along with this Il'ar from the East. *Its well that I have good lieutenants.* Hap wasn't happy with suddenly being cut-off and trailing Yakov's main army. It made him feel useless. Priest Duran rushed back into the tent.

Hap looked up inquiringly. He asked, "Is there anything else Priest Duran?"

"I'm sorry my lord Regent, but I just this moment received another message. Baron Yakov followed Baron Filip's forces during the night, they are attacking. A horse is being sent to pick you up and take you to your estates. It will be here in about a candlemark," he said breathlessly.

Hap asked disbelievingly, "A candlemark?"

"It's one of the Eastern horses, Regent. I was told you needn't pack anything."

"They don't think they can hold the estate." It was a statement more than a question and not necessarily directed at the priest. "Call my son, Tunis. Have him attend me. Thank you."

Tunis entered as the priest left. "Father?"

"Tunis, *So like your older sister Angeline, May she be with Fiona, hovering just outside of what's happening, ready to pounce. Let's hope your fate is kinder,* come in. Were you hovering right outside the flap?"

"No, Father. But I saw the priest go suddenly rigid and rush back into your tent. I knew something was up."

"Good. Get the camp ready to move. Make all speed to the estate. Uri followed Enri during the night and even now attacks. After you have given the orders find Nils and return here."

"At once, Father," said Tunis and hurried out to comply.

Alone, Hap took time to worry about his wife Mona. She was dutiful in all things, but entirely dependent on him to give orders when needed. It was the one drawback from her upbringing in O'Kelly's clan where the males gave the commands and the women obeyed, but he would soon be at his estate. At least for however long it remained his.

Tunis returned with Nils P'edar. Outside Hap could hear the bustling sounds of camp breaking. "Sit down, Tunis." He waited until his son sat to continue. Nils remained standing. "I'll soon be leaving, going back to the estate. It will be the job of the two of you to move the men south while avoiding Baron Yakov's troops."

"What's the ultimate goal?" asked Nils.

"Grimval. I wanted to beat them to my estate, but they move too fast. I'm counting on gaining a day while they sack the place. You should then be able to hook up with me before Mill Town. Tunis, I know you grieve for your sister, but do not engage Yakov unless you must. Priest Duran has a means of communicating with me. We will rejoin."

The two men stood. Hap clasped his son's forearm then drew him into a hug. He looked over at Nils, imploring him silently to look after his son. Nils nodded his understanding.

Half a candlemark later Tunis and Nils sat their horses next to Regent Hap Simon at the head of the Army's column. They were watching a dark speck slowly spiral down from the clouds.

"Why did the East get them and not us?" asked Tunis aloud.

"Covetous, my son?" asked Hap. "They are on our side. Why not instead count our blessings and look to that which is ours alone?"

"You mean like Harvest storms? There was a good trade," said Tunis with a trace of sarcasm.

The wind in his face exhilarated Hap. Almost he was able to agree with his son's covetous nature concerning the horses. All too soon they were gliding downward. He could see his estates on the horizon and Filip's too few forces arrayed against Yakov and the Westerners. From this vantage point he could see that once Uri's army on the west side reached the river bridge there would be no stopping them. A swift fighting retreat was the best that could be hoped for. He now rued the decision to 'build a bridge that will serve my grandchildren' as he had boasted back then.

The scout that had brought Hap's horse peeled off, dropping down towards the command tent below. Hap had no idea how to guide his mount which was just as well, the horse had a mind of its own and was bearing straight for the estate's manor building. It landed in the courtyard next to another of the Eastern horses. His manor attendant ushered him into the main Hall. Sitting at the table on the dais was Mona, Baron Filip and a stranger. *It must be the Easterner Il'ar.*

Hap got the impression that the young man was used to getting his way, but was still diplomatic about it. Only the up cast to his eyes gave any indication of his origins, though they could easily be taken for those of the Free Goatherders. Neither race spent much time among the Central Landers.

Mona spied him first. "Hap!" Rising, she hurried into his arms. "I'm glad you are safe. I was so worried," she said tears glistening, threatening to spill over She looked up at him, "Tunis?" she asked.

"He is fine, love. We will speak later." Hap had no idea when later might be. "I'm glad to see that you are well." He gave her a brief hug then released her. They walked to the table. He addressed Enri, "How bad is it?"

Enri rose. "Regent Simon. I'm glad you are here. May I introduce Il'ar. He is son to the High Priestess El-lina."

Hap bowed slightly to the Easterner who merely looked at him with knowing eyes. "My pleasure and my thanks, Il'ar, for all the aid and assistance you render." He turned back to Enri. "Now, answer my question."

Sloan Quinn grinned at the directness of the Regent. Enri straightened slightly though he had a twinkle in his eye.

"I see the Regent is growing into his position. Good, though that is not the answer to your question. Bad, is. We have two large forces bearing on us." He motioned Hap to look at the map as he punctuated the positions of the enemy forces and those of their own. Sloan and Il'ar added their perspectives and suggestions as well.

Hap listened silently but with great interest. He responded with just a little, perhaps more, disbelief, "As I understand it, what I am hearing is that they are getting stronger, individually, the closer Mieze gets to us."

"According to what my mother says, Mieze is entering into what she terms as 'Ascendency.' Her moon lowers in the sky and turns a bloody red. The abilities of her followers are augmented during this period while a feeling of doom and despair saps the will and strength of her enemies. All will peak when Mieze is at her fullest," defended Il'ar, who had made the suggestion.

Hap asked, "How long does this last?"

"For the entire moon phase," said Il'ar solemnly.

"Then we must act swiftly. The first thing that I want you to do is to evacuate Mona and the rest of the children. Take the private barge and send them to Mill Town." He turned to Mona, "If we don't meet in a half moon go to Grimval. Baron Suleiman will take you in."

Sloan Quinn saluted his Regent and departed. Hap continued asking questions of Enri and Il'ar. The answers weren't very pleasant. The forces loyal to the Sinclairs were being pressed on all sides. Baron Reis attacking the Free Goatherders from the west, Baron Iago attempting to punch through the western mountains of the Grimval Valley, and Baron Yakov driving Hap's men steadily southward. Of all the forces, only Baron Uri Yakov had the direct support of Western troops and they were a hammer.

While Reis was relentless in his attacks against the Free Goatherders, his advance was costly and slow. It did, though, have the effect of keeping the Free Goatherders at home. Hap knew he could not count on any support coming from that quarter. His only hope of survival was to make it to the Grimval, but it would have to be an orderly retreat. A headlong rush would only bring Yakov to the gates of an unprepared Grimval. He asked, "What are your plans for the bridge?"

Enri once again gave way to Il'ar who outlined the preparations.

18

WYBEE AND JONATHON

Scrubbing the decks was no fun for Wybee. His back hurt from bending over the holystones, the block of sandstone was biting into his hands, and his knees felt like they were one immense bruise, tender to the touch. He looked over towards Jonathon. The heir appeared to be faring little better. Both continued working without complaint. The task had; however, given Wybee plenty of time to think, but the answers had thus far proven elusive. Why Tierra no longer spoke to him or why she felt so far away still remained a mystery.

Jonathon hadn't said much since Tierra had spoken to him telling him that his parents had died. Even now as he bent over the holystone scraping it back and forth across the patch of deck in front him, he said little. Wybee figured that he was just trying to cope. The pressure of being the heir and helpless to stop the Central Lands from being overrun had to weigh heavily. And where was the hero? Tierra had given Wybee specific instructions to give to him, but he was nowhere to be found. Not even rumors.

"You boys had better move down a little. You're wearing a hole in my deck!" groused the captain as he walked by.

Na Na trailed after him carrying two spoons, a small stew pot, and two trenchers made of bread. "Time for lunch, boys," she said as she handed them their trenchers and spoons. She watched them critically as they shifted to a sitting position. Wybee reached out for his bread bowl while Jonathon sat listless.

Wybee offered, "He still hasn't gotten over the news about his parents."

"Poor lad. We'll be in Mill Town by tonight, maybe there will be some better news," she offered lamely. All the news recently had been bad, but one could still hope.

Wybee dug hungrily into his stew. He had been listening to the sailors as they made their way up river. The talk had been about one defeat after another for the Central Lands. About how Fiona had forsaken the land and retreated to the East or how the people who converted were being treated fairly. Wybee wasn't so sure about the last one. Before Tierra had quit speaking she had warned about conversion. It wasn't going to end up well for those who did or so she had said.

Talk also eddied about the numbers of refugees they had been encountering on the road. The vast majority had fled south clogging the roads until the armies of Baron Filip and Baron Yakov had driven them off into the countryside. There was little doubt where they were going. Grimval. Word had gotten out somehow and flew with the speed of rumor that there was safety to be had there. "None gets into Grimval unless Baron Sulieman wants them in," was the word on everyone's lips or so said the sailors. *Na Na is part of the O'Kelly clan. She'll get us in.* Wybee fervently hoped so.

A candlemark before sunset Wybee's barge docked at Mill Town. The city was crowded to overflowing with the lucky people who had manage to take passage on the previous barges and the river was crowded with barges returning northward. Na Na came on deck wearing a frown.

"The ride's over. We have to get off, boys. The Captain has been ordered back to the Regent's manor."

Wybee looked around in dismay. While they had been on the barge there had been relative safety and speed. On the road they would be amongst the throng once again and on foot. Wybee worried for the strength of Na Na's legs. He worried about Jonathon's mood. He worried about Tierra. He worried about time, especially having enough of it. *The hero will come!* Wybee couldn't complete his task without him. *He has been promised.*

"Yes, Na Na," he said. He roused Jonathon to his feet and together they retrieved their meager belongings.

With their barge being one of the last to arrive, every available inn or room had been taken. There was no place willing to crowd in three more travelers. The City Guard had been polite but firm in directing the unhoused to the roads leaving town. Darkness found them on the road south of town heading for Grimval.

The three had kept to the floor of the river valley following the river southward. To do otherwise would have put them into the rolling foothills of the ever rising Goddess Fangs mountains and Na Na's fears about the strength of her legs was proving true. Even though the boys carried all their goods, the going was hard on the middle-aged woman. They spied a small copse of willow near the river's edge that had not yet been claimed by any travelers and settled in for the night.

The barge captain, pleased with Na Na's cooking, had been kind enough to provide them with three turnings of provisions, "This will get you to the valley entrance, kinswoman. I wish I could do more," he had said handing over the fare.

"Love of the people, Captain," said Na Na Mac Duff accepting the gift.

"Wealth and many children," he responded smiling at the two boys.

Na Na had been too tired to cook. The three dined on meat strips and hard biscuits washing them down with water from the river. No fire had been set. They wanted to attract no attention from unsavory refugees.

"I'm sorry, boys, but when we get to the fortress at the mouth of the Grimval things will be different," she soothed as much for herself as the boys.

Wybee agreed, "We know, Na Na."

Jonathon, still in his mood, said nothing. He merely put his blanket in the deeper shadow of a willow and lay down. Sleep was near when a loud snap echoed through their meager camp. All three froze. Wybee felt a weak stirring of wrongness. A menacing voice spoke quietly from just within the copse.

"Well, it must be my lucky night. Which makes it unlucky for you. Get up and move to the center where I can keep an eye on you."

Na Na and Wybee complied, huddling close together in the center of the copse. A single figure stepped out of the shadows holding a long wickedly bladed knife. He was dirty, unshaven and reeked of his own odor. He also had a red tinge around the edges of his eyes.

"Now, just toss that food pouch over here and maybe I'll let you live," he said gesturing with his blade. As his gaze passed over Wybee, a flicker of recognition passed across his face. "Except you, boy," he hissed. He shifted his weight to reach out and to grab Wybee.

Suddenly a look of confusion overtook his face. His step faltered. Blood began to trickle out of the corner of his mouth. He stumbled and fell nearly on top of the two. Standing behind him in the shadows was Jonathon calmly wiping the thin blade of a small rapier-like sword. Satisfied that he had cleaned it, he returned to his blanket followed by the eyes of Na Na and Wybee.

"It was my father's," he explained, speaking for the first time in turnings. "He told me to never be without it. Lieutenant Gilroy taught me how to use it."

Unlike Na Na whose breath was just now returning to normal along with her heartbeat, Jonathon had spoken calmly and clearly. Offering that and nothing more.

"Bless your father and your lieutenant," said Na Na, "But we must try and get some sleep."

The night noises returned to the chirruping and buzzing of night insects with an occasional splash from the river. This was punctuated by the soft breathing of Jonathon as he settled comfortably in his blanket. Na Na and Wybee lay fitfully, the dead intruder still lying between them. The rising of Mieze with her angry redness filled the night sky, warring with the remaining silvered splendor of Fiona as she set. A red tendril of light penetrated the copse, illuminating the dead intruder. A thin spiral of smoke rose from the body. Then in a flash of red, the corpse disintegrated leaving behind only ashes. There were no further visitors that night.

The dawning brought a brisk sunny turning, promising of autumn delight and easy traveling. Already the temperature had started its seasonal decline heading inevitably toward the cold wintry season and as they got higher into the Goddess Fangs the blankets would be put to another use, warding off the chill of the day. But that wouldn't be for another hand of turnings or more. At the moment, breaking fast with a warm meal and drink helped to ease away the concerns of last night's visitor.

Wybee explained for the third time the disappearance of the dead man's body. "Jonathon, it just disappeared in a flash of red."

"How?" Jonathon had been pressing the question as if continuing to ask it would produce another more satisfactory answer.

Wybee exasperated, "I don't know! Only that it felt wrong,"

"Felt wrong?" asked Jonathon hopefully.

The sense of wrongness hadn't come from Tierra. She was still dormant in the back of Wybee's mind only faintly stirring on occasion. The worry hadn't turned to fear yet, but Wybee's sense of absolute rightness had been eroded. "No. Not like that."

"Everyone is still fleeing south," stated Jonathon. His matter of factness was sobering as if he had completed his mourning and was now able to look the world in the eye and assess it critically. "That means our armies have been unable to halt Baron Yakov's advance. I wonder how well prepared Baron Sulieman and O'Kelly are?"

"That's rather adult thinking for such young boys," said Na Na as she busied herself repacking their provisions. "Such ponderings are for our rulers and leaders, not for the likes of us."

"Yes, Na Na," said Wybee taking the pack of food and slinging it across his back. Jonathon helped her up and they took off down the road. The river road was well traveled but not overly crowded. The trio managed to find a spot where they could walk without fear of being overheard.

The sun was high in the sky, its weakening warmth unencumbered by clouds. Na Na decided to stop for their mid turning meal. They spread a blanket under a deciduous tree, not far from the road, whose leaves were beginning to turn but still provided some shade. Na Na sat massaging her cramping calves waiting for the rocks to heat so she could fry some travelers bread. Wybee and Jonathon had wandered a short distance away huddled together.

"Look, Wybee, we were dumped off the barge because the army needs them to escape. If we stay here we can meet back up with them. I'll be with one or more of my uncles. That's better than running off to Grimval, and who knows what when we get there."

Wybee was unsure. He looked back towards Na Na. She had been good to them when they needed it. She was intent on getting back to Grimval and her valley. She had lost her own boys. It would crush her to have himself and Jonathon desert her now.

"I don't know, Jonathon. Is the hero there? What about Na Na?"

The question seemed to take some of the confidence out of Jonathon. "She can stay with us. We'll all be safer with my uncles."

Wybee was about to argue the point. Instead he staggered back a step and cried out in pain, clutching his chest as he dropped to a knee. In his concern, Jonathon forgot about their agreement to hide their identities. Fear flooded his features. He dropped down beside his companion.

"Wybee! What's wrong?"

Wybee struggled with the pain, gasping for breath. Finally he choked out. "Jonathon, Tierra! She's dying!"

A shadow moved across Jonathon blocking out the sun. He looked up to find Na Na standing over them. She was sharing her glances between the boys and those still on the road some of whom was watching them.

"Keep your voices down," she said. "Let's see if we can move the lad back under the tree."

Jonathon and Na Na half carried half drug Wybee back to the blanket under the tree. In the dozen or so steps it took, Wybee managed to get his feet under him, but he was still weak. At the blanket they lay him down. Na Na stood over him menacingly, glaring at the travelers on the road. If any had entertained assisting, they changed their minds and continued on their way. None came near. Satisfied that no threat would come from that direction Na Na softened.

"Now, lad, what was that all about?" she asked Wybee.

Wybee was relieved to be lying down. He felt as if some of his very life essence had been taken from him. *Tierra must have been in dire need to take life from me. But I am her vessel. My life is hers to take.* He opened his eyes and saw Na Na standing above him still waiting for his answer.

"I'm not sure, but Tierra..." he began before faltering to a stop.

"So you're mixed up in that. Both of you?" she asked addressing herself now to Jonathon. Jonathon said nothing, but couldn't hide the stubborn resistance his posture settled into.

"Yes, Na Na can see it now. Such young lads to be thrown into the affairs of goddesses and men. Too young. Little do you know about the pains and travails of birth or death for that matter, though all are learning now. Well, that explains why you were about to bolt. No, no, don't deny it. Na Na raised two boys of her own. I can see the nervous itch of honorable intentions. I can also see that there is more about you that you haven't said." Na Na waited a moment to see if there would be any explanations.

"Nothing to say, then? Very well, just remember this. Na Na cannot help choose the right path without a look at the map. But this I do know, a fleeing army is no place for young lads."

Having spoken her piece, offering what she could to the boys, she turned her attention to Wybee. He looked pale and drawn, but had no discernible injuries.

"Jonathon, if you would be so good as to get some water, I'll do what I can for Wybee," she said.

—⁓⁓—

Jonathon started at the use of his real name, but he went to the river to fetch Na Na some water. The river was about a league across. He could easily swim it as long as the current wasn't too strong, but could he pull Wybee along with him? He looked up the river searching for a narrowing, but there was none in sight. As he looked down river he saw a barge making its way around the slight bend. His face lit up with joy. He started racing down river waving his arms.

"Grand Mother! Grand Mother! Stop!"

The sound of his shouts caused a commotion on the deck of the barge. A tall willowy man ducked into the cabin. Jonathon recognized a bow being strung. Then he saw a woman step out of the cabin and look his way. There was no mistaking the bright red hair of Mona Simon. He had found his grandmother. She turned away from him and spoke some harsh words that he could not discern. The barge did not slow down. Jonathon stood, struck dumb. She wasn't going to stop.

—⁓⁓—

The tall willowy man stepped into the cabin of the barge. "Madam?"

He was nearly bowled over by the compact form of Mona Simon who was making her way on deck. Though nearly fifty cycles in age, she still maintained grace in her appearance and manner. Her hair still flamed red, a gift of her O'Kelly heritage, and while it was her predisposition to obey men, he knew her temper could still flame as well.

"Out of my way, Worrel. I hear my grandson calling." There was no stopping Mona on her way to the deck.

He followed her through the door stopping just outside. Turning shoreward he immediately spied the young boy running along the bank waving his arms. He also saw a bowman out of the corner of his eye reaching in his quiver for an arrow. Mona saw it too.

"I know the voice of my grandson, Captain. As well you should," she said in her most regal.

"Milady, I know best how to handle this. Just go back into the cabin," said the Captain.

"Captain, if that man fires upon my grandson both he and you will be strapped to the anchor and thrown into the river," said Mona coldly, menacingly.

Worrel was proud of her. *Well said, Milady!* He knew that ordinarily, Mona would have complied with the wishes of the Captain, but this time she stood firm rather than flustered, gazing steely eyed at the man.

"Aye, I know it, Milady," said the Captain.

For the first time Worrel noticed the red tinge around the iris of the Captain's eyes. *Fiona, help us, he's converted!* A quick glance at the bowman confirmed his worse suspicions. He had also. Mona must have seen it as well as she turned and ran to the railing.

"Jonathon! Run!" she warned.

The *tun* of the bowstring sounded a moment later. The arrow struck Mona high in back between the shoulder blades. The force carried her over the railing and headlong into the river.

Shock rooted Worrel to the spot for a moment. He simply could not believe that the barge captain would have the baron's wife fired upon. The flash of Worrel's knife demonstrated his recovery. It buried itself in the throat of the Captain. Worrel faced the bowman, sword in hand. The bowman offered no resistance, merely smiling as Worrel's sword slid in between his ribs. Collapsing, he joined his fellow convert on the deck. The penetrating gaze of Worrel swept the deck looking for any signs of disobedience or conversion. He found none. With a voice laced with pain and frustration he ordered, "Let's get this cleaned up! Get someone in the water, look for the baroness! Beach this barge! Let's move!"

—⟨⟨⟨⟩⟩⟩—

"Jonathon! Run!"

The words of his grandmother jerked Jonathon's head up. Horrified, he watched as she left the barge and plunged headfirst into the water with an arrow in her back. He straightened to his tallest. In his mind's eye he knew. His eyes filled with bitter hatred. "There's converted on that barge. They killed my grandmother. I can't prove it, but I swear that it is true. They will pay."

He didn't move as the barge slowed, turning shoreward. He watched in agonized silence as a crewman leapt into the river searching for his grandmother. He was beyond feeling.

19

SHEM

The light through the open window was fading. The faint breeze stirred the heavier herbal scented air, which Shem found relaxing. Too relaxing actually. Shem had been lying wide awake in his bed for the better part of a candlemark trying to decide what the mysterious pull, beckoning to him, was. What had been the meaning of Vlad's withdrawal? Was he now free of the Sun Father?

Shem tried sitting up. Big mistake. Dizziness and a sharp pain in his forehead forced him back down. He didn't know what was in the draught the healer had given him, but he knew he wasn't going to take any more of it. He could not afford to be immobilized. The doorway to his room slid open. The healer entered and behind her Selene. Shem caught the smile before it enveloped his entire face and forced it to more moderate proportions.

"I know that wasn't for me, but I'll ask how you are feeling anyway," said the healer coming to his bedside. Her eyes flicked to the sheets and blanket down by his waist. "I see that you have tried to get up. It will pass. For now I need you to remain in bed," she explained leaning over Shem and peering deep into his eyes. Apparently satisfied she straightened and placed her hand over his chest to feel his heartbeat. She frowned.

"You're well enough, physically," she said reaching for her bag of powders.

"No draughts."

She stopped at the intensity of Shem's voice. The two locked stares. The contest of wills lasted little more than moments. The healer backed down.

"Very well. I'll check back later. Before the council meeting. We'll deal with the dizziness then." So saying, she turned on her heel and left. Selene stepped up to the side of Shem's bed.

"She's afraid of you or rather of what's inside of you."

Shem strove to keep the concern out of his eyes. He didn't want to show weakness in the presence of Selene. *I fear the Sun Father as well, but I fear failure more.* Shem put on a brave front, "Should I fear what's inside of her?"

"She would have to carry the council. That's seems unlikely, but I don't know," answered Selene truthfully. She hurried on, "I have heard some news. It's all bad." She left the offer dangling.

"Any of it about Wybee?"

"No, Shem. I'm sorry,"

"Any guidance from the high priestess?"

Selene shook her head sorrowfully. Shem studied her. With the Council meeting soon, Shem wouldn't have long to await his fate. He knew he had no friend in the healer. He hadn't seen Ip'star in over a turning. Ma Ne had pressed hard to come to this council, but he had never actually expressed support of Shem. His Holiness seemed a fair man, but fair did not necessarily mean support. Only Selene had stood with him. *Will you come with me?* He didn't know where to go, he didn't know where Wybee was, and he wasn't sure about any friends he had here in Sho ku, but he decided one thing. He was going his own way even if the council decided against him. *Alone if need be. I will not fail.*

The healer returned before the setting of the sun. With her was Ya Ma and Ma Ne, both in what must have been ceremonial garb. The tight fitting black garb of Ya Ma was similar to what he had worn the night Shem had met him, but now had a silver badge depicting a dagger, a star and a clenched fist holding crossed arrows on his left breast. Looped across his shoulder was a decorative but still functional garrote. His face scarf was loosed on one side and hung down the left side of his face.

Ma Ne's robe was more colorful and flowing, befitting of a well to do Goatherder. Dyed bars of silver and green slashed diagonally across his chest from left shoulder to right foot. It was held closed by a sash of black through which his ever dangerous sword was secured along with two long daggers. He wore no emblems. The faces of both men were masks of stone.

The healer walked purposefully towards the bedside table and dipped a bowl of water out of the basin. She rummaged through her herb pouch selecting a paper of herbs.

Shem said, "No draughts."

The healer poured the contents of the paper into the bowl and swirled it around. "This will remove any lingering traces of the dizziness," she explained, her back still to Shem.

Shem repeated a little more forcefully. "No draughts!"

The healer looked around locking eyes with her patient. She put the bowl back on the table. "Very well. Get up and follow us," she smirked.

He remembered the wave of dizziness from the last time he had tried to get up. Then his movements had been unthinking and swift, the onset of the dizziness immediate and overpowering. This time he moved slowly. *It's been half a turning. Surely the draught will have weakened with time.* It had not.

By the time Shem had sat completely up, the room spun slowly before his eyes. Closing them only made it worse. The room spun quicker and quicker threatening to overwhelm him. He snapped his eyes back open. The healer stood before him holding out the bowl.

"It will make you whole," she offered.

Shem had no reason to believe the healer. He gritted his teeth. "No."

Moving deliberately, he swung his legs out of bed and set them on the floor. Sometime during the turning the woven mat beside his bed had been kicked away and not repositioned. Shem's bare feet came into contact with the cold stone. Immediately, the mysterious pull that had been beckoning Shem strengthened and added will and determination to his efforts. Shem slowly rose to his feet, the dizziness held in check. Still there, still dangerous, but it was now controllable.

Shem turned slowly to face the healer. Her features were inscrutable, but for a moment registered of surprise. Shem grinned, not in happiness, rather resolution. It was almost menacing. He knew he was about to be led to the Council, but his heart and the touching longed for the mysterious pull.

The healer spun on her heel. "Follow, if you can," she said over her shoulder, striding quickly towards the door.

Shem looked around for his clothes. He couldn't be expected to attend the Council dressed only in some over large shirt. He spied his weapons leaning up against a wardrobe. Ma Ne followed his gaze.

"None may stand armed before the council," said Ma Ne.

"I was looking for clothes."

"What you now wear is sufficient," said Ya Ma.

The first step was shaky. Shem carefully concentrated on first lifting then shuffling his foot forward. The next was easier as was the one after. By the time he reached the door his confidence had risen. He was nowhere near normal, but able to move without the constant threat of falling on his face. Ma Ne nodded towards the left. Shem stepped through the door and turned. He heard the whispery steps of Ma Ne and Ya Ma following. Waiting at the end of the corridor was the healer. She watched Shem take a few steps, frowned and continued on.

"I don't think I'm supposed to be able to do this," said Shem. He received no reply. He hadn't really expected one. Ma Ne hadn't proven to be much of a conversationalist and Shem wasn't really sure that when he did speak if it was a compliment or a complaint. *Maybe it's all Goatherders. No matter, I won't be stopped.* The stone passageway became a narrow flying bridge ending at the second from the top level of Fiona's Temple. Shem now knew where he was. Soon he would find out why. Entering the temple foyer he found Selene, Ip'star, and a woman he had never met. That she was a Free Goatherder was beyond doubt. The slant to the eyes, the straight dark hair, and the inscrutable expression, though somewhat softened, all pointed to her heritage. They broke off their conversation when Shem arrived.

"Wait here," instructed Ma Ne. The two guards entered the Temple chamber.

"Shem, I would like you to meet Tonya Marcus, wife of the late Baron John Marcus," introduced Selene.

Closer inspection revealed signs of recent weeping, now suppressed. He was afraid to bow. He wasn't sure he would be able to stop once he lowered his head. "My sympathies, Baroness,"

She waved away the words, "No longer a baroness, Shem. I have become Ton Ya of the Free Goatherders once again. I hear this council was called because of you."

Shem replied with a sigh. "I'm afraid so, Ton Ya."

"You should be proud, Shem. Among us the hero or protector as we call you has long been anticipated and of late, much discussed. Or so I'm told," she said.

Shem nearly succeeded in keeping the sarcasm out of his voice. "You have a strange way of showing it."

"So it must seem. I would tell you the tale of the Protector, but it would spoil my grandfather's ceremony, and he's been waiting a long time to tell it," said Ton Ya mischievously.

Shem had almost missed it. He had been surprised by Ton Ya's open display of emotion. She had been the first he'd seen break out of the taciturn mold. *It must have been the time she spent with the baron.* "Your grandfather?"

"Yes. John always took such pride in it. Stealing and conquering the granddaughter of His Holiness, Leader of the Free Goatherders." She spared a moment for a fond memory. "I'm pleased to have met the Protector," she finished.

"I am pleased that you are again healthy, and I hope, ready to continue," said Ip'star in his turn.

Shem could feel as well as see the sincerity in the greeting. Choosing to leave the state of his health unanswered, he replied, "Thank you, Ip'star."

The door of the temple chamber opened. Ma Ne and Ya Ma flanked the opening. From within the chamber intoned a deep ominous voice.

"Protector, enter and be judged."

Selene stood beside Shem. She reached down and squeezed his hand hard before releasing it. Shem, Selene, and Ip'star started forward. Selene and Ip'star were barred at the doorway by Ma Ne and Ya Ma who then backed into the chamber and shut the door. Shem was alone.

He stopped a few paces inside the chamber to look around. He heard the door close behind him. The soothing scent of incense, the same he had experienced earlier, almost made him loose his grip on the dizziness. He staggered a step before recovering. He heard the footsteps then finally saw Ma Ne and Ya Ma as they made their way across opposite sides of the room to join the table arrayed before him.

It sat before a luxuriously draped background depicting the history of the Free Goatherders. The stark contrast of colors, vibrantly vivid, with each panel painstakingly embroidered with dyed goat hairs represented different stages of their history. One panel in particular stood out. It showed a blazing streak of green across a cobalt sky. Shem was awed. He knew little of his own history or that of the Central Lands, only folklore, and that verbal. He had never seen an entire people's history laid out for all to see.

His gaze shifted to the table. Sitting in the center was His Holiness looking much the same as the last time Shem had been brought before him as did the ancient priest on his left. On his right, sat a man in his prime that Shem had not met before. His face was a little flatter than the others, otherwise indistinguishable. The end seats were taken by Ma Ne and Ya Ma. The table was unadorned, with two exceptions, a silver moon mounted on a pedestal and the depiction of a man holding a green planet on his shoulders attempting to raise it over his head.

Off to Shem's left was a smaller table with two chairs. Only one was filled and that by the healer. While her facial expression was unreadable, her body language indicated fear, worry, and concern. Shem already knew no help would come from that direction. The only other person in the room that had any extensive contact with Shem was Ma Ne. Shem wasn't sure what to expect there.

His Holiness unfolded his arms, drawing his hands out of his voluminous sleeves. One held a small gong and the other a striker. He set the gong down in front of him, between the two statuettes. He struck the gong. It rang with a single pure note pitched to cut through discourse.

"The Council is met. Shem of the Central Lands has been brought before us. Can any vouchsafe for him?" The normally soft voice of His Holiness now held authority and strength without any increase in volume.

"I have traveled with this man. He is known by all that meet him as Shem," replied Ma Ne.

"What else do you know about him?" intoned His Holiness.

"That he claims to be the *Hero* of Tierra. We know this individual as the *Protector*. I have determined that he believes this to be true," said Ma Ne.

"Can anyone else speak of this?" asked His Holiness.

The healer rose from her chair and addressed the Council. "I have examined this man. I have felt the touching of Tierra. Further—"

"Just answer the question asked," interrupted His Holiness. "Does he believe his claim?"

"Yes, Holiness."

He turned his attention to Shem as the healer took her seat. "Do you, Shem, fully understand the claim you make?"

Shem was impressed with the tone of the Council. None raised their voices, none shouted. All spoke with a calm serenity, even the healer, even after being chastised. Shem tried to emulate them.

"Holiness, I do not believe I understand anything fully," he began haltingly, "Only that I know what I'm doing is right and I shall do it to the best of my ability." Shem felt a surge from the unknown force as if it were pleased with his answer. If any on the Council felt it, none showed it.

"Then let me explain what I can," began His Holiness.

The healer rose from her chair interrupting, "Holiness, I must protest."

"Must, Cam Phor?"

"Apologies, Holiness, but this man carries a danger."

"Your time to speak will come, Cam Phor. Please be seated." His Holiness waited until the healer had sat before continuing. "Shem, the Life Giver has long been known to us. Blessed Fiona herself revealed this to us many lifetimes of man ago. She also let be known to us the manner of her rising. That this rising would be challenged and that the Life Giver had need of a Protector. Lastly, that this Protector would pass through our lands. You claim now to be that Protector. Let us say you are. After you leave this Council what will you do?"

Shem's inner mirth vanished. He had thought this to be the tale of the Protector that Ton Ya had told him to expect. He had found it amusing that the healer had been put in her place, so as not to disturb the long prepared telling. He answered the question quickly, without thought, letting his heart speak.

"First, I would find that which calls me so urgently at this moment. After, Tierra, though I don't know where to look or what to look for. I would find Wybee who is supposed to be my conduit, whatever that is."

The calm of the Council was nearly shattered. The healer had started at Shem's first words. Uncertainty and fear nearly overwhelmed her. She began to rise, but halted as her movement attracted the eyes of everyone else at the table. She sat back down.

His Holiness returned his attention to Shem. "It would seem to this Council that you are like a kid lost from its dam. Not knowing where the sweet grass is or the way back to the river. Is this so?"

"It is," said Shem. He stared at the featureless expressions of the Council as if daring them to chastise him for telling the truth.

His Holiness turned serenely to the healer. "Cam Phor, your time to speak has come."

The healer rose. "This man has been touched by the Life Giver. That is beyond doubt. Why, might be another question. This man tells the truth—-as he knows it. This man has also been bonded by the Sun Father, high priest of Mieze. Which bond is the strongest? I do not know, but I fear. He could undo all." The healer sat down.

His Holiness turned back to Shem. "What have you to say to this?"

Shem burned. He burned with shame for being accused of being a puppet of the West. He burned because he knew he could not and would not deny that bond. He burned because once again it looked like he would fail. He stood his straightest and threw back his shoulders.

"I am not Shem 'o the West. I am Shem, hero of Tierra! I will not fail," the last came out as a low growl from deep within Shem.

The small gong sounded once again. His Holiness gently placed the striker beside it. "This Council has heard the words of Shem. It has heard the words of Cam Phor. It has long read the ancient words. It is time to decide."

The Healer rose from her table and tucked her hands in her sleeves. She silently glided from the room. The Council members settled themselves into what comfort their seats would allow, all eyes on Shem. After the door closed behind the healer, His Holiness looked to his right.

"Hen Was, you are the free people's representative. The first vote falls to you; however, you were last to have arrived receiving the least council. You may wait until last if you desire."

"Holiness, I have read the text. I have heard the words. I vote no."

"Priest Ro Ber, you represent the Blessed Fiona. How do you vote?"

The vote by Hen Was did not bother Shem that much. The two had never met, but the vote of the priest was important. Shem had spent a lot of time traveling with High Priestess El-lina. He knew that she believed in him and would have instructed her priests likewise. The Free Goatherder priest looked decidedly uncomfortable. *Do not desert me*, pleaded Shem inwardly.

"Holiness, I have read the text. I have heard the words. I vote... no."

The word fell like a hammer blow upon Shem's ears. *This can't be happening.* He stood in stunned silence fighting to keep upright. He barely registered the ritual words as Ya Ma also voted no. It was now Ma Ne's turn.

"Ma Ne, as protectorate of the Cap Tan you represent the peoples of the Central Lands. Further, it was your actions that brought the Protector before this Council. How do you vote?"

Shem steeled himself. If Ma Ne refused support then the last five turnings would have been a complete waste.

"Holiness, I have read the text. I have heard the words. I vote no."

"This Council is unanimous," declared His Holiness.

The sudden surge from the mysterious source was the only thing that kept Shem upright. Despite his resolve, the fact that none stood with him was devastating. The single note of the gong announced the finality of the Council meeting. Shem had been refused whatever help Ma Ne had brought him here to receive. But that wasn't really correct. *All Ma Ne had actually said was that he wanted to bring me to the Council so they could hear what I have to say.*

The Council members waited for His Holiness to stand before following him out of the chamber. As he began rising Shem asked.

"What is to be my fate?"

His Holiness's voice actually contained mirth. "Whatever you make of it, Protector."

"Then I'm free to go?"

"You were never held, Protector. You were our guest. Has anyone treated you differently?" asked His Holiness.

Shem wanted to scream out "Hen Was! Ya Ma! Ma Ne! You!" but that wasn't actually true. Instead he said, "A certain healer comes to mind."

"Ah, yes. That second bond. I understand you refused the antidote. If you have changed your mind, I'll send the healer to you," offered His Holiness.

At least I'm free. Shem bit back the harsher words he had nearly blurted out. He knew better than to poke a sleeping predator. "No thank you, Holiness."

He watched as the Councilors filed out. None made eye contact with him. He made his way slowly to the door. Temple guards opened it for him as he approached.

Outside in the foyer his friends, *or what passed for friends in this group,* Shem was no longer sure, waited for him. They read his expression and knew the unbelievable had happened. Shem addressed Ton Ya first. "Your grandfather didn't tell me the story of the Protector."

"If I can help in any way, just ask," was all she said.

"How bad was it?" asked Selene.

"Unanimous," said Shem continuing to walk towards the exit. He planned to go to his room and gather his belongings. After that he would search out whatever it was that was calling to him, and let them try to stop him.

Walking was easier now, no longer requiring immediate attention. Shem increased his pace arriving at his room without incident or interruption. Once inside he went directly to the wardrobe to don his clothes and weapons. Fitted out, Shem drew his sword and went through some simple forms. *So far, so good.* As long as he moved slowly, he could remain clear headed.

A soft knock interrupted his concentration. He spun quickly on his heel sword in front him at the ready. Orientation vanished into a swirling maelstrom. Shem dropped to a knee leaning on his sword for support. The door slid open. Selene entered.

"A moment of devotion?" she asked hopefully.

"If it would help," gasped Shem. Slowly, still leaning on his sword, Shem rose to his feet. He walked carefully over to the bed and sat down, taking off his boots. Bare feet on the floor seemed to help his recovery.

"There was something in the healer's draught that robs me of my balance," explained Shem. "I had hoped it would pass, but it hasn't."

"That's why you took off your boots?" asked Selene quizzically.

Shem looked up. Selene hadn't come into the room any further. She stood just inside the doorway. Shem could see her concern, that she was serious. "You don't feel it?"

"I feel your pain. I see your doubt. Is that what you're asking?"

Shem settled his feet firmly and rose from the bed. Now that his feet was in contact with the bare floor, he felt better, stronger. He knew that he would be unable to hold his own in a sword fight, but that knowledge could be masked. "The Free Goatherders are hiding something. Something of power. I can feel it. I can feel it through the stone. It's calling me. It wants to be found."

"So you are going to find it," said Selene, "Despite the Council voting to withhold it from you."

"I am."

"And despite the fact that you can barely stand?"

"Yes."

"Is that wise?"

Shem gave her a little grin, it looked strained. "I've never been known for my wisdom. All I know is that I have to find it."

"Then I'm going with you," Selene pronounced.

"No."

Selene took a step back at the intensity of Shem's response. Shem was immediately sorry. He hadn't meant to speak harshly, not to Selene. He tried to make amends. "Selene, it could be dangerous and as you say, I can't even adequately protect myself."

"Which is all the more reason to accompany you," she replied firmly.

Shem did not want to tell Selene that her presence would divide his attention, or that it would take all of his concentration to maintain what stability he did have if it came to a fight. "Whatever it is calling me, it is not Tierra, herself. It is of her, I'm certain, but not her. Otherwise, I would welcome you."

"It shall be as you say. Shem, protector of Tierra. Be careful." A sad smile played across Selene's lips, one that did not reach her eyes. She placed her palms together and gave Shem a small bow.

Shem watched the retreating figure of Selene. *She thinks I'm pushing her away.* Aren't you? *No! Well, yes. I don't know.* Shem pushed the argument out of his mind. He didn't have time for it right now. He said softly, "As much as I can be." She closed the door behind her.

Shem stood outside of his door looking both ways down the hall. *Quit looking with your eyes. Let your feet tell you which way to go.* Shem concentrated on his feet. He would have liked to have closed his eyes to concentrate better, but feared the dizziness returning. Yes, he was sure of it. Whatever was calling to him was inside the mountain. Shem turned to his right and made his way down the hallway following the pull.

The strength of whatever it was calling to Shem had grown stronger, more insistent, with every step. For some reason he had expected some elaborate labyrinth, or a crisscrossing of paths designed to confuse. Isn't that the way these things are supposed to be? But nothing had been simple yet concerning Tierra. Instead, the way had been short and straight. Arcing downward into the heart of the mountain, it turned only when it encountered a massive vein of iron ore. It was at the turn that Shem hesitated. He sensed something or someone around the corner. Gathering all his strength and determination, Shem rounded the corner and came face to face with Ya Ma and Ma Ne. They were guarding the door to a chamber hewn out of the rock.

"State your purpose, Protector," said Ma Ne.

"I've come to answer the call."

"The Council has forbidden it," said Ma Ne.

"No, the Council has voted not to assist me. His Holiness said I was free to go wherever my fate leads me."

"Your fate has led you to your death," said Ya Ma.

Shem stared into the depthless, emotionless eyes of Ya Ma. He replied calmly. "Then the Council does the work of Mieze."

The sword of Ya Ma flashed out of its scabbard, the point centered at the base of Shem's throat. Shem didn't flinch as he faced down Ya Ma. If this was to be his fate, so be it. He was glad Selene wasn't here to witness.

"You dare name that name here," said Ya Ma menacingly.

"The truth may be spoken anywhere," said Shem. He had no idea where the words came from, but they felt right. And they had an effect on Ya Ma and Ma Ne.

"Dare to win," said Ma Ne. Ya Ma withdrew his sword, returning it to its scabbard. Both men stepped aside.

"What you seek is behind this door. Discover your fate," pronounced Ma Ne. As one they drew their swords in a slow deliberate movement.

Shem took a deep breath. *This is it.* He stepped forward bare-handed. If they were going to cut him down, he wouldn't have been able to stop them anyway. Three steps brought him to the door. He pulled the latch. Nothing happened. He put his palm flat on the door and gently pushed. The door opened inward. He sensed the movement of Ma Ne and Ya Ma as they positioned themselves behind him.

The room was about five paces square resembling a large closet. Two lamps burned some scented oil, but produced only enough for dim light. A pedestal in the back of the room below the lamps was the only other furnishings. A figure with its back to Shem stood before the pedestal. Shem took two steps into the room and stopped. Ya Ma and Ma Ne followed, stopping a pace behind. The figure turned.

"We meet again, Shem. Have I ever told you the tale of the Guardians?" asked His Holiness. He stood confidently facing Shem, arms folded, hands in sleeves.

Shem was confused. No one seemed surprised that he had come in defiance of their vote, nor did his presence invoke anger. Instead of imprisonment or death, His Holiness had offered to tell him a tale. *What game is this?* He didn't know how to proceed. What was clear was that the source of what he was seeking was somewhere in the vicinity of the high priest of the Free Goatherders and behind Shem were two very proficient killers ready to strike if he made a wrong move.

"It's one of our oldest tales," continued His Holiness, "allow me to tell it." Two chairs made of stone appeared beside the men. "Please, be seated."

Shem looked at the chair beside him then back up at His Holiness.

"It's Tierra or possibly the Pointer sensing our need and providing, but I get ahead of myself. Sit and listen."

"It was in the earliest of our turnings, during the carving up of the Central Lands. The barons were just coming to their power and claiming their different baronies. We of the Free Goatherders, desiring above all else our autonomy, managed to remain undiscovered here in our mountains. Then one night, blazing across the heavens was a glorious green light approaching from the northwest. We watched in amazement as a piece separated from the main body and began arcing down. It passed over our village bathing us in its green luminance before passing over the mountain and striking the ground. It struck this mountain. It made the tunnel you walked down including this chamber where it finally came to rest."

Shem believed the last statement. He could feel the fragment pulsing with every part of his body, but especially in the center of his chest where Tierra had touched him. He was very much aware of the fragment and even more, its desire. It desired him. And he it.

"The high priest of Fiona was with us at the time. As the green glow over the mountain subsided he went into a trance. We heard the words of the Blessed Fiona from his mouth. 'You have witnessed the inception of Tierra. Long will she lie in the bosom of the Land, nurturing, until the day of her awakening. Guard that portion of her that is yours for a Protector will come. In need will he come. Provide for him, so that Tierra may live.' Blessed Fiona went on in much wisdom that night, but that is another tale. We continued to follow the teachings of Fiona, but pledged our lives and our souls to Tierra, Life Giver, As a clan we set set out to find Tierra. Upon discovering this valley and the mount where rested the Pointer, we were named the Guardians."

The tale was more cryptic than clarifying to Shem. It certainly didn't explain his treatment at the Council nor the fact that finding this chamber had been no difficult feat. Who he was should have been obvious to the Council members, so why the charade? Unless the bond to Vlad made him damaged goods. *Could I have in some way disrupted the plans of the goddesses?*

"Hardly," said His Holiness.

It took Shem a moment to realize that the high priest had answered the question he had just asked of himself. A moment of panic set in with the realization that His Holiness could read his thoughts as Vlad did. *This is why they hesitate.*

"Forgive me. I misspoke a moment ago. The true words of the Blessed Fiona were, 'In need will he come, bare of feet and lacking knowledge.'" His Holiness looked down at Shem's feet.

Realization, then relief, flooded through Shem. "This is the test. The Council meeting was a charade." Shem's eyes narrowed in displeasure. "Why the healer? Why the act? There could have been a simpler way."

"It is our way," said His Holiness. "We will speak no more of this." He stood. Shem did likewise. The stone chairs vanished. His Holiness unfolded his arms, drawing his hands out of his sleeve. In one hand he held a wooden box.

"This is the Pointer, though I believe the old language actually calls it *Gedeelte*. It is yours." His Holiness held out the box.

A portion of Tierra. It could tell me where to go, what to do. Shem felt the rightness of possessing the artifact. He reached out his hand.

"A last word of warning, Shem. If you are not he or if you are rejected, your body will be consumed by the Gedeelte leaving nothing but a pile of ash. Choose."

Shem's hand stopped. His Holiness had not called him Protector. *Is it the bond with Vlad that makes him doubt? Have others tried and failed?* He wriggled his toes. Beneath the soles of his feet he felt a gritty substance. Shem wanted to look down but kept his gaze fixed on the figure before him. The planted seed grew rapidly. Shem's hand moved ever so slowly first towards the Pointer then away. *Was this all some drunken dream? Did I make it all up? Am I nothing more than what my brother always accuses me of?* Ma Ne's voice menaced from behind him.

"Face us, Shem."

Once again no honorific was used. Shem knew that behind him stood two very good swordsmen. He knew he could not face both with a chance to win, especially not in his weakened condition. He had hesitated to grasp the box and now had to pay the price. He felt himself slipping in to failure again. Frustration and embarrassment broiled through him. He bellowed, "No!"

His hand went to his sword. He spun on his heel to face Ma Ne and Ya Ma. Immediately the dizziness returned. Shem staggered sideways. He saw the two swords begin their movement towards him. The box containing the Pointer flew out of His Holiness's hand and into Shem's. The dizziness flash-burned its way out of Shem's core. Replacing it was clarity, speed and power. Shem straightened. His left arm had raised up to block a blow from Ya Ma. Shem wished he had a shield on it. A small thin oaken shield materialized repelling the blow of Ya Ma's sword. Shem's sword arm stiffened. His sword became an extension of his arm, an extension of his will.

He had been a good swordsman before, but now with the Pointer he was more than he had ever been. Faster, stronger, more agile. He could sense the blows before his opponents knew they were going to use them. He easily deflected Ma Ne's cut and with a sweeping circular motion that collected the blades of both men, threw them back a step.

Ya Ma and Ma Ne recovered their balance. They sheathed their swords and bowed.

"The Protector must dare to win," said Ma Ne.

"Dare not and he loses," said Ya Ma.

"When Tierra awakens she will have need of the Hjerte," proclaimed His Holiness. "Welcome, Protector. If you would, we would like you to take your seat at the Council."

"Take it, Hero." The small muffled voice came from Shem's stone pouch. "Hey! You wanna open this thing?"

He let the little man of the Nem Elt-til out of his pouch. The little man flew up to Shem's shoulder. Shem rolled his eyes and groaned, "Not you."

"I've missed you, too, Big Boy. I don't know how you've managed to survive without my guidance. Who are your friends?"

The Council met the next morning. The healer was not present. Her place at the side table was taken by Selene and Ip'star. Shem sat to the right of His Holiness, Priest Ro Ber moving down one position. A small chair had materialized for the Nem Elt-til who had become the darling of His Holiness. He sat on the table between Shem and His Holiness.

"You know, Holiness, I'd ditch this loser here, but he'd be lost without me," declared the Nem Elt-til.

Shem asked innocently, "Do you have a name yet, little man?"

"Back off, Hero! One needs only to look at you to know you can't rush perfection. I swear, Holiness, I can't for the life of me figure out why the Life Giver chose him, but that's why she made me. To make up for his shortcomings."

"Nem Elt-til, after this is over I would count myself blessed to have you sit by my side," His Holiness laughed out loud, shattering the illusion of the stoic Free Goatherder.

"At least you can count. That would be an improvement," rejoined the little man nodding his head in the direction of Shem. "But alas, my curse is to see this one through," he said. "By the way, Hero, that's a nice gee gaw you got there around your neck."

Shem fingered the Gedeelte, which now hung from a leather thong. An iridescent green jewel shaped in a rough approximation of an arrow, it flashed through the green spectrum changing hues depending on the light that struck it. It lightened the heart of all who gazed upon it, giving hope. Above all, it throbbed with life. The moment it touched Shem's hand, Tierra had stirred, recovering somewhat. She still wasn't a shadow of what she had been, but even an occasional thought from her was an improvement. Shem's heart warmed a fraction where she had touched him.

"Yes, it is," said Shem. Now that it was in Shem's possession, he felt more complete. The whole person that he hadn't been since the night his parents had died and himself captured by the Westerners. His body tingled with its newfound power. Shem had no idea what else if anything had changed about him since the Pointer's contact. He hoped the Council would be able to provide some insight.

The chime of His Holiness's gong silenced conversation. "The Protector is among us," he announced.

Eyes turned to Shem. Shem saw no remorse in any of them and he showed none back. Shem imitated the stoic nature of his hosts. "I would know if you have knowledge to the extent or limitations, if any, of the Pointer."

"Hey! Bonehead! You missed your cue. This is where you are supposed to introduce me!" The Nem Elt-til jumped indignantly to his feet. He strode to the center of the table, looking into the eyes of all present. His gaze lingered on Selene. "Now there's a vision," he said.

Shem groaned inwardly. The Pointer had not only empowered him, but the creation of Tierra as well. Before he had been obnoxious, now he was impossible!

"I am a creation of the Life Giver, Tierra. I am of Nem Elt-til." He spoke normally and all heard his words. "On behalf of the Life Giver I thank you for the Gedeelte." He used the old word which meant 'part of the Hjerte' or portion. "Now let's get real. Our main goal here is to get the Hjerte. Do you know where it's at?"

"Taciturn and succinct," said His Holiness, both chiding and praising his new little friend. "In answer, roughly. That is why the Pointer was provided. To get you the rest of way."

"There are a few other little things I'd like to know," said Shem to the Nem Elt-til, "A few facts. Maybe fill in a gap or two. You don't mind do you?"

"Whatever you need, Hero. I was just trying to save you some time. We only have so much of it, you know?" he said, making the last part a question.

Shem knew. He only had a moon to find the Hjerte and half of that time was gone. *The Pointer will help speed up the rest of the journey.* Already the Pointer had enabled Shem to sense certain facts like the amount of time for the journey. It had proven the right of much of El-lina's advice, and it was definitely wanting him to go southeast towards Grimval Valley. But whether that was towards Wybee or the Hjerte, Shem didn't know. He hoped His Holiness would have some information about it. "You offered to tell me the tale of the Protector. I would like to hear it."

"It was an empty promise, Shem. You know the tale. You are living it and the end has yet to be written."

The air released from Shem's hope.

Selene rose. She was dressed in a long white hooded robe with a single black stripe around its edge indicating her first level status. She reached up with one hand and pulled back the hood, her golden locks lit by occasional green glints as light from the Pointer flickered across them. Her other hand held a small wooden box. Shem smiled. He knew the box contained her spider.

"If I may address the Council?" she asked.

"Speak," said his Holiness.

"I have spoken with High Priestess El-lina. She tells me that the Central Landers have been pushed back past Mill Town. She doesn't expect them to hold."

Shem frowned. The rest of the council showed no emotions, but the air became heavier in the Council room.

"Shem, she suggests we leave immediately for Grimval. Priest Fitzpatrick will be waiting for us. Wybee has been found."

Wybee has been found. Thank you, Tierra. Shem nodded his agreement and rose from his chair.

"Hero, you will need transportation. We stand ready," said Ip'star rising from his seat.

"Thank you, Ip'star. I accept."

"The duty of Protectorate of the Cap Tan has passed to me. I will accompany you. Our last knowledge put the heir with

Wybee. Perhaps he is with him still," said Ya Ma rising from his chair at the Council table.

Still smarting from his treatment by the Council Shem wasn't sure he wanted Ya Ma along. He'd had about enough of their ways and rituals, still his skill with a sword could prove invaluable. To any more than that, Shem did not want to commit. Besides, he knew that refusing would not stop Ya Ma from getting to the heir's side. He said, "As you will."

The single, pure note of His Holiness's gong sounded throughout the chamber, stopping any further discussion. "This Council has not been dismissed. You will all take your seats." Those who had risen sat. His Holiness continued, "The Protector wished to know of any limitations of the Pointer. First, it must be acknowledged that the Pointer has never been wielded. It is not fully known what it can do, let alone what it cannot. It is merely a portion of the Hjerte. It is not the Hjerte. It's powers are not without end. Second, the Pointer is a part of the Hjerte. As such its power may also be summoned by the Life Giver at need. Lastly, the Hjerte is a creation of the Life Giver. Should her rising not occur then the Hjerte itself, all its creations, manifestations and those touched by its power will simply cease to exist. It will be as if they never were."

"That is all that is known. Some scholars have speculated otherwise. Some think that the Protector's use of the Pointer would draw power out of the Life Giver thus weakening her, but speculations are not facts." His Holiness looked over the Council.

Priest Ro Ber spoke. "Goddess Mieze wishes to prevent the rising. This is known. She will do all in her power to stop the Protector." Priest Ro Ber peered intently at Shem. His statement was a reminder to all of the bond that Shem shared with the Sun Father. "We believe that she will try to use up the power of the Pointer if she cannot control the Protector."

His chill words echoed into silence. Shem felt as if he were being weighed on the scales. Once again His Holiness surveyed the Council. None had any further questions or information to share. He picked up the striker, "May the blessings of Fiona and those of the Life Giver go with us all. This Council is adjourned."

As the gong sounded its clear, pure note through the chamber Shem was already rising, the Nem Elt-til perched on his shoulder. The doors of the chamber were opened by the guards as Shem approached. He swept through and turned towards his room. When safely out of earshot he asked the little man. "You were created by Tierra, you should know. Is what they say true? Can the Pointer be overused?"

"I don't know, Hero," he said without his usual cocky attitude. "But you were given the Pointer to do a job. I say let's do it."

"Even though we risk being as if we never were?"

"I never was to begin with. What about you?" asked the little man.

"Nothing to brag about, though I don't let that stop me," said Shem. The Nem Elt-til laughed. His laughter lifted Shem's spirits, but did not alter his concerns.

Shem caught up with Ip'star and Selene at the bottom of the "hundred steps". The four Eastern horses stamped eagerly, anxious to be flying once again. Shem didn't remember much of the last flight. Mostly a lot of lurching and swaying about and the horse's displeasure. Certainly nothing to be eager about. They were joined by Ya Ma who seemingly just materialized before them.

"That's a neat trick, Goatherder," quipped the Nem Elt-til, back to his usual self and perch on Shem's shoulder.

"It is nothing, little man. I did not wish to be seen until now. I was always there. Your eyes just slid away from me."

Ip'star helped Selene into the saddle of Fugol, her previous mount. She stroked the side of her winged steed's face. He seemed content. Cyst came up to Shem, snuffling face and chest. Not smelling any ale he stood still while Shem swung into the saddle and strapped in as he saw Selene do.

Ip'star laughed, pleased with the prospect of soon being in the air. "I wasn't sure how that was going to work out, Hero. Cyst was ill pleased by the burden of your last flight. He might have refused to carry you."

Shem basked in the power of the Pointer. He felt good about himself. "Can't say that I'd have blamed him, but for now, those turnings are over."

Ip'star explained the most comfortable positions of the saddle to Ya Ma. "Just settle in and let Rodor do the work. Move with him. It's much the same as riding on the ground, only different."

"The same, but different. Spoken like a scholar," said Ya Ma declining to tie himself to the saddle.

"Where are we going?" asked Ip'star swinging into his saddle.

"Grimval Keep. It lies at the foot of Grimval Falls. It's the only way in, now that Barons Sulieman and O'Kelly have closed the Valley," answered Selene.

The group was about to lift off, but their departure was delayed by the last moment appearance of Cam Phor, the healer. She walked directly to Cyst and Shem. Shem looked down with skepticism and more than a little distrust. His new found power also hinted at something else. Something...He could not quite put his finger on it, but it had a distinct Western flavor to it. Shem searched her eyes but could find no traces of Vlad. "Yes?"

"You may have been named Protector and claimed the Pointer, but your trial has yet to occur, Shem O' the West."

20

Regent Simon's Estate

Il'ar spoke into the web of Priest Conyn. "Mother, we could use some help."

The priest's tent was unoccupied. With the exception of Il'ar the remainder of the Central Lander leaders were busy loading their troops onto the barges that were now arriving to carry them down river. They couldn't stand against Baron Yakov and his forces without prepared defenses, especially not after Baron Yakov reunited with his Un Tier. Retreating down river should give them enough time to prepare. Even if it meant going all the way to Grimval fortress. This last had caused some consternation with the Regent as well as Baron Filip. Neither wanted to fly in the face of the enemy all the way to Grimval and beg on the doorstep of Barons Sulieman and O'Kelly for safety. They had thought it more honorable to stand and fight even if it meant defeat.

"We are getting too good at running," the Regent said during the last council. "We should stand at Mill Town and close the road while we still remember how to fight."

Il'ar had argued. "Can you close the river, too? If you cannot then they will have an avenue around us. Sooner or later they are going to take to the river. Mark my words, we need to get ahead of them. Gain enough time to prepare the field."

"Time is one thing we do not have a lot of," sighed Priest Conyn. "At least not according to the high priestess."

"Then we must do what we must do," relented Regent Simon.

The sheen of the web faded then grew brighter as it locked on to High Priestess El-lina.

"Il'ar, you are well?" asked his mother.

Il'ar spoke quickly, knowing that the web could fail or his mother could be blocked. He also knew she spoke to many others as well. "I am well, Mother. Hard pressed, under strength, and fleeing south, but well. What of the muster?"

"Soon, Il'ar," said El-lina.

"Mother, the Central Landers weary of 'soon', weary of running, weary of defeat. They begin to despair. I cannot continue to sell 'soon'."

"It's the best that can be done at present, Il'ar."

"Then we shall go to Grimval and trust in Fiona. What of the awakening?"

"Tierra hangs on, but barely. The hero is on the cusp."

In his cups more likely. "We will do what we can, Mother." Il'ar watched as the sheen of the web faded.

He found the Regent and Baron Filip down at the docks supervising the loading of the barges as they came in. He joined them. "She said soon."

"Soon may not be soon enough," said the Regent turning back to the barges.

Il'ar invoked his mother's title to lend weight to his words. "Do not despair. The high priestess said the hero is on a cusp. We must make haste to get to a defensible position."

"You are, of course, suggesting Grimval Fortress," said Baron Filip.

"Yes."

"Leaving my son to make his own way from the rear. Cutting him off." The Regent hadn't made an issue of Tunis, until Il'ar had suggested going directly to Grimval fortress. Since then Il'ar could see that it plainly grieved him to abandon his son.

"I'm sorry, Regent, but the faster we go towards Grimval, the faster the enemy chases us. Your son will be the safest among us." Il'ar could see his attempt at soothing words had had little effect. Disruption, upheaval, war, it illuminated the worst in mankind. Dealing with the pain was never easy. That was why in the East they fought no wars among themselves.

"Pass the word among the barge captains, we head for Grimval," ordered the Regent, relenting.

The troops began filing aboard.

—◦◦◦—

Sunlight filtered through gaps in the lean to. One persistent ray was warming Ham's eyelid and no amount of hand waving was going to dislodge it. Ham reluctantly opened his eyes. He had been having the most wonderful dream sitting on the right hand of Vlad, the Sun Father, as he passed judgment on the Central Landers. His brother, Shem, groveled on the floor at Ham's feet, looking much the same as he always did after a drunken revelry, begging for Ham to rescue him.

The present slowly supplanted Ham's dream. He looked around the edge of his lean to, surveying the camp. He had over a hundred of the Un Tier. He estimated that the Central Landers on the other side of the river had three times that number, but they were trying to hold off Baron Yakov's forces who had started out with an equal number of Central Landers plus five hundred of the Sol Dat. What Baron Yakov did not have was heavy infantry. All the remaining Un Tier were with Ham on this side of the river.

The flying mounts of the Easterners were troublesome, but switching to nighttime operations had neutralized their advantage, relegating it to a nuisance. A dangerous nuisance to be sure, but not the huge tactical force it could have been on the battlefield had they sufficient numbers. Ham searched the sky for the tell tale speck of the mounted watchmen. He saw none. Rising, he collapsed the lean to. There was no need to pack it. He would just erect another one when needed. Ham was rapidly gaining an appreciation for the methods the Un Tier employed in the field. Travelling light, no bulky cumbersome wagons stretching out for leagues behind them, now that was the way to fight a war. As long as it was a quick one. This night Ham intended to shorten the duration. "Clan Leader U'cha, get 'em up and get 'em going. We're moving out."

"The light still shines, soft skin Ham. We'll be seen," came the growling hiss of U'cha nearby.

"Yes. I'm counting on it. Let them see—-and fear."

"Up! Up and on for the glory of Mieze and the Sun Father," bellowed U'cha with his hissing laugh. The march to the bridge had begun.

Ham watched a single speck orbit on the east side of the river tracking their progress. Half a candlemark later it was replaced by another as the first went to report speed and movement of Ham's forces. Ham chuckled, "That didn't take long."

⸺◦/◦/◦⸺

In the very back of Shem's mind tucked safely away in a corner that he had claimed over twenty cycles ago, Vlad witnessed the start of the heroic attack of Shem against the two Free Goatherders. He had felt the mysterious pull inside of Shem and Mieze had directed him to determine the source and strength of this power. Vlad wasn't sure, but he thought he had detected a moment of sharp concern from his goddess. *If this... pull.. or whatever it was, elicited fear from his goddess then Shem must be prevented from acquiring it.* At the moment, it appeared the Free Goatherders were going to do just that.

The moment the Pointer touched Shem's hand a blinding whiteness streaked with green flashed across Vlad's consciousness and completely surrounded the bond. Only being engaged with the Auge Ose saved his bond from being burnt out of Shem's mind, that, and the fact that the bond had been made so early, and buried so deep, Shem's mind no longer considered it foreign.

The eye of Mieze reacted instantly with an angry red glow of power that reinforced Vlad's will, enough to protect him. The bond of Vlad was now tightly sealed with no access to Shem's will, rendering it nearly useless. Vlad withdrew.

"Sun Father." The voice of the Goddess Mieze implanted itself in Vlad's being. "The one called Shem is now in possession of the Gedeelte, a portion of the Hjerte. He will be going to the place called Grimval. He cannot yet control what he has. He must be stopped before he discovers how."

⟞⟋⟋⟍⟋⟍⟋⟍⟍

The awareness eased itself into Ham's thoughts. They hadn't been on the march for a candlemark yet, and still had two more before the sun set. Ham hoped to be far enough along by then to let the Un Tier rest during the light of Fiona. U'cha had been insistently suggesting it, claiming that the silvered light would rob the Un Tier of their power. Ham had reluctantly given in, remembering how fast his forces would move under the red light of Mieze.

"Ham," came the calm voice of Vlad. "Your brother has become a problem."

Become? He always has been. Ham sniggered.

"Your opportunity has arrived. The chance for personal satisfaction and the favor of the goddess. This is what you will do."

Ham listened intently. From time to time the ghost of a smile snuck through his solemn demeanor. Orders issued, Vlad departed the mind of his tool. Ham's mission had changed. There would be no resting during Fiona's moon.

The grumbling of the Un Tier began just after sunset. They had been setting a steady pace for the Easterners to report. With the darkness Ham increased it. He had to fulfill Vlad's plan before Baron Yakov became aware that he had arrived at the estate. There being no Central Landers on this side of the river to oppose him, Ham continued to push the Un Tier under the silvered light of Fiona. "There will be glory in the end, Clan Leader. Glory you won't have to share with anyone, even me."

The thought tamped down the dissent and U'cha began a low guttural song of praise to Mieze. It was taken up by the rest of the clan. The candlemarks sped by as did the leagues between the clan and the bridge. With the rising of Mieze the bridge came into sight.

Ham declared, "Clan Leader, you have done well. Even under the cursed silver light, the clan has made better time than last night. You have earned the right to be first."

"What will the soft skin Ham be doing?" asked U'cha.

"The Sun Father has given me a task. From this point on, you command," said Ham. He paused as U'cha absorbed the fact. A thought occurred to him, a way to keep ahead of Baron Yakov. "A suggestion if I may, burn it to the ground."

U'cha strode a few steps onto the bridge, which arced up over the river high enough to allow barge traffic to travel beneath it. He turned and faced his people just as Mieze cleared the horizon bathing all in its menacing red light and silhouetting the clan leader.

"Clan U'cha, Blessed Mieze and the Sun Father have ordered all to bow. All shall bow! Or face the wrath of Mieze and Clan U'cha."

The clan cheered. The noise was deafening, alerting those at the estate that their doom approached. U'cha turned and as one the clan swept up and over the bridge. Ham followed at a more sedate pace.

He knew that the clan would encounter an empty estate. The Sun Father had told him that the Central Lander force had evacuated earlier during the sunlight hours leaving just a shell behind. His countrymen had done nothing but run since the beginning. *If this is all they are capable of, they deserve this fate.* Ham crossed the bridge and turned towards the dock. He hoped the enemy had not been too efficient in destroying everything left behind. He needed something that would float.

His search ended about halfway down the docks. A dory, a high walled two-seater, was tied to the wharf with only its prow visible above the water. Ham seized the prow and rolled it over. The bottom had been stoved in, but not too badly He could patch it up enough to limit the leak while retaining visible damage. He grasped the dory with both hands and heaved it up out of the water.

The ease with which the boat left the river surprised Ham, nearly toppling him over backwards. He had expected much more resistance from the water. He looked up at Mieze. It was larger than he had ever seen it. The light reflected a more distinct red that he had ever experienced. It made his body tingle. He felt more alive at this moment than any other in his life. Under the light of Mieze, there was nothing he could not do. Ham threw back his head, raised his arms, and howled; his voice joined the cacophony of the U'cha clan as it ran rampant through the estate grounds. Regent Hap Simon's manor house caught fire adding its light to the night sky as Ham slipped his hastily repaired dory into the river and headed south.

I'con and Lieutenant Cutler stood at attention before Baron Uri Yakov enduring a blistering barrage of profanity laced epitaphs. Uri described at great lengths what would be happening to their dead bodies should they fail him again. "All they know how to do is run! Catch them!"

"What of their troops behind us? They could fall on our rear," began Lieutenant Cutler.

"What of them?" interrupted Uri, "Do you think I am concerned? I am not. We must overwhelm those that are before us and quickly. Now prepare to move out."

"But our troops need to rest. We've been on the march the entire night," said Lieutenant Cutler.

Uri knew this to be true. The Sol Dat forces were gaining strength and stamina with each passing turning. Uri had only managed to keep up with Enri's force because of them. Traveling at night, their speed outmatched those of the Central Landers, but with the rising of the sun the Westerners had to stop and wait for Lieutenant Cutler's people to catch up. This turning had been no different except Enri had called up barges and the Central Landers had escaped southward in the interim. The Sun Father was not going to be pleased. Uri did not look forward to that conversation. He had to do something. Something he didn't like. Split his forces, again.

"They'll get no rest this turning. Have them start making rafts. They can rest when they get these rafts on the river. I'con, mid-turning you take the Sol Dat and get to the manor. I want that entire estate burning. I want to see it light up the night sky."

"Yes, milord," they said and left the tent, glad to be away from the irate baron.

It's too bad you didn't join us, Enri, but no matter. I'll catch you now. Since the first encounter outside of High City, led by Enri, his countrymen hadn't proven willing to stand before Uri and his army. They were especially unwilling to stand against the Un Tier. If it hadn't been for the Easterners and their flying mounts Enri wouldn't have survived that encounter, or if the Sun Father hadn't insisted he keep the bulk of his brutish warriors on the West side of the river Uri would have crushed his once friend. *Maybe I give Enri too much credit. It may be the Easterner. Enri would have stood firmly believing that Fiona would give him the victory.*

"Baron Yakov, attend me." Vlad had arrived.

Uri winced. The Sun Father had not bothered to ease in. He was just there. Uri knew he was in trouble, again.

"You have failed me soft skin. Your countrymen still live."

"Not as many and those that do continue to flee south. Soon there will be nowhere else to go. They will have to fight. I have a plan."

Uri steeled himself as Vlad none too gently probed his mind for the details of his plan. Vlad saw that the funnel of the river valley had only one destination. The fortress of Grimval, his final destination. Moving by land and river would drive the soft skins there the sooner.

"Very well. I have sent out a calling. Reinforcements will be arriving soon. And soft skin, this is your last chance." Vlad withdrew.

Uri waited for the blinding flash of pain that usually accompanied Vlad's mercy. He was not disappointed. Picking himself up off the ground he finally exhaled, irritated that he was relieved. What was Vlad reducing him to? In the private part of his mind he thought, *There will be a day of reckoning, Sun Father!*

The Sol Dat left at mid turning followed by Uri's horsemaster and what mounts they had left. He was to keep up with the Westerners as best he could. So far there had not been any of the Eastern watchers in the sky and Uri hoped it remained that way. He was getting tired of everybody and their brothers watching his every move, assessing every action he took. He even found himself thinking that perhaps... *squash that thought!* He could not afford to let even a lingering hint of regret escape what little part of his mind he had walled off for himself.

The building of the rafts took the rest of the turning. The first one, carrying Uri, didn't push off until nearly nightfall. They poled southward during the light of Fiona which had waned a bit of late, at least in comparison to the increasing size and brightness of her sister moon, Mieze, which simply dominated the night sky in size and brilliance. The rising of Mieze emphasized the reddish yellow glow ahead of him. Reaching upward from the surface like an outstretched hand in eager anticipation of the Westerner's goddess. It grew larger as he grew nearer.

A candlemark later, he was floating under the stone bridge of Hap Simon's estate. The smell of ashes and burning timbers had long overtaken the river smells of decaying vegetation and green algae. Mingled with the odors of burning, the acrid taste of smoke clung to his clothes, hair, and tongue as the constantly shifting breeze brought drifts of smoke across him. Through it all the manor and all its outbuildings blazed providing contrast to the increasing angry red tint of Mieze. Above the crackling and popping of the flames carried the shouts of Sol Dat combating the bellows of Un Tier.

"Lieutenant Ham should know better than to let them sack the place, they need to keep moving!" he said aloud even though it had been his very intention to do the same thing. He yelled to the raft behind him. "Put to shore. Take a break. I'll be back shortly."

Uri tied up at the next pier and climbed ashore. Skirting around the smashed and charred detrius of wanton destruction that littered the pathways of the estate, he headed in the direction of the loudest bellows. He found Clan Leader U'cha and Clan Leader I'con arguing hotly while the estate burned all around them.

"U'cha commands! U'cha clan will stay until nothing stands!"

"The soft skin baron says follow the running rabbits until they stand or go to ground!"

"We stay!" said U'cha.

Uri confronted his clan leaders. "Where is Lieutenant Ham?"

"Soft skin Ham gave U'cha command. Soft skin Ham had a task," said U'cha.

Uri pondered the response. *A task. His own or for someone else?* He didn't bother asking U'cha. The Clan Leader would only know what Ham had told him. He heard the whicker of horses outside the flickering light of the flaming manor. That decided him.

"Stay here until I return. Send someone to the horse master and tell him I want his best mount," he spoke to both clan leaders, letting them decide who had received the order, then left for the river. He found Lieutenant Cutler at the pier where he had tied his own raft. "You command. Float until daybreak then beach and hide the rafts. I'll find you then."

"Yes milord," said Cutler.

Uri returned to his clan leaders. The estate would probably burn for another candlemark or two, but he had seen enough. He had to keep moving. *There is a growing list of only partial enjoyments from my victories.* He mounted the waiting horse. "We follow the enemy while the light of Mieze shines. South for her glory!"

The Westerners gave a mighty cheer and headed down the road at a brisk pace following Baron Uri Yakov. *When I catch you, Ham, it had better be a good tale.*

21

GRIMVAL

The exhilaration of being aloft, free of the confines of the surface, with the wind in one's hair and the majestic view, were lost on Shem during the flight to Grimval. Not even the soaring heights of Mount Fiona, which they had to fly around, moved him. He did catch glimpses of bliss on the faces of Selene and Ip'star, but his thoughts had dwelt mainly on the words of His Holiness and Priest Ro Ber. The power of the Pointer could be used up or taken by Tierra and Mieze's plan of making the hero waste what he had. Even his newfound confidence hadn't been able to totally suppress that kernel of doubt. *Wybee will be in Grimval. He can talk to Tierra. She will know.* Armed with that knowledge Shem pressed on. Finally events were going his way.

"Come. Come. Come to me. Come to Grimval."

Shem looked around for the source of the compelling call. He was about to answer when he realized that it came from within him. It didn't feel like any of the times Vlad had spoken to him. His voice was harsh, usually derisive or demeaning. *Was it Tierra?* Whomever it was, Shem put it out of his mind. He was already on his way to Grimval.

One mountain looked much the same as another to Shem as they continued basically eastward following the Little River as it carved its way through the foothills of the Goddess Fangs. The only change to the monotony was when they spied three groups of river craft rowing towards Mill Town for all they were worth. Ya Ma dropped back beside Shem pointing to the craft.

"Soldiers of Baron Reis. For half a moon they have tried to push through our land. For half a moon they have failed. Watch, Protector. See where the river narrows ahead of them? How the cliffs overhang? That's where the trap will be sprung."

The lead boat swept into the narrow passageway. Like a swarm of hungry gnats a volley of arrows rained down on the boat from the cliffs. The second and third boats tried to veer out of the passage. Chaos ensued. The narrow passageway soon resembled a Gergens Knot as the group franticaly tried to avoid entering the passageway with its hail of death from the cliffs, but the river current was every much an enemy as the Free Goatherders. Ships from the following groups accordianed into narrowing passageway causing all the craft to slow. More arrows flew from the cliffs, some trailing the glitter of fire. One by one the boats burst into flame. The men on board leapt from the craft looking like ants boiling out of their mounds. None survived. The Free Goatherders had held the river.

"Baron Reis continues to try, but we will not let him or his men cross our lands," said Ya Ma.

Then the mountains quit, sloping down to a wide valley where the confluence of the Little River and the Majestic River gave birth to Mill Town. Barges plying upriver strung out in a long line as they poled their way against the current. Keeping pace along the river road were mounted soldiers. Shem knew that they were headed for the fortress at the foot of the Grimval Falls. Everybody was. He did have to admit that the retreat was orderly. The populace gave way to the soldiers parting before them and then reforming after they had passed. Why people allowed themselves to be herded instead of dispersing to the countryside was beyond the understanding of Shem. It certainly would have made the soldiers travel easier. Reaching the Grimval River, the group swung southwards and would have rapidly outpaced the soldiers below, but Ip'star slowed up.

Rising from the valley floor was an eastern mount. It climbed swiftly up to join the group. Ip'star led them in a lazy circle waiting for the scout to join them. Ahern, lieutenant to Il'ar sat the mount.

"The stars shine brightly, Ip'star," he said.

"Never so brightly as upon you," responded Ip'star.

Ahern bowed in acceptance of the praise. "Were that it were so. Il'ar would know if all is well?"

"I've seen brighter days," said Ip'star, "but not many."

He waved as Ahern peeled away and descended towards the mounted column. The report complete, Ip'star led the group in a direct path towards Grimval's fortress.

The good graces of Cyst had kept Shem within earshot of the Eastern pair. He hadn't been fooled by their charming manner and he knew that more had been said than the mere words he had overheard. He quickly caught up after the meeting had been concluded. "What troubles you, Ip'star?"

Shem had noticed the change in the way Ip'star looked at him the moment he sat with the Council during the last meeting. It was as if Ip'star had been looking for something in Shem and had finally found it. Shem felt a justification. He hoped his new respect would overcome the reluctance the Easterner had been concealing. Not receiving a reply from his first question, he tried a different tack.

"Why have there been no scouts til now?" Shem asked. "I would have thought that you at least posted outriders."

"I can only surmise that reinforcements have not arrived," said Ip'star with a shrug. He added, "We can expect a visit from Il'ar soon."

"Would it have anything to do with brighter days?"

"If your wits are as sharp as your ears, Il'ar is going to have to make some adjustments," chuckled Ip'star.

The glistening rainbow which perpetually hung over the Grimval Falls announced the end of the flight. Below a makeshift tent city was springing up as the Central Landers who had been fleeing the coming of Mieze and the Westerners finally found themselves with nowhere else to run. The city filled the valley floor on both sides of the river and was slowly spreading up the slopes of the heavily forested mountains. But dominating all was the sprawling stone fortress of Grimval which began at the foot of the falls.

The main gate was on a rocky islet in the middle of the river. Over topping it on each side was a gate tower extending three heights of men. It was filled with bow windows and arrow slits. Atop each of the towers sitting behind the crenellated battlements was an arbalest capable of throwing a small tree. A curtain wall spanned the river on each side of the main gate, arches built into the walls to allow river traffic during times of peace, but which were now closed, barred by wooden portcullises. Drum towers secured the corner rising fang-like on either bank of the river, many tens of heights of men, filled with arrow slits promising a rain of death in any direction, and guarded the portage gates on the shore sides as well as the curtain wall, which ended at the base of the cliff. It was the cliff faces that made the fortress at Grimval unique in all the Central Lands. As the portage roads made their way switching back and forth up the cliff side, they were periodically protected by walls most with small turrets serving not only to provide covering fire for road travelers, but also to hide the numerous caves, which honeycombed the cliff. At the top a series of crane-like structures protruding over the cliff expedited the raising and lowering goods not ported by wagons and looking for all the world like saliva dripping from the tusks of an Un Tier. Indeed, from the air, the entire complex resembled the gaping maw of a hungry predator.

Selene pulled up alongside Shem. "That gives a whole new meaning to 'Grimval'" she said, shivering.

"Why don't the barons allow the people in?"

"The high priestess bid them to close the valley to the converted," she said.

Shem persisted. If these people were still there when Yakov arrived the valley floor would become a massacre field. "How are they supposed to do that?"

"I don't know," she said.

Ip'star and Ya Ma dropped back even with Shem and Selene. Ip'star led them into a lazy spiral as he searched for a place to land. Below their arrival in the skies before Grimval had caused a stir. Men had begun gathering on the battlements, stringing their bows. Ip'star kept them well out of range. Selene pointed down to the docks which were empty except for one barge that looked to be decked out more for pleasure than commerce.

"How about the docks?" she asked.

Ip'star shook his head, "The horses would cause too much of a commotion. Let's swing towards the fringes and find a place."

"Drop me off here," said Shem. "I'm going to the main gate and see what they have to say."

It wasn't really an order, but Ip'star wasn't going to gainsay the Hero of Tierra. He led them down low, over the river and landed on the docks next to the pleasure barge. As he had suspected, curious people started gathering to stare in disbelief at the winged horses. Shem and Selene dismounted.

Shem asked Selene. "Where are you going?"

"Someone has to look out for you," she said.

"I couldn't think of anyone I'd rather have than you," said the tiny voice of the Nem Elt-til who had climbed out of Shem's stone pouch and had flown up to his shoulder. He eyed the winged horses as they leapt up into air, "Show offs," he muttered.

Shem asked innocently, "What was that?"

"I said, let's go do some heroing," he replied.

Selene smiled, "What a cute little man."

"Did ya hear that, Hero?" said the Nem Elt-til puffing up.

Shem felt a twinge of emotion. *Am I jealous?* He put the thought out of his mind as he led them to a bridge at the base of the curtain wall. The refugees parted before them creating a clear path. He contemplated trying the portage gate. *No, I'll not enter the back door like a servant or a common merchant.* The bridge rose over the culvert and ended up on the berm. He looked up at the hoarding suspended over the outer curtain wall and noted the Valley men watching them from the murder holes between the buttresses. *This will be a tough nut for the Westerners to crack.* They made it to the gate house as the last rays of the setting sun were vanishing over the mountain tops.

The huge gates rose half the height of the curtain wall and were made out the fire resistant timber that Grimval was famous for. They were closed tight. Shem couldn't see, but felt positive that the portcullis behind it was down and secured as well. The only other entry was a postern gate, little more than a door built into the main gate to allow entry of a few without opening the larger gates. He looked up to the top of the gate house and called out, "Gatemaster! Two for entry."

"Three," said Nem Elt-til.

"Shut up," said Shem.

"None may enter," came down from the top of the gate house. Shem saw a smallish nondescript man staring down, "by order of the Cap Tan unless they can prove that they are not converted."

Cap Tan? Do they have the heir as well as Wybee? Shem's hopes rose. "I am Shem, Hero of Tierra!"

"Good for you, but words are not proof. Be gone!" Shem heard the sniggering laughter of the fortress defenders. He puffed up.

"I am Selene, First Acolyte. I would speak with Priest Fitzpatrick," called up Selene, stifling Shem's angry retort.

"I'm sure you would, First Acolyte," the Gatemaster called down with more respect than he had offered Shem. "Come back with the rising of the sun."

Shem extended his senses. *There! And that one as well.* "I sense two, Nem Elt-til. Behind the second merlon on my side, the third merlon on your side," said Shem softly.

"I agree, Hero. Whack attack?"

Shem considered it for a moment, then said, "There's no way to prove it until Mieze rises. I say we come back then."

"Spoilsport," said the Nem Elt-til.

Decision made, Shem called up to the recalcitrant keeper of the gates, "We will be back, Gate Master." He led Selene back to the bridge as the Gate Master returned to his gate tower.

"Where to now?" asked Selene.

Shem felt confident that the big barge at the docks was the barge the heir had arrived on. Hopefully there would still be someone on board. "Back to that fancy barge,"

Worrel answered their hail and allowed them on board where they found a woman approaching middle cycles who called herself Na Na. They were soon joined by Ip'star, Ya Ma, and Il'ar who sniffed the air as he met Shem. Shem had no personal recollection of their first encounter, but he had heard. He vacillated between irritation and embarrassment. Na Na was visibly impressed by the assemblage. She had never before come into contact with people of such high stature until the last turning. Since then, everyone she met had been or would be a mover and shaker of events. She was giddy breathing the rarified air.

"I knew there was something about Jonathon," she said. "He was so much more serious than other boys his age. And to find out he was the Cap Tan, well, you could imagine my surprise."

Shem stated the obvious, "Yet, you were not allowed entry,"

"It all happened so fast," said Na Na. "Captain Worrel tied up at the dock. By the time we finished, Priest Fitzpatrick and a representative from the barons were already aboard. When they found out who Jonathon was they whisked him and the body of his grandmother away. Jonathon insisted that Wybee be taken as well."

"That makes sense," said Il'ar who was familiar with court protocol, "but the proof requirement seems stringent."

"Jonathon's grandmother was killed in front of his very eyes by converts on this barge," informed Worrel quietly.

Shem asked softly, breaking the reverent silence caused by the last statement. "What about Wybee?"

"Something has overcome the lad. I'm not sure what," said Na Na. "He collapsed one morning and has yet to fully recover."

Ya Ma had sat quietly up to this point. The closest he had come to breaking out of his demeanor had been when Shem recounted the Gate Master's words.

"What will you do now, Protector?" he asked.

"Now, I intend to sleep. At the rise of Mieze I'm going back to the gate." Shem briefly outlined his discovery of two of the converted on the castle walls and what he was going to do about it.

"It sounds risky, Hero," said Il'ar still hesitating slightly at the term.

"Go for a weapon," challenged Shem. "If you beat me to it, I'll listen."

The two men locked gazes. Shem waited motionless. Il'ar made a move. His hand had travelled mere inches before he was looking cross eyed at Shem's knife hovering under the tip of his nose.

"A true warrior does not need a demonstration, Protector," chided Ya Ma.

Shem's eyes never wavered from Il'ar's. "It would seem I owe you an apology, Hero," said Il'ar calmly.

Shem put his knife away chastised by Ya Ma's lesson. "And I, you, Il'ar."

"Captain Worrell if you would permit me the use of your cabin I would greatly appreciate it," said Selene.

"Of course, First Acolyte, but I have turned it over to Lady Na Na," he replied.

Na Na blushed at being called a Lady, "You go right ahead, dear," she said.

——⟨⟨⟨⟨⟩⟩⟩⟩——

Selene went into the cabin and closed the door. Inside she pulled the box containing her spider out of the sleeve and opened the lid. She noted the bright sheen of the web and concentrated on Priest Fitzpatrick. The web faded briefly before returning to its original luster.

"Priest Fitzpatrick, First Acolyte Selene from High City. We are at the Cap Tan's barge. We have been denied entry."

"It's not surprising, sister. The young Cap Tan is adamant about keeping converts out of the fortress. Witnessing the death of his grandmother has affected his judgment, at least for now."

"Now when we need it most."

"Sister, if our tasks were easy they would not be worth doing."

"Yes, Priest Fitzpatrick. We will be returning to the gate with the rising of Mieze. The Hero plans a demonstration. It would be beneficial, perhaps, if you were there to witness."

"I will do what I can, sister."

"Has there been any word from the high priestess or Priest Duran?"

"None that would be uplifting or helpful this night. I am sorry," replied the priest.

Selene bowed her head in disappointment. She said a brief prayer to Fiona and one to Tierra as well. She knew that Fiona would not mind. She said nothing else as the web slowly faded with the breaking of the contact. Selene returned to the deck of the barge.

Shem had already fallen asleep, curled up in an out of the way section of the deck. Ya Ma and the Easterners were comparing notes with Worrell on the state of the retreat and the moral of the army. Selene declined to join and walked to the stern of the craft. She admired the soft silvery glow of Fiona's light as it bathed the countryside which was just now starting to flicker with the pinpricks of cooking fires. She started at the tiny voice on her shoulder.

"I feel that I should have a memory of the flickering lights, but I do not," said the Nem Elt-til wistfully.

"Fireflies. It reminds me of fireflies. Their backsides glow with the setting of the sun. It is believed to attract the attention of the opposite sex."

"If your backside was to glow, it would definitely attract my attention," said the Nem Elt-til. "But tonight I fear the attention being attracted means to take life, not give it."

Selene smiled at the compliment. "You're incorrigible, but unfortunately correct. Will Shem be able to do it?"

"That depends on what *it* is, I suppose. He will easily accomplish the death of the two converts. If he doesn't I will. Will he accomplish the awakening? That's why he was chosen," the Nem Elt-til looked slyly at Selene. "Will he capture your heart? If he doesn't, I will!"

Selene laughed at the audacity of the little man, but in her heart she rooted for Shem.

⸺◦/◦/◦⸺

Shem awoke the moment the red tinge of Mieze became apparent. He rose and stretched the kinks out of his muscles. Looking towards the north he noticed that Mieze had not yet broken the horizon. *When it does it will shock us.* He couldn't explain how he knew, but he did. He moved swiftly across the deck waking the party. Ya Ma was already awake.

"You risk much, Protector," said Ya Ma.

Shem challenged, "Do you have a better way?" Ya Ma remained silent. Shem continued, "Dare to win."

Il'ar approached. "Hero, I would have a new first impression," he said extending his hand.

Shem clasped the forearm of the Easterner. He agreed, "I as well, Il'ar,"

"Then let us make one," said Il'ar.

They bid farewell to Worrell and Na Na. As they stepped onto the dock making their way to the bridge Mieze began to rise above the horizon. The sky became a battle ground between the normal darkness and the redness of Mieze. There was no contest.

"Fiona, preserve us!" gasped Selene looking back.

Shem looked back. He froze. Mieze had nearly doubled in size since it's last rising. It would fill nearly a fifth of the sky when it rose to its full. Shem could feel the oppression and doubt emanating from the goddess's orb. He knew it would only grow stronger, sapping the strength of her enemies while strengthening the will of her followers.

"Protector, your time has come," said Ya Ma breaking the spell.

Resolved, Shem again led the group to the bridge. He felt his steps were slower than before as he struggled against the will of Mieze. He felt doubt trying to find a firmer foothold within himself. He gritted his teeth and continued on. *I will not fail!* By the time they reached the main gate Mieze was halfway through its rising. The stars faded before her approach, as all traces of the silvery goodness of Fiona was overpowered by the evil redness. Shem stood as he had before and hailed the gate.

"Gatemaster, I would have entry!" His words seemed weak even to his ears. He hailed again, stronger this time. "Gatemaster, come forth!"

The guards manning the battlements were the first to present themselves. Shem quickly found the two converted. They manned the same positions as before. Shem reached up and unwound the sling wrapped around his forehead. He reached into his pouch and selected two stones.

"Hey! Be careful," cried the Nem Elt-til climbing out of the pouch and flying up to Shem's shoulder. He glanced up at Mieze then up at the gatehouse and its two towers. "Great, I take a nap and everything goes to..."

"Why do you disturb my rest, Hero?" sneered the Gatemaster from above. "Have you found your proof?"

"I have. Observe."

He dropped the sling to its full length, spun, and released. The second stone dropped into the pouch. Shem spun and released. Despite the evil influence of Mieze, the action had been faster than the eye could follow, but not fast enough to prevent the second convert from firing his bow. The first stone flew true, striking the guardsmen in the temple below his helmet. He collapsed behind the merlon. The second passed the arrow on its way down striking the convert squarely between his eyes. He disappeared behind the merlon. Shem raised his arm. An instant before the arrow struck home a shield materialized on Shem's arm deflecting the arrow, which would have impaled the Nem Elt-til, up and away from the party.

"Hero, you scare me," said the Nem Elt-til.

"Take aim!" screamed the Gatemaster.

"Hold!" came the commanding voice of Shem.

From behind the merlons where the converted had fallen rose a wisp of smoke then a flash as their bodies burned to ash.

Shem called out, "There is your proof, Gatemaster. That which you would prevent is already among you!"

"That proves nothing, Hero," screamed the Gatemaster.

"Hero, bi-ig problem. Those weren't the only two. Not now," said the Nem Elt-til glancing up at Mieze.

"Gatemaster." The voice of Priest Fitzpatrick gripped the attention of the Gatemaster, barely. "It proves the Hero knows who is enemy. Which is more than I can say for you."

Shem ignored the priest and the Gatemaster. "Selene, warn them. There are more among them. I know who they are. This is their last chance to live, to reaffirm Fiona or Tierra. Do it now."

Selene stepped forward. There was no denying Shem's request even though it was the job of Priest Fitzpatrick to call for repentance. Shem placed his hand on her shoulder. She began with a trembling voice, choked by the power of Mieze, but each word became stronger and stronger feeding off itself and Shem and the Pointer.

"Soldiers of Grimval, heed me. Your hearts are troubled. Your eyes see Mieze as they have never seen it before. Your minds doubt all that you have been told or taught your entire lives. You know the true path. Do not doubt! Do not disbelieve. Confirm Fiona in your hearts or confirm Tierra who seeks to rise among us. Do it now or suffer the fate of those two who were among you."

Selene's voice faded to silence. The soldiers in the fortress looked around. Some had fallen to their knees, others just looked confused, many fired their bows in defiance. Shem raised both arms into the air palms outward in a warding gesture.

He bellowed, "No arrows will strike this night!"

The Pointer flared bright green cutting through the bloody red murk of the night air. The air pulsed. The streaking arrows skipped away at the last moment as they encountered the will of Shem made solid above their heads. The air pulsed a second time, rippling up and through the fortress, leaving a series of red flashes in its green wake beginning with the Gatemaster. It was all over in seconds. Mieze cleared the horizon hanging angry and red above the scene as if gloating over the death that had been brought about because of her and promising more.

"Open the gate," ordered Priest Fitzpatrick.

Il'ar placed his hand on the shoulder of Shem. "Impressive, Hero."

Shem felt anything but impressive. He hadn't consciously called on the Pointer. It had acted on its own in response to Shem's need. At the time Shem had no idea what was going to happen only that he needed to protect his friends and expose the converted. He also felt a little drained. *How much of the Pointer was used? How much remains?* There had to be a way to control the output of the Pointer, to direct its power instead of simply unleashing it. *Wybee will know. He can ask Tierra. He has to!* The postern door opened. A man stood before it wearing the plain brown robe of an initiate. He placed his hands palms together and bowed deeply to Shem.

"The One and his party may enter."

———

The dim light of the brazier did little to lighten the dark of the room nor did it completely dispel the chill of the harvest season. The healer bathed the forehead of the slight form lying on the bed before her, wiping away the vestiges of the fever-like symptoms that still had Wybee in its grip. The onset of the fever had begun with the fading of Fiona in the night sky. Surprisingly, Wybee didn't feel sick, only weakened. A slow steady drain of his energy.

"I am sorry, Wybee."

The words were a whisper barely discernible. Wybee's pulse quickened. It had been several turnings since he had felt her stir within his mind and even longer since she had spoken.

"Tierra!" he said. In his mind he shouted it out with joy, but to the ears of the healer it was a low pitched mumble.

"The Hero nears. He has the Gedeelte. This night will be hard on you."

The voice vanished. Weak as it had been, it lightened Wybee's mood. *Tierra is still alive. The Hero's coming. All will be well.* In his excitement he completely disregarded the warning. Above the constant rumble of Grimval Falls, he heard raised voices shouting from the gate house. His eyes fluttered open.

"Rest, child. It's just someone contesting with the Cap Tan's ruling. They will soon depart," said the healer.

Wybee felt a pulse of energy pass him, energy that felt like Tierra but slightly different. "Whom do you serve?" it demanded as it swept by. On the heels of the questing pulse of energy Wybee screamed as he felt another chunk of his life's essence depart from him. The healer ran from the room.

Priest Fitzpatrick arrived a short while later. Following in the priest's footsteps was Jonathon, concern etched on his face. Priest Fitzpatrick held back, allowing the two friends time alone.

"Wybee, it's me Jonathon. Can you hear me?" he asked taking Wybee's hand in his.

Wybee gave the hand a weak squeeze. He managed to whisper, "The hero is come."

"Yes, he is here. A big strapping warrior with chips of flint for eyes and a hard voice, asking for you. I will send him in, but first I wanted to see if you were well. You had another one of those spells, didn't you?"

Wybee gave Jonathon's hand another weak squeeze. He didn't want to tell Jonathon what he was now beginning to suspect. That he had misunderstood his purpose. Yes, he was to be Tierra's voice for the Hero, but that was secondary. "I would like to see him, Jonathon. Finally. I would like to know what took him so long!"

Jonathon smiled down at his friend, recognizing the attempt at humor though the delivery was barely audible.

"Okay, Wybee. I'll send him in. He cleared the fortress of converts. He can make sure we are safe."

"That's good, Jonathon," said Wybee, releasing Jonathon's hand.

Jonathon turned to leave. On his way out, he admonished Priest Fitzpatrick, "Do not let Wybee over do it."

"As you will, Cap Tan," said Priest Fitzpatrick.

Shem entered as Jonathon left. He looked around the sparsely furnished room before centering his attention on the wan form lying on the bed. With a nod of acknowledgement, Priest Fitzpatrick made his way to the door. Shem walked to the foot of the bed to allow Wybee to see him without having to move.

"I'm Shem. So you are the one I've been searching for across half of the Central Lands. It's no wonder I've had such a hard time of it. There's not much of you to find," said Shem with a smile.

Wybee could feel the Pointer lying hidden under Shem's shirt. It strengthened him just to be near it. He started to rise to a sitting position. Shem came up to the head of the bed and rearranged the pillows for support. He took the chair at the side of the bed.

"I was told you were big and strong, with hard eyes and voice," said Wybee with a firmer voice than he had before. "I can see that you are big. I'm Wybee."

"Do not confuse size with strength, Wybee. A big man can be weak and a small lad can have the heart of the world."

Wybee smiled. "I believe that is what you are searching for, Hero." He felt good about the big man, could feel the goodness within him. *I can see why Tierra chose him.* Wybee probed a little deeper. There was more. Shem was troubled. His kindly cheerful manner masked a lingering doubt. Wybee knew what it was. He wondered if Shem would still have the courage when it came his time. *I wonder if I will.*

"And I believe that you are supposed to tell me where to go. Though to tell the truth that has been the job of my brother until lately. I didn't like most of the destinations he suggested," said Shem.

Amusement twinkled the eyes of Wybee. He was glad the hero had finally found him. He wished it had been sooner if only for the pleasant company. "That will be the easy part, Hero," said Wybee. "Everybody in this fortress knows where you need to go. The One has become part of their folklore."

"The One. That's what I need, another name. It's getting to the point that I don't know what to answer to," Shem sighed, "No one calls me Shem anymore."

"*Waa-a, Waa-a, Waa-a.* I'm really touched, Schlep," quipped the Nem Elt-til climbing out of Shem's pouch and flying to the edge of the bed.

"That's Shem," corrected Shem.

"Whatever, who's the kid?" asked the Nem Elt-til.

"Nem Elt-til." Wybee studied the little man intensely, recognizing him immediately for what he was. A creation of Tierra. *Probably designed for a specific purpose.* The Nem Elt-til returned the favor.

Wybee asked, "How many are you?"

"One at present," answered the Nem Elt-til, dropping the abrasive nature which he apparently reserved for Shem. "Many at need, though I'm no longer sure of that."

Wybee nodded his understanding. "I am Wybee. I am Tierra's voice for the Hero." He left off the rest of his thought, *When I'm not just a vessel, but if that is my purpose then so be it.* The Nem Elt-til flew up and perched himself on the pillow next to Wybee's ear. He spoke in low tones.

"I am honored, Brother. We all serve for her needs. Some more than others. Vaar Tu, Her vessel, I name you. Now, we have to take care of Bo Bo here."

Wybee giggled at the manner in which the little man treated Shem. He turned his attention to Shem as the Nem Elt-til flew off the pillow and up to Shem's shoulder. "I'm sure you have questions. Ask, Shem. I'll see if Tierra can answer them."

"She is still alive?" asked Shem speaking quickly, without thought, saying the first thing that came to his tongue.

"Alive? I would say that Tierra *is.* In answer to your question, yes, she still is."

"Can she teach me to control it?" asked Shem. There was no need to explain what 'it' was. Both knew.

"You would control a goddess? For that is what the Gedeelte is or at least a piece of her. None of the other stones have ever shed a piece. None of the other goddesses were willing to share such an intimate and uncontrolled piece of themselves. Free will." Wybee paused to catch his breath. "It does the will of the goddess, because it is the goddess, but on a smaller scale. You could possibly ask Tierra to tell it to do specific tasks, but she already knows what needs be done. You merely unleash her." Wybee noted the change in Shem's posture as frustration crept in. *That wasn't what Shem wanted to hear.*

"It would be nice to know what the result is going to be in advance," groused Shem. "The Council of the Free Goatherders fears that I will use it up before the awakening," said Shem. "They say I need to learn to husband its power."

Wybee sank back into his pillow. He could see that Shem feared the words of the Council. He wished he could reassure the big man. *Tierra, is it sufficient?*

"For the task? Yes, but the hero can call upon it for other uses. Already it is diverted, protecting him from his other bond. He must not repeat what he has done this night, otherwise it will have to be replenished... from other sources. My sister Mieze has set many difficulties in our path. Her Ascendency emboldens her. She has passed her increased power on to her followers in order to stop me, to stop my surrogates. That decision will cost many innocent lives. Perhaps even the hero's."

Perhaps even mine, thought Wybee.

"Yes. I am sorry, Wybee."

Wybee lie back deeper into his pillow, his eyes closed, his worst fears realized. The awakening of Tierra hung by a precarious thread. Keeping that thread intact would fall to Shem, whom Wybee now had to tell that the weapon the hero had been given could no longer be used without great sacrifice. He showed no trace of feelings when he spoke.

"Shem, Tierra says that the Pointer is sufficient for the completion of your duty. There is, however, a risk

"Then the Council was right," said Shem. "I could squander the Pointer."

"Yes."

—◁◉▷—

The dory leaked like a sieve and needed bailing again. The water level had reached the bench that Ham sat on and the side boards were sitting lower and lower. Soon it would capsize, but Ham couldn't bail nor could he use the makeshift oar for fear of the noise. The Central Lander barges were little more than a league ahead of him. Ham considered making for the west shore and abandoning the boat to continue on foot, but discarded the idea. It would take too long to make it to Grimval afoot. He simply did not have the time to spend waiting behind the Central Lander forces. So far, the night sky of Mieze had protected him from being discovered, but the dawning would arrive soon and Ham had to figure out a way to get in front of those forces undetected, preferably with the dory. The leaking boat made the decision for him.

Just before sliding under the water's surface Ham grasped the sides and rolled the boat over. Ham was pleased by the new strength he had under Mieze's red moon and the ease with which he accomplished the maneuver. Pulling the dory behind him he made for the west shore. When his feet touched the muddy bottom he pulled the dory over him and punched out the leaky patch to give him a field of vision. Staying just within the reedy growth along the bank Ham slowly walked upriver. His main concern was that someone would notice that the dory was drifting against the current. *If they would just beach the barges for a candlemark or two I could get ahead of them.*

His wish was granted a candlemark past dawn. Up ahead, Ham could see that the barges were headed for the eastern bank. He slowed his pace and crept on. The next two candlemarks passed with excruciating slowness, but Ham was finally able to get ahead of the Central Landers and out of sight ahead of them. He kept to the reeds and under the boat for the rest of the daylight hours. Still, he made good time.

At dusk, after resting a bit and taking time for a meal and to patch the boat once again, Ham took to the river. By the rising of Mieze he was nearing Grimval. He felt a surge of energy ahead him. The menace of the energy burst caused him to halt. He didn't know what had just happened, but whatever it was would have been deadly. This he knew. He rowed the boat to the west bank to see if it would be repeated. The voice of Vlad came to him.

"That was your brother, Ham," said the Sun Father. "That is but a sample of the power he now possesses. Had you been caught in it, you would have been destroyed utterly. You must make him use that power again. Every time he does it lessens his ability to bring about his goddess. She teeters on the edge of existence. Do not fear him, Mieze will protect you."

"Yes, Sun Father. I understand."

"Do not expect assistance from any converted in the fortress, there are none. Otherwise proceed as planned."

"Yes, Sun Father."

The presence of Vlad faded. Ham remained on the bank pondering the new information. He knew Shem would have been formidable even before the acquisition of his new found power. What he now counted on was that Shem would not be able restrain himself. *I will have to goad him into using his new weapon. It shouldn't be hard.* Not having any support inside the fortress was a different problem. Ham rested under the light of Mieze soaking in his own enhancement from his goddess.

A candlemark later Ham once again punched out the patch, turned the dory over and crawled underneath. He made his way along the bank towards the fortress until he came to the docks which served the unloading of cargo headed to the portage gates. Ham estimated the distance to the culvert leading into the fortress and decided that he could easily make the distance underwater. He also noticed that the number of guardsmen were steadily growing. Something was afoot. He couldn't stay where he was much longer without increasing the risk of discovery. Taking a deep breath he submerged and swam for the culvert.

He hadn't taken into account the increase of the current trying to squeeze a river through two narrow outlets. It hadn't been noticeable before. The docks had deflected some of current towards the center of the river, but the closer he had gotten to the islet which held the main gate and split the river in two the stronger the current became. The roar of falls filled his ears even underwater and each stroke was more difficult to call a gain. His breath was running out. He dare not surface for risk of discovery by the guardsmen on the wall and he dare not fail for fear of the Sun Father. He considered dropping the bundle draped around his neck containing his knives and sword. Surely it wouldn't be too difficult to find another. This was a fortress after all. Finally he saw the portcullis in his blurry vision. He surfaced nearly out of breath. The portcullis was inset into the wall providing him with cover from the guardsmen above him. He gripped the wooden bars to test them for strength. They broke with an audible snap. *Thank you, Mieze.* Ham knew no one had heard the sound. The roar of the falls covered up a multitude of sins. One could barely hear themselves think. He was glad that he did not work here as a guardsmen, but he supposed one got used to the sound and compensated for it in other ways; still, better to work at the top of the falls than the bottom, best yet, don't work anywhere near it.

Ham matter-of-factly broke off another section of the wooden river gate and squeezed through. On the other side he had a good look at what was ahead him. It was not promising. Both banks had steep sides reinforced with algae covered stone that would be wet and slick. There would be no scaling of those banks. On the shore side just past the culvert rose the tall tower, jutting into the river and filled with arrow slits. *The current will be strongest there.* Beyond the tower a bridge connected the islet to shore. There had to be a maintenance stair at the bridge. If there wasn't, he would be in trouble. Ham took a deep breath, ducked under the water, and kicked off.

The current was strong, but the strength he received from Mieze was stronger. He made it past the tower and kept going until he felt a lessening of the current. Surfacing, he found himself at the edge of the falls pond, where the swirling water had yet to organize into the current of the Grimval river. He looked up. He had passed the bridge, but not by much. As he had anticipated a stair had been cut out of the rock in order to allow work parties to make any necessary repairs to the bridge. He clambered ashore and stood dripping wet under the bridge. Satisfied, he thought to himself, *So far so good, but these wet clothes are going to be a problem.* The problem being he didn't have time to wait for them to dry.

At the top of the stairs Ham studied the night sky. He judged that he still had about two candlemarks left under Mieze. That should be enough to get him to the top of the falls and, he hoped, to safety for the daylight hours. He switched his gaze from the sky to the way before him. The path, it really wasn't big enough to be called a road, leading away from the bridge led to the portage road which could then be followed in a zig zag fashion up the cliff side. Traffic on the road was practically nonexistent only a stray pair or singular person making their way up or down the passageway which was wide enough for wagons to pass going each way. It appeared that shops and inns also lined the portage road once it started up the side of the cliff. The dripping of his wet clothes nearly stopped, Ham stepped out from under the bridge and started up the path. He quickly discovered that he need not have worried about his clothes. The mist hanging in the air from the falls would have dampened them anyway. The few people he passed, those not wearing a waterproof cloak, also had dampened clothes. Thankfully, in Ham's opinion, none of them seemed to pay him a thought.

A curtain wall with a solitary tower rose from the base of the cliff protecting the portage road and the structures behind it which were carved out of and into the cliff's face. They were not all inns or shops, barracks, armories, and even, *yes, bakeries!* were interspersed among them as well with an occasional market place. Behind their closed doors and with the mist of the falls hanging heavy in the air, Ham could smell spices and the beginning aromas of fried meat pies and breads being prepared for the coming turning's business. Nostalgia tugged at Ham as he remembered how after his time in the army he had wanted to become a shop keeper. *It can still happen,* he thought to himself. *After I take care of the problem my brother has become.*

"Ham?"

Shock, surprise, then wariness flashed through Ham jerking him out of his reveries. Familiarity tugged at his conscience. *I know that voice.* Slowly, Ham turned towards the voice calling to him, but not before he loosened the sword in his scabbard, which now hung from his waist. Recognition flooded through him. "Sheila! Thank the goddess, what are you doing here?"

22

ARMY ARRIVES AT GRIMVAL

The rising of the sun brought the first of the Central Lander barges around the bend. Regent Hap Simon stood amidships with Baron Enri Filip taking in the sight of the massive fortress with its fang-like towers and menacing open maw. The Regent shuddered. "I remember seeing the fortress for the first time when I was a child," he said to Enri, "It scared me witless. I refused to enter thinking it was going to devour me and I would have to spend the rest of my life in its bowels, but now I'm glad to see it."

"And I," replied Enri. His gaze shifted to the sprawling encampment before its walls. "I had hoped that Jonathon would have relented and allowed the people entry."

Hap sighed fighting back his disappoint with his grandson. *You have been taught better, child. I will set it to right.* "Priest Fitzpatrick says that Jonathon is adamant, though why they obey a child of nine cycles is something else that I intend to find out."

The arrival of the barges caused a stir in the populace. A few started following the barges towards the dock, spreading the word that the army was finally here to protect them. The few became many. By the time the Hap's barge reached the dock a crowd had gathered to see who would step off. As a deck hand scrambled to set the gangway in place Hap looked around for anyone from the fortress.

"It doesn't look like Jonathon sent anyone to greet us," remarked Enri.

Hap glanced up at the gatehouse. All he saw were guardsmen. *There! On the east tower gate.* Jonathon stood flanked by Barons Sulieman and O'Kelly. *Are they so fearful they won't even leave the fortress?* thought Hap. *Do they fear Yakov or the people, I wonder.* Hap looked to the Captain of the barge. "A fanfare if you please and announce me."

A blast from the horn of the bugler silenced the murmurings of the crowd. "Make way for the Regent Hap Simon of the Central Lands! Make way!"

The murmurings picked up again, though never quite reaching the level of a cheer. Hap wasn't sure whether to be pleased or alarmed. He stepped up to the gangway and raised his hands for quiet. "People of the Central Lands, the army arrives as I speak. We will make our stand here at Grimval. Baron Uri Yakov and his Western horde will go no further! This I swear! This I pledge to you! We will retreat no further!"

The noise of the crowd grew reaching the level of a cheer, just barely. *They would be happier if they were inside the walls,* thought Hap. He turned to Enri, "Have Sloan Quinn set up a perimeter at the bend in the river. On both sides, mind you. We will protect these people. They expect it of us."

"Aren't we going into the fortress? It would be much easier to defend the walls than it would the countryside," said Enri.

Hap glanced up at his grandson once again. The boy still hadn't moved from the tower gate. *I'm not sure what's going on with you, Grandson. I'm not sure you will even let us in.* "Yes, it would, but if we cannot gain entry for the people, we stay out. We have, what, two turnings?"

"Probably closer to one and a half. Those beasts move fast under their cursed moon," said Enri.

"Then tell Sloan to hurry. I'm going to the main gate and try to talk to my grandson." Hap strode down the gangway surrounded by five members of the Cap Tan's Hand and made his way towards the bridge. The people gave way before him. Crossing the bridge to the berm he looked up at the tower gate. Jonathon was gone. *I trust that means he will meet me at the gate.* Hap continued with his retinue until he stood before the main gate with his guards in formation behind him.

"Who stands before the gate?" called out the new Gatemaster.

Hap stood silent. He was Regent of the Central Lands. The fool of a Gatemaster had heard the crier announce him from the barge. He refused to beg to be let in to a fortress of his own land.

"Announce yourself by the command of the Cap Tan!" called down the Gatemaster.

Hap remained silent. Archers appeared along the crenellations though none nocked an arrow. Hap said softly "Stand easy, Lieutenant Gilroy. None will fire."

"Aye, Regent," said the lieutenant ensuring that his sword was loose in its scabbard. His men did the same.

Come to me, Jonathon, willed Hap. It seemed the moment stretched out for a candlemark, but it was actually only a heartbeat or two before the postern gate opened.

"Grandfather?" asked Jonathon.

Hap dropped to a knee and spread his arms wide in invitation, "Come here, son. It's alright now."

Hap hadn't really expected Jonathon to rush into his arms, but he had hoped. *There's too much hoping going on here. Not enough doing.* His expectations imploded with Jonathon's next words.

"It is well that you kneel before me," said Jonathon.

Anger, frustration, and finally pity flashed through Hap Simon's very soul. *This war has cost my grandson dearly. More than any child should have to pay in a lifetime! Damn you Uri Yakov! And your minions! I swear by the Blessed Fiona and the new Tierra, you will pay!* Hap rose swiftly, towering over his grandson. He studied his eyes, dismayed at the hardness he found there. He received a further shock when another figure stepped out of the postern and took up a defensive position behind Jonathon. It was a Free Goatherder. Hap directed his words as much to the Free Goatherder as he did to his grandson. "So, the Free Goatherders have already sent the Protector. I knelt as kin not as liege. Jonathon, if you would take the reins of leadership, be the Cap Tan, it will be before a Council of Barons. That is our law and not even the destruction of our people can alter it. Do as you will, but until then I am still Regent of the Central Lands."

"I hold the fortress. None may enter unless I am sure they have not converted. I am sorry, Grandfather. I will have no converted within these walls." Pain and conviction in equal measures were readily evident in the eyes and voice of Jonathon.

Once again pity filled Hap Simon. *At least he called me grandfather. He is not yet lost.* He knelt once more. "I kneel again as kin, grandson. Will you not embrace me?"

Jonathon hesitated, but only for a moment before walking into Hap's arms and putting his arms around him. Both slowly increased the pressure of the hug.

"You are only nine cycles, Jonathon. Are you sure this is the path you wish to travel?"

"Grandfather, I saw what they did to Grandmamma. They shot her down like a rabid animal! In the back! Before my very eyes. They were going to let her body just float away down the river!" sobbed Jonathon. "There will be no converted in the fortress. None may enter unless I am sure. None!"

Hap asked gently. He had to know the strength of Jonathon's resolve. "Not even I?"

"I'm sorry, Grandfather. I can see no other way."

Hap's heart nearly rent in two at his grandson's anguish. He felt the righteous anger burning within himself for the hurt caused. There was only one choice. "Then call a Council. Let's do it right. We can ill afford to be split at this time. If I may, do it quickly. The enemy is on our heels. We haven't much time."

Jonathon released his grandfather and stood back. He brushed his eyes with the back of his hand and stood straight. Hap rose as well. Jonathon spoke formally.

"I call a Council of the Barons. Here on this berm in one candlemark to declare as Cap Tan. Bring whom you will." The ritual words spoken, Jonathon turned and walked back into the fortress followed by Ya Ma.

Hap bowed his head to hide the tears that trickled down his cheek and turned away to return to the barge. The Cap Tan's Hand followed him.

On the way back to the barge Hap raged inside. Raged at the lost innocence of Jonathon, raged at Uri Yakov for starting this war, raged at the goddess, Mieze, for giving Uri troops, and most of all raged at himself for letting down his family. How did it ever come to this? Children weren't supposed to be left alone in this world unprotected. They weren't supposed to watch their grandparents murdered before their eyes, they weren't supposed to suffer, not like Jonathon suffered. It was obvious now that no one was going to enter the fortress that wasn't already there and he wasn't going to try to force the issue. They would just have to fight on the outside. And prospects weren't good. He hoped the fortress would provide covering fire with their arbalests. That would help some, but first things first. He had to prepare for the Council.

—◦◦◦—

Shem stood outside the main gate in the chill of the harvest morning watching as the tables were being set up for the Council of Barons. He fervently hoped that it would not be the charade that the Free Goatherder Council had been. He didn't believe that his patience would stand for another one of those. The precouncil meeting with Jonathon hadn't gone well. The boy Cap Tan had insisted, demanded, and then ordered him to use his power to cleanse the peoples outside the fortress. Shem had steadfastly refused giving no reason for his denial. He couldn't openly admit that his power was limited, it would devastate the morale of the Central Landers. They were calling him 'the One' while reassuring themselves that they were now invincible. How could they lose, the One is here. Our salvation has arrived, the One is here. Only the calming influence of Selene kept Shem from unloading on the boy ruler, that and he would have had to deal with Ya Ma who had taken up his position as Protectorate of the Office of the Cap Tan and was never far from the young ruler.

Beside Shem stood Selene. She split her time between Shem and Priest Fitzpatrick who had taken her under his wing after her short sermon before the gates. Shem wasn't sure, but he believed it had something to do with preparing her for elevation to the priesthood. What he did know was that he was glad to have her at his side for the Council. Shem looked down at his shoulder and caught the Nem Elt-til winking lewdly at her. "Like you have a chance, little man."

"More than you, big boy," he said. "At least I told her I wanted her."

Exasperated, Shem rolled his eyes, but did take a peek at Selene. *She is beautiful, but about to become a priestess. What chance do I have?*

Shem's reverie was broken by the arrival of the Baron Enri Filip and Il'ar led by the Regent Hap Simon whose stern features radiated resolution and not much of a desire to compromise. Shem briefly recalled his treatment at the hands of the Sinclairs. True, none of these here had ordered it, but none had done anything to stop it either. Like the Councils of the Free Goatherders, Shem considered this one a waste of time. Following them in procession were Priest Conyn, Worrell, and the now Lady Na Na who looked about the berm trying to imprint this memory in her mind for her grandchildren, if she ever had any. The leaders stopped at the center table, Hap in the middle flanked by Il'ar and Enri, and stood waiting behind their chairs for the arrival of the Barons Sulieman, O'Kelly, and the presumptive Cap Tan

Jonathon Sinclair. Priest Conyn, Worrel and the Lady Na Na stood at a side table with Selene, Shem, and the ever present Nem Elt-til perched on his shoulder. Overseeing all were five members of the Cap Tan's Hand, led by Lieutenant Gilroy who placed his men in the places most strategic.

The postern gate opened. Shem watched as Priest Fitzpatrick led the way followed by Barons Sulieman and O'Kelly. O'Kelly looking like the shepherd who abandoned the ninety nine for the one and was pleased about it. Last out of the gate was Jonathon, shadowed by Ya Ma. The young would-be ruler strode purposefully to the middle of the table opposite his grandfather. As ranking priest Fitzpatrick opened the council.

"In the sight of the Blessed Fiona and in the shadow of Tierra this Council Barons his hereby convened to determine the Cap Tan of the Central Lands. Regent Hap Simon presides. May the glory of the goddess bless this council and their will be done." Fitzpatrick had stressed the plural. The inclusion of Tierra was a departure from the benediction, but none voiced dissent.

"Pleased be seated," said Hap. "In lieu of our current time restraints we shall proceed directly to the matter at hand. Who approaches the Council?"

Jonathon rose, but before he could speak the postern gate opened once more and four soldiers stepped out carrying a bed. They brought it directly to the main table and set it down. Wybee looked up from the rumpled blanket. He apologized to the Council.

"Forgive me, Sirs. Tierra bid me attend."

Shem felt a stab of sympathy for the pale sickly child whose voice barely rose above a whisper but collected the attention of all. Despite the best efforts of the fortress healers, the conduit of Tierra, the child Shem had been searching for during the best part of a half a moon, still languished. His bed was set just behind Jonathon, sandwiched between the young Sinclair and Baron O'Kelly who fussed with Wybee's blankets.

Instead of addressing the Council, Jonathon turned to his friend. "Wybee, you should be back in the keep. You're not well enough to be out here in this chill."

"You would argue with Tierra?" asked Wybee.

To Shem it appeared that Jonathon was about to do just that until the disapproving gaze of Baron O'Kelly brought the young lad up short. "No," he said finally relenting. Turning to the Council Jonathon began.

"The Regent, my grandfather, Baron Hap Simon has done an excellent job holding the Central Lands together since the death of my other grandfather, Cap Tan Chet Sinclair and my father, Ex Cek Malcolm Sinclair. But times change. The world stands on its head. A new goddess is being born. A new goddess whose high priest will be Jonathon Sinclair. She has told me this. At her awakening I must be Cap Tan." Jonathon sat down. Baron O'Kelly smiled knowingly.

That Jonathon had been schooled and was now being controlled, at least to judge by his body language, by Baron O'Kelly was blatantly obvious to Shem. *If I can see it the rest can as well,* thought Shem. *The baron also wants to control me.* His attempts had not been concealed nor had he pushed that hard, but at the moment, O'Kelly and Priest Fitzpatrick were his strongest allies.

On the other side of the table Regent Simon sat stone faced but determined. Baron Enri Filip looked inclined to agree with O'Kelly, at least in the area of Tierra. Every time she was brought up, he leaned forward, eager to hear what would be said. Shem wasn't sure where he stood on anything else. Il'ar tried to appear above the fray. He gave the impression that whomever ran the Central Lands was really of no great concern to him as an Easterner, who ran the war was, or so Shem believed. The tightness around Il'ar's eyes also betrayed a losing of patience.

"Political theater. You gotta love it," whispered the Nem Elt-til into his ear.

Shem replied, "Like the plague. Both of which should be avoided if at all possible."

"Speaking of Tierra..." began Enri.

"I must insist we stay attentive to the business at hand. Choosing whether or not to elevate Jonathon to Cap Tan," interrupted Hap. "Let us not forget we still have a war to administer."

Il'ar spoke up for the first time. "Your forgiveness, Regent. The selection of your ruler is your own affair and need not concern me or those of the East. Doing our part in the coming battle is. If the fortress would allow my Avians to bivouac above the falls it would put us in a position most advantageous to us all."

"I have already said that none may enter unless I can be assured that they have not converted. What assurances can you give me, Il'ar of the East?" asked Jonathon.

Il'ar sat back in stunned disbelief.

"Jonathon, Tierra would have it so," said Wybee so softly that it went almost unheard.

Ya Ma stepped forward and whispered into Jonathon's ear. None at the table could hear the words, but Jonathon's face flamed in embarrassment.

"I meant no disrespect, Il'ar of the East," began Jonathon haltingly, "Your word will be assurance enough. If would be so kind as to give it, your presence here will be excused."

There was no disguising the coldness in the voice of Il'ar when he rose and spoke. "I, Il'ar, second to the high priestess of Fiona and next in line for the Eastern throne, pledge that not any of my troops have converted to the Goddess Mieze. Not now, not ever in the history of our nation!"

"Thank you, Il'ar," said Jonathon meekly.

Il'ar marched proudly away from the table and toward the bridge unable, or unwilling, to hide his resentment in his stiff stride.

"Grandson, are you sure you want this? The weight of the Cap Tan is a heavy burden," asked Hap gently. Jonathon nodded mutely. "I second the proposal," said Hap with a sigh and a sharp glance towards Baron O'Kelly. "Any further discussion?"

Disappointment dominated Shem's feelings toward the proceedings. *This isn't the time to put a child in charge. Especially with the council fractured underneath the surface.* Shem paid little attention to the remainder of the doings of the Council. *Let these men do as they will. My business is with Tierra.* Right now all he wanted was to spend a little time with Wybee. As near as he could figure he only had two turnings until the moon Mieze would be at its fullest and most menacing. Whatever it was he was supposed to do had to be done by then and only Wybee could tell him what that was and where. He rose to go to the boy.

"Shem! I am asking you once again this time as your duly proclaimed Cap Tan. You are the One. The hope of the people. Cleanse them. Cleanse the army. Only then will I open the gates," said Jonathon.

Shem found all eyes on him. Apparently the question had been asked more than once. He looked at Wybee but saw only sorrow in the expression of the poor boy. Anger began building within him. He didn't have time for this. "I have already told you Jona..."

"Cap Tan!"

"High Priest," said Wybee collecting everybody's attention. "You are High Priest first, Jonathon. Would you squander that which has been given for a lesser goal?"

"But the people, Wybee," said Jonathon.

"Then let them in," said Wybee simply and without judgment.

"I cannot," said Jonathon after a moment. He hung his head. "I cannot."

"Then do not try to place the blame at the feet of Shem." Wybee motioned to the soldiers who had brought him out. "I will leave now. My purpose here is done."

Shem marveled at the composure of Wybee and how everyone hung on his words. He was also thankful. His building anger for the headstrong young ruler would have led to a confrontation and that had now been averted. He informed the Council, "I'm leaving, too. You have your battle to plan and I have mine. May the Goddess Fiona and Tierra be with you all. Cap Tan?"

The last had been more of an acknowledgment than a request, but Jonathon merely waved Shem away without comment. Shem followed the guardsmen as they carried Wybee back into the fortress.

⸻

"I would like to thank everyone for their support in the matter of the One," said Jonathon. It was not exactly a pout, but not too far removed.

Hap felt sympathy for his grandson but didn't let it show on his features. *You will learn that leaders and leadership do not always go hand in hand, Jonathon. Your people are not trained animals who jump at your every command.* A quick look around the table revealed that the Cap Tan's remark was not going to be addressed. "Let us turn to defense."

Priest Conyn spoke up from side table. "Cap Tan, one of the Easterners wishes to land on the berm without being feathered from the walls."

Jonathon looked up and spied the mounted messenger orbiting above, out of bow range. He turned and signaled to the watch commander. "He is welcome," he said to the priest.

Priest Conyn spoke into his box containing his spider web. A moment later the winged horse landed on the edge of the berm. Dismounting was Ip'star. He rushed over to the table and gave a brief bob of his head to Jonathon.

"Cap Tan, scouts report that the Westerners are approaching by river and road. They will be here by nightfall. They have been reinforced by a group of Un Tier, two hundred strong with an equal number of Sol Dat."

Hap was devastated. He knew that Baron Yakov's forces had reformed again at his estates giving him a hundred of the dreaded creatures to go along with his own forces and about two hundred of the Sol Dat. The reinforcements would make them nearly a thousand strong. He didn't hold out much hope for his forces outside the walls of the fortress. Not now with so many of the brutes and not near enough of the mounted Easterners to counter them. He waited a moment to give Jonathon a chance to respond, but all he did was nod in acknowledgement. "Cap Tan, if I may, it is not too late. Bring everyone inside."

"No," he said forcefully.

Hap regretted for a moment seconding his grandson's proposal to become Cap Tan. *His stubbornness will cost the lives of thousands of civilians!* He let the resentment go, much as he had the news of his wife's, Mona's, death. There would be time to grieve later. If he survived. "Can we at least expect troops?"

Baron Sulieman spoke for the first time. "Hap, I have ordered a reserve force readied. As we speak they take their places. If your lines breach they will be released, otherwise we will do what we can to support you from the fortress. The range of our arbalests reach to the bend of the river."

"Thank you, Ichabod. Cap Tan, I have one last request." Jonathon looked up. Hap continued, "I would take Worrel and the Lady Na Na into the fortress. Worrel has served my family faithfully since before you were born. He watched over you during visits to my estates and the Lady Na Na has done you a great service in getting you to Grimval. I would have you reward them appropriately."

Hap watched Jonathon with apprehension wondering if he pushed his grandson too far with his request, but he had to know how far Jonathon was in Baron O'Kelly's councils. *If he looks to Camdene for this decision then....* Hap didn't have time to complete the thought.

"What reassurances do I have, grandfather?"

Hap felt the weight of Central Land's people fall across his shoulders, practically suffocating him. *What have I wrought?* Jonathon's fears of the converted had rooted too deeply. Family and personal dedication meant little to him in the face of that fear. This was even worse than losing Jonathon to Baron O'Kelly's influence. Far worse. *I shall have to demonstrate fealty to him and hope he knows it for what it is.* "I will vouchsafe for them with my life."

"Very well, Grandfather. I believe the rest of us have matters to attend to. This Council is adjourned."

Jonathon had weighed the words of his grandfather's carefully before responding, never once looking to anyone for advice. For this Hap took solace, but it was a small victory. He rose stately and made his way back to his men.

—◦◦◦—

The soldiers set Wybee's bed down in his room within the Keep. "Will there be anything else, Vaar Tu?" asked their leader.

"No, that will be all. My thanks," said Wybee.

Shem asked, "Vaar Tu?"

"Yes, that's what everyone around here has begun calling me," said Wybee with a pointed stare at the Nem Elt-til perched next to Shem's ear. The little man shrugged his shoulders innocently.

Shem observed, "The way they say it it sounds important."

"In the old language it means 'vessel' as in vase or container."

Shem turned to find Selene standing in the doorway. A wide grin split his face as the pleasure of seeing her flooded through him. He quickly recovered his composure and was rewarded with a sly smile.

"The time draws near, Shem. Priest Fitzpatrick has been instructing me in the histories of the One and the Hjerte. Would you like to hear them?" asked Selene.

Shem basked in the pleasure of merely hearing her voice, albeit guilty pleasure. "Do they tell me where to find it?"

"That's the surprising thing. Everyone here knows where it is," she said with a laugh.

That was the second time he had heard that particular statement. If it hadn't been Selene he would have felt that she was laughing at him. *Everyone but me!* He thought though he couldn't help but be amused. He glanced over at Wybee who was grinning through his tiredness. Shem said, "Not everyone."

"You are standing over the chamber now, Hero," spoke up the Nem Elt-til. "If you'd quit drooling over this vision of loveliness here," he said giving a bow to Selene, "You would have felt it."

Shem felt his face warm with the blush that was rising from his neck to his face. He stilled himself and concentrated on the Pointer. *Yes. Yes, I can feel it. The Pointer is tugging me downward.* "It's below this keep?"

"Maybe Selene would like to show you the chamber?" asked Wybee. She nodded. "Good. A word of warning, Hero. Do not try to raise the Hjerte. Not yet. After you have visited the chamber return here and Tierra will explain what you have to do and when."

Selene led Shem down the hallway towards the center of the keep. The hallway opened up into a good sized room with a high ceiling. Shem wasn't sure what the room was used for, there were no furnishings to speak of just a few chairs scattered around a couple of tables in no orderly pattern. Standing in the very center was a narrow little guard shack. It had no markings, no guards, or anything else to indicate its importance. Truth be told it looked out of place, a building within a building. He poked his head into the shack.

"Be careful," said Selene.

Just inside of the doorway were some stairs. In fact if one were unaware they could step inside the shack and fall down the stairs that began just beyond the door and spiraled down for as far as Shem could see before finally disappearing in the inky darkness.

Shem pulled his head out of the doorway. A sudden movement down a hallway opposite of the way he had arrived caught the corner of his eye. He turned to look, but whatever it was had disappeared. He asked the Nem Elt-til, "Did you see that?"

"Yeah, someone ducked into one of the rooms down the hall. I'm not sure, but the pretty young thing he had his arms wrapped around might have had something to do with it," said the Nem Elt-til.

Shem didn't know what it was, but something about the words of his companion didn't ring true. He thought about going to check, but if he were wrong he would be barging in on well, it would be an embarrassment that not even being *the One* could save him from.

"What's wrong?" asked Selene.

Shem responded, "Nothing. Nothing. So, the chamber is down these stairs?"

"Yes. Watch your step and grab one of the torches inside the entry," said Selene.

Shem stopped inside the doorway. Off to his left was a basket of unlit torches. He grabbed two and continued down the stairs, Selene trailing behind him, and the little man still on his shoulder. After several circuits he came to a landing. Taking his flint and striker out of his pouch, he lit the torch. The light revealed a passageway carved out of stone leading away from the stairs. Selene came up next to him and lit her torch from his. Faint sounds of movement echoed from the passage. Shem strained to listen. Something was out of place. He wracked his memory trying to locate the missing pieces. *The falls. The roar of the falls is gone.* Above ground that roar was constant, so much so that now he was underground, where it was masked, it felt strange not to hear it. He gestured down the tunnel, "Do you know where that leads?"

"Not exactly, but according to Priest Fitzpatrick it goes under the falls pond to some storage chambers and then some stairs going up inside of the cliff face. It's used to haul goods to and from the city proper that need to be kept dry. At present Baron Sulieman is using it for troops to reinforce the Regent," said Selene. "Let's keep going."

After the landing the stairs were carved out of rock and continued spiraling down. As Shem led them down he couldn't stop thinking about who built them. Shem remembered the tunnel leading to the Pointer and how His Holiness had said that the tunnel only appeared straight to the Protector and the Guardians. That was obviously not the case here. He asked, "Was this made by the Hjerte?"

"Yes. This is where it landed. It not only buried itself deeply, but caused the land to rise, creating the waterfall and closing off the Grimval valley. Later, the Priesthood carved these stairs down to the chamber and built the keep on top of it. Originally to hide the location, but it took so many laborers that it couldn't be hidden and became part of the Grimval folklore. Some even make pilgrimages to the 'Chamber of the One'. Others more foolish or self deluded have tried to dig it up. You'll see," she said.

The torch was near to guttering out when the three reached the bottom of the stairs. Light was shining out of the doorway which contained no door. Shem was confused. The soft humming of the Nem Elt-til didn't help. The mood of the little man had gotten increasingly more cheerful the deeper they had penetrated. Shem didn't see anything cheerful about the place. Other than the stairs themselves none of the rock had been improved, not the walls or the ceilings. It was dark and close. Not even the Pointer reacted any differently other than a slight tug towards the chamber and there were no guards. *If this Hjerte is so valuable why are there no efforts to safeguard it?* Shem and Selene doused their torches and entered.

The inside while brightly lit by some crystalline globes embedded in the stone, globes which shone with a chemically induced inner light, was as unimproved as the stairway had been. The room itself was circular and large enough to fit about a hundred persons without difficulty. Around the edges of the walls rock dust of cycles unnumbered had collected and lay undisturbed. Only in the center was the dust cleared, with a few exceptions, and that by the feet of numbers uncounted that came to visit the chamber. In the very center of the otherwise unfurnished chamber was a marble plaque, and about the plaque were the heads of pickaxes lying in circles of green ash.

The Nem Elt-til flew off Shem's shoulder as they entered and made a beeline for one of the globes. He was mesmerized by the glow.

Shem chuckled and said aloud, "Like a moth to a flame."

"What was that?" asked Selene.

"Nothing."

—⊷⊷⊷—

The aged, decrepit-looking man who bent over the Auge Ose, gripping it with wrinkled claw-like fingers as much for support as for contact with the jewel, in nowise resembled the hale and vital Sun Father of nearly three quarters of a moon ago. His hair had fallen out along with most of his teeth, but neither bothered him as he rarely ate anymore anyway, his life being sustained by his Goddess Mieze until the fulfillment of his purpose which would come within the next two turnings. His eyes; however, were different. They still burned with intensity. Intensity and the desire to become a demigod.

He watched as U'cha and his three hundred Un Tier neared the bend of the Grimval River. Beyond that bend were the forces of Regent Hap Simon arrayed on both sides of the river in a feeble attempt to halt the coming onslaught. Behind U'cha followed I'con with his hundreds of Sol Dat and mounted troops of Uri Yakov. On the river advancing in makeshift rafts were the five hundred Central Landers. The pieces were nearly in place. The army would attack that night with rising of Mieze. He shifted from his view of the coming battle to find Shem.

"He is in the Hjerte chamber," came the voice of Mieze. Such was their bond now that there was no wrenching away of the stone, but the smooth flow of two entities merged. The chamber came into view, the focus sharpened revealing Shem and Selene standing in the center of the room. "He is about to sense the Hjerte," said Mieze. "When he does, I want you to compel him to begin the awakening. He doesn't know it, but it is too soon. Get him to do it now and he will fail or at least use up enough of the Gedeelte to render it incapable of performing the awakening at the proper time."

Vlad felt the presence of Mieze fade into the background. He slid easily and silently into Shem's bond and waited.

—⚡⚡⚡—

The plaque was chiseled stone and the only stone in the chamber that had been improved. Its face had been smoothed and polished. Within the improved area were chiseled the words, 'The One will come. Tierra will awaken. People will weep. Balance restored.'

The shiver shook Shem's entire body as he stood over the stone reading the words. "Simple enough,"

"So others thought," said Selene indicating the scattering of undisturbed green ash piles.

Shem cut his eyes quickly to Selene, searching. *You've been with me nearly every step of the journey!* he thought. "Do you doubt?" There was a moment's hesitation. Shem felt as if his world were about to collapse.

"No," she said looking at the ash piles, "But I do worry."

Shem exhaled in relief. "Thank you." He gave her a little sheepish grin. "So do I." His gaze returned to the plaque as he dwelt on the inscribed words. *'The One will come.' That's definitely me. ' Tierra will awaken.' Well, no time like the present.* Forgetting Wybee's admonition, he reached out with the Pointer, imagining a thin tentative strand making its way through the stone. He felt the Hjerte buried deep beneath his feet.

As the first tentacles of power touched the stone, Shem felt it stir. Instead of welcoming him an urgent warning surged out, racing back up the thin tendril of power he had sent down, nearly flooring him. "Stop!" Shem was confused and from the midst of the confusion he felt the presence of Vlad pouncing. *No!* screamed out Shem in the agony of his mind, but the compulsion had him completely in its grip. He had to raise the Hjerte now.

Like an arrow the Nem Elt-til flew straight to Shem. He tried frantically to get Shem's attention, buzzing around his head, beating him with his tiny fists. "Stop! Stop, you moron!"

Shem tried desperately to stop, but Vlad's control was complete. He watched seemingly detached as his will refused to obey his commands. His forehead beaded with sweat. The ground began to shake.

The Nem Elt-til turned to Selene who was rooted to the spot unable to immediately comprehend what was happening. "Do something, darling! Break his concentration!"

"How?" she stammered.

"I don't know! Kick him, kiss him, I don't care, but do it now!"

A slight vibration beneath her feet broke Selene free of inaction. She threw her arms around Shem's neck and kissed him on the lips as passionately as she knew how.

Shem was at the limit of his strength. He could hear Vlad's gloating laughter as he directed Shem to increase the summons. He could do nothing to stop it. Then Selene's lips were on his own. An instant of pleasure filled him, but it was brushed aside by a new entity.

"Shem, I am Fiona. Let me in."

Yes. Acceptance was all that was required. Shem's mind was brushed aside as the power of the Goddess Fiona surrounded the compulsion squeezing it back into the bond of Vlad and sealing it along with the Sun Father. The shaking of the ground ceased with the halting of the summons. Fiona withdrew. It took a moment before Shem realized that Selene was still kissing him. He waited a moment more before raising his arms to embrace her. As he feared would happen, Selene broke off the kiss. She backed away, searching his eyes.

The warmth of Selene's lips still lingered on his. He wondered what her eyes were searching for. Then the realization of what had just happened sunk in. *I almost ruined everything! What a fool I am!* "I'm alright, now. Somehow Vlad's bond broke free of the Pointer."

"That's because you used it to try and raise the Hjerte! What were you thinking, bonehead! Or are you even capable of thought?" groused the Nem Elt-til. He said to Selene, "Let's get him out of here. Quickly. Before he does anything else stupid."

23

THE BATTLE BEGINS

The long patrol was nearly over. Mounted upon Anwar high above the river valley Il'ar had thus far not sighted the huge brutes that he knew was below him marching towards the fortress. He could clearly see the makeshift rafts being used by Baron Yakov's Central Landers along with his mounted troops keeping pace on the road, but of the Un Tier or even Sol Dat naught could be seen. Earlier reports had indicated that the speed of their march would bring them to the fortress possibly as soon as night fell. Il'ar knew that he should have been able to see them by now.

"They must have taken to the woods, wouldn't you say, Anwar?" The winged horse snorted his agreement.

Looking up at the sun he judged that he had about three candlemarks of daylight remaining. He decided to return to the bivouac. Turning Anwar about, he caught a glimpse of sunlight reflecting from the wooded hillside. Then another as a group of Un Tier, trying to stay hidden, skirted a small clearing. *I believe a little reception is in order.* "Target acquired," he said. "Let's go home, Anwar."

By the time he landed outside the city atop the fortress, which was the home of the Baron Sulieman, Il'ar had made his plans, but first he had to contact his mother. Outside his tent he found the guardsman, Rafal. The Easterner Prince didn't ask him how he had made his way into their camp without the approval of the young Cap Tan, he didn't really want to know, or why the guardsman had taken such an interest in seeing to his needs; all he knew was that he was there and it would be more trouble than it was worth to send him back. Besides Rafal would probably just find another way to return. The young man was that resourceful. "See to it that I am not disturbed, Rafal."

Inside the tent he opened his box containing his spider and its web. "Mother, I need to speak to you." The web dulled instantly and almost as quickly shone brightly.

"Il'ar, be quick. Something monumental is about to occur and I haven't much time."

His pulse quickened. *So it's about to begin.* "Yes, Mother, here as well. Where are the rest of the Avians?"

"Tomorrow's dawn. You have to hold out until then."

Il'ar suppressed his disappointment. "You ask much of me, Mother. I do not know how many of us will still be alive by morning."

"I ask much, Il'ar? Or is it the times we live in that ask much of us? Do you think the goddess asks too much?"

Chastised, Il'ar replied, "No, Mother. Tomorrow then. Give my regards to Father."

The sheen of the web dulled indicating that his Mother had broken contact and returned to whatever her duties had been. Il'ar and his less than twenty Avians were on their own. He reached out to Anwar. "Anwar, have Ahern come to me."

Within the candlemark Il'ar was airborne once again with fifteen of his men. He kept only three on the ground to provide scouts for the morning. Messages had been sent to the Regent Simon and Baron Sulieman alerting them of the presence and location of the Un Tier and Il'ar's planned aerial attack. The Easterners did not want the Central Landers firing on them in the confusion and excitement of battle.

The Un Tier would have to come off the ridge and onto the valley floor to get around the bend of the Grimval River; otherwise they would have to descend the sheer cliffs where they would be helplessly exposed, opened to the combined firepower of the fortress and the Regent's troops. No, they would not attack from that direction. They were heavy infantry and needed flat ground where their superior exoskeletons and massed formations could wield fear, as well as might, to their advance.

Advantages that Il'ar meant to deny them as long as he could. The defenders didn't have to wait long. The Un Tier broke cover at the base of the tree line just before the bend in the river. Il'ar expected them to take a moment to reform and attack in mass. He was surprised to see them continue forward bellowing in small frenzied groups intent on overrunning all in their path. Il'ar and the Avians descended towards the attacking Westerners, armed with the new compound bows provided by Baron Sulieman they could take up stations above and in front of the Un Tier and pour down lethal firepower. Instead Il'ar intended to lead them in one sweep before splitting his forces sending Ahern and six more up to high cap to be used in relief or where needed.

The first sweep was executed nearly to perfection. Dropping out of the sky like a meteor shower only to slow as they leveled out at a height about halfway down the ridge line, the Avians annihilated the exposed lead elements of the Un Tier breaking the ill conceived assault before it encountered any of Regent Simon's forces. The ragged cheers of the Central Lander ground forces accompanied the retreat of the remnants of the enemy as they made their way back to the cover of the trees leaving over forty of the brutes lying dead or dying on the field.

Il'ar gave the signal to Ahern to break off and take his men up and away. They swerved off just before a flight of enemy arrows descended like rain from the ridge top. Il'ar looked about in surprise as three of his riders and two mounts fell out of the sky. He saw the second cloud of arrows emerge from the tree tops near the ridge line and veered his remaining Avians towards the west side of the river safely out of bow shot.

"It's going to be a long two candlemarks, my friend," said Il'ar patting the neck of Anwar. "Pity, whoever is in charge of those archers is more clever by half than the Un Tier leader." Anwar huffed his agreement. Il'ar signaled to wing leader Shura, "Your command. I'll be back shortly," then descended towards the Regent's command tent.

⸺◦◦◦◦⸺

Did I do the right thing seconding Jonathon? Or will he now become just the puppet of Camdene O'Kelly? Does Camdene have the best interest of the Central Lands in his heart or is he dedicated to the awakening of this new goddess to the exclusion of all else? Hap still wrestled with the thought. That his grandson had undergone a significant life experience was beyond doubt. He did seem much older now than his mere nine cycles, but was that enough? *Besides there is a war to be fought and I didn't have the time to drag the Council into a prolonged debate.* There seemed no good answers to Hap. The cheers coming from Sloan Quinn's men on the west side of the river brought Hap back to the here and now. He and his men who were dug in around the bend on the fortress side were out of sight of whatever was happening. He itched to know what was going on.

I'll know soon, he thought as he watched one of Sloan's runners pushed off in a dory to cross the river and report. At the same time an Avian rounded the bend descending towards his camp. The Avian arrived first carrying Il'ar who leapt from his saddle and hurried towards him.

"Regent, they're here. Un Tier leading. They broke out of the woods around the bend. The first group made a dash for the road, but we turned them back, killing about forty. They retreated back to the edge of the woods. There are more, probably Sol Dat, in the trees around the ridge top. Mounted Central Landers and on rafts come up behind them. The battle will begin in earnest by nightfall."

"Forty of the beasts dead. Thank the goddesses! At least those that are on our side," said Hap. "Do we know how many remain?"

"No, Regent. They've learned their lesson about coming into the open in the daylight. For now at least they stick to the woods," said Il'ar.

Hap looked around at his defenses. He had amassed the bulk of his troops across the road believing that only a fool would try to descend the cliffs. But his own men would be hit hard by the concentrated Mashers when they did attack. His only hope was for the Avians to thin their ranks, which would not happen under the moon of Mieze or Fiona either for that matter. He did not look forward to the setting of the sun.

"Regent, we do have a chance to reduce the Central Lander troops, especially those that continue to raft down the river. I don't know why they expose themselves in that manner. Perhaps to keep up with the speed of the Westerners, but we can hit them from the air. They are vulnerable. The risk is that the Un Tier will attack right away when they see the skies are empty above them." Hap wavered, uncertain. His uncertainty must have shown because Il'ar continued. "Tomorrow morning two hundred of my countrymen will arrive."

Hap mused while his thoughts raced, weighing the options. "I wonder how many of us they will find still alive?"

"As do I, Regent," said Il'ar reluctantly.

Hap feared to be left without the air cover of the Avians, but he also feared to lose the chance to reduce his enemies forces, even if those enemies are Central Landers. His thoughts suddenly found themselves on a different road. "Ironic, isn't it? To so soon find myself in a situation similar to Jonathon's. Do I protect myself or others? Play it safe or dare to win?" Beneath his feet he felt a slight shaking of the ground. Somehow, he knew he was out of time.

Hap made his decision. "Good luck, Il'ar."

"And to you, Regent," replied Il'ar taking his leave.

"Sound the alarm. Everyone to their posts!" ordered Hap to his runner. Hap watched Il'ar take flight to the sound of horns calling men to their posts. The dory crossing the river reversed its course. His camp became a flurry of activity. He prayed aloud, "May the goddess have mercy on us all."

—◆◈◆—

The return up the stairway and through the halls to Wybee's room had been uneventful. None had been met or even seen. It was as if the temple was deserted except for themselves. Entering Wybee's room they found him lying back, head deep in his pillow, looking even worse than he had when they had left. Priest Fitzpatrick sat at his side.

I have done this to him, thought Shem, ashamed. *My lack of control has caused Tierra to take even more from the poor lad.* Shem wasn't sure when exactly he had come to that conclusion, but it was now obvious to him. Wybee was going to be little more than a sacrifice to Tierra, a backstop for Shem's lack and mistakes. He bowed his head as he approached the bed, a tear escaped the confines of his eye and rolled down his cheek. He took Wybee's small hand in his and raised his head to look directly at the frail child. "I'm sorry, Wybee. I lost control of it. Vlad was waiting and when he pounced I couldn't fight him off. I'm sorry." He felt the slight pressure of Wybee's hand squeezing his in reassurance.

"Do not sorrow for me, Hero. We must all fulfill our destinies as the goddesses would have us to. I am proud of you. We survived. You will be better prepared for tomorrow. It must happen before the rise of Mieze. Do not forget that." Wybee's voice was little more than a whisper, barely audible above the constant drone of the falls. His eyes cut towards Selene standing beside Shem at his bedside. "Tierra begs you to thank her sister for her aid. It was most welcome. She says she will see her on the morrow." The Nem Elt-til flew down from Shem's shoulder and landed lightly on Wybee's chest who gave him a feeble smile. "And you, Eens Luwe, vindt ze grappig. Morgen worden er voor hem. U zal worden hard nodig." (You, Sly one, she finds funny. Tomorrow you must be there for him. You will be sorely needed.)

The Nem Elt-til bowed reverently to Wybee, "Vaar Tu." He flew back to Shem's shoulder and gave Selene a lewd wink.

Confused, Shem looked from the priest to Selene. Sadness lurked behind their eyes. Even the Nem Elt-til was a little subdued just beyond his bluster. *What did Wybee say? What was the meaning behind his use of the old tongue, for surely that is what is was? What does he not want me to know?* The trio allowed themselves to be herded out the door by Priest Fitzpatrick who said his farewells before returning to Wybee's room and closing the door. "What did he say?"

"He said I'm a funny guy and you should be glad I'm around," boasted the Nem Elt-til.

Shem was skeptical, "Doubtful."

"The Nem Elt-til is essentially correct, Shem. Not literal, but close enough," said Selene.

The sounds of battle horns being blown broke off any further discussion. The stirring sound heated Shem's blood. He hurried towards the door and, finding it still daylight, made his way to the gate tower. Selene remained behind. None denied the One entry anywhere and he soon found himself atop the tower looking out towards the bend in the river. While the gate tower gave an excellent view of the berm and the docks it wasn't designed to be tall enough to see to the bend. Frustrated, Shem eyed the taller tower on the east bank of the river. *That's where I need to be.* He dashed down the stairs and across the curtain wall.

Atop the taller tower, Shem could see all the way to the river bank. He judged that there was about a candlemark of daylight left. He could see the preparations of the Regent's men. Three rows of pells, sharpened stakes driven into the ground to slow down the advance of the Un Tier or mounted troops, crossed the road and extended from river to cliff side. Behind them men with pikes and feather staffs, spears spring loaded with hand-length spikes, then shield bearing infantry, finally archers. Shem noted that the Regent had not bothered to mount any of his troops. *It's just as well,* he thought, *there wasn't any room along the road between the river and cliff to maneuver them anyway.* As he stood watching, the Avians disappeared around the bend. "Why are they leaving the field? The battle will be here."

"They go to attack the rear," said the Nem Elt-til.

Shem didn't ask how his friend knew. *Friend. Yes, he is my friend. I've known that all along, too.* Shem moved to the rear of the arbalest and asked the sub-leader of the weapon, "Do you mind if I take a shot?"

"You are the One. Take as many shots as you like," he replied.

"It won't be long now," Shem said to no one in particular. His words proved true. Nearly as quick as the Avians left sight the warning horns sounded. Shem aimed the arbalest at the middle of the road where it rounded the bend.

"Your pardon, Expected One, but the bolt will never reach that far," said the soldier a worried frown upon his face. "It will fall among the Regent's troops."

Shem was confident. "No it won't,"

The first Un Tier rounded the corner. Shem fired, willing the tree trunk sized bolt to its target. It struck the beast in the center of its chest hurling it back into those following it. A cheer rose from the top of the tower. Pleased, Shem ordered it reloaded.

"I don't think this is such a good idea," said the Nem Elt-til.

Shem was adamant, "I can't stand by and do nothing."

Over the dull roar of the falls and the creaking of the arbalest ropes being drawn back Shem heard the bellowing shouts of the Un Tier as more of them rounded the bend and headed towards the Regent's line. They were met with a withering fire of arrows from the defenders. The compound bows provided by Baron Sulieman were having an effect, but not near enough. While many fell, many more kept coming with the arrows sticking out of their thick hides. The reloading of the arbalest complete, Shem aimed at the leader and fired once again willing the bolt to its target. It struck just before the Un Tier reached the pells, punching all the way through the enemy soldier and into the one following him. Amidst the cheers of those on the tower, the Nem Elt-til shouted into Shem's ear.

"You are using the Pointer, Hero. You can't afford it!"

The reminder doused Shem like a pail of cold water. On the other hand, the Pointer had done what he wanted done. No big show, no drama. He wanted it, willed it, and the Pointer did it. He filed that away for future thought. "You're right, let's go." He turned the arbalest back over to the control of its sub-leader. "Don't try to do what I just did. Stay within yourself, blessings of Tierra, Sub-leader."

His battle lust dampened, Shem left the tower as the Un Tier began smashing their way through the pells.

⚓

Back in the air, Il'ar allowed himself a few moments to ponder all that had happened during this turning, which was not even over. It could be summed up with one word. *Bleakness, and promising to get even worse.* His men had done well fending off the first attack, but he had been surprised by the arrows coming from the ridge top. *Carelessness kills!* He had been too wrapped up in trying to turn back the Un Tier assault and now three of his riders were dead and the bulk of the attack had yet to come. He didn't hold out much hope for his chances or for those under his command. The enemy numbers were simply too overwhelming and the headstrong little Cap Tan refused to listen to reason, refused to bring everyone behind the walls to safety. *Too late for that now.* At least attacking the Central Landers on the river and road should hold no surprises, he hoped. All they had to do was hold out until morning when his mother's promised reinforcements would arrive. And pray to the goddess that they could.

Wing leaders Shura and Ahern had divided the remaining Avians between them and were making lazy sweeps on the west side of the river keeping the Western forces at bay. Il'ar swung wide of the bend and joined them.

"We heard the horns," said Ahern resolutely. "What are your orders?"

Il'ar knew his orders were going to be considered ruthless, even he thought they were. "We attack the rafts. Kill as many as possible before nightfall. Any questions?" Neither Wing Leader responded. "Very well, move out."

Grim-faced, Il'ar took the lead with Shura's wing on his left and Ahern's on his right. They descended out of the blazing globe of the almost setting sun. The soldiers on the rafts, each with three to four aboard, never saw the approach of the Avians. The first they knew of the attack was the rain of arrows that had sprouted out of their chests as they fell into the river. Shura and Ahern split off each taking a different segment of the river and leaving death and devastation in their wake. They stayed on station until their arrows ran out.

Il'ar felt sick inside as he watched the waters of the Grimval River turn red from the amount of blood being spilled into it. He had stayed above the flights directing the slaughter, as it could be called nothing else, and had not fired an arrow, but his hands were as bloody as everyone else's. He had ordered it. *Those soldiers would have done the same to the innocent civilians trapped outside the fortress walls if they had had a chance,* he thought trying to justify his actions. It was an apt comparison. The rafted soldiers had been unable to mount an adequate defense, the rafts being too unstable a platform to accurately return fire from, and so they had died in droves. He signaled to regroup the wings.

As they climbed higher to get above the ridge top and the Sol Dat archers at the river bend ahead of them Il'ar looked back one last time. He estimated that fully two thirds of the Central Lander foot soldiers had been slain. A sudden motion caught out of the corner of his eye claimed his attention. Wing Leader Ahern was pumping his index finger down vigorously. Below them barely visible in the dim light Il'ar saw that the Un Tier were about to break through the pells. He raised his lancet to signal the wings and banked Anwar towards the western shore in a diving slow roll. The wings followed stringing in behind him one closely on the tail of the one in front.

Il'ar pulled out of the dive just above the river and set his lancet. The diving maneuver had increased the speed of the Avians who now just barely above the ground flashed towards the Un Tier. But not fast enough. The archers of the Sol Dat had seen them and loosed a volley. The arrows fell behind Il'ar but he knew they fell among the wings. He concentrated on the lead Un Tier and drove the lancet through the body of the beast before he pulled up in a climbing turn towards the eastern bank narrowly missing the sharpened stakes. He looked back to see how many had made it. He was disheartened to see only three others. The ones who had been immediately behind him. The rest had fallen, but not before breaking the charge of the enemy. He watched the withdrawal. With heavy heart he headed for the bivouac. His force was spent.

—◁❀❀▷—

The attack of the Easterners had exacted a heavy toll on Baron Uri Yakov's old troops. Many of them he had either trained himself or had a hand in certain areas. Most of the officers and sergeants were *or rather had been,* thought Uri, Guardsmen of the First File, graduates of the first class of his arms school. Now they floated down the Grimval River feeding the fishes and the insatiable appetite of the Sun Father's desire for death, especially Central Lander death. Not even seeing the body of Lieutenant Cutler lying in the shallows had moved Uri. He had been harsh in his orders to the survivors to leave the bodies where they lie, form ranks, and march on. He had listened to their grumbling with deaf ears and coldly continued his advance.

Upon arriving at the bend in the river his irritation had not been for the loss of the Un Tier lives but in the piecemeal manner in which they had attacked. So great had been his anger that Uri had actually called out to Vlad to ask for U'cha's punishment and Vlad delivered. U'cha had been burned to ash before Uri's eyes, though it had come with a stern warning that such would also be his fate should he fail. He had quickly organized the remaining Un Tier and launched a coordinated attack. Twice he had nearly broken through. The first was thwarted by some amazing shooting from the tall tower on the east side of the river. Fortunately for Uri the arbalest had only shot twice. The second time his Un Tier had been turned back by the cursed Easterners, but it had cost them, dearly. Uri no longer considered the flying horses a viable threat even in the daylight. He had survived the potent blows of his former comrades and now that night had fallen he was about to see the breaking of Baron Simon's defenses.

"Baron Yakov, pull the Un Tier back and wait for the rising of Mieze."

The insidious voice of Vlad was soft spoken instead of the usual domineering and demanding tone that he used to instruct Uri and somehow that made it more powerful. Uri wanted to ponder the meaning of that but dare not. He hadn't even known that the Sun Father was with him and that frightened him. He kept his feelings under as tight a control as he could and prayed that it would be enough; but, strangely, he wasn't sure who to pray to. Nevertheless the order was to be obeyed and obeyed immediately. "Clan Leader U'dog. To me."

The Un Tier clan leader shambled over, his nonchalance igniting a brief moment of irritation in Uri. He quickly suppressed it. *Forget it, Uri, this fool will be dead before the night is done.* "Stand down, Clan Leader. We will wait until Mieze rises so that she may witness the glory done in her name. Pass the word." Uri waited until the Un Tier had left before summoning his other leaders, I'con and Lieutenant Kim whom Uri had promoted to replace the deceased Lieutenant Cutler. "I'con, Lieutenant Kim, a moment." The two leaders promptly attended the baron. "We suspend our attack until Mieze rises." Neither leader made a comment. Uri continued. "I'con, your archers are to be commended in bringing down the cursed Easterners. They now have another important job. Before Mieze rises move archers up to both flanks. They will provide suppressing fire to the center. Lieutenant Kim, when the attack resumes wait until the Un Tier break through the pells. When they do, ride hard through the openings, hard and fast. I want you to hit them like a hammer."

"Yes, my lord!" said Lieutenant Kim.

"I'con, hold your fire until the horsemen charge. Then fire in front of them. After they clear the pells send the rest of your men after them. I want this to be swift. Do not waste time fighting the footmen. Leave those to the mounted soldiers. After you clear their lines strike for the civilians. Kill as many as you can. Terror and confusion. That is what I want, that will win the battle for the glory of Mieze and the Sun Father." Uri added the last just in case Vlad was still in his mind listening. "Go now. Rest while you can."

I'con nodded his understanding then departed.

"Yes, Sir!" replied the Lieutenant.

Uri watched in satisfaction visualizing the blood red night to come. Not all the redness would be from Mieze's moon.

───✖───

Ham woke in a strange place with strange sounds in his ears. A constant buzzing roar and occasional whump, though not exceptionally loud, tickled his eardrums and generated exotic thoughts of faraway places that he had never seen but had been told tales of when he was a child. Tales to warn him against being in those places. He tried to open his eyes, then realized they were open. It was just dark as pitch. Reality gradually crept in, taking the place of the sleepy dreams that had enwrapped him. Sheila. He was in Sheila's room in the Grimval fortress. The buzzing roar was the sound of the water crashing down from the falls into the pool underneath and the whumping noise was... an arbalest! There was a battle going on! He sat up quickly. Judging from the darkness and the lack of the deep defining redness that would have accompanied Mieze, Ham determined it was early nightfall. The heaviest fighting would be yet to come.

He lay back and collected his thoughts assessing what he knew and what he had yet to do. Being found by Sheila had been a stroke of luck. She had been one of the lucky few who had been granted sanctuary before Grimval had closed its gates to outsiders and, after Shem had destroyed the converted inside the walls, the only one Ham felt he could trust. In addition to sheltering him in her arms, as well as in her room, she had been the one to tell Ham about the Chamber of the One and had shown him how to get there. That had been an adventure. Fortunately, he had seen Shem before Shem had spotted him. He and Sheila had barely ducked into a doorway in time. *And speaking of which, it's time I got moving before Sheila gets off work.* Still he could not help but admire Shem for what he had accomplished. He had had a different air about him, no longer walking around apologetic but purposeful and with determination. *He really is Tierra's hero. It is a shame I have to kill him for it.*

So far the trip down from Sheila's room halfway up the west side of the falls had been uneventful. Infused with the excitement of being undetected behind enemy lines, Ham took great care to walk purposefully but not hurriedly. He didn't want to be stopped and asked why he wasn't manning the walls. As he stepped onto the bridge to the islet he heard the sound of marching troops. *Reinforcements. It would appear that the battle is going well for Yakov.* With a renewed sense of satisfaction and a smirk on his face, he hurried across the bridge.

Rounding the corner of the Keep Shrine, Ham pulled up short. A guardsmen stood watch at the entrance. A momentary pang of panic gripped him. Tamping it down he continued. When he got to the door, he took off his nearly shapeless, floppy hat while he wrung his hands.

"State your business," said the guard who looked as if he would much rather be on the walls or at one of the inns like the one Sheila worked at.

Trying to sound his most pitiful he whimpered, "I'm on my way to the chamber to pray the One will save us."

"A big strapping fellow like yourself?" said the guard with more than a little derision. "You should be on the walls."

Ham shrugged and looked in the direction of the east bridge where Baron Filip's forces were still crossing. The guard followed his eyes to the marching column of soldiers. Ham said, "I reckon I will be soon enough."

"Go on," said the guard. As Ham passed him he heard, "Say one for me." Ham smiled as the seed of fear he planted took root.

The brightness of the chamber hurt his eyes. Ham had not taken a torch, preferring the darkness as his cloak. He was amazed that the globes shone without any visible flame. *I wonder if Mieze has marvels like this?*

"Yes, and many more," said the voice of Vlad in his head.

Ham looked about the circular chamber displeased at its size. "This is where we shall be tomorrow," said Ham. His brother was pretty good with that sword of his. There was even room for him to use his sling which was something that Ham did fear. "I had hoped this space would be small. Shem will have plenty of maneuvering room."

"A matter of no import. When Mieze rises on the morrow you will be undefeatable. Your task will be to encourage your brother in whatever way is necessary to use the power of the Pointer against you. It is limited and must be wasted. If that is not possible you must kill him. Will that be a problem?"

Ham's smile was grim, full of himself and loathing for his brother. Despite the new determination Shem displayed, Ham was confident. He took one last look around the room committing it to memory. "What must be done, must be done. What of the battle outside?"

"That is of no concern to you. Mieze has strength enough for war and more. To return here to do your duty is that which is most pleasing in her eyes."

Ham knelt. "It shall be done."

How easy it had been. With a mere thought he had extended the range of the bolt and made it fly with deadly accuracy. Something that easy couldn't possibly have used up that much of the Pointer. Easy, that was the problem. It was so easy it was seductive. Shem could have stayed atop the tower and fired all night without another thought, and in so doing ruin everything. Everything he had fought so hard for. Even the slight amount of power he had used to extend the range of the bolts could prove to be the cost of failure. Failure always came cheaply.

Sleep had been impossible. There had been nowhere to escape the sounds of battle. Even over the constant noise of the falls it permeated everything. The cessation of the fighting had been even worse. The relative quiet had tormented him. He felt he should be doing something! Anything. So he found himself alone on a curtain wall halfway up the west side of falls overlooking the valley floor which would erupt once again with the rise of Mieze. He watched as a lone figure made its way down the portage road and wondered if that person was as aimless as he was at present.

Shem looked up at the night sky looking for Fiona. The silvered moon's light was faint. So much so that it barely cast any illumination at all, and what there was would quickly be swallowed up by the angry red of Mieze when it came, which would be very soon. He would have liked to have had someone to talk to. To ask them why this time was chosen? Why when Mieze was at her strongest and Fiona her weakest? Shem had never had any religious instruction. His family's farm had been on the edge of civilization. The nearest hamlet had been three candlemarks away. The border to the West had been closer and after his farm had been burned and he carried off to live with U'bad's clan any chance of learning about Fiona other than Westerner's curses had been impossible. Still, it wasn't clergy he wanted to talk to. He wanted a friend.

"Shem? Is it really you?"

Surprised, Shem turned to see who the voice belonged to, the young female voice that had called so softly to him. The voice was vaguely familiar, but he couldn't make out who the hooded figure standing beside him was. Selene was the only one who he knew in the fortress and this was not her. Recognition arrived, along with the taste of lamb chops. Shem couldn't believe it. "Sheila? What are you doing here?"

"It is you!" she said excitedly. "Ham will be so thrilled."

Shem's words tumbled all over themselves in his confusion and disbelief. "Ham is here? How? When?" He could see that his words passed right over Sheila as she continued on enthusiastically.

"I heard that you are the One! That you are going save us just like you rid the fortress of the converted. Oh Shem. I'll be able to tell everyone that I know you, that I knew you even before you became the One. It is true isn't it? You are the One, aren't you? Ham will be so glad. I know he will." Sheila's rush of words come to a halt. She cocked her head and looked at Shem, puzzled. "Shem? Are you okay?"

Shem's mind turned over what he had just heard. He wasn't sure if it was coldness, dread, or disappointment that he felt, but it must have shown on his face. *I doubt thrilled is what my brother will feel, but how did he get in? And when? Was he immune to the power of the Pointer? How far will he go to stop me?* Somehow Shem knew it was no coincidence that Ham was here just as he knew they would meet and when they met it would not be for pleasantries. "Okay? Yes, yes, I'm fine. Just surprised is all. Ham, you say."

"You have a strange way of showing it. I thought for a moment you were going to throw me off this wall!" she nearly pouted.

"No, no. That's great news and it's really good to see you, Sheila. I'm so glad that my brother and his...uh...my friend, I meant to say, has survived this madness. At least this long. How about your sister or father?" Shem instantly regretted the question. Sheila's face fell and she hung her head. "I'm sorry, Sheila. I shouldn't have asked."

"No, it's okay. I'm not sure about Janet. I haven't seen her since I fled, but my father... I think he converted."

Shem's eyes glistened in sympathy. He could blame it on the waterfall if need be. *I'm not surprised about your father. He never was one to make a stand if it meant the disruption of his business.* Shem tentatively put his arm around Sheila's shoulders and gently pulled her close giving her a hug. "I think you should go on home now, Sheila. Mieze will be rising very soon and I think she will be particularly menacing tonight."

"Okay," she said pulling out of the hug. She looked up at him, pleadingly, "You are going to save us?"

Shem took her hands in his and gave her a warm comforting smile. "Of course. I'm the One."

Sheila's tear-brimmed eyes lit up with renewed pleasure as she let go his hands and left the wall.

Mieze's rise was sudden. The darkness went from nearly black to an intense blood red in the blink of eye. The same blink shattered the silence of valley as the remaining two hundred of the Un Tier rounded the corner of the bend bellowing and cursing as they crashed into and through the pells to engage the pike men, smothering them like a rolling tide. Immediately behind the Un Tier came the remaining soldiers of Uri Yakov, mounted with lances lowered followed by hordes of the Sol Dat.

Shem, still atop the curtain wall half-way up the western side of the falls, watched the well orchestrated attack. He was impressed with the precision of the troop movement. He knew it was the influence of Uri Yakov. In all the cycles of his life in the West with the Un Tier, they had never been able to work together with anything approaching the precision of a mob. He yearned to be down among them doing something. Anything would have been better than the frustration he felt watching the destruction of the Regent's valiant forces. He felt the Pointer as it awakened at his breast.

"Easy, big fellow," came the voice of the Nem Elt-til at his shoulder. "This is not our fight. You can't do everything."

Shem released the Pointer's growing influence on him, grateful that it actually obeyed him, but he couldn't stop the bitterness that crept into his voice. "It would seem that I can't do anything!"

"Your time will come," said the little man.

Shem was not soothed. In fact his bitterness grew as the archers of the Regent fell back after firing their initial volley, themselves under attack by the arrows of the Sol Dat. It wasn't so much the enemy fire that caused their retreat, rather the fact that the pike men and those with the feather staffs, which had actually proven effective but once used not easily rearmed especially when it was stuck in the bony chest of an Un Tier, had fallen swiftly away once the mounted soldiers poured through the gaps in the pells. The archers couldn't shoot without risking hitting their own troops.

The shielded infantry fared better, but not much. They were simply no match for the mounted troops who once they broke through turned either right of left to clear the areas behind the pells or went to the aid of the few remaining Un Tier. This type of headlong suicidal strategy coming from Baron Uri Yakov surprised Shem. He had actually graduated from the Baron's arms schoo,l and knew that this tactic was not what was taught there. It was however effective in achieving its one goal. To break through the pells. The most shocking ploy was yet to come.

The Sol Dat charging hard on the heels of the mounted troops veered neither left nor right once they passed the pells. Neither did they engage the Regent's troops, but rather made straight for the civilian populace encamped all along the valley floor. Realization of what was about to occur slammed into Shem's awareness making his blood run at first cold then boil over at the calculated cruelty of it all, wholesale murder on a grand scale. This was more than Shem could stand. He couldn't stand idly by while innocents were slaughtered. He made to leave the curtain wall.

"Where do you think you are going?" asked the Nem Elt-til.

"I'm going to help."

"All by yourself. You. I suppose you think you can make a difference," stated the Nem Elt-til flatly. "Or is it just your conscience that you want to ease?"

The stinging rebuke slammed into Shem the force of a falling tree. His anger and frustration immediately transferred to the little man. Face dark and clouded with the effort to suppress the need for physical violence, the need which threatened to explode out of him, Shem spun to face his friend. Whatever it was that Shem intended to do was halted by the horns of Baron Enri Filip. Shem and the Nem Elt-til turned to watch.

The men who had been on the west bank of the Grimval, and newly marched over when it was apparent that Uri had concentrated his forces on the east side, charged forward to engage the Sol Dat. The flanks of the Regent's forces began sliding back towards Enri's in an effort to assist and regroup. They met just north of the docks and held, barely. Uri's army continued to pound against them, beating them back step by step. Empowered by Mieze's bloody red rays, they were relentless and fearless. When it seemed they were about to break through, the Regent's lines horns sounded once again. Baron Sulieman ordered the portage gate opened and his reserves, five hundred strong, poured out under the covering fire of the arbalests which were now in range.

It appeared to Shem that a stalemate was developing. Uri's army would have a difficult time advancing now that it was in range of the walls. Every step closer it managed only made the conquest that much more difficult. The archers on the walls would be able to join the arbalests. How long this situation lasted was another question. The Western army's strength did not seem to flag even though their numbers gradually decreased while the will and strength of the Central Landers waned, sapped by huge moon of Mieze.

Shem couldn't recall how long he had stood watching, but he knew he had seen enough. He also didn't know where his previous anger had gone, but it had drained off while he and the Nem Elt-til stood vigil on the wall. Untold hundreds, even more counting the civilians, lay dead or dying on the valley floor. It was beginning to sicken Shem. He asked aloud, "Why?"

"You are asking more than I can account for, Shem," said the Nem Elt-til.

It nearly escaped Shem's notice that his friend had called him by his name instead of whatever insult came to mind. He was too numb to reply. He turned and left the wall.

—◦◦◦—

The pounding had been relentless and still was. It seemed to Hap that all he had ever done in life was fight this battle. Step back, swing. Step back, swing. Unable to move forward, unable to hold their ground. Constantly they were driven back. Defeating the foe in front of you was the only goal, but always another of the cursed Westerners was instantly there to take the place of the one just fallen.

Step back, swing. Thrust. Step back, swing. Sometimes it was one of Yakov's horsemen, but mostly the bat-like ears of the Hunters, or Sol Dat as they termed themselves. Glowing in the red rays of their goddess's moon. Chanting their goddess awful songs of death. *I hate the color red!* thought Hap.

Step back, swing. Thrust. Step back, swing. At the start of the battle, Hap had invoked Fiona's mercy, but it became quickly apparent that there was only one mercy available this night,

Death. *If this is your Mercy, Fiona, I don't know how much more of it I can stand.* He was near to exhaustion and it was probably a candlemark or more until dawn, with its promise of aid.

Step back, swing. Thrust. Step back, swing. Enri's reinforcements had helped to hold the line and prevent it from being cut in two after the initial onslaught had driven Hap back, and Sulieman's timely appearance along with supporting fire from the walls and towers had buttressed them when it looked like his lines would break. Now there was no one else to count on. Not until morning. Step back, swing. Thrust. Step back, swing. Out of the corner of his eye Hap could see the docks. They didn't have much further to be driven back. At the base of the curtain wall they would stand their last.

Step back, swing. Thrust. Step back, swing. *I remember blue skies. My arm is tired.* Step back, swing. Thrust. Step back, swing. *The cool winds of Harvest drying the sweat from my brow. The rush of excitement as Jonathon's fishing line grew taught before suddenly jerking off to one side or the other.* He refused to think of his grandson. *The sweet scent of flowers in the Planting season. Goddess, but this place stinks! Sweat, blood, excrement. Fear. Pain.*

Hap wondered why the short sword of the Sol Dat standing before him was now red and dripping blood.

—◈◈◈—

The room was dimly lit. Only two candles burned at the head of Wybee's bed, and they did little to combat the chill of the early morning. Wybee lay resting, or so hoped Selene, who sat at his bedside and had been since she and Shem had returned from the Chamber of the One. Her concern for the wan little boy had grown to sympathy during the candlemarks she had sat in vigil. The door to Wybee's room opened. Selene looked up and through the shadows saw Shem enter. She felt a warmness stir within her as she remembered her lips on his and how he had reached up to gather her in his arms before she broke off the kiss. *Stop that! Keep your mind on the task at hand,* she chastised.

"It's okay, Sister," came the soft voice of Wybee. She turned back to the frail child. His tired face grinned back, "That is the reason for Tierra's awakening. So that all may learn to love one another again."

Selene felt the warmth of her blush claiming her face, glad that the darkness hid it from Shem. She patted the hand of Wybee and looked back at Shem who stood just inside the door an uncertain expression on his face. *He looks ragged, in need of rest.* "Come on in. Have a seat. You've been up all night, haven't you?"

"I've been on the wall. The Regent doesn't fare well. He's been driven back past the docks," said Shem wearily. He sank gratefully into a chair next to Selene.

The frustration and anguish in Shem's voice struck a chord of sympathy in Selene. Sympathy for the Regent, for Jonathon, Wybee, Shem, and Priest Hotig. Priest Hotig. The realization that she hadn't spared a thought for her old mentor saddened her. *Look where the road has led, old man. The awakening of Tierra has put the Central Lands on the brink of destruction. Only Shem can raise the Hjerte and only She can put an end to all this.*

"Why do you look at me like that?" asked Shem.

The question caught her off guard. She blurted the first thing to come to mind, "You look terrible. You need to rest, get some sleep."

"Thanks. You, on the other hand, look beautiful, especially when you blush, but I need to talk to Wybee first." Shem said, trying to smile but not quite pulling it off.

"What is it that concerns you, Hero," asked Wybee.

"I don't know how I'm going to do it."

The matter-of-factness of the statement gave strength to its finality. No one spoke. Feeling as if the very floor beneath her feet had disappeared leaving her core beliefs without a firm foundation, Selene fell back to the one thing she could absolutely trust. Her faith. "You have to know how, Shem. That's why you were chosen."

"It's not the physical act itself. I have that figured out, but if I release the power Vlad will be free to try to stop me. I'm not sure I have the ability to raise the Hjerte and fend off the Sun Father at the same time. If somehow I do, my brother Ham is here as well. One thing I know as absolutely true is that he is one of the converted. I don't know if he entered after I cleansed the fortress or if he was here and the cleansing had no effect on him. Neither case is very encouraging. If he entered after, then how? And how many came with him? If he was here and not cleansed, what else is he capable of? I'm positive that he will be there in the chamber to try to stop me."

"Everything you need is within you, Hero. Search your heart. Tierra would not have chosen you otherwise. You will know what to do," said Wybee.

Selene was dumbfounded. *That's all the advice Tierra could give?* She watched Shem for some sign as to how he would take Wybee's words. She expected an explosion. Instead he sat looking sorrowful.

"But Wybee, if I do this thing it will kill you. It will use you up," said Shem with a catch in his voice.

"Do not concern yourself with my well being, Hero. We all have our part to play. I've had the room next door prepared for you. There is a bed and a washbasin. Get some sleep. Remember, it needs to be done before Mieze breaks the horizon." With that Wybee closed his eyes and drifted into sleep.

Selene rose and took Shem by the arm. She put her finger to her lips for quiet and escorted Shem out the door. She could see the hurt in Shem. She hurt for him because of it. Standing before Shem's door she asked, "Are you sure about your brother? That he is here? That he is converted?"

Shem eyed the guard at Wybee's door. "Not here." He opened the door to his own room and motioned for Selene to enter. Once inside with the door securely fastened he resumed, "I met my brother's girlfriend, Sheila, on the wall about halfway up. She used to work at the Wayfarer Inn at Third Stone, her father owned it. She was excited about meeting me." Shem paused. He let loose a short lived chuckle before continuing. "Usually she could care less, but anyway, she let slip that Ham was here and something about how thrilled he would be to see me. She doesn't know."

Selene stepped into the pause, gently prompting, "Doesn't know what?"

"That Ham had converted to Mieze or that the last time I saw him, when we were both being held prisoner by Chet Sinclair, he told me that if we met again one of us would die," finished Shem, the last with a note of remorse and sadness in his eyes.

Selene began, "Oh, Shem! He didn't mean it."

"Yes, he did. What he doesn't know," interrupted Shem. The sadness and remorse faded replaced with coldness and determination, "is that I intend to win."

Tears threatened to spill over Selene's lids. She reached out and hugged Shem fiercely. *Please Tierra, don't let it cost him his soul.* She wanted to do more to comfort him. Instead she released him, led him to his bed and saw to it that he lay down. Then she went to her own room and cried.

❦

As the last rays of Mieze faded from the night sky, frustration was foremost in the mind of Uri Yakov. He was not going to defeat Regent Simon. Not while he sat at the foot of the walls of Grimval Fortress. The rock throwers were near to completion but not even those would be enough to penetrate the fortress defenses in time for the next rising of Mieze, the deadline set by the Sun Father. Uri deplored the useless waste of men caused by the tactics he had been forced to adopt at Vlad's orders.

"Soft skin! Your army will disengage and pull back. The calling has arrived. Do nothing as they pass through your lines."

Uri winced in pain. Vlad had been abrupt, heedless of anything but his own desires. Worse than that Vlad had taken control of his men. Uri watched as his army stopped fighting and took a step back without any orders from him. He knew now he had lost favor and with that came a price. It was not long in coming. Wave after wave of pain assaulted him as he collapsed to the ground unable to stand. Each wave stopped just short of killing him. He felt the gleeful gloating of Vlad as he took his revenge. All of his failures were revealed a split second before the pain rendered him incapable of thought only to revive him before the next arrived. At last they stopped.

"So you regret your allegiance to Mieze, do you?" came the insidious voice of Vlad.

Uri's heart nearly stopped beating. He knew it only continued because Vlad wanted it to. He no longer felt any fear. "Yes! Yes, I regret it. You've lied to me! I'll—-"

"You'll do nothing, soft skin, unless I allow it. For now you will watch. At the conclusion of this battle after Mieze basks in her victory, you will be displayed before all while slowly, limb by limb, your body will be reduced to ash with you capable of feeling every excruciating moment."

Uri was raised from the ground and held in stasis watching over the battlefield.

Central Landers in groups of ten to twenty, some armed some not, moved into his line of sight and walked towards the broken and smashed pells.

As the morning sun broke free of the hills around Grimval Valley, Vlad's army took two, then three, then four steps back from the remaining men of Regent Simon, Enri Filip and Ichabod Sulieman. The totally exhausted defenders made no move to reengage.

The groups of the Central Landers answering the calling continued coming in a steady stream, growing in numbers. Vlad's army stepped back further and further from the valley's defenders. Those answering the calling passed through the corridors and took up positions facing the defenders. It took two candlemarks before they stopped arriving. In all Uri estimated that there must have been over three thousand. Three thousand of Mieze's converted filling the valley against less than two hundred outside the walls loyal to Fiona.

They did not attack. As one they began chanting.

"Mieze, Mieze, Mieze, Vlad, Vlad, Vlad."

It went on and on, deafeningly loud, drowning out even the dull roar of Grimval Falls.

You will lose, Sun Father! thought Uri with all his soul. *Tierra will awaken. And when she does, you will have to deal with me!*

———◄◖/◗/◖►———

"Mieze, Mieze, Mieze, Vlad, Vlad, Vlad."

Ham woke to the sound of the first chant. Even halfway up the cliff face in Sheila's room he could hear it clearly. He turned. Sheila was still asleep, exhausted from demonstrating her pleasure at having Ham with her once again. Ham rose and dressed.

Outside he went immediately to the top of the curtain wall that made up the back of the inn in which Sheila stayed and worked. At the top he could not believe his eyes. The valley was filled with thousands of Central Landers all standing before the walls. Some were soldiers with all their weapons, some farmers with sharp implements, others merchants or money lenders, all were demonstrating their faith. It was awe inspiring. He felt a desire to join them, instead he returned to Sheila's room.

"Ham, where have you been? What's that noise?" asked Sheila sleepily.

Smiling, Ham said, "Salvation."

"Shem? But they are chanting Mieze. How can that be Shem?" asked Sheila, confused.

Anger flashed through Ham at the mention of his brother's name erasing his good feeling of a moment before. He calmed himself before asking, "What makes you think salvation comes from Shem?"

"Don't you know? He's the One! I saw him last night. He said he was going to save us," she said rising out of bed. She turned away from Ham and reached for her robe.

A calculating coldness descended on Ham. He drew his dagger and hid it along his forearm. "Did he? Where did you see him?"

"Next to the inn. I saw him going up the steps to the wall so I followed. I couldn't believe it was your brother. I had to make sure and it was!" Sheila said excitedly. She tied her robe, turned and walked up to Ham. She continued, "I told him you were here and that you'd be so happy for him."

He put one arm around Sheila drawing her close. He covered her mouth with his own and plunged his dagger into Sheila's abdomen, yanking up to make sure it did its job. He watched, a little disappointed that it had come to this, as Sheila's eyes widened in surprise before clouding over in death. He withdrew his mouth from Sheila's and said without emotion, "I can't begin to tell you how that makes me feel."

Having cleaned up Sheila's room as quickly and quietly as he could, Ham left for the stairway going down to the Chamber of the One. He had decided to hide there until the time came.

―――❧❧❧――

It was mid turning and Il'ar was worried. He paced restlessly back and forth within the confines of his tent atop the falls. His Central Lander valet, Rafal, had wisely taken up a position outside the tent flap more to warn any visitors than to protect the Easterner Lord. *Where were they?*

His mother, High Priestess El-lina, had promised that the Avians would arrive that morning and as of yet none had. Worse, the new child Cap Tan had summoned him for an explanation. It was bad enough that the turning before in a desperate, but successful, attempt to reduce the Western forces, he had led his wings to battle losing all but three of his riders, but to now have to answer to a child that Il'ar thought needed a good paddling for some of the decisions he had made, only deepened his irritation.

"Mieze, Mieze, Mieze, Vlad, Vlad, Vlad."

The incessant chanting of the thousands of Central Landers standing before the walls of Grimval Fortress chanting the name of their goddess did nothing to improve his mood. He wished that they would shut up. Il'ar felt useless. *Where are you, mother?*

"Il'ar?" The voice belonged to Ip'star one of his few remaining riders. "We shouldn't keep their Cap Tan waiting."

Il'ar stopped pacing and glared at his visitor. He hadn't heard Ip'star enter the tent.

"They will arrive, Il'ar," assured Ip'star. "I don't know why they are late, but they will arrive."

Il'ar took a deep breath and slowly exhaled, draining away some of his foul mood. "I hope so, Ip'star. Though even they may be too little now. Let's get this over with."

The two men stepped out of the tent. They were stopped by Rafal. "Il'ar, this came a moment ago." He handed a parchment scrap over to the Eastern Leader.

Il'ar perused the note. He asked his valet, "Do you know where Wybee's room is, Rafal?"

"Yes, Il'ar. I'll take you there," he said.

Il'ar scanned the eastern sky, a habit of many cycles riding with the Avians. *Nothing!* The sky was emptier than the makeshift corral they were now passing. Anwar, one of the few remaining Avians, was waiting as Il'ar came near. He nickered and nudged Il'ar looking for some attention. Il'ar stopped to scratch his mount between the ears. "I'm sorry, Anwar, I haven't any sweet cane."

"Il'ar, I have this," Rafal pulled a reddish root vegetable out of his trouser pocket and handed it to Il'ar. "Will it do?"

Il'ar examined the tuber. He held it up to his nose and sniffed. It had a sweetish scent. "What is it?"

"A sweet root. Its fresh. Just picked today," said Rafal.

Il'ar held the root up to Anwar. He sniffed it, took it out of Il'ar's hand, and crunched down. The crunching sounds increased. Anwar shook his mane and huffed in enjoyment. Il'ar smiled, enjoying Anwar's pleasure. He gave his mount one last pat and turned away. "Well at least someone's happy today. Where did you get it, Rafal?"

Rafal fidgeted, eyes darting side to side, giving Il'ar a nervous look. "My father taught me to be... ah... resourceful, sir," he said.

Il'ar laughed. "Remind me to keep you around after this is over," he said to Rafal then turned to Ip'star, "Inventory my tent."

In an improved mood, at least on the surface, the group left the corral.

The guard at the Keep Shrine checked the scrap of parchment before allowing Il'ar and Ip'star to enter. Il'ar raised his eyebrow at the increased security, but said nothing. They were met at Wybee's door by Priest Fitzpatrick.

"Any word?" he asked.

Il'ar didn't need to ask who the priest was referring to. He shook his head in the negative.

"Ill news, Milord. It won't be well received. It leaves us with only one hope," said Priest Fitzpatrick.

Il'ar put his hand on the shoulder of the priest in a consoling manner and with his voice full of resignation said, "As I understand it that is all we have ever had."

Wybee's room was well lit and contained most of the remaining important personages of the Central Lands. Jonathon sat by his friend's pillow occasionally stroking his hand in a comforting way. Baron O'Kelly hovered near Jonathon looking ready to swoop down to the rescue if necessary. Ya Ma, was also close by keeping his eye on Baron O'Kelly, Baron Sulieman, Priest Fitzpatrick, Acolyte First Selene, and Il'ar himself. Missing was Regent Simon who was still outside the gates, and Shem, arguably the most important person.

The atmosphere was gloomy as if a depressing darkness had settled over all, with the possible exception of Ya Ma, robbing them of any hope of ever seeing warmth or sunshine again. Il'ar knew his news or lack thereof was going to add to it. He saw no reason to delay the inevitable. He acknowledged Jonathon with a slight bow. "Cap Tan."

"Il'ar, second to High Priestess El-lina, next in line to the Eastern Throne, welcome," said Jonathon.

Il'ar wondered if the Cap Tan was trying to make amends for his earlier embarrassment at the Council or just practicing his manners. One thing was for sure, he wasn't exuding confidence. He was about to respond when Anwar broke into his thoughts. A glimmer of hope awakened in him. *Are you sure, Anwar? No, no. I do not doubt you. Thank you my friend. Yes, of course, another sweet root.* Il'ar turned his attention back to the young Cap Tan. He said with a mixture of pride and relief, "Cap Tan, I bring news of the high priestess."

Il'ar expected his announcement to change the mood of the room, but it was lost in the stopping of the chanting. Heads turned towards the valley entrance. Ears cocked trying to pick up the sound that had been ever present for the last six candlemarks. Il'ar wasn't sure who said it but he heard, "Thank Fiona for that, at least."

"What do you think it means?" asked Jonathon.

"It means that they now know that I am here." As if materializing out of thin air High Priestess El-lina stood in their midst. Il'ar could see that even her presence did little to dispel the dour mood of the room. She walked over to Wybee studying the sickly child. "So this is the thread we all hang on," she said cryptically.

"Tierra bids you welcome," said Wybee weakly. "She hopes to see her sister soon."

"Fiona would rejoice in that," said El-lina, "as would we all. Cap Tan, I bring family and news. Ma Ne and the Guardians hold the ridges to the east. Your cousin Tunis has closed the exit to the valley behind the forces of Uri Yakov. The Westerners are surrounded."

Jonathon did not respond. He stared at the doorway. Il'ar turned to look. Standing just inside the door was Baron Wilbert Lucas, uncle to Jonathon. Il'ar looked back to Jonathon. The Cap Tan smiled. Baron O'Kelly frowned.

"Il'ar, you have done well with few resources. I have brought the Avians," said El-lina.

Il'ar sighed with relief. He felt useful again. "Thank you, Mother."

The door to Wybee's room opened once again and Shem stepped through. "What was all that racket about?" he asked directing the question to no one in particular.

"It was the calling. The Goddess Mieze invoked it to bring her faithful to the valley to help her channel her power. Tonight when her moon rises she will be at her peak. Unstoppable," said El-lina.

"I suppose that is why Wybee told me that Tierra must awaken before the first rays of Mieze are visible," said Shem blandly his attention riveted on the bosom of El-lina's low cut tunic.

She reached up and grasped the Azure that was nestled there. She drew Shem's eyes to hers. "Yes, that is why."

"This calling, is she allowed to do that?" asked Shem.

El-lina paused, looking oddly at Shem. Finally she answered. "Ordinarily, no, but this is her moon of Ascendancy. Fiona was powerless to stop her. It did allow her to help you, though, the last time you were in the chamber. She will not be able—-or allowed—-as you put it, to intervene again."

"I see," said Shem slowly. "Well, I suppose I ought to get this over with."

Il'ar was intrigued by the interchange, but couldn't for the life of him figure out what had just happened. He did wish that the hero had shown a little more enthusiasm, though. All this dour resignation was not conducive to a happy warrior spirit, besides, he was in the mood for miracles. One thing was certain, this was not the same Shem he had met south of High City half a moon ago.

Shem gave a last, sad look at Wybee. He turned to Selene. Il'ar could see the tears glistening then brimming over as she rushed into his arms, hugging him fiercely. He hugged her back then left the room.

The chanting began again.

—⟡⟡⟡—

The rest had done Shem good, though it could have been better. When the chanting began he had felt Vlad's bond pulse in time with it. He feared that when he released the power of the Pointer, he would be unable to withstand whatever Vlad had planned for him. It was only the intervention of the Goddess Fiona that had saved him the last time and help from that quarter would not be available. Shem had to do it on his own.

Nagging at the back of his mind was another question. Was that necklace worn by the high priestess her connection to Fiona? Shem recalled that during the time he had spent traveling with her even when she was disguised as the Peddler she had often reached for it, hidden as it was beneath her tunic. Usually before she had some revelation or instruction from her goddess. Was that coincidence? The Hjerte was a jewel or stone of some sort as well. Which meant that Vlad also had to have one. The focus for Shem had always been to raise the Hjerte, but could he separate Vlad from his? Shem wished he had thought to ask Wybee about it, but it was too late now.

The little guard shack was before him and inside it the stairway leading down to the Chamber of the One. He checked his weapons. Knife on his hip, second one in his boot, sword in its scabbard, Pointer around his neck, sling around his forehead, all were where they were supposed to be. He checked his pouch to ensure he had some stones to sling. As he opened the flap and stuck his hand inside side he heard the indignant squawk of the Nem Elt-til.

"Hey, be careful you ham-fisted lummox! Don't you ever knock?"

"Sorry," mumbled Shem in surprise which quickly turned to umbrage, "What are you doing in my pouch?"

"You're not very observant, are you? I live here!" said the Nem Elt-til.

Shem asked in total disbelief, "In my pouch?"

"What do you want me to do? Nest in your hair?" The Nem Elt-til flew up to Shem's shoulder and looked critically at the shoulder length locks. "I suppose I could, but you don't wash it often enough for me."

Shem spluttered indignantly, "You can't nest in my hair! Besides, I'm going to awaken Tierra and I'm going alone."

"Good luck with that! You need me, big boy," said the Nem Elt-til.

Shem stopped. The Nem Elt-til had saved him on numerous occasions, Shem couldn't deny that, but this time was different. This time he had to face his difficulties or his destiny, as he reasoned it, by himself. He had to. Vlad had too long needed contending with. Shem realized that now. He couldn't continue knowing that the ever-present, looming shadow that was the Sun Father could strike him from within anytime, anywhere. The bond must be broken. Besides, Tierra had chosen him and it was now time to justify that. Lastly, there was Ham.

He had to survive the coming fight with Ham. Despite his declaration to Selene about winning, Shem didn't harbor any hatred toward Ham. Ham was the only family he had left, but somehow Ham didn't feel that way. He had been resentful from the first day Shem had come back into his life after escaping from U'bad's clan. He hadn't even believed Shem at first. Not until Shem had proven his knowledge of Western ways by bringing back trinkets scavenged from Un Tier campsites. Giving Ham all the credit had worked for a while, but it had apparently not been enough. After his conversion, Ham's deep-seated resentment had turned to hate. Shem sighed. He didn't want to kill his brother, but he couldn't figure out any other way.

"I knew you would see it my way," said the Nem Elt-til misreading Shem's sigh as capitulation.

Shem softened. He would have placed his hand comfortingly on the Nem Elt-til's shoulder if it were possible. He truly liked the little man and didn't want to hurt his feelings. *Not that the Nem Elt-til ever considers mine,* thought Shem ruefully, *but this is my time. This was what everything has been racing headlong towards.* "You speak truly, my friend, but that is precisely why I must go alone."

The Nem Elt-til flew off Shem's shoulder and hovered in front of his face, studying it intensely. Apparently making up his mind he said, "Good luck, Hero," sounding this time like he meant it.

Resolved, Shem stepped into the guard shack and began his descent down the stairs. *No torch,* he decided. Not knowing where Ham was, he did not want to give away his position by lighting up the stairway. Carefully and as quietly as he could, he made his way down. It was slow going in the darkness. Every so often he would stop and listen before continuing on. Near as he could figure he had at least three candlemarks before the sunset and then at least four before Mieze rose after that. He did not know how long it would take to do the awakening, but that uncertainty wasn't worth the cost of stumbling headlong into danger. The rumbling of the falls grew fainter the deeper he went until at last he could hear it no longer. The same could not be said about the chanting. It seemed to pulse its way through everything. It wasn't loud, it was just there and a little unsettling, like his plans for the coming battle.

Shem stopped to rest, sitting on the cold stone steps. It wasn't that he was necessarily tired, but he had a few things to square within himself. He thought back to his conversation with Wybee concerning use of the Pointer, or more specifically, controlling it. Wybee had said that Tierra knew what he needed, but if he was specific in his desires, would she do it his way? It would be a lot easier to wield his weapon if he knew what the weapon would do beforehand. If he could master it's use then perhaps he could conserve the amount used. There was also the little incident at the farmstead graves when his sword refused to obey his muscles. He could ill afford a repeat of that in the chamber. Finally, though he didn't yet know how, he had to figure out a way to separate Vlad from his connection to Mieze. Could he follow it back from the bond to its source? Shem settled into a comfortable position as he visualized the coming confrontation.

—◦◦◦—

At the bottom of the stairs, in a little nook at the base of the wall and the stairwell, waited Ham, thankful that his earlier reconnoiter had paid off. After leaving Sheila's room he had made his way down to the Shrine Keep and found it still guarded. He didn't believe his story of paying homage in the chamber would work again, so he went instead to the portage gate. He had discovered that the portage tunnels had a spur that led to the Chamber of the One. It hadn't been guarded before and wasn't now. He entered and made his way to the stairs leading down.

Bolstered by the chanting of those outside, Ham's steps grew stronger. He thought it amazing that he could still hear the chanting even though the rumble of the falls had faded. He basked in the rhythmic waves as they enveloped him giving him a sense of invincibility.

"Yes, Ham. Feel the power of the Goddess Mieze. The calling. It was sent for you. To counter the Gedeelte carried by your brother. As long as they call, you can draw upon Mieze and she has much to give. Tonight the Ascendancy is at its fullest. Tonight with the rising of Her moon you will be undefeatable."

The voice of Vlad faded from his mind. Ham had what he had wanted, without even realizing it, from his earliest childhood. The means of paying Shem back for that night when he had sat over him with that bloody rock in his raised hand. Not the petty pleasure of letting him get what he deserved for slight infractions, but once and for all. Ham continued down the stone stairs that led down to the chamber with a smile on his lips and a feverish intensity in his eyes that bordered on insanity. He waited to hear the footfalls of his brother.

—◦◦◦—

Selene closed the door to Wybee's room. She could no longer bear the oppressive silence, the suffocating wait that blanketed them, all except Wybee who had fallen into a light sleep. For all the earlier talk of the One bringing their salvation the room had all the cheeriness of the Acolyte's Hall awaiting the results of their last jury.

Il'ar had left earlier to see to the newly arrived Avians and to get reports on the new troop placements, Jonathon had left as well to talk in private with his Uncle, Baron Wilbert Lucas, accompanied by Ya Ma with Baron O'Kelly scampering after them. With Selene's departure that left only the High Priestess El-lina and Priest Fitzpatrick to keep vigil with Wybee.

"Are you ready?"

Selene knew the voice of the little man by now and did not bother to turn to look at him perched upon her shoulder. "Ready for what?"

"To go rescue our favorite chump," he said.

Despite her gloominess, she smiled. "He said he had to do it alone."

"Like that's going to happen. You heard the Vaar Tu. He needs us," snorted the Nem Elt-til.

Selene recalled the words. Wybee had told the Nem Elt-til to stay by Shem and that he would be sorely needed, but no mention had been made of her. On the other hand nothing was said against her going and she wasn't going to let a hurried hug be her last memory of Shem. She summoned up her hopeful optimism, rejecting the possibility of failure. "Let's go. It's a good turning for a rescue!"

—◦◦◦—

An exhausted Sloan Quinn gazed over the body-strewn battlefield. They littered the road, the docks, the gentle slope leading to the steep cliffs lying where they had fallen. Here and there were heaps designating the spots where heroic efforts had occurred, but mostly they lie in singles or pairs. It wouldn't be long before the stench of decay set in. The Westerners had not bothered to drag their dead or injured with them while they disengaged. Nor had his own forces been able to extract their fallen as they had steadily retreated to the curtain wall of the fortress, none save the Regent. Sloan had seen him pierced by the sword of a Sol Dat. He had been able to drag him free, somehow, but who knew anything for certain during the heat of battle and he now lay severely injured at the base of the wall, weak but alive. Then the fighting had just stopped. Uri's army pulled back making way for the hordes that simply stood before them.

Sloan thought he recognized some of the people in the horde from High City. There was a merchant who he used to buy fried pies from, he thought he saw the smithy who had forged his last sword, and even an old childhood friend who had farmed around Fourth Stone. It was an eerie feeling as they just stood there with blank faces looking off into nothing. Who knew what they saw before their eyes? Sloan didn't. He was just sure that whatever it was wasn't the reality he saw with his. Then the chanting began.

Sloan had looked around for Priest Conyn or Baron Enri Filip during the lull. He considered it a lull as victory was at hand for the Western forces if they would just reach out and take it. Neither the baron nor his long time priest was to be found. Sloan had desperately wanted to know the meaning of all that was happening. He also was hoping to be able to establish communications with the fortress to try and get them to open the portage gate long enough to extract the remainder of the Central Lander army. Neither had occurred. All he had left was about three hundred or less, tired and injured troops facing untold numbers of his own countrymen who simply stood in front of them chanting, chanting, chanting.

Sloan wished they would shut up, but feared them doing so.

24

CHAMBER OF THE ONE

The Pointer urged Shem out of his reverie by informing him that it was nearly nightfall. He had but four candlemarks left to achieve the awakening of Tierra before the rising of Mieze. Shem had been contemplating the fight before him. Foremost on his mind had been separating Vlad from the power of Mieze. Would it lessen his abilities? Was it possible to fight Vlad and Ham separately? And where was Ham now? Without answers, it had been nearly impossible to plan every aspect of the impending fight, but Shem had done the best he could, and now had what he hoped was something workable. With a heavy sigh Shem rose and proceeded down the stairs.

Other than the chanting which was felt more than heard, Shem descended in silence. He entered the Chamber of the One and walked to the plaque. The Pointer's energy strained to be released. Surprisingly it did not surge downward though the position of the Hjerte below him was firmly set in his mind. Shem could feel the artifact's desire to be free. Cognizant of Vlad's bond and the fact that Ham had yet to make an appearance, Shem let a trickle of the Pointer's power out and directed it downward towards the Hjerte. As the first tendril touched it a warning again surged frantically upward. "Stop! Stop!" At the same time Shem heard the voice he had been dreading.

"Hello, Brother."

Shem kept his back to Ham. He didn't want to face him. He didn't want to see what he heard in his brother's voice, his desire to kill Shem. He had hoped to face Vlad first. That, at least, wouldn't have been a face to face confrontation. Now he knew that Vlad had been waiting for Ham to strike first, forcing Shem to fight them both at the same time, making him use the Pointer's power just to stay alive. Of the two, Shem considered Vlad the more potent foe. He had to get him to open the bond.

Shem had recalled how Fiona had surrounded Vlad's compulsion before forcing it back and sealing the bond, a seal that would be broken when Shem exerted power. He knew that he did not have near the strength of a goddess, but perhaps he could surround himself with a shield that would give him enough time to try the plan he had devised while on the stairs. Hopefully it would not use up too much of the Pointer. He directed the Pointer to shield his mind, then without turning around released a ball of energy at Ham. The small sphere of contained force slammed Ham against the chamber wall. *It had worked!* The Pointer was following his commands.

As expected Vlad eagerly pounced, trying to overwhelm him quickly. He nearly succeeded. Shem staggered under the amount of mental force that Vlad unleashed against him, hammering against his shield which barely held. Shem sent a thread back along the bond. He saw a skeletal frame, hardly more than skin and bones grasping a large, ruby red stone on a pedestal that glowed an angry red and beat in time to the chanting. Desperate and with little time remaining, he sent a burst of power through the bond to try to break the contact. He felt as much as saw the green light that exploded around the globe. He felt the surprise of Vlad who nearly broke contact with the Auge Ose, for Shem now knew that that was what the ruby globe was. He also felt a lessening of Vlad's attack against his shield. Shem began to slide into unconsciousness. He fought it with every ounce of strength he could muster without calling on the Pointer. He had to stay alert enough to confront Ham whose attack he expected at any moment. He clung to awareness as he sank to his knees drained both by Vlad's attacks and the amount of power he had released from the Pointer. He thought it strange that the Pointer was now draining energy from himself as well. Had he used up Wybee already? He prayed to Tierra that it was not so.

He heard a faltering of the chanting. His attack against Vlad was working. Now was the time to separate Vlad from the Auge Ose. He sent another burst knowing that he did not have the power to spare. Darkness stepped closer and closer to him.

—◦∅◦—

The pit of the Auge Ose glowed a bloody red, pulsating in time with the chant of the calling. Erik descended the steps. He knew that he would find the Sun Father there. Vlad had not left the pit for over half a moon. He no longer ate, no longer drank. He stayed clasping the ruby as it slowly consumed him. Erik feared that Vlad would die before the rising of Mieze, the culmination of her Ascendency. He feared even more that he would not. He had long known that Vlad had killed his father and he intended to return the favor. And return it before the Sun Father became a demigod.

At the bottom of the stairs Erik witnessed Vlad, encompassed in the glow of the Auge Ose, launch his attack on Shem. He watched in surprise as the ruby was suddenly encased in an emerald green glow, momentarily shocking Vlad into almost releasing his grip. A second green burst did break the grip of Vlad leaving him stunned for an instant. *This is my opportunity.* His father had died a slow agonizing death. Erik had hoped to return that favor as well, but one did not rebuff opportunity merely because it did not fit one's fantasy. He slid his dagger out of its sheath and into the vitals of Vlad the Sun Father.

—◦∅◦—

The chanting of the calling faltered. Uri felt himself lowering to the ground. Excitement surged through him along with hope. Hope for one last shot at the Sun Father. *He's losing! The Western bastard's losing!* He noted the confused and uncertain faces of the Sol Dat. Bereft of Vlad's iron control their confidence had eroded. The stasis that held Uri vanished. He staggered a few steps before regaining his balance. Determined not to waste this opportunity, he drew his sword and charged forward. "Men of Yakstown, follow me!"

He didn't look back nor did he bother with the Western soldiers. The calling had faltered and he intended to halt it for good. That they were Central Landers did not cross Uri's mind. They were one of the sources of Vlad's power and he meant to see that they could not be tapped into again. He and his men fell upon them with a vengeance.

Those who had answered the calling did nothing to defend themselves. Uri and his men slaughtered them until the chanting stopped. He had won. At least this fight. Towards his rear came the sounds of another attacking force. The Central Landers loyal to Fiona were launching a counter offensive. He turned his men towards the Sol Dat and raised his sword. "For Tierra!" he yelled calling on the name of the only goddess he had not renounced.

An angry, hysterical, female voice screamed in Uri's mind, "None renounce me and live!" A flash of red encompassed him. When it was gone, the reddened ashes of Baron Uri Yakov were all that remained.

⁂

The struggle was difficult, one of the hardest things Shem had ever tried to do. He knew he couldn't lose consciousness. The temptation to use the Pointer to heal himself was great, but Shem was afraid. Afraid that he had already used too much of its limited resources. He looked up from the floor where he now sprawled.

Ham was picking himself up off the floor of the Chamber of the One. He stood still a moment to bring his labored breathing under control. Shem could relate. His own breath came in shallow gasps. Watching Ham dust himself off, Shem marveled. The force with which Ham had slammed into the wall would have killed a normal man, or at least rendered him unconscious, but all it had achieved was to stun him and that only for a few moments. Shem's eyes followed Ham's slow advance until he towered over him.

"Surprised? Did you think that my goddess had no gifts to give? I have no need of limited trinkets. Mieze provides all," he gloated, reaching down and grabbing Shem by the shirt. Effortlessly, he raised Shem up with one hand, holding him suspended in the air. Their gazes locked on one another.

No words were spoken. None were needed. Ham's crazed stare told Shem that his brother was gone, forever lost. His widening grin, more menacing than pleasurable, proved the truth of that. Shem slumped in Ham's grip, his body going lax.

Ham released Shem, who crumpled to the floor in a heap.

"Yes, I like that better. You see, Shem, I've seen you lying on the floor helpless before me. The Sun Father showed it to me. Aren't you going to get up? Don't you want to fight me? I want you to. I want to do to you what you did to me on that night, Shem. The Sun Father showed that to me, too. How you tried to kill me to save yourself!"

Shem managed to make it to his knees. *Buy some time.* He gasped, "That's not true, Ham. Vlad showed you what you wanted to see, not what happened."

"Liar!" said Ham kicking Shem viciously in his exposed ribs. "He showed me the truth! And now you're going to pay." Ham drew his sword, holding the point to Shem's throat. "Beg before I kill you."

Shem bent over clutching his aching ribs. He couldn't fight Ham in this condition, not without drawing on the Pointer. He knew it and worse still, Ham knew it too. But he wasn't giving up. He tried to reach his brother one last time. "I'm not going to fight you, Ham."

"I've already won, Shem. I told you to beg," he said.

"Heal yourself. Raise the Hjerte. Now is the time."

Shem had no idea who the sweet seductive voice belonged to, but it sang to him. It gave him sage advice. He longed to obey it, but a nagging doubt lingered. Twice he had touched the Hjerte. Twice it had warned him away.

"Heal yourself. Raise the Hjerte. Now is the time."

The chanting stopped.

For a moment it was if time didn't exist. Ham stood transfixed, eyes sightless, listening to some inner voice. Shem felt his sling loosen from his forehead and drop away.

"The cavalry's here, big boy. Do your thing," came the voice of the Nem Elt -til in his ear.

Shem thought furiously. The words of Wybee drifted into Shem's rapidly racing thoughts, *We all have our part to play. The birth of a goddess requires sacrifice.* Shem tried mightily to remember who had said that, but couldn't bring it to mind. *No matter,* he thought, *what is, is.*

"Heal yourself. Raise the Hjerte. Now is the time."

Where's the path? The words of Wybee floated in his mind, harsh in comparison to the sweetness luring him. "All you need is inside of you. Search your heart."

Shem knew his time was rapidly running out. He didn't know what had stopped the chanting, but he knew it would start again and when it did his opportunity to act will have passed. The first stirrings of panic nibbled around the edges of his determination. His mind went back to the night he had pledged his allegiance to Tierra. Free of the alcoholic haze he saw for the first time what had actually transpired. The materializing of the emerald green kernel. How it embedded itself within his chest, within his very heart. *Of course! How could I have missed it.* The revelation lifted Shem's hopes. He said aloud, "The touching. It's been the touching all along."

The sweet seductive voice, which had been luring him ever so delectably, became shrilly audible, echoing through the chamber. "Kill him! Kill him now!" The booming command of Mieze freed Ham from his inaction.

Shem staggered to his feet. He saw the Nem Elt-til flitting around Ham's head. He saw Selene wildly swinging his sling about trying to use it like a club. He knew he had only moments before Ham swept them aside. Shem summoned all the remaining power of the Pointer and funneled it into the emerald kernel that resided in his chest. All other sensations faded as the warmth of the Pointer's power caused the kernel to come alive, greedily absorbing all that could be given it. The touching continued expanding in his chest, swelling and swelling, near to bursting. Then the Pointer was spent. In a blinding flash of emerald green the touching released its accumulated power.

The flash staggered an infuriated Ham who was swatting ineffectively at the buzzing little man. He cried out in pain as the Nem Elt-til fired a small arrow into his eye. The arrow was followed immediately by the sling, stone in pouch, striking Ham in the same eye, driving the little arrow in even deeper. Ham's sword clattered to the stone floor as he clutched at his wounded eye.

Shem knew he should advance, take advantage of Ham's temporary weakness. He had no doubt his brother's injury would prove only superficial and now that the Pointer lay dull and cold against his chest, he needed to press home against every chink in Ham's armor. Still, he stood motionless, awaiting, as always, Ham's judgment.

"We could use a little help here," shouted out the Nem Elt-til. "Now would be a good time."

Shem stood motionless, confused. *Did I do it? Did it work?* Other than the green flash Shem could discern no change. Until. It was the faintest of tremors. Having already touched it twice, Shem was well familiar with the location of the Hjerte. It was stirring. The lights from the globes illuminating the chamber winked out.

Poo-ooom!

Shem staggered forward propelled by the concussive force of whatever had happened behind him. He threw his arms over his head to ward against rock chips falling from the ceiling of the chamber. The Gedeelte burst into a blindingly bright green.

Bright as the Gedeelte shone, it was but a pinprick compared to the emerald shaft which had punched its way from the chamber floor up and through the roof. Within the shaft the Gedeelte was rising.

Muscles, pumped with adrenaline and the sure knowledge of a coming fight, bulged from Shem's chest, arms, and legs. From somewhere a slight breeze lifted a lock of his hair and blew it back past his shoulder. He looked and felt every inch the hero. Drawn by the light and beckoning shelter of Shem's protection, Selene and then the Nem Elt-til made their way to stand behind him.

"You did it, hero," said the Nem Elt-til from his perch on Shem's shoulder.

From his other shoulder he felt the hand of Selene exuding confidence as she stood head to shoulder with him. Shem felt proud. Tierra had awakened. Now he could deal with Ham, however bittersweet that would prove to be. Jaw set, Shem drew his sword. "It's over, Ham."

Ham dropped his hands from his wounded eye. Blood from the ruined orb trickled down his cheek in counterpoint to the defiance blazing from his uninjured eye which now glowed with a reddish hue. Shem watched. A ruby patch began to form over Ham's ruined eye protecting the socket from the elements. Ham reached out his hand. His sword rose from the cavern floor into his grasp.

"You're wrong, Brother. It has just begun," laughed Ham.

Ham cast his attention towards Selene and the Nem Elt-til, the two responsible for his wounding. He raised his sword pointing it at the pair. A red tinged ball of energy formed at the hilt and raced down the length of the sword shooting outward.

Shem raised his forearm. A stone shield materialized on his forearm deflecting the energy upward to crash into the roof of the chamber. Rock chips fell among the trio.

Shem felt a tremor through the soles of his boots. It was as if the bones of the land twitched.

"Your are correct, Hero. The land is restless. It misses the Hjerte. Now that it is gone it will revert back to the way it was before. You and your friends should leave."

The voice of Wybee left him. The void replaced with yet another subtereanean rumble. This one was obvious to all. More rock chips fell from the ceiling this time intermingled with droplets of water. He felt the tension in Selene's hands as she gripped his shoulders tighter.

"If we spread out I think we can take him," said the Nem Elt-til.

He heard the nervousness concealed behind the Nem Elt-til's bravado. When he spoke it was barely above a whisper. "We need to get out of here. Stay behind me as I ease over towards the door.

Outwardly unconcerned about the instability of the chamber, Ham cut off Shem's access to the door of the chamber. He stalked the trio determinedly. Ham's quick glance upward confirmed Shem's sense that the Hjerte was rising through the chamber roof.

"Don't think that rock's going to save you, Shem," said Ham.

He launched a furious assault seemingly striking from all sides. Shem blocked every attempt, some with his sword, others by allowing the Pointer to generate whatever needed armor was necessary, especially for his friends who still crouched behind him. Surprisingly, a number of Ham's strikes were directed at the emerald pillar. Shem used his brother's momentary preoccupation to maneuver himself between Ham and the chamber's exit. His attack thwarted, Ham stepped back, catching his breath. Idly, he wiped moisture off his forehead.

Shem knew that this was his best moment of escape. Ham was winded and he and his friends had a clear path towards the chamber exit. But when it came down to it he found that he couldn't give up on his brother without a final attempt to save him.

"You are right, Ham. The Hjerte is not going to save me. Tierra is. There's still a chance for you."

"Funny, I was going to offer you the same thing, but I decided I'd rather not share," said Ham between breaths.

The whole chamber lurched suddenly. Up, down, left, right, it seemed to move in every direction at once.

CRA_A_ACK! CA-AR-OOM-M-M.

The floor and ceiling of the chamber split wide seperating the brothers. Fissures honeycombed the ceiling, each crack dripping a steadily increasing stream of water. Shem could hear kerplunks as rubble fell into the gap and splashed into the water below. The time between the splash echoes getting shorter and shorter as the water rose.

"If you have an exit stratgey, hero, I'm all ears," said the Nem Elt-til

"Take Selene. Make for the stairs. Quickly you haven't much time. I'll keep Ham occupied. Go now!"

Shem reached back and shoved Selene towards the chamber entrance. He kept his eyes on Ham.

Shifting his sword to his left hand, he gathered a ball of emerald energy in his right, "Let's finish this, Brother."

"With pleasure," replied Ham, a similar red tinged ball building at the hilt of his sword.

Shem was ready first. He hurled the energy at Ham. The magical sphere caught him chest centered and exploded in an emerald blast. Through the explosive blast strode Ham, numerous red balls of energy lined up on his sword.

He raised his arm in the direction of Shem just as a column of water geysered up through the chasm seperating them. Ham lost his footing as the land convulsed. Balls of energy flew into the chamber roof above him. Down came tons of rock and water. Shem turned and ran.

He barely made the chamber door in time. Behind him he willed the door sealed. The Gedeelte made it so, stopping the flooding waters. Shem knew it wouldn't hold for long. A quick glance upward told him it wouldn't matter if it did. Water was cascading down the stairwell as well as detrius from the ground shaking. He dodged and splashed around some larger pieces of stone and made the stairs. He sprinted up staying just ahead of the rising water. Ahead of him he spied Selene and the Nem Elt-til.

They were huddled on the edge of a precipice made by a partial collapse of the stairs. Selene sat holding her ankle. Tears and blood from a couple of abrasions competing with the falling water streaming down her face. Shem had the Gedeelte make a shield above them and hastened towards the refuge.

"She got struck by a falling rock, Hero. Busted her ankle. Of course it did save us from being swept away when the stairs collapsed."

Shem looked down. A bone had broken the skin and was protruding out. He had broken a bone or two during his time being raised by the Un Tier. He knew the pain Selene was in. First he needed to protect them from the rising water. He extend the shield downward encasing them all in an emerald bubble. Then he gingerly took Selene's leg and foot in his hands. "This is going to hurt, I'm sorry."

At the first gasp of pain a glow encased Shem's hands and Selene's foot. Three pairs of eyes watched as the bone, pushed into place, began to knit. The bleeding stopped and Selene's skin reformed around her ankle.

Shem asked anxiously, "How do you feel?"

"Better, thanks," replied Selene her eyes growing wide as the water rose all around them. "Your brother?"

Shem ducked his head. There hadn't been anything he could do. Ham had been too far gone. Too completely in the clutches of Mieze to break him free. He shook his head negatively, "The last I saw him he was firing balls of energy all about the chamber and it was collapsing around him. No hope."

The land must have agreed. With a sound of finality it gave a last groan and shake to settle the contents of her upheaval. When it was over the green bubble was completely buried in rock.

"This kinda sucks," offered the Nem Elt-til as he surveyed their surroundings. "What I'd really like is for us to be at the top of the falls looking down at all this."

With a soft pop the friends disappeared.

—◦◊◦—

"Mieze, Mieze, Mieze, Vlad, Vlad, Vlad."

It was the only sound heard in Wybee's room. It hung over all like an ominous pall drowning out even the roar of the falls, dampening the spirits of El-lina and Priest Fitzpatrick. Still the silent vigil continued. It had been five candlemarks since Shem had left to bring on the awakening.

Wybee stirred. A low moan escaped his lips. Then another.

El-lina wiped his brow with a cool cloth. "It begins."

"He has been a brave child and has suffered much for Tierra," lamented Priest Fitzpatrick.

"Yes, as have many others. The world travails at the birth of a goddess."

"But why did she choose a time when her sister was at the peak of her power?" asked Priest Fitzpatrick.

"Shem often asked me that question during the time we traveled together. I have no more of an answer now than I did then. A goddess does as a goddess will."

The falling face and slumping shoulders of the priest told El-lina that the emptiness of the platitude satisfied Priest Fitzpatrick no more than it ever did Shem, but it was all the high priestess had to offer. She simply didn't know why. El-lina felt the discharge of energy originating in the chamber far beneath their feet. The chanting faltered then came to a halt.

Wybee's breathing ceased. Sadly both clergy looked to Wybee watching as his sacrifice came to its conclusion. El-lina began to offer a benediction, but the words forming on her lips fell into silence as an emerald green glow began to encompass him. They uttered not a sound as the glow coalesced into a bubble around him, thickening until the two could no longer see into it.

Mesmerized El-lina had no knowledge of the amount of time that had passed. Wonder and amazement filled her as the green orb continued to grow. Waves of emotion emanated from the globe, love, kindness, understanding, the sense of green things growing, goodness, and other feelings not so easily recognized but necessary to all living things.

The room rocked from an explosion far below. An emerald green shaft appeared encompasing Wybee and taking him upward into the night sky.

"Can it be?" she asked aloud. "Was Tierra with us all this time?"

El-lina was astounded when Tierra answered. "Yes, child. I wanted to experience the fleeting cycles of those who will worship me. I am much pleased, but must now deal with my sister."

El-lina rushed out of the keep. They alone had witnessed the birth of the goddess, and now desired to keep the awe inspiring vision within their sight as they fled the keep for the safety of the eastern tower.

⸭∞∞⸭

"The Westerners will not be able to breach the walls of Grimval, Uncle," declared Jonathon passionately. He earnestly believed this. He had to. He had run out of other options. The moon of Mieze was about to rise and complete the Ascendancy. Tierra's hero looked to have failed.

The tiny room at the top of the east tower swayed. It caught no one's attention. Nor did the muffled sound of a lid popping off a pot under too much steam barely cut through the constant roar of the falls. The bright green light knifing through the arrow slits of the tower walls managed to garner the attention of Jonathon, but it was the voice of Wybee that broke off the conversation he was having with his Uncle.

"Jonathon."

He looked all around, searchingly. "Wybee?"

"Yes, Jonathon, it's me."

Jonathon peeked at his Uncle who bore a hopeful look. "Are you in my head?"

"Yes, Jonathon. It is done. The One was successful. Tierra wishes to speak with you."

Jonathon brought his hand up to scratch his head. He was delaying. Wybee had never had the ability to speak to him in this way before. He didn't want to ask, but one thing he had learned since he became Cap Tan was to face problems when they were small otherwise they would only get bigger. His throat tightened. It was all he could do to choke out the next words. "Wybee, did you die?"

Wybee's words, when they came were wondrous, filled with awe. "No Jonathon, not in the way you mean. The Nem Elt-til had the right of it. Vaar Tu, he named me. The vessel. You see, I was always Tierra, only I didn't know it. It is true I no longer inhabit the body of Wybee, but I am not dead. I am more alive now than I ever was. The Hero did it, Jonathon." The shaking and rumbling of the ground was definate and pronounced this time. The light green rays penetrating the arrow slits grew brighter in intensity. Even the roar of the falls altered slightly as if the water had been diverted from its natural course. The voice of Tierra changed, becoming the voice Jonathon remembered from the tunnels. "The awakening has been achieved. It is now time for you to be high priest. I want you to go to the top of this tower. You must address our people."

The globe that had been Wybee had risen far above the falls and centered itself above the eastern most tower, a single intense ray of light illuminated the form of Jonathon. He stood looking over the field of battle. So bright was the light of the newly risen goddess that the valley floor was lit up as if it were midturning. Instead of the expected ruby light of Mieze in full Ascendency it was bathed in the vibrant green of renewal, of Tierra. All fighting had ceased while faces, some rapt, some in disbelief, others in terror stared up at the tower awaiting the coming of something momentous. Before Jonathon was the Hjerte. He tentatively reached out and placed one hand on the jade stone. When he spoke it was with the power of Tierra.

"People of the Central Lands, behold! Tierra has awakened! Rejoice at her coming. People of the West, lay down your arms. The battle is over. It is time to go home."

Bereft of the diabolical will that had been driving them the Sol Dat and remaining Un Tier milled about aimlessly, weapons dropping from their hands to lie ownerless on the blood soaked ground. Most tried shielding their eyes from the brightness of Tierra as they made their way down river away from the fortress, away from the valley, away from the assembled troops of the Central Lands, but mostly away from the damning presence of Tierra.

Jonathon looked out over the assemblage. Carnage and suffering filled the valley and its inhabitants, but not his vision. Supplied and butressed by Tierra, what Jonathon saw was a stronger united Central Land full of hope and promise. It was time to start the healing. His conversations with his uncle had revealed to him how much hurt his decisions had cost the people of the Central Lands. His grandfather's selflessness had pricked his conscience as well, though his new role as high priest was probably the most telling. One could not hide the truth from a goddess nor should the truth be hidden from the people. Wybee had taught him this, though he had not done a very good job of learning. It was time for amends.

"Do not harm the Westerners as they leave. Do no harm to those who answered the calling. They were once our brothers and sisters, and with the good graces of Tierra, they will be again. Open the gates. Send forth the healers. Let all who wish to enter do so with the blessings of Tierra."

After having delivered Tierra's message, Jonathon left the top of the tower bound for the eastern portage gate accompanied by Baron Lucas and Ya Ma. He wanted to see his grandfather again. As they neared the portage gate, they encountered a small group led by El-lina and Priest Fitzpatrick. They were all covered with a streaky film of rock dust. He looked out across the falls pool and gasped. The Shrine Keep and its small rock island had sunk into the pool. All that remained was a thin strip that held the curtain wall.

"What happened?"

"All that I can surmised, Cap Tan," offered El-lina, "is that the Hjerte was the anchor holding the islet in place. When it was raised, the land reverted to its original state."

"Any other survivors?" A sniggling factiod teased around the edges of Jonathon's rememberance. It came to him a moment later. With a catch in his breath he asked, "The Hero?"

El-lina and Priest Fitzpatrick merely shook their heads.

Jonathon felt their anquish, but had already had a full plate of loss. He filed away the Hero's demise for later consideration and turned to go out the gate. He found his grandfather off to the river-side of the road, lying in the grass. A temple healer knelt before the prone body. Fearing the answer, Jonathon asked, "Is he alive?"

The healer looked up, then back down to his patient. "He has lost a lot of blood. His bandage needs changing, but yes, Cap Tan. He is alive... for now."

Regent Simon's eyes blinked open. He raised his hand slightly, offering it to his grandson. "Jonathon?" he asked weakly.

Jonathon knelt beside his grandfather and took the proffered hand squeezing it to reassure him. His tears flowed freely. He knew the blood soaked bandages wrapped around his grandfather's abdomen and chest soaked up the life essence, which was slowly seeping out. He had but one hope. Head bowed, voice tight with pain he said, "Tierra, save him."

"The flesh is not willing, Jonathon. I'm sorry."

Regent Simon's hand gave Jonathon's a feeble squeeze. He tried to smile, but the effort was too great.

"Grandfather, I was wrong to keep the gates shut. I am sorry."

"And I to press so hard. All is well, Grandson. Do not grieve," whispered Hap. He closed his eyes and slipped into the beyond.

Jonathon's head fell to his chest. Waves of guilt and anguish rose up out of his chest and swept through his entire being. He wanted to wail, to stand up and stomp his foot demanding a new outcome, he wanted to deny all that had just occurred, but the dignity of his office prevented it. Instead he kept his head lowered while his tears made their streaky wet, glistening tracks down his cheeks. He held to his grandfather's hand until the healer quietly touched his hand.

"Jonathon." The soothing voice of Tierra reached out to him.

Jonathon was too hurt to respond to the voice in his head. He released his grandfather's hand and slowly rose. The voice shifted to that of Wybee.

"Jonathon. I know you suffer, but others suffer as well. Call for repentance. Those that accept will be healed and cleansed of Mieze."

Jonathon did as he was told, but did not stay to watch. Numb, he walked slowly back into the fortress. He heard the voices praising Tierra but did not share in the celebration of Tierra's good graces. He made his way to the eastern tower and collapsed into the first bed he found.

—◦◦◦—

None would see the rising of Mieze that night, overshadowed as she was by the awakening of Tierra. None heard the cosmic cataclysm that erupted in the heavens above as Mieze lashed out in one last desperate attempt to thwart her sister. None saw Mieze submit. It was all hidden behind the globe of Tierra as she bathed and cleansed the Central Lands freeing it from the taint of her sister's ambitions. At least for now.

AFTERMATH

The celebration was in full swing and had been for the last two turnings. The enticing aroma of roasted meats, spicy stews, and fruity sweetmeats permeated the gathering. The great hall of Baron Ichabod Sulieman was full to overflowing with guests that wandered in and out, there being as many tables set up outside the hall as within, strolling minstrels or acrobats, and those repentant who had answered the calling and were now searching to reconnect with lost friends and family members. The hall was well lit with torches which provided a little warmth to take the edge off the harvest season chill as well as to provide illumination.

At the front of the hall was the Baron's Table. Cap Tan Jonathon Sinclair, sitting in the seat of honor, presided over the festival-like gathering. It was his first turning in attendance. The previous turning while the rest of the barons had buried the dead and paid tribute to the many fallen, he had been ensconced in a shrine observing the Ceremony of the High Priest, a mostly private affair between himself and Tierra. There he had been officially presented with the Hjerte and had received initiation into the priesthood. The ceremony had wrought a significant change in him.

He had entered a sorrowful, grief-stricken young boy and had left at ease with himself and his new duties. Well, he was mostly at ease. His mind still drifted occasionally to Shem. None had seen the hero or any of his party since the night the Keep Shrine had collapsed into the falls pool at the base of the Grimval Falls.

Like Jonathon most at the table knew of Shem and his party but few actually knew them. Only El-lina and Ip'star had spent any significant time with Tierra's chosen. Strangely, neither of them seemed overly saddened.

"What now, Cap Tan?" asked Baron Sulieman who was leaning forward to speak around Baron Lucas.

It appeared that Jonathon hadn't heard the question. He took a moment to take in the festive atmosphere and the guests sitting with him at the table, High Priestess El-lina, Barons Lucas, O'Kelly, and Sulieman, Il'ar, Ip'star, Priest Fitzpatrick, and of course, Lady Na Na and Worrell. Many had heard the question and seemed eager to hear the answer. Truth was there was much to be done. Assessments had to be made about how much damage the Westerners had inflicted on Yakstown, High City, and Grimval Fortress; what was the state of the farmsteads along the border; casualties had to be counted; and justice dealt to the families of Barons Arn Reis and Juan Iago. But at the moment Jonathon did not want to deal with these issues. There would be plenty of time for those.

"Jonathon?" prodded Baron Lucas.

He looked first to his uncle Lucas then El-lina. The question had been a plant, the answer carefully constructed to generate trust in Jonathon's leadership. He knew the answer and finally spoke. "This turning we continue to give thanks to the Goddesses Fiona and Tierra. It is to them that we owe the victory. On the morrow, I shall pay my final respects to Regent Simon and Baron Filip. After that, journey to High City. As soon as it is presentable we shall hold a Council of Barons to determine our future course. Tierra desires a Conclave of all the lands to try and work out our differences. It is her desire that we seek harmony among our people."

"Do you think the West will attend?" asked Baron O'Kelly.

A group of laughing and squealing children ran past the Baron's Table chasing after something flittering in front them.

Jonathon squirmed in his seat as he felt a pang of jealousy. He looked to Baron O'Kelly and shrugged his shoulders.

"They will or they won't, it is not for us to make their decision. In the meantime, I say let's enjoy ourselves," said Wilbert, stepping in and redirecting the conversation.

Jonathon sat back so as not to disturb the ambience flowing around him. His people deserved this time. He sneaked a peek at the children cavorting about the hall and sighed. So many people had given so much for him. Even up to paying the ultimate price. *Tierra let me be worth it,* he thought

"You will be, Jonathon," she said.

Epilogue

"Where are we?" asked Selene.

"We?"

Confused, Selene looked about for the source of the unknown voice. She could see no one. Even worse she didn't recognize her surroundings. "Where are my friends? Why am I in bed?"

She saw a head pop up above the mattress. The small figure climbed up and perched herself on the chair next to the bed. At first Selene took the the figure to be a little girl, but the eyes were too old, too knowledgeable. At least for a moment. In the next the seriousness was replaced with a twinkling merriment.

"There were no others. Just you. I can be your friend," offered the woman.

Relax. Take it easy. There has to be a rational explanation. Selene tried again. "Where am I?"

"You are in the Hospice of Gentle Care. I'm Ziggie."

The name meant nothing to Selene. She was still lost. "How did I get here?"

"I was hoping you would tell me," said the little woman.

———

The foothills and valleys all looked the same, but it didn't matter to Shem. He walked the path unerringly, guided by the pointer around his neck. The arrow knew where it was and where it wanted to go. Home. Shem's memory of this place was foggy. He wasn't sure how he had gotten into Sho ku the last time, but he knew that if he continued to follow the pointer the inhabitants of Sho ku would find him. What he didn't know was how he had arrived in the valley to begin with. One moment he was buried in a cave-in the next he was staggering beside a stream trying to catch his balance. The only thing he knew for certain was that this journey was none of his doing, but as long as he was on it he would find out what the pointer wanted.

⚋⚊∅∅∅⚊⚋

The Nem Elt-til had left the woods behind some two candlemarks ago. He had fluttered up and out of the bowl it had been situated in and looked out upon an expansive sea of grass rippling in a light breeze. He headed in as westerly a direction as he could determine buzzing between the seeded heads of grass stalks.

"It would be nice to be a little larger so I could fly faster," he said aloud.

"Waa, waa, waa. Whine, whine, whine. Poor poor pitiful me."

The Nem Elt-til spun around trying to locate the voice behind him. He looked down. A smallish lad with pale blond hair, his head barely reaching the seed stalks, looked up at him. The Nem Elt-til lowered his head, his voice respectful, filled with deference, "Vaar Tu, I..."

"I know exactly what you were doing, Quit bobbing around. I need to talk to you." Wybee held out his hand. The Nem Elt-til landed on his palm. "Bob. Yes, I like that. You were complaining, Bob, about how hard life is. How difficult the path. How if I just had this or could do that then things would be easier. Aaaaant! Wrong answer. You have everything you need and it is readily available to you."

"Then why can't I..."

"There you go again."

Bob took a deep breath. He supressed his rising frustration, especially since he was being cut off whenever he took a step down that path. He looked Wybee in the eye and said with all seriousness, "Vaar Tu, what is happening to me?"

"Ta Recht," said Wybee trying not to smirk.

Bob sat down hard on Wybee's palm, his breath exploding out of him. "Now? Really?"